ALL THE SKILLS

— BOOK TWO —

HONOUR RAE

Podium

For my readers on Amazon, Royal Road, and Patreon.
Thanks for the opportunity to write my daydreams.

Cover design by Miblart

ISBN: 978-1-0394-7022-4

Published in 2025 by Podium Publishing
www.podiumaudio.com

Podium

ALL THE SKILLS

— BOOK TWO —

PART 1
THE GEMSTONE EGG

CHAPTER 1

How could you let this happen?" Valentina groused.

Not for the first time in his life, Whitaker thought about turning his card's considerable power on the other hive leader. One good push ought to do it. The slopes were steep. Valentina's birdlike bones would snap like dry twigs on the sharp rocks.

As for the dragons . . . Crag was younger, stronger, and heavier than Valentina's dragon, Elissa. He could win handily in a bloody match.

Then Whitaker could rule the hive as he saw fit without Valentina's nattering in his ear.

This was just a daydream. The truth was Valentina wouldn't hit the slopes. The air would catch her, or the ground would turn springy and spongy under her. Then she would be up and throwing fire and lightning in Whitaker's face.

But the two seconds between him shoving her off and her return might be worth it.

"Well?" Valentina demanded, tapping the point of her cane impatiently against the stone. "What do you have to say for yourself?"

Oh. That question hadn't been rhetorical.

"How about you keep your tongue behind your teeth for once?" he asked, though none of his exasperation showed on his face. More and more dragons and riders were showing up by the second. While none dared to stand close enough to hear their bickering, he didn't rule out any spying cards at play. "I can't be expected to pay attention to every Common who disappears after their rider dies."

Again, Valentina tapped the point of her cane against the rocky earth. This time, chips of stone flew away.

"That's always been your problem. You've never cared about our lower-tiered dragons. Now, look what that's gotten us, eh? A dead purple and a lost egg."

Whitaker dearly wanted to roll his eyes. He had never heard Valentina give a sniff about purples before. They were classic Common dragons with only a few showing up in the Uncommon ranks. There might be one or two Rare purples in other hives, but in Whitaker's estimation, that was a waste of a good card.

"Be quiet," he said again. "I'm trying to concentrate. The body's practically mummified, and I'm trying to ease it out without breaking any bones."

It may be only a purple, but Whitaker wasn't a complete idiot. If the hive leaders weren't seen to be showing respect, the other dragons would protest.

Crag, his dragon, was currently resting several ledges up. He was too large to move any closer without his weight upsetting the loose scree and possibly causing a rockfall. Several Rares that comprised his personal retinue of attendants surrounded him. The dragon heads were gathered together, and they all looked like they were plotting.

Again, Valentina tapped her cane. This time Whitaker felt the ominous vibration of an earthquake through the soles of his shoes.

"Better to be quick about it. That egg is likely dead anyway, as long as she's been in there. If you paid more attention to the rider rolls, you would have seen a gap in the nesting schedule. Then this whole unpleasantness could have been avoided. We could have had two Rares at once! Imagine wiping the smirk off of Harvest Moon's leaders' faces . . ."

Through decades of practice, Whitaker ignored her. Instead, he focused on his Legendary Telekinesis card's power.

He was having a hard time moving the purple's corpse out of the tunnel, even using Crag's linked Material Manipulation card to widen the tunnel within.

The purple felt unusually heavy. Perhaps she had been dead so long, the organics in the body had fused with the rocks.

Whitaker certainly wasn't going into the cave to check. He was pushing fifty and in no shape to go scrambling up a thinly supported rock ledge. The delicate rock face was the same reason Crag couldn't lift him there, either.

That purple had certainly found an inconvenient place to creep off to and die.

"No doubt we'll have all the female dragons slinking around for days, afraid they'll die from egg binding, too," Valentina continued. "If they can't trust their leaders to take care of them, who can they trust?"

"Their riders?" he asked, voice dripping with sarcasm. "If that silly purple bothered to link up with another rider, she would have had someone watching over her— Ah, finally."

The dragon's body had been wrenched loose from whatever had kept it snagged down. Hand extended, Whitaker twisted his wrist, eyes half shut as he carefully floated it out.

"You will have gotten the entire body out in one piece, I hope," Valentina said. "We've collected quite an audience. There's no need to punctuate our failure."

Whitaker appreciated that she was willing to admit it was her failure too. Though he said, "Dragons die all the time—"

"To scourge, yes. But here, in their homes, they expect to be safe."

Whitaker didn't answer.

Down below, where a crowd of dragons, riders, and morbidly curious hive dwellers had gathered, there came a sudden hush.

The back half of the dragon's body floated out. He had gotten it all in one piece and hadn't had to break any limbs along the way. The purple looked dehydrated and mummified but strangely peaceful. Posed, as if she were sleeping.

She was curled around nothing. Damn it. Whitaker had left the egg behind.

Ah, well, he would get it next.

Using exaggerated care, he floated the body over the ledge, down the slope, and to a spot just before the flat area where the bulk of the crowd had gathered.

There were more gasps and tiny cries from those who recognized the dragon.

"That's Cori!"

"Cori!"

"Oh, poor Cori!"

Again, Whitaker had to struggle not to roll his eyes. How *convenient* that people were concerned about the creature only after learning of her death, and not while she had been missing. This wasn't his fault.

In fact, the stupid purple was being shown great honor by the marked attention of the two Legendary hive leaders. Valentina was nosy and officious, and should have died when she reached a decrepit age—approximately three decades ago—but she was right that the hive would be in a minor uproar over the purple's death.

They asked their dragons to risk their lives, cards, and riders every time there was a scourge-eruption. This hive was to be their sanctuary. The one place they could be safe.

Having a purple die while laying eggs was not the image of competence the leadership wished to give.

He and Valentina were lucky the Uncommon rider who'd stumbled across the body hadn't run yammering to her other low-tier friends. Instead, she did the right thing by immediately passing the news up to leadership.

Whitaker let the body rest so gently on the stone before the crowd, he didn't stir up a mote of dust.

Either that or Valentina was helping him by keeping the dust down.

"What of the egg?" the old woman snapped.

"You want me to float out a dead egg in front of them, too?" he asked sardonically.

"They're not stupid. And it will serve as a reminder to the other laying females that they need to be in a designated spot should the worst happen."

Valentina had just been arguing the opposite point, which was very much like her. The Uncommon rider who'd reported the body had been hysterical, stating the egg was a Rare or better, which was preposterous. A Rare out of a Common? A Common *purple*? One that had been left to the elements for how many months?

He would be lucky if the egg didn't crack en route and shower everyone with rotten goo. Whitaker had accidentally cracked a rotten egg once as a child. It was not a smell he would ever forget.

But.

He couldn't very well leave the egg there. Not unless he wanted to seal up the cave to entomb it.

And Valentina had a point. Damn her.

So Whitaker ignored the continuing cries and beginnings of sobs from down below and turned his attention to the egg. Thanks to his and Crag's combined powers, it was barely an inconvenience.

Or it should have been.

He held out his hand and lifted. And continued to try to lift.

"What in the world?" he gasped.

"What's the problem?" Valentina snapped.

"It's like trying to move a mountain." Suddenly, he wondered if this was the thing Cori's husk of a body had been caught on.

That would mean . . .

Valentina frowned at him as if concerned Whitaker was trying to pull a prank. Then she looked up to the cave. She was even less able to climb up there than Whitaker, though Whitaker would have paid very good shards to watch her haul her ninety-year-old body up.

But Valentina was a Legendary card wielder. She was plenty powerful just by staying in place.

"Where is it?" she asked.

"There's a small chamber at the back of the tunnel. It's open to the sky—"

Whitaker went silent as his telekinesis senses went wild. From above came the sounds of rock grinding on rock, and Whitaker got the impression of a thousand different pieces spinning and relocking into place.

"You're going to smash the thing, fool woman."

"Quiet, child. Let me work."

Valentina's eyes were half closed. Then, without any warning, the cave floor flowed out from the entrance into the sky via a ribbon of rock. Tons of weight and material floated in midair, supported only by Valentina's pure elemental might.

The rock gently broke apart and drifted back into the cave save for the end of the ribbon, which supported a single small object.

It was more like the size of an ostrich egg than of a decent dragon egg, and so deep black that for a moment Whitaker thought it must be rotten all the way through.

Until the moment he felt the *power* of the egg.

Then he knew that young Uncommon rider had not been hysterical.

From her place on top of the hive, Valentina's dragon, Elissa, flexed her might. The bright day's sun was instantly blanketed by clouds, and a roll of thunder rumbled through the sky.

Crag, too, tipped his head back and roared. Every speck of solid material for a mile vibrated just the tiniest bit as he announced:

"LEGENDARY!"

Whitaker turned to Valentina. The woman's lips were pinched as she guided the egg, still on its raft of stone, downward.

"How is this possible?"

"Pick your jaw off the floor," she snapped, though he noticed she sounded winded. That little stunt had cost her. "I don't know either, and I don't care. But if you want to keep this egg, you put out a call for everyone in our territory with a Legendary card to come. Now. And for the sake of Common shards, don't let anyone under-rank near that egg. We don't need a massacre on our hands."

She turned and walked off.

"Wait, where are you going?"

Valentina continued walking, cane tapping on every other stride, though it didn't look like she needed it. "To talk with that silver rider. You felt the power of that egg. I want to know how she's still alive."

Valentina picked her way down the steep slope toward the massing crowd down below. Some kind souls had already returned with flowers to lay them tucked up against the purple's hide.

Valentina thought of herself as a strong woman, but she didn't care to look at the poor beast directly. It had deserved better. Surely there must have been some farmer or forgotten child that wouldn't have minded linking up with a purple?

If Whitaker had been doing his job, the purple wouldn't have slipped through the cracks.

Though . . . it was not all his fault, Valentina supposed. The man was full of himself but dreadfully overworked. Considering the troubling amount of scourge-eruptions recently, that work was increasing.

Which was why they needed a Legendary egg. A new leader to help them carry the load.

So did every other hive. They'd fight for it, too. They'd pull every underhanded trick in the book to make this new egg and rider theirs.

Valentina was determined that whoever linked with the thing would be one of their own.

Once people saw she was coming, they rightfully edged back. Some pretended to be very busy.

Now, where was . . . ah. There. Valentina raised her cane and pointed. "You, there! I intend to speak to you!"

About a quarter of the crowd froze like scourge-mice under the gaze of a dragon.

With long practice, Valentina pulled on the wind and moisture in the air. Mist collected at her feet, and she stepped onto a cloud. That cloud sank down the slope much faster than she had been able to move before, even with the rocks rumbling out of her way.

It was a fancy way to travel, but nowadays her bones ached when she drew too hard on her mana.

It was worth it today. Her quarry had not escaped.

"You." Valentina pointed her cane again. Closer now, she was able to center on a young Uncommon rider. She was pretty enough, with clear dark skin and curly hair pulled fetchingly back in a puffy tail behind her head. Her big brown eyes went wide at the sight of Valentina.

"You're the one who found Cori, weren't you?" Valentina had always prided herself on her ability to remember names. And mentioning the dragon made it look like the leadership cared more than their regular actions hinted at. "Well? Come here, girl."

The girl swallowed and looked back over her shoulder at something—likely her dragon. A gangly young silver stood not far away.

"That was me, ma'am. I'm Kenzie, and that's Marteen."

"One of our recruiters, yes?" Valentina asked. Hands resting on her cane, she craned her neck to look up at the girl, though Kenzie was not tall. "What brought you to these slopes, eh? Surely, you weren't recruiting the rocks."

The girl looked hesitant and glanced over her shoulder again. "It was . . . ah . . ."

"Me."

A teenage boy stepped out from behind Kenzie. Though he was taller than the recruiter, Valentina hadn't noticed him before.

Stealth card, she assessed. And a strong one if it could hoodwink her.

She took an extra moment to regard him. He was reedy in a way that suggested he had more growing to do. Dirty-blond hair, middling-color blue eyes, but there was something about him . . .

Something familiar.

A hazy memory came and went: scissors snipping fabric.

Ah, yes. *That* tragedy.

"Ernest Kane, isn't it?"

He blinked. So did Kenzie. They both looked shocked and chagrined enough for Valentina to guess why the two of them had been up here alone.

"I've noted your presence around that glittery Rare egg that's been causing us so much trouble," Valentina continued, which was only half a lie. She'd noticed him before. "But what I want to know is how did an Uncommon rider and a Rare recruit survive a brush with a Legendary egg, hmm?"

"I . . . uh . . ." Ernest hedged.

"Luck, ma'am," Kenzie said. "*Ernest* was heading for it, but I stopped him. I felt the strength of the magic—I'm linked to a silver, you see. And Marteen's always been sensitive that way. She shares it with me."

The fact that the girl was babbling what was obvious was telling. Valentina rested her gaze on the boy. How old was he? Every teenager looked like a wet-nosed child to her nowadays.

Old enough to fit her mental timeline. Had it been nearly eighteen years already?

Interestingly the boy didn't offer an excuse of his own. He just blurted, "The egg's okay, right? It . . . it's been alone for some time."

Valentina snorted. "It may be as big as an oversized chicken egg, but a Legendary is made of sterner stuff."

The boy's shoulders slumped in relief.

Interesting.

Valentina would have to think about this. She knew of the Kane family—despicable people, put in charge of a despicable job—but if the boy had loyalty to Wolf Moon . . . Perhaps the boy took after the maternal side of the family.

He could be molded.

But he would find himself in fierce competition with noble brats much more powerful than a mere baron.

Valentina's cane poked Kenzie in the sternum. The dragon rider winced but didn't step back.

"You were lucky," Valentina said. "We could have very easily had three corpses today, not just the one."

"Why?" asked Ernest.

Kenzie elbowed him.

"Because Legendaries take only the strongest," Valentina snapped. "Do you know how many boys and girls my Elissa's egg killed before I stepped up? Six! Sucked the air right out of their lungs. Or fried them with lightning. Tried to bury one alive, too. Whitaker's Crag got all the way to hatching and practically melted an entire observing noble family, from the grandfather all the way to the baby, before he linked. So you think on that, boy, before you write your father for a Legendary card." Not that she expected a borderland barony to have that sort of wealth.

Or perhaps . . . perhaps they did.

That had been a strong **Stealth** skill.

She turned to Kenzie. "As for you, I expect you know your job?"

The girl had gone slightly ashen. "You want me to recruit Legendary wielders, ma'am?"

"No!" Valentina prodded her again with the end of her cane. "Every noble will be willing to scratch each other's eyes out for a taste of that egg, even if their brats risk being horrifically killed. No, your job is to make sure *that*"—she swung around and jabbed at the purple corpse—"never happens again. Find us more Common and Uncommon riders. And maybe a decent Rare recruit that will interest that glittery egg, if you can manage it."

Valentina shook her head, frustrated. She could practically hear the arguments of the other hive leaders now—Wolf Moon couldn't find a partner for their current Rare. How could they be allowed a Legendary?

She was exhausted by the thought of it, and loath as she was to admit it . . . Valentina found herself tiring easily nowadays.

Not that she would ever let anyone other than Elissa know.

Without waiting for an answer from the shocked Uncommon rider, she called up another cloud around her feet.

Then Valentina took to the air.

She may be old and tired, but she still had style.

CHAPTER 2

Kenzie waited until the exact second after Leader Valentina ascended to the upper ledge to rejoin the egg. Then she whirled on Arthur.

"Ernest Kane?"

The only response Arthur could give was a sickly smile. He was stunned, too. First by finding the dead dragon, second by the leader's reactions and the confirmation that the tiny dark egg was a Legendary. And now against all luck and logic, Valentina had known his fake name.

He couldn't keep his gaze from flicking up to the ledge. The leaders were having an animated discussion around the egg. Possibly on how to safely move it.

If Legendary eggs were so dangerous, how did anyone ever manage to link up with one?

Arthur's non-answer wasn't good enough for Kenzie. She gripped his upper arm tight.

"How deep in the dragon-soil pit are we?"

"We're not."

"You're *not* a noble!" she hissed.

She was wrong there. Well, in a way. That reminder was enough to sober him. He finally ripped his attention from the egg to Kenzie.

"You know I had to get close to some of the nobility," he said carefully, aware people were milling around. "Baron Kane is a minor noble from the other side of the kingdom. The chances of anyone looking up the records of his children are slim."

"And if they do?"

Arthur found he didn't have an answer.

Kenzie let out a breath. "Okay," she said, "you know the best thing to do when you're caught in a lie?"

"Uh . . ." He dearly hoped she wasn't about to say "Tell the truth."

But he should have expected better from Kenzie.

"You double down. Come on." Still gripping his arm, she pulled him away.

"The bells aren't ringing," Arthur said.

Kenzie gave him an odd look. They had left the hive slopes behind and were currently walking through the city. Marteen had elected to stay on the slopes and mark a vigil over Cori's body.

Arthur thought it was odd. Dragons died not infrequently during scourge-eruptions. And while there was some sadness, it was nothing like this. When he'd asked Kenzie about it, she remained tight-lipped.

"The dragons see dying to scourge as different." She hadn't elaborated past that.

The farther Arthur got from the hive slopes, the better he could think. And he realized it was too quiet.

"Shouldn't there be celebrating?" he asked. "The whole city throws a festival whenever a new Rare is laid and a second one when it's linked up with someone."

Kenzie bit her bottom lip. "I don't think the hive will waste resources on celebrating this Legendary egg until they know they can keep it."

"Keep it?"

She shrugged. "Wolf Moon Hive is small, and we've got two Legendaries. Yeah, Valentina is as old as dirt and Whitaker's not much better, but I've heard of bigger hives swooping in to take Legendary eggs from smaller ones before."

Arthur had to battle down a flash of anger at the thought of strangers—of anyone—taking what ought to be his.

. . . What ought to be the Wolf Moon Hive's, he meant.

Kenzie continued. "So I bet they'll be keeping it quiet—well, as quiet as anyone linked with dragons get. Our dragons will probably be gossiping come the next scourge-eruption."

"Then where are we going?" he asked.

"I told you. We're doubling down on the Ernest Kane story, which means you need to move full time into the hive—"

"What!"

"And shed some of your assets." She stared so openly at his chest that he had to resist the urge to cross his arms. Of course, she wasn't staring at his muscles—or lack of them—she was looking pointedly at his heart.

"You want me to bring the kids out," he said slowly.

"You heard Valentina. We need recruits." She held up a hand as he started to object. "Look, I haven't pried much into your dealings because I want to be able to tell a Truth Seeker that I didn't know what you're up to. But you're already known to Valentina. And if you attract too much attention, someone might hire a Treasure Seeker strong enough to defeat your storage card. The decent thing to do is to make sure those kids aren't in there."

"The fact you might get some recruits out of the deal has nothing to do with it, right?" he asked sardonically.

Kenzie laid a hand over her own chest as if shocked.

But she also had a point. The borderland village kids didn't experience time while in his storage, so there hadn't been a reason to bring them out while the theft of Duke Rowantree's cards was on everyone's mind.

But Lional and Penn Rowantree had finally packed up and returned to their duchy—presumably to find another way to fix their shattered finances.

The hive leadership now had their hands full with the new Legendary egg. Meanwhile, that Rare egg was on the verge of hatching, and dozens of noble kids would be vying for its attention.

No one would pay attention to a few extra Common and Uncommon recruits. Or orphan brats showing up outside a scourge-eruption.

"All right." He sighed. "I already talked to Freyja. She can't house them all in her orphanage, but can place the rest in others around the city. I trust her."

"The hive has plenty of room," Kenzie said leadingly.

"That will be up to the kids," Arthur told her firmly.

It had been some months since Arthur had seen Freyja's orphanage. While the grounds and the inside were as neat and tidy as always, the entire place felt . . . smaller than it had when he was younger. Even the hallways were narrow and cramped. He had to resist the urge to shift his shoulders, feeling like his own clothing was a touch too small.

When he'd left, Arthur had given the management of the kitchen to the care of another orphan he'd trusted. He resisted the urge to pop in and check how things were going.

Freyja received him and Kenzie with a smile and led them back to her office, where she closed the door.

She turned to Arthur. "Now, before we begin, should we expect any effects from the storage?"

"Effects?" he repeated.

"Depending on your storage power—you're not the only one with such a card," Freyja said with a wave of her hand. "Several on the Lobo evacuation teams transport their civilians that way. Though I'm told it can be jarring for those who have been stored . . ."

Kenzie stared at Arthur, looking a little sick. Apparently, this hadn't occurred to her.

"No." He shook his head. He had only given Freyja the bare bones of the story. She hadn't asked many questions about how he had rescued the children, which he found interesting. "Time doesn't pass for people in my storage. To them, it'll be one eye blink they were in the village, and the next here. But they may be . . . overwhelmed by city life."

That was an understatement. He'd at least had his travels with Red's caravan to get him used to life outside the borderland village. For these kids, the transfer would be instant.

Freyja visibly relaxed. "We can deal with confusion."

"And . . . they may be underfed," he added.

"We can deal with that, too. I trust you remember the kitchens?"

That earned a reluctant smile. "I do. Okay, I'll start with the twins first."

Mentally, he reached for the list.

Retrieving the children went both better and worse than he feared. Better because they were all healthy and, as he said, unaware of their time spent in storage. So there was a bit of disorientation from all of them. From their perspective, they had just said goodbye to their parents in a small cottage at night and in the next moment found themselves in an office in daylight surrounded by strangers.

The twins were sensible girls and had each other to draw on for strength. They were also willing to take a preliminary recruitment chip from Kenzie. Freyja insisted on keeping them at the orphanage for at least a few days to "find their feet" before she would release the twins to the hive.

It was very much the same for the next couple of children who were younger, but still old enough to have received a card.

The babies and toddlers were easy enough as well. Freyja immediately called for her staff to warm bottles, and most were happy to be fed milk that hadn't been watered down for once.

The problem came with the younger children, from four years old to nine, who all were alarmed to find themselves somewhere new, and who immediately wanted their parents.

Freyja swooped in to handle these too, but their crying still cut Arthur to the core. He knew he had done the right thing. He'd given these children a new home and a real chance at a good life. But the brokenhearted weeping of one girl who kept calling for her mother was hard to hear.

He left the moment Freyja gave him the nod to make room for the rest of the orphanage staff.

Kenzie, who must have been made of harder stuff, stayed to talk up the hive to the older kids.

Arthur practically fled out the door.

"I did the right thing," he told himself. But he didn't feel like it.

As soon as he hit the streets outside the orphanage, he broke into a jog . . . then a run.

At first, it was only to get away. Then, for a whole other reason.

New Skill Gained: Running (General)
Due to your previous experience and your card's bonus traits, you automatically start this skill at level 5.

Huh. Something new to level. Who would have guessed that running could be a skill?

It looked like his new Master of Body Enhancement card was getting to work.

He smiled to himself and pushed faster. Not that it was easy in these packed, busy streets. He got a few yells aimed his way, and he suspected he would soon get a dodging skill.

One of the canals lay ahead. He had walked along the stone borders hundreds of times before, and he'd always been tempted to see if he could jump it.

Now, that might earn him a skill.

Arthur lengthened his stride and hit the edge, leaping into the air . . .

And fell short.

Wolf Moon Hive's short summer was ending, and the water had already taken on an icy chill.

Spluttering, Arthur reached the edge just in time to earn:

New Skill Gained: Basic Swimming (Sailor/Fisherman Class)
Due to your card's bonus traits, you automatically start this skill at level 3.

"Level 3?" he grumbled. "That's not fair. I have had some swimming experience."

He was about to heave himself up when someone stuck a slim hand in his face.

"Come on, Your *Grace*," said a sarcastic voice. "I'll help you up."

He looked up to see a pretty young woman grinning down at him. Her hair was like fire in the setting sun, and she looked distinctly amused.

She also seemed familiar, but he couldn't place her face.

Arthur wasn't too proud to turn down the lift. He grabbed her hand, and she hauled him, dripping, out of the canal.

"Thanks," he said.

"That was dumb but entertaining." She grinned again. "Ernest Kane, right?"

He felt his smile freeze. "That's right, but how . . . ?"

"Cressida Icehouse," she said. "I watched your duel against Mattew Rockhound."

Then it hit him. She had done more than watch. This girl had been the referee and the one to finally beat Penn, Arthur's cousin.

This girl was one of the young nobles.

CHAPTER 3

By silent agreement, he and Cressida walked back toward the hive. Arthur's boots squelched with every step, but at least he no longer left a trail of dripping water. A cold wind picked up out of nowhere—not unusual for the Wolf Moon Hive. It didn't feel good on wet skin, but he could endure.

No, Arthur's first problem was that he didn't actually live in the hive with other nobles. The apartment he used to share with Horatio was several blocks away.

Arthur's second problem was that he was awful at talking to girls. And Cressida was very, very pretty.

She wore a flowery dress with some sort of cinch fabric thing in the middle that put emphasis in all the right places. Her red hair was pinned up, showing clear, soft-looking skin on the nape of her neck and a trail of freckles. Arthur was visibly trying not to shiver in the air chill . . . or stare.

"Our little group hasn't seen you around the Rare egg much," Cressida said, breaking the silence between them. "I'd heard rumor that you left the hive entirely."

"Just been keeping to myself," Arthur muttered, ducking his chin as if in embarrassment. That last part had been a helpful hint from his **Acting** skill. "I didn't think I made a particularly good showing at the duels, so I wasn't sure if I would be welcomed back."

He meant to be self-effacing, so he was taken aback when Cressida gave him a surprised and mildly annoyed look. "Is that all? Everybody loses their first few duels, even those who have combat cards. Do you know how many hours of practice it took to get my flame summon to listen to me?"

He shook his head.

"I don't mind telling you that I was awful," she said. "Now . . . Well, I'll show you."

She flipped her hand in a circling gesture. There was a flash of orange, and a miniature bear made of fire appeared. It was no bigger than an apple and stood up on its hind legs to peer up at her. With a chubby face paired with round ears, it was . . . a little cute.

"Help out my friend. He's freezing, so be gentle," she told the bear.

Arthur blamed the cold for making his thoughts slow and stupid. "Wait . . . what?"

In the next second, the miniature bear galloped through the air right at him. Arthur backed up a step and raised his hand to swat it down, but Cressida warned "no" and caught his wrist.

Her hand was fever warm from her fire summon.

The bear tucked its head and barreled straight at Arthur's chest. The moment it hit his shirt, it dispersed into a puff of steam.

Warmth rolled over Arthur as if he had walked into a steam sauna. Wisps of steam rolled off of his shoulders, and all of his muscles loosened at once.

The sensation lasted for a few heartbeats before it faded, leaving Arthur's clothing all the way down to the socks in his boots damp instead of soaking wet. The chilly wind was much more manageable.

He glanced at Cressida, who grinned back at him, dropping his wrist. "My little bears make me popular in the winter," she said. "My father's land is north of here, nearly at the ice fields, so we endure long winters."

She was perhaps underselling herself a bit. The ability to instantly warm someone would be invaluable in the northern ice country.

Arthur's next question came out before he had time to think about it. "Your father must be insane to let you go. Why are you trying to be a dragon rider?"

Her friendly expression closed off. She didn't look cold, exactly, but the smile that she gave him was practiced and poised. "To do my duty and fight the scourge, of course. Aren't we all here for that reason?"

"Yeah. Of course," he said, too quickly.

She gave him a look out of the corner of her eye, then seemed to shrug. "Anyway, you should come back into the fold. Now that they'll be forcing the Rare to hatch soon, the rest of us should have a chance."

"I thought there was still a line for who got to meet the hatchling first?"

Some of her humor returned. "There have been quite a few dropouts by people who were more interested in making connections with nobles rather than being a dragon rider." Another side-eye glance. "I hope that you aren't one of them."

"I'm not—"

"Good! Then we'll see you tonight at the promenade?" She clapped him on a shoulder. "I've got to tell everyone of your *grace*ful dunking."

He groaned and she grinned, striding ahead. There was a knot of gossiping noble girls not too far away, and she looked intent on joining them.

Oh, that's why she had been nice. She now had a good piece of gossip to share. Horatio had carped endlessly about how small and boring the Wolf Moon Hive was. If that was true, the visiting nobles must be bored out of their minds.

Arthur rolled his eyes, and when he was certain Cressida wasn't looking, he ducked down the next side street and broke into a light jog. He intended to take as much opportunity as possible to level his new skills.

Arthur grinned into the wind as he ran. He didn't think it was his imagination—he was running a touch faster. Each stride felt smoother, too. It was as if his joints had been lubricated with cooking oil, and he simply knew how to set his foot exactly right on the ground to increase the proficiency of each stride.

As he dashed through the streets, he didn't focus so much on where he was going but *how* he ran. His back straightened, stomach tightened, and he felt like he could draw every breath that much more easily into his lungs.

New skill level: Running (General)
Level 6

His grin widened.

He was already half in love with his new Master of Body Enhancement card, and he had only just begun to explore its powers.

When he reached his apartment, he practically flew up the stairs, taking two at a time. He didn't earn a skill from stair-climbing, but he thought that he might with a few more repetitions.

Stair-climbing might seem like a silly skill, but so was **Card Shuffling** and that had saved his life.

Arthur had thought about that moment with the guard off and on over the last few weeks. He would have never expected a mundane skill to come in handy. To actually allow himself to pluck a card from someone's card-anchor deck. That had been a failure of imagination. After all, hadn't he come close to defeating a summoned creature with his **Butchering** skill?

His Master of Skills card was utility only, but the concept of "utility" could be stretched—especially once a skill leveled high enough.

That was the excuse he gave himself, a few minutes later, for why he leaped back and forth from his cot to Horatio's empty cot and back again. Just like a little boy would when pretending that the floor was on fire.

But Arthur was not a little boy anymore, and the wooden cots groaned with every landing, as did the floorboards. Then the downstairs neighbor gave a muffled yell and thumped the ceiling with a broom.

One more leap, Arthur promised himself.

He sprung from his bed to Horatio's and heard a sharp crack from the cheap, protesting wood underneath.

New Skill Gained: Leaping (Performer)
Due to your previous experience and your card's bonus traits, you automatically start this skill at level 4.
Do you wish to add this to your Performer Class?

Arthur pumped his fist in the air in triumph but dismissed the message. He did intend to add his next skill to the class, but as a Tier-1 non-crafting class, all the levels averaged out with one another. He'd lower his overall score. He intended to level up his **Leaping** skill first.

Was there a difference between jumping and leaping?

Arthur was about to find out—the downstairs neighbor be damned—but a slip of paper caught his eye. It had been pushed under the apartment door. He would have noticed it before, but he'd been too excited to check out his skills.

Stepping off the cot, he picked it up. It was a note penned in Kenzie's handwriting, likely delivered by a paid courier.

Ernest Kane would have a spot at the hive. I got you a room on the second level. Pack up and get out of that hovel you call an apartment.
P. S. Remember that egg is probably hatching tonight. Be there.

It looked like Ernest Kane was about to make an appearance.

CHAPTER 4

Arthur walked into the Rare hatching room, the site of the promenade, and stopped short in surprise.

The last time he had been there, the line to stand in front of the Rare egg had circled the room. Many more noble scions and hangers-on had filled up the space in the middle, chatting and talking. That hadn't counted those who had taken their socializing and arguments into the hive's small dueling space to settle grudges. He heard the list of those allowed to spend time with the egg directly to encourage it to hatch had been nine pages long.

That had been several weeks ago. Arthur had chosen to lay low and let "Ernest Kane" fade into the background.

It seemed he had missed an exodus.

The room had barely a quarter of the people it had held before, and that was a generous estimate. There was no longer even a line of people waiting for the egg. Now they clustered at the stage in loose groups, chatting and barely throwing glances up at it. Others milled around, exchanging gossip and drinking.

Arthur knew what had happened: Those who had come here to meet with their peers and arrange deals under informal circumstances had gone back home. The rest either had nowhere to go, hadn't yet concluded their business, or actually wanted to try for the egg.

It was a depressingly small number overall, and it made him feel insulted on behalf of the Rare hatchling.

His indignation turned into mild chagrin when he remembered he wasn't really trying for the egg either.

A young woman peeled off from a tightly gossiping group and walked over. It was Cressida, and she looked stunning in a green dress and a fiery red-orange necklace that reminded him of her flame bear.

She smiled as she approached. Arthur found himself smiling back.

"I trust you washed the canal reeds out of your hair," she asked in greeting.

"Just for you," he lied, having not had the time or the extra coin to waste on a bath. He didn't *think* he smelled like canal water. In any case, Cressida didn't flinch away when he held his arm out to her.

She took it, but she was the one to steer him deeper into the room. Not to the group of gossips she'd just left, but up to the stage.

The egg was just as impressive as it was the first time Arthur had seen it. Standing nearly as tall as his waist, it looked like it was crusted with a rainbow of gemstones. This was an illusion, as dragon eggshells were made of normal egg material. But the look of it was said to indicate a shimmer-quality dragon inside—a Rare or powerful card holder.

As he got closer, Arthur saw striated cracks running from the top downward, though none of the shell had chipped off. It looked like it was in the beginning stages of hatching. The baby not yet pipped.

By all rights, it should be surrounded by onlookers. Instead, the well-dressed nobles watched nearby with careful disinterest.

Where are the common folk? he wondered, glancing around. He didn't spot anyone not dressed as if they had a personal tailor.

Arthur himself was likely the cheapest dressed among them, but he covered it well with an expensive vest and a new shirt.

No, there weren't any common folk here other than Arthur and the guards.

He supposed it made sense. People who went to the expense and effort of getting enough shards to create a Rare card typically sold them for a top price, traded them, or used them to advance their rank in a guild. People paid money for Rare craftsman's wares, and towns that hired Rare guardsmen attracted high-quality residents.

The hive life still seemed luxurious to Arthur, who had grown up in a border village meant as a working prison, full of uncarded people plagued by sickness and starvation.

"What do you think?" Cressida asked.

He blinked, realizing he had been lost in his own thoughts. "In general or . . . ?"

She swatted his arm playfully. "The egg, of course." Then she turned back to gaze at it, tilting her head. "I think it'll be an illusion type."

He suspected the same but didn't want to admit it. "Not earth type, with all those gemstones?"

She made a face. "There is no way a dull brown dragon pops out of an egg that spectacular."

"Earth cards have their uses," he said, not liking her snobbery. "I hear they are invaluable helping farmers manage their fields and can turn the ground itself against the scourglings."

"But it's the nature greens who force-grow crops in emergencies," she countered. "And I've heard some have deadly spore powers that can rot entire swaths of scourglings where they stand. And," she added, "this egg is supposed to be a high-grade shimmer. Green shimmers have portal powers."

"I've never understood that," Arthur said, just to be contrary. "How do grass dragons get teleportation?"

"They don't have powers over *grass*, they have powers over nature strong enough to create a stable hole from here to there." Cressida flicked her hands. "It's not teleportation. I've heard of a Rare purple who had teleportation."

"You don't like purples, either?" he asked, catching the note in her voice. He didn't know how to talk to girls, but he found it very easy to tease Cressida. Unlike most of the others there, she seemed strongly fixated on the dragon.

The noble girl faltered. "It's not that I don't like them. But . . . have you ever heard one speak? They're not conversationalists."

Arthur smiled, remembering Tess.

"Purples aren't that bad," she continued so defensively he knew he must have hit a nerve. Then she lowered her voice, tilting down to speak lower—almost into his ear. "I heard one of the hives just had a Legendary laid by a purple."

He glanced at her in surprise. The hive leaders must be suppressing the news to non-dragon riders. That wasn't going to last for long.

"Yes, it was here."

"Here? Are you sure?"

When he nodded, Cressida bit her lip and threw a glance up at the Rare egg. She looked guilty. "Why in the world haven't they announced it?"

"Waiting for this egg to hatch, I suspect." He hoped it wasn't that the Legendary egg got taken away to another hive.

If that were the case, he'd have to follow it.

Something tingled on the edge of his awareness. Arthur started to turn unconsciously without fully realizing why. He caught sight of a cluster of nobles about thirty feet away. In the usually empty room, they stood out.

He caught the murmur of upset voices and realized several of the boys were trying to calm down and separate two others who were glaring daggers at one another.

Cressida followed Arthur's gaze and then snorted through her long nose. "Here we go again."

"Again?" Arthur asked, but his question was answered a moment later.

"That's enough! I can't let this insult stand!" One of the boys threw out his hands, and crescent-shaped shimmers of force extended from his palms. The friends who were trying to calm him down were pushed, staggering away.

The other boy, who looked like he'd had triple portions for every meal of his life, shouldered free from his own friends.

He stepped up, and the challenger didn't give an inch. The result was they stood nearly chest to chest, yelling insults in each other's faces.

Arthur couldn't catch what they said coherently—it was typical noble talk of family honor and refusing to let some insult go. Nothing he hadn't heard a hundred times before when too-drunk nobles thought they weren't getting the respect their bloodline deserved.

He looked to Cressida. "Shouldn't they take this to the dueling room?"

"They would if this had anything to do with the egg. This is just an inner family grudge match." Standing next to him, she slipped her arm around his and pointed. "See, that's Viscount Cornfellow's third son. I've heard he has a terrible gambling problem. Anyway, the big one, Granton, is only the son of a baron, but he's the firstborn and the barony is in the rich inner lands, so—"

She didn't finish before Big Granton sneered and stomped his foot.

A stone rolled out from under the impact as if he'd thrown a rock into a pond. Arthur was watching for it, and still, the jolt was almost enough to knock him off his feet.

The issue was, this wasn't a mere Common or Uncommon earth skill. It was Rare, which meant Big Granton's earth manipulation card had some more tricks to it.

The ripple wave hit the walls and reflected back. And because the walls were unevenly spaced, some ripples hit and reflected before others. Soon ripples were hitting other ripples and reflecting off one another, which created more jarring ripples in a cascade effect that shook the entire room.

Chairs and tables were toppled over. People lost their balance completely and fell over several times while trying to get up.

Arthur crouched down, trying to lower his center of gravity as much as possible. Cressida tried to copy him, but her feet slipped out from under her.

He reached for her, only for her to wrench out of the way, pointing back toward the stage in alarm.

"The egg!"

The gem-encrusted egg had come loose off the pedestal and rolled across the stage. The nearby guards lunged to grab it, but they both were knocked off their feet from an ill-timed double jolt.

"No!" Cressida shrieked. "Help it!"

She flung out her arm, and a large bear made of living flame galloped forward on smoky feet.

"Cressida, don't! You'll burn it!" Arthur yelled. She hadn't summoned the gentle warming bear. This was the powerful combat version—he had seen it used to take down Penn. It was both powerful and deadly.

Fortunately—or unfortunately—it was also incorporeal. The bear ran at top speed and just managed to reach the edge of the stage as the egg did.

It reared up on its hind legs as if to catch the thing . . . and the egg fell right through, leaving a smoky hole where the bear's torso had been.

The egg toppled over and fell, likely to shatter into shards on the unforgiving floor.

Except it didn't. A white tablecloth whipped itself from a nearby table and billowed under the egg.

The brilliantly jeweled egg stopped in midair.

Arthur managed to climb to his feet in between jolts.

New Skill Gained: Balance (General)
Due to your previous experience and your card's bonus traits, you automatically start this skill at level 5.

He barely glanced at the notification. His gaze flicked from the caught egg to the side entrance.

Leader Whitaker stood there as steady as a rock, even though several stone ripples flowed under his feet. His hand was outstretched as he held the egg safe in midair.

Valentina walked out from behind him, took one look at the scene, and sniffed. "That is quite enough."

She tapped her cane once, and the ripples simply stopped. They sank into the floor as gently as water draining away.

The power of a Legendary versus a Rare.

With a flick of his wrist, Whitaker wrapped the egg securely in the tablecloth and gently returned it to its spot. Several more cracks marred the shell.

"Now, who's bright idea was this?" Leaving Whitaker to deal with the egg, Valentina shuffled across the floor, cane tapping every other step.

She was a tiny thing with flossy gray hair tied into a thin braid that went down her back. It should have made her look girlish. But there was a presence about her that spoke of power. It was in the way her voice carried louder and farther than it should, how the spilled water formed puddles as she passed them by, and the distant torchlight bent and flared toward her, throwing wild shadows across the room.

Valentina was angry, and the elemental powers she commanded with her Legendary card conveyed that quite clearly.

People drew back as she approached, including the viscount's son.

The only one who stayed in place was Big Granton—and that was because every eye was on him.

The boy's face was spotty with a flush, and sweat beaded his brow.

"It was my card," he said, chin up and ready to take his punishment.

And why not? Arthur thought bitterly. Nobles were never truly punished. Whatever fine or scolding Valentina leveled on Granton wouldn't erase the fact that, for a moment, everyone had been affected by his card's power. Unable to keep their feet, they had been helpless. And all from one stomp of his foot.

You couldn't buy that type of intimidation for a hundred Rare card shards.

Valentina shuffled up to him. Soft slippers were visible under her floral gown, but they did nothing to soften her appearance.

"So," she said in a normal volume that nonetheless could be heard by every ear in the room. "You thought you would throw your weight around a little, hmm? Give us all a show?"

He shook his head. "I apologize for the disturbance. I tried to warn Cornfellow—"

"That you have no control?" she asked lightly.

His lips twitched into a scowl, but his expression smoothed a moment later. "Once released, the energy must dissipate on its own. It's not my fault my card is powerful."

Arthur hissed from between his teeth, and from the shuffling and murmurs, he wasn't the only one.

Sometimes cards had drawbacks—some were so specialized they became unbalanced, and some were a flat-out double-edged sword. The more powerful the card, the greater the potential risk.

Arthur's Return to Start trap card was a lesser version of this. If he was attacked using a card power, he would be instantly transported to a set point without a limit for distance. That set it apart from most teleportation cards which had a strict distance limit. The instant transportation upon being attacked had saved his life.

The downside, naturally, was Arthur couldn't be certain what counted as an attack. A Sickness Seeker running an intrusive charm without Arthur's knowledge? A prank where someone charmed a paper animal to bop him on the head? A pickpocket using a Sneak card to get fingers on his valuables?

Arthur could never be sure, and until he finally traded for a Common card—at great expense—that could be used to nullify one card in his heart deck at will, he had been on edge.

It was thanks to that Nullify card that he hadn't been yanked out of the room when the Earth Ripple charm went off.

Granton continued. "It was a mistake to set off the card in a room with so much stone. I didn't realize the ripples would reflect so easily on one another."

Valentina shone a grandmotherly smile at him. That was what made her next words all the more biting. "No, you stupid boy, your mistake was thinking you would make any kind of dragon rider with a power you cannot control."

Granton's flush deepened. "I'm certain that any dragon who linked with me would have a card to fit my own—"

"By that, you mean to magnify your power." Valentina shuffled a step closer. "If you think I would allow anyone with an uncontrollable card anywhere near a scourge-eruption with civilians running for their lives, you had better think again."

"That's hardly fair," he began.

She turned away. "How many of you noblelings have seen an active scourge-eruption with your own eyes? Not the aftermath, not the rotten land or diseased people. How many have seen the cone? Come on. Raise your hand. You want to be dragon riders, and dragon riders are not shy."

Reluctantly, Arthur raised his hand. Two others did as well.

Perhaps he should have kept it to himself, but that had been a pivotal day in his life. Not acknowledging it felt like a betrayal.

Valentina's eyes fell on him for a moment. He looked back steadily.

After a moment, she turned back to Granton. "You're out. You aren't fit to link with a Common slug, much less a Rare dragon. Furthermore, for endangering a hive egg, you are sentenced to two weeks of hard labor in the dragon-soil fields."

The boy sputtered. "You can't do that!"

With one flick of her finger, a small puddle of spilled water lifted off the ground and slapped Granton across the face. His head snapped to the side, and he took a step back in shock.

"You'll find that I can," Valentina said. "Guards, get this idiot out of my sight."

The two guards that had been attending to the egg stepped off the stage to collect Granton.

Arthur suspected one of them had a subduing charm up his sleeve, as Granton didn't make much of a fuss.

"Now," Valentina said, "if there is anyone else among you with a similarly uncontrollable card, or feel they may not be suited for a life of killing scourglings, please leave. Well? Anyone? The door is open." She pointed helpfully.

There were some looks shared, but no one made a move to go.

The other leader, Whitaker, spoke up from his place by the egg. "I'd take her seriously, ladies and gentlemen. If she finds out you're lying and you're unlucky enough to link with the hatchling, she'll just slit your throat and have the dragon choose again."

A few uncomfortable coughs came from the audience. This time, three people left, shoulders hunched and ashamed. Arthur and everyone else did them the courtesy of pretending not to watch.

"Well, then," Valentina said, sunny and cheerful again. "Now that that's over with, let's get this egg hatched. You, you, and you. Terra Smithstrider, Ruban Hawker, Ernest Kane." She pointed to the three who had raised their hands to indicate they'd seen live eruptions. "You're up to greet the hatchling first."

CHAPTER 5

You lucky dog," Arthur heard from Cressida's direction.

He shot a look at her and shrugged. He couldn't deny it.

Some of the nobles here had been working for weeks in duels and basic showmanship to earn the coveted honor to meet the hatchling when it emerged. Now, thanks to the whims of the hive leadership, he stood in their place.

Too bad there was zero chance of him linking with the dragon.

Dragons could not link cards with people who held a higher-tiered card in their heart. From what he understood, the stronger magic was incompatible with a dragon's magical core.

Unlike people who had heart decks, dragons were hatched with a card at the core of their being. This was the new card they brought into the world and the one that continued on after their deaths. While they could collect more cards like any other magical being, their core card was the one they could never trade out.

It would be like Arthur trying to trade out his skin. Not only would it never work, it would get gruesome real quick.

One question that remained a mystery was how the dragon developed its new card while it matured in the egg: if it was influenced by the cards around it or if it was laid preordained with a certain card already in its core. There were solid arguments for the first theory, as baby dragons regularly hatched early—inexplicably fully formed—when they sensed the perfect partner card nearby. But others who took their time to hatch, like today, still found their riders and linked cards together to form a stronger power.

Arthur wasn't sure what he believed, but he knew with two Legendary cards in his heart, the Rare dragon wouldn't give him a sniff.

As he ascended the stairs, his mind was filled not by the egg in front of him, but by the tiny Legendary egg he'd seen today. What kind of a card would fit that dragon?

Did he dare try to link with it? Would it even want him if he did? And what if the Legendary dragon picked someone else? Then Arthur would be known as a Legendary card wielder—something that the "son" of Baron Kane or Arthur the nobody bartender should not be.

"Line up, you three. Tallest to shortest," Whitaker said with a wink toward them.

That grouping left Arthur in the middle between Ruban and Terra.

The groups of nobles had clustered together at the front of the stage. Even though he knew logically that every eye was on the egg, he still felt the weight of their gazes.

He never thought of himself as shy of crowds before.

Whitaker waited until Valentina ascended the stage. She didn't walk up the short stairs like a normal person. Instead, she conjured a cloud to float her up the three and a half feet.

Arthur thought he saw Whitaker roll his eyes. His derision was gone a moment later as he held out his hand to the egg. Once again, it floated into the air.

"Normally, we allow dragons to hatch on their own, but this one started cracking its shell two days ago. It's too valuable to the hive to allow it to go into distress. If it is weak, linking usually helps bolster its health. Now, you three are to greet the dragon first. It may be woozy and confused. If it shows no interest, then you are to step away and allow the next three to come up."

At that, he swept his gaze down to the well-dressed mob crowding up against the stage.

"Well? What are you waiting for? Form an orderly line. First come, first serve. Hurry up!"

Whitaker had just told them to be organized, but Arthur caught quite a bit of shoving and elbows. The first ten or so were boys with what he suspected were Body Enhancement cards.

Cressida had managed to secure herself a place behind them, however. The boy who stood behind her was rubbing at a char mark on his arm.

Whitaker waited until the line was formed and then turned his attention back to the egg. His outstretched fingers twitched. Abruptly, a thin piece of metal shot out of his pocket and wedged itself delicately in between a jagged crack in the shell.

After that, it took no time at all. Whitaker's sliver of metal cut the shell away as if it were made of fabric. Whitaker's dragon had a Legendary-level material-altering card. That, paired with Whitaker's Telekinesis card, made for an effective combination.

Without even touching it, he managed to peel away the shell like someone would take off a jacket. Only a slick off-white membrane was left, the dragonet's limbs visibly pushing against it. Arthur wasn't sure if Whitaker used his metal tool to split open the membrane sac or if the dragon managed to do the last bit.

Either way, the sac opened, and the dragon tumbled several inches to the floor in an ungainly wet mass.

It was . . . very, *very* pink.

Vividly pink. Shockingly see-it-coming-from-a-mile-away pink. Wet and newly born, it seemed to glow with that same inner light Arthur had seen with Sams.

The dragonet's head and body were delicately thin. Feminine was probably the right term, as it extended two long wings which blushed to a pale rose color on the underside. She opened large blue eyes.

The tough boys who had muscled their way to the front of the line all drew back as if horrified.

Arthur was a little surprised, too. Though he hadn't daydreamed about linking with this dragon, he had wondered what color and power it would have. His best guess was a brown earth or naturalistic green.

Pinks were generally knowledge-based or meta-wild cards.

The little dragon lay on the ground, neck stretched out as it gasped for air. Arthur could see the frantic pulse of its heart in the veins under its thin skin.

He wondered if maybe they should have let it hatch in its own time.

Without thinking, Arthur bent to help it, even if he could only lift its head to breathe easier. He had never raised any of the **Nursecraft** skills past the most basic levels, but common sense told him someone should clear the egg goo from its nostrils.

He should have known better. The baby dragon recoiled weakly from his outstretched hand.

"No," she said in a feather-soft voice. "Your card . . . isn't right . . ."

Arthur stopped, torn between helping the creature and backing away.

"Move aside, Ernest," Valentina said. "This one isn't for you."

"I wasn't trying to link it—" Arthur stopped before he dug a hole for himself. Bowing his head, he moved to the side.

Whitaker looked to the other two. "Well? What are you waiting for?"

Terra and Ruban jumped, but under Whitaker's scowl they did what they were told and stepped forward, though they both seemed reluctant.

The baby dragon let out a pained mewl of distress, flexing too-big wings as if she wanted to fly away from those two. They quickly backed off.

"Hurry now," Whitaker snapped, looking down into the audience. "Who's up next?"

Some of the nobles—the brawny boys especially—were easing their way toward the exit. Pink dragons weren't a favorite among those who wanted strength and power.

Whitaker's face darkened.

Valentina was a bit more direct. With a crack of air, a rime of frost froze the door shut an instant before the first noble reached to open it.

"Anyone who touches that door earns themselves an automatic week in the lowest level of the dragon-soil pits. I don't care who your fathers are."

"Let me through!" Cressida pushed past two boys, each thicker than two of her put together, in an effort to reach the stage.

One boy moved aside, and she ran up the stairs, hand outstretched with palm open to the dragon.

"No," the pink rasped, big blue eyes seeming to look past her.

Cressida froze. "What do I do? What card do you need?"

"That's not how it works, child. Stand aside for the next," Valentina snapped.

The pink dragon didn't answer Cressida. It only lay there limply, breathing in wet gasps.

Arthur reached to press against Cressida's shoulder and was surprised when Cressida allowed herself to be moved away.

People started to ascend the stage one by one, most looking intimidated and unenthusiastic. But they were complying. The pink had little to no reaction to any of them.

Cressida stared after the dragon helplessly, fists clenched. With a shock, Arthur realized she truly wanted this dragon.

"I'm sorry," he started to say, but she cut him off.

"What do you think it meant?" Cressida hissed. "You find the right card, you link with a dragon. Pink isn't that too far off from red, and reds are fire based. It could still choose me, right?"

"Red is more energy and transformation," Arthur said.

"Transformation is mostly the oranges," she countered.

"There are gradients. Aren't pinks supposed to be smart?"

She whirled on him, nostrils flared. "Are you calling me stupid?"

Oops.

Arthur held up his hands in a peaceable gesture. "You know what I'm trying to say. Don't pinks usually link with a scholarly card?"

Her lips pressed together, and she nodded once in sharp apology before turning back. "We can't let this stand. Surely someone in this tiny hive has a card it will like. Or . . . do you think the shops will have one for sale?"

Arthur didn't answer. The line to stand by the pink was halfway gone, and it was obvious the dragon wasn't reacting to anyone. Those who had walked past were allowed to leave.

Whitaker stood to the side in deep conversation with someone in a Sickness Seeker uniform.

The Sickness Seeker approached to scan the hatchling with a haze of green magic coating his hands. The dragon whined and tried to get up—to move away from his magic.

As it did, Arthur caught a hint of black veining on its pink belly.

The Sickness Seeker caught it too. He backed up with a gasp.

"By my first card, that dragon is scourge-touched!"

CHAPTER 6

One of the girls let out a short, sharp scream.

The nobles near the hatchling drew back in horror. One scuttled to the side so fast he toppled off the edge of the stage and fell with a crash.

This created a cascade effect where everyone else hurriedly backed away. Within a few seconds, some outright ran for the door, Valentina's threats forgotten.

Even Cressida gasped and did a half shuffle-step to the side before she regained control of herself.

Arthur stood stock still. Stunned.

Valentina and Whitaker stood on either side of the Sickness Seeker and either seemed to be berating him for his lack of tact . . . or questioning how in the world this was possible *while* berating him.

The little pink dragon lay limply on the stage, alone and forgotten. It didn't have the strength to hold up its head. Arthur didn't like how its mouth lay open as if gasping for air.

He couldn't let this stand.

He strode forward, having to sidestep to avoid people who'd taken the leaders' distraction as an opportunity to run away.

"What are you doing?" Cressida demanded. She followed behind him against the current of people.

"The scourge can't get to us. We're carded," he snapped, frustrated not by her but by the actions of those around them. Had everyone lost their minds?

Within moments, nearly the entire room had emptied except for him, Cressida, the leaders, and the Sickness Seeker.

"I know that," Cressida said, though she seemed heartened by his words and increased the length of her stride to walk along beside him. "I asked what are *you* doing."

"The dragon's dying. I'm giving it some time."

Arthur remembered the black veins that had crawled through his friend Ernie's body. He vividly recalled how it had felt to stand next to his bedside, personally protected from scourge-sickness thanks to his own card, while he'd been helpless to save his friend.

Arthur only received his Master of Skills card because of the actions of a dragon. The very least he could do was to help another one.

The little pink dragon stirred uncomfortably as he approached. She looked like she wanted to shake her head at them—she sensed they didn't have the right cards—but had already become so weakened she couldn't make the effort.

"I know," Arthur said. "I'm not here to link with you. I'm here to help you."

The dragon wheezed in a breath, ribs inflating like a bellows. "It hurts . . ."

The scourge-sickness, its own weakness, or the fact it hadn't found someone to link with yet? Arthur suspected all three.

How to explain this to a child? "I'm going to work magic over you, to give you more time. It won't hurt, but you shouldn't fight the magic."

The hatchling let out another wheezing gasp. "Time . . . to find the right card?"

"Yes."

With a last wheeze, she closed her eyes. But not before her head edged up and down in a nod.

That was all the permission his card required.

Reaching out, Arthur pressed gentle fingers on its vivid pink scales. In the next moment, the hatchling dragon disappeared into his storage space.

That got everyone's attention.

Cressida gasped. The healer cried out in horror. A violent gust of wind whipped Arthur around. Suddenly, he was face-to-face with a very angry Valentina and Whitaker.

"What did you just do?" Whitaker demanded.

His tone was flat, but only a fool would discount the dangerous glint in his eye.

Arthur held up his empty hands in front of him. "The dragon is fine. I have a storage utility card. Nothing ages while it's stored in there, so I thought—to give it more time—"

"Show me," Valentina said, voice cut with ice.

Arthur winced. It was impolite to ask someone to reveal the details of a card. Thankfully, he had the choice to display only one of his cards in his heart deck, not all of them.

Concentrating on his heart deck as his father had once taught him to do, Arthur gestured outward. With the flick of his hand came the ghostly outline of his Personal Space card, complete with details.

Personal Space
Rare
Utility
The wielder of this card is granted an extra dimensional space, 30 x 30 x 30 sq. ft. in which to store objects. As this space exists outside of time, the stored contents will experience no aging once placed inside. Contents will resume aging normally when removed. This dimensional space is only accessible by the card wielder, and objects inside cannot be sensed by lower than a Legendary-rank seeker.

"It's a Rare power," Whitaker said. "You just got damn lucky, kid. Unlinked, newly hatched dragons are fragile. You could have poisoned it by storing it with a lesser card."

Valentina was not so forgiving. "What gives you the right to touch a dragon which already rejected you?"

Arthur drew himself up, even though a part of him wondered the same thing. "Forgive me, but I've seen scourge-sickness before. It acts fast, and the dragon seemed to be fading. If you have someone with another storage power or a healing card, I can pull the dragon out in a moment. You can see the card's description. No time will have passed for it."

Valentina narrowed her eyes. "That's twice in one day I find you in the middle of hive trouble. I don't like this pattern that's emerging *or* your arrogance in thinking you know what's best. You"—she pointed a finger at him, and it was as if a spear of air hit his chest, knocking him back a step—"are involving yourself in high-level dragon-rider business when you're a nobody."

Arthur wanted to argue . . . but he couldn't. He knew it had been a risky move, but it hadn't stopped him. At least the pink dragon was safe until they could find a solution.

Cressida seemed to be thinking along the same lines.

"Will this give us time to find a proper healer for the dragon?"

Valentina and Whitaker looked back to the Sickness Seeker. The man winced. "Not in this hive, I'm afraid."

"What do you mean?" Arthur demanded.

"Surely you have veterinary staff on call?" Cressida said on the heels of his words.

"It's not a cold or a scrape, it's the *scourge*. It's the antithesis of worldly life." The Sickness Seeker's tone had taken on a cadence, as if this was something he'd said many times before, either in a lecture or a sermon. "No low-tiered Sickness Seeker or Sickness Destroyer can handle it. This takes true healing on a higher level. It will need a Legendary healer or better."

Whitaker muttered a curse under his breath, turning away to run a hand down his face. "That means Harvest Moon Hive."

"No!" Valentina said before the healer had time to nod. "Harvest will lend us a healer and take the Rare as payment, if not the—" She stopped short and scowled. Though Arthur could guess what she was about to say. *If not the Legendary egg as well.*

Valentina's ire turned to Cressida. "Why are you here, Lady Icehouse? I understand Ernest feels the need to stick his nose in high-level business, but your friends have already fled." She gestured toward the door in disgust.

Cressida lifted her chin. "I'm staying because I intend to link with this dragon."

Whitaker barked a laugh. Valentina's scowl deepened. "Don't you have some sort of a flame summon card, child? Do you think that would be attractive to a *pink* dragon?"

"Then I'll purchase a card that's acceptable," Cressida insisted. "An intelligence enhancer or a tactic card . . ." She trailed off at the looks of doubt on the leaders' faces.

Reluctantly, Arthur agreed. The chances of the perfect Rare card that just so happened to be for sale were slim. And once Cressida put it in her heart, she would have a hard time taking it out again. He knew that by painful experience.

"Enough of this nonsense." Whitaker turned back to regard Arthur critically. "Your little stunt got my attention. But do you think we'll let you walk around the hive freely with an unlinked Rare hatchling in your storage?"

Arthur knew he couldn't allow himself a moment of doubt. "Yes."

The leader's eyes narrowed, and Arthur was very aware that he could strip the meat off his bones with the strength of his telekinesis. That was, if Valentina didn't get to him first. But the elderly woman remained silent, watching this play out.

After what seemed to be an age, Whitaker said, "Why?"

"If you had someone with a better storage space you could trust, you would have sent for them by now," Arthur said. "You read my card. As long as the dragon is stored, it's safe. Only a Legendary Seeker or better could find it there. Furthermore, this gives you time to quietly pay a healer to arrive, or make other arrangements." He glanced at Cressida, who smiled thinly back.

"All of which we could do with you locked up," Whitaker said easily.

"But you won't want to draw attention to where the dragon's gone." Arthur's heart was pounding in his chest, but he didn't allow the panic he felt at making this up as he went along to show on his face. Besides, he still had one winning card up his sleeve. "You're the only ones who saw me store the dragon. And there's one other thing."

Whitaker's eyes narrowed another degree. He looked like a snake about to strike. "What would that be?"

"You know I'll be loyal to you. I . . . I won't take off with the pink because I don't want it." He took a breath. "I want a chance at the Legendary egg. And I know I have to keep in your good graces to get it."

Valentina spoke up, voice droll. "Am I to believe the most *honorable* Baron Kane had an extra Legendary card he just happened never to tell anyone about? Especially after what happened when he lost the first?"

"I wouldn't ever disclose family secrets, ma'am."

He half expected one or perhaps both of the leaders to strike him down for insolence.

Instead, Whitaker turned to Valentina. Arthur didn't see what expression passed over his face, but the old woman raised her eyebrows.

"It's a cheap price for the cooperation, Val," Whitaker said.

The old woman scowled but then turned back to Arthur. "I can't guarantee you the first try at that Legendary egg. Once we open those floodgates, every high noble son and daughter will want to try their luck. The competition will make these Rare promenades look like a puff of breeze in the face of a hurricane. Do you understand?"

He nodded.

Valentina turned to Cressida. "And you, girl. Do you want a shot at the pink? Then you had best keep your mouth shut about what you've seen tonight."

Cressida nodded, though her eyes were sparkling. Arthur had the feeling she was itching to run down to every card shop in the city and start throwing coins around.

"Then, *Ernest Kane*," Valentina emphasized the name, "I charge you to keep our little pink dragon safe."

Arthur's knees kept him steady right up until the moment he walked out of the room. He leaned against the stone wall, breathing hard.

Also, he had a notification.

He'd gained another level in **Acting**.

CHAPTER 7

Oh, decided you still work here, huh?" was Bob's greeting as Arthur walked in through the back kitchen door.

Arthur shrugged. "Hive duties come first, Bob. You know that."

"Don't play virtuous recruit with me. I don't know what scam you're playing, but you've got no more eye for that damn egg than most of those nobles." Bob eyed him while he spoke, rubbing a dishrag over a mug that had been thoroughly cleaned. "But it was supposed to hatch tonight, right?"

Arthur wasn't surprised Bob had mostly figured him out, or that he knew hive gossip. He was a canny owner and had built a place for people to talk freely.

"Yes, but there were complications," he said, hedging. "I can do a few hours in the mornings here, Bob, or the cleaning shift in the evenings. But I gotta stay in the back."

Bob's eyebrows shot up. "You want to keep out of sight? What happened? Your scheme go sour on you?"

"Something like that." In reality, his "scheme" was nowhere near done. But Ernest Kane could not be seen at the front of the house, bartending.

Arthur had extended an olive branch, however. Bob was always having trouble hiring good staff for the early-morning prep-work shift. Arthur had done his fair share as a new-hire kid, freshly graduated from classes. He knew the work and mostly didn't mind it.

"Fine," Bob said. "You start tomorrow morning, first shift."

"You don't need help now?"

"No. It's dead out there. Take a look."

Now it was Arthur's turn to raise his brows. He stepped to the entrance that separated the kitchen area from the main tavern and pulled the heavy fabric aside.

Sure enough, only a few patrons sat at the bar—and those kept well away from one another. The tavern was almost eerily silent.

"Rumor's been circling," Bob said to Arthur's silent question. "Some say scourge-infection's taking hold here in the heart of a hive. It's put a chill up men's spines."

So, some of the news had leaked out. Not a surprise considering how fast the nobles fled. Arthur bet a fair few signaled for purple dragon transport to get them home at once—and weren't shy in saying why.

"Carded men and women have nothing to fear from scourge-diseases," Arthur said. "And this hive has been free of scourglings for centuries."

Bob finally abandoned the glass he'd been wiping dry and switched it out for another. "People know that here." His free hand touched his temple. "But not here." His fingers moved to his heart. "They'll likely get over it soon, once the shock wears off. But until then . . . well, no one is in the mood for celebration."

Bob's words stayed with Arthur as he made his way out of the hive. To his annoyance, he found that they resonated with him, too.

A whole new world of skills had just opened up to him thanks to his Master of Body Enhancement card. Not to mention how it paired with his current Master of Skills card . . .

But he found he didn't have the appetite for it.

So much had happened over a short period, and he hadn't yet had time to process it all. The black egg. Scourge's appearance in the hive. How was that even possible? Oh, and the little fact that he was carrying a dying baby dragon in his storage.

With that in mind, he focused on his Personal Space card. It happened to come with a convenient list.

(2) bags of beef jerky
(1) woolen shirt
(1) winter jacket
(2) silver coins
(1) pair of boots
(1) pink shimmer dragon (F)

Interesting that his card had not labeled the dragon as scourge-touched, yet had included that it was of a higher shimmer quality and its gender. Arthur hadn't been able to tell if it had a shimmer—that was, a sparkly aspect from a dragon's normal base color, considering it had still been wet with egg goo.

And it didn't mention the dragon's name. Was that because Arthur didn't know the dragon's name or because the dragon itself didn't know?

Some dragons gave their name, and some allowed themselves to be named. From what Arthur understood, it was mostly the Commons that allowed their linked partners to choose a name for them. The higher-ranked dragons had minds of their own.

Arthur supposed he would be one of the first to find out. Valentina told him to be ready to come to their call at a moment's notice.

Of course, she didn't share her ultimate plans with someone as low as Arthur, but he suspected the two leaders were on the hunt for healers who knew how to keep their mouths shut, and Rare card wielders with knowledge-type cards.

Well, Valentina told him to be ready at a moment's notice, but she hadn't ordered him to stay in the hive. She was a Legendary elemental card wielder linked with a Legendary weather dragon. He was certain she could find him whenever she pleased.

With that in mind, Arthur made his way down to the hive's ground level and through the gates out to the city.

The last month or so while he'd waited for the heat to die down after the theft of the cards had been . . . trying. He hadn't dared go to his regular haunts or places nobles were likely to show up.

So Arthur had gone exploring and found a gambling hall that didn't ask too many questions about age.

They might if Arthur ever came away winning big jackpots, but he was much too careful for that.

The gambling hall he chose tonight was set at the dead end of a canal, where the water had nowhere to drain to or from. It took on a greenish look and a rotten smell. The men who regularly visited weren't much better. Most had the smell of the dragon-soil fields on them, which meant they were serving a criminal sentence.

Arthur's game, when he wanted a challenge for his Gambling Class, was blackjack.

While he had a card-counting skill, the house couldn't be entirely trusted. Neither could the players, for that matter. It introduced randomness in the game.

Arthur still came out ahead—most of the time—but he had to work for it. And he made sure not to take too much from the house.

Unfortunately, one of the players sitting at his table didn't have the same self-control. Arthur wasn't sure what trick he tried, but a card-anchor stone in the middle of the table suddenly whistled like a teakettle. The chair he sat in lit up with a strong glow, and three burly men converged on the fool.

Arthur winced as the man was dragged to the back of the gambling hall. Likely, to be taught a lesson.

It soured his taste for the game. He walked away after the next hand, only up by two silvers.

By then it was so late at night it was practically dawn.

Arthur hesitated before he picked a direction. Should he return to his old apartment or take Kenzie's advice and keep to his new room in the hive like a proper noble son?

Before he could fully decide, he heard shouting. That wasn't too unusual for this part of town. The fact that the voice was female was a little odd, though. Thankfully, she seemed only blisteringly angry and not in distress.

The voice rounded the corner, and Arthur blinked in surprise when he saw Cressida striding alongside a man in scholar's robes and, from the sounds of it, tearing verbal stripes off his back.

I wouldn't want to be in his shoes, he thought, amused.

A moment later, Cressida looked up and caught Arthur's eye. She turned back to the scholar and snarled, "Fine. You've always been useless to the family. I don't know why I'm surprised."

Then she turned on her heel and stomped toward Arthur.

He would never, ever say so, but she looked much like her flame bear: hunched angry shoulders and hands so tense they were almost claws.

Arthur watched her come up to him, knowing he hadn't done anything wrong and yet absolutely sure he was about to be in a world of trouble.

Shoving down the unmanly urge to turn tail and see if he could acquire a **Quick Escape** skill, Arthur stood his ground.

Something—likely a nudge from his Charming Gentleperson card—made him say, "Cressida, how nice to see you this night—uh . . ." He glanced at the sky which had a growing hint of dawn. "Morning?"

This earned him a scowl as she closed the distance between them. "Don't tell me you've been on the hunt, too?"

"The . . . hunt?"

"For cards!" she snapped, throwing her hands up in the air. "Not like there's anything good around here. Have you ever seen a hive city this tiny? They have only a handful of card shops. And of course, they're scattered in all directions, and it seems *somebody* has cleaned them out."

She glanced over her shoulder as she spoke, still frowning at the retreating figure in scholar's robes.

"Was he an attendant?" Arthur asked. He could imagine a noble lady like Cressida would not be allowed to walk around unaccompanied in the middle of the night in a strange city. Then again, she had a Rare combat card.

She shook her head. "A cousin, and not a favorite one." Her dark look returned. "Why don't any of the shops have anything but cards suitable for farmers?"

"They're not that bad," Arthur said, a little stung.

She gave him a *look*.

"They have a great selection," he insisted out of a sense of local pride.

"Ah-ha!" She wagged a finger at him. "You *were* searching for knowledge-type cards for the dragon!"

She was slightly too wild-eyed, and there were darker bags under her eyes now visible in the light.

Arthur spoke slowly. "You heard me make a deal with Valentina. My goal isn't a Rare dragon."

She blinked and then slumped, rubbing at her eyes. "Of course. Forgive me. It's been a long night, and when I saw you out here, I assumed . . . well, it doesn't matter."

"You've been searching for cards all night?" he asked.

She nodded. "Either the lack of variety around this hive is criminal, or others have gotten there first and bought out the supply of knowledge cards."

He very much doubted that. The other nobles and Rare hopefuls had fled at the thought of a scourge-infected dragon. Cressida might be the only one in all the hive willing to try her hand.

"I even went to my cousin Jayer." She waved a hand in the direction of the scholar. "You know what they say about the scholar's guild, but he's such a stickler for the rules . . ." She made a frustrated sound in the back of her throat. "It's ridiculous. I'm hitting walls wherever I go!"

"No, I don't know what they say about the guild," Arthur admitted. "Remember, my father's barony is in the back end of nowhere."

"Well, I'm not talking about the blue rumors of what they get up to under those robes." Cressida's smile faded when he didn't smile back, obviously not understanding. Her eyebrows went up. "Never mind. I'm talking about the scholar's library, of course. They hoard knowledge and meta cards like a broody hen over her eggs—you remember that small brouhaha five years ago?"

"We don't get much news out in the back end, either," Arthur said.

He touched her elbow to guide her down the street in the direction where he knew several vendors set up carts to provide early-morning food. The ones that provided baked goods kept early hours. And frankly, Cressida still looked wild-eyed from her night of frantic searching. She could use something to eat.

They turned the corner, and Arthur saw several carts setting up. The smell of baked goods rose in the air.

"That smells wonderful," Cressida said. She strode forward as if she was about to demand to be fed right then and there.

Arthur pulled her back. "They're still setting up. We're early, even for the bakers. Tell me about what happened with the scholars."

Cressida gave him a sidelong look. "You say you're from the back end, but so am I. It was the talk of the kingdom."

He shrugged. Perhaps it was in noble circles, but five years ago he had been living in a border village that was little more than a death camp. He didn't know how to read, and no kingdom criers came to deliver the latest reports. "Maybe I've heard but forgot. Tell me anyway, and I'll buy you a pastry."

Her smile was slight. "You drive a hard bargain, Ernest, but . . . I suppose that's all right." Then, to his surprise, she once again wound her arm through his so they could walk together along the canal which bordered the street. This time, though, she pulled him close and spoke softly to keep the conversation between the two of them. "You have at least heard of the scholar's grand library?"

Arthur nodded, even though he hadn't. He didn't want to come off as too ignorant.

"Well, what's lesser known are the smaller regional libraries scattered across the kingdom. That way, if a scholar wants to pursue a niche subject like, oh, the study of a variety of hazelnut specific to a region, they go to that library, stick an appropriate card in their anchor tattoo, and research to their heart's content."

Arthur nodded along. This made sense. He also wished his old orphanage headmistress, Freyja, had explained that scholar's guilds had access to card libraries. Likely, it wouldn't have changed his mind about not joining, but he might have found some use for them . . .

"Well," Cressida continued, "some of the scholars have been getting lazy over the last decade or so. And"—she lowered her voice further—"it's said the king's inquisitors weren't spot-checking the libraries as they ought."

Arthur thought he knew where this was going. "The cards rotted?"

Cressida nodded. "Not just a few, either. By the time it was discovered, and a survey was taken . . . several whole libraries were practically useless. Thousands of cards were gone, including many Rares, and, it's said, several Legendaries."

Arthur grimaced.

Cards didn't exactly rot like a piece of fruit left out, but it wasn't too far off, either.

Magic cards left sitting out without being added to a person's deck and used eventually lost their integrity and crumbled away. Common cards, which held the weakest magic, were said to be safe for up to six months unused outside of a deck. Uncommon cards, several years. The length went up from there.

To lose powerful Rares, or, even more unthinkable, Legendaries was . . . criminal.

"Several high scholars lost their heads," Cressida commented.

He nodded, feeling that was just punishment.

Each of those cards represented power and health to someone who was uncarded. It could mean the difference between life and death out at the borders.

It was distasteful the scholars hoarded them for themselves but not a surprise. Nobles and families of great wealth did it. But to then let those cards rot, unused . . .

All those cards were forever gone from the world. All that magic was wasted. Sets that could never be completed . . .

Not that the king condoned card sets. But still.

By this time, they had reached the vendor carts. Arthur used a few coppers from his hard-earned money to purchase sweet rolls and a bitter hot tea that was famous for pepping people up in the morning.

Something interesting happened at his first sip.

Thanks to an infusion of black tea, your base stamina has temporarily been increased by one point. This is a temporary effect and will result in a three-point temporary backlash once the effect wears off.

Time left: 4 hours 59 minutes, 59 seconds.

You have gained a body enhancement: Exhaustion Resistance (Stamina)

Due to your previous experience and your card's bonus traits, you automatically start this enhancement at level 7.

He blinked. A body enhancement. Not a skill. That was interesting.

Also, was that why he sometimes felt worse after drinking morning tea? This had hardly been his first all-nighter or the first time he had sipped the strong tea to combat it. Though now that he thought about it, he did usually feel awful by the afternoon. He thought that was due to his lack of sleep.

Also, exhaustion resistance was a valuable enhancement to acquire. How did that differ from skills?

His thoughts were derailed as Cressida made a very . . . distracting sound on her first bite of pastry.

"This is divine," she exclaimed, and then promptly tipped a copper to the smiling vendor.

Then, slipping her arm within Arthur's again, she hastened him down the street. Arthur was happy to go with her. He had a shift at Bob's, but otherwise, his day was free until the hive leaders called for him. Besides, it seemed Cressida had something in mind.

As soon as they were some way down the street and not likely to be overheard, she asked, "How is the dragon? Is he okay?"

"*She*," he said, "And yes. Time doesn't pass for whatever I store, so she's in the exact same condition as last night."

"She," Cressida repeated, a little wonder in her voice. "I wasn't entirely sure, but I hoped . . . Can you possibly bring her out? Just for a moment? Not in the street in plain view, of course. But . . ." She trailed off as Arthur shook his head.

"That wouldn't be a good idea," he said, voice low.

"I wouldn't tell anyone—"

He shook his head and glanced around, though he didn't see anyone. "Do you think," he said carefully, "Whitaker and Valentina would just let me skip off through the hive and the city without somehow keeping an eye on me? With an unlinked Rare in my storage?"

Cressida's green eyes widened, and she looked around, but Arthur already knew she wouldn't see anyone. He hadn't gotten an indication he had a follower either. Nothing from his skills, no sounds he couldn't explain, not even a feeling of being watched.

Just his logic.

He had a **Stealth** skill, but a specialist with a strong **Stealth**-based card—one who used mana to aid them—could beat any skill.

Cressida seemed to come to the same conclusion. After a moment's fruitlessly looking around, her gaze returned to him. She leaned in close and whispered, "Then be sure to watch the shadows."

"The shadows?" he repeated.

She nodded and cut her eyes to the side, back down the street. "Stealth powers bend the light around them, but they don't always work well in the shadows." Then, in a louder voice meant to carry, she said, "Yes, Ernest, you may accompany me back to the hive if you wish."

He found he didn't have a choice in the matter. Not that he minded.

They walked along the slowly wakening streets and finished the rest of their pastries.

"So," Arthur said, "you never told me what you wanted from your scholarly cousin. Forgive me, but the conversation looked . . . intense."

Cressida frowned, but Arthur got the impression it wasn't at him. "I told you about their scholarly libraries. They have one here. A rather good-sized library, for the size of this place," she sniffed, reminding him of his friend Horatio. He had been dismissive of the size of the hive and city, too.

"And I was hoping to take a look at some of their cards. See if there was the possibility of a trade."

Arthur translated that as *bribe*.

"He said no?"

She sniffed. "Unequivocally. Said that only those in the scholar's guild were allowed access to the library. That's an excuse dipped in dragon soil. As a girl, I was allowed access to my village's scholarly library."

Arthur knew the reason why. "Could that be because you are the daughter of a powerful noble?"

"And I am still the daughter of a powerful noble," she snapped, turning, frustrated, to glare at him. "That's how these things work."

He very much wanted to tell her that "the way things worked" was unfair, and she was being a brat for throwing her family's weight and reputation around to gain access to restricted areas.

That was the type of thing Arthur Rowantree would say. Ernest Kane would agree with Cressida.

He couldn't make himself do it.

To his surprise, Cressida did not double down on her assertion. The fight seemed to drain out of her. She sighed, leaning against him a little. "It doesn't matter. Even if I could convince the scholars to trade . . . I don't know if I would be picking the right card for her." Her eyes went to Arthur's chest, almost as if she could see the dragon inside.

"Dragons only choose based on the cards in your heart, not in a card-anchor tattoo," Arthur confirmed.

"Not that I would ever get a tattoo," she said loftily. Again, she deflated. "I suppose I could pick a short list and try them in my heart deck one by one. If the cards were only there for a moment . . ."

Arthur shook his head vigorously. "Have you ever taken a card out of your heart?"

He felt Cressida shudder in revulsion as she shook her head.

"I have," he said.

She turned to stare at him. "What? When? *Why?*"

"I was just a boy, and the card had been in my heart for less than a day. But . . . part of it had already become part of me. It hurt like a constant bruise." He tapped his chest meaningfully. "And it didn't get better until eventually, I put the card back."

Cressida continued staring, shock mixed with a bit of admiration in her gaze. He could tell she wanted to press more, but Arthur wasn't going to tell the entire story.

"The point is, whatever you stick in your heart becomes part of you," he added. "That's why we use card anchors for temporary powers."

"Everybody knows that."

"There's a difference between knowing something and experiencing something," he said with emphasis. "If you get the chance to choose from the library . . . I suggest you pick something that you can live with. Because once you put it in your heart, I don't think you'll be able to take it out again."

Slowly, Cressida nodded, and they walked the rest of the way to the hive in silence.

All the while, Arthur kept his attention on the shadows, looking at them out of the corner of his eye.

Nothing seemed odd, and if he was being followed, the person doing it wasn't so careless as to let the long cast of a morning shadow stand out.

At least, until they got to the hive entrance.

The guarded archway was bracketed by several torches that had been lit during the night but hadn't yet been put out for the morning.

The morning sunlight was still just dim enough to allow the fires to cast crazy shadows. And in them, just for a moment, Arthur caught a glimpse of a head and shoulders that didn't belong to him or Cressida. And it was too far away to have come from either one of the standing guards.

He exchanged a few words with the guard on duty and glanced casually back the way he had come. No one stood visibly behind him, but he had no doubt: Valentina and Whitaker were having him watched.

CHAPTER 8

Arthur felt like he had been asleep for five seconds before he heard a knock at his door. He woke, bleary and disoriented at his new surroundings. It took him a startlingly long time to remember Kenzie had gotten him a room in the hive.

It was small and by no means fancy. An inner room without a window. He was lucky it came with a cot to sleep in.

But he had lived in much worse circumstances.

The knock at the door came again, and Arthur peeled his face off his stiff pillow long enough to call out, "Yes? Who is it?"

A rattle of keys was his answer, and Arthur sat up just in time to see an unfamiliar man stride into his room.

He reached for a belt knife that had been attached to his pants . . . which lay crumpled on the floor, too far away to easily grab. In his mind, he toggled the option off his Nullify card to activate his Return to Start card just in case —

The man bowed.

"I'm sorry to bother you, sir. Leaders Valentina and Whitaker request your presence at once."

Arthur gaped. "Of . . . of course," he said, finally focusing on the man's uniform and seeing the insignia of a hive attendant.

The crisscrossing tunnels through the levels of the hive were a nightmare to navigate for locals, much less visiting nobility. This man had likely been sent not only as a messenger but as a guide.

"I'll be out in a moment," Arthur said pointedly.

The man nodded, and with a swift, curious look at Arthur's humble surroundings, he made his way back out and closed the door.

Arthur slumped, mentally reactivating his Nullify card over his trap card. Not that his Return to Start would have done him any good. He hadn't keyed in a new location as an escape point, should the worst happen. So, it would have automatically returned him to the last place he woke up: his bed.

"I have got to be smarter," he muttered to himself. Especially now that the hive leaders' eyes were on him.

With that in mind, he dressed quickly in his newest, cleanest clothing. His outfit wasn't comparable to what nobles usually wore. He would have to hope they thought the Kane barony was too poor to properly support him.

Then he tore a small corner from a spare piece of paper he had been jotting notes on. He once again reached for his Return to Start card.

Would you like to key in a safe location point?

Arthur mentally selected yes and focused on the small square of paper.

A moment later, a tiny card mark—the image of his Return to Start card—miniaturized to the point most details were lost, appeared on the piece of paper as if inked there.

He slipped it into his pocket. On his way, he intended to drop the tiny corner piece in the tunnel system.

Should the worst happen in the next couple of hours, he would at least give his attacker a surprise.

It would have to do, and he would rekey in a better location as soon as he could. Bob's tavern, perhaps.

When Arthur stepped out of the room, freshly dressed with his hair combed back, the messenger gestured down the tunnel. "This way, sir."

They passed by windows on the long walk up, and Arthur saw it was late afternoon, coming into the evening. He had been asleep longer than he thought and blamed the stamina penalty for his fogginess.

That, too, was starting to wear off. A quick check showed he was only one point down from his usual base. Which was good, because the messenger seemed to be leading him almost up to the top of the hive.

Arthur needed every bit of his stamina for the long climb.

Nobles and other people of means paid a dragon rider—usually a purple—to carry them up the slopes if they had business on a high level.

The man sent to fetch him took Arthur the long way up the flights of stairs. Worse, like everything else in the hive, the way was twisted and meandering. They would take a stairway up and walk the length of a tunnel or two until they came to the next stairway to take them to the next level.

Arthur had never been past the seventh level. At level ten, he no longer walked on the bare floor but thinly carpeted pathways. That carpeting became newer and thicker as they continued upward.

Soon, he spotted murals painted on the stone walls: idyllic scenes depicting dragons in flight or mimicking the landscape around the hive in various seasons.

As they went higher, those murals were replaced with paintings that could be removed and cleaned.

Furniture was added along the tunnels too, for sitting and relaxing. Windows were cut directly into the rock to give views out in every direction. Doorways led out to grand, sweeping balconies that seemed to extend so close to the clouds he felt he could reach out and touch them.

Delicious smells melted out of the kitchens. Though Arthur thought he ate very well as it was, he was extremely curious to try the dishes of the upper class.

They were so high up that some of the windows sported delicate fractals of ice on the outside. Thanks to the fireplaces here and there, Arthur didn't feel a bit of a chill.

No wonder Kenzie always talked about earning a place at the upper levels. They did well for themselves here.

Nevertheless, it was a long, arduous trek. Both he and the messenger sent to retrieve him were puffing for air by the time they reached their destination.

Arthur was mildly disappointed he hadn't earned a stair-climbing skill.

The messenger led him, finally, to a wide tunnel that ended at wooden double doors. Beyond, he heard raised, annoyed voices.

Another servant cracked the door open at the man's knock. The two spoke quietly, and Arthur heard, "Ernest Kane."

The second attendant quickly ushered Arthur in.

Valentina and Whitaker stood in the middle of the room, surrounded by a ring of men and women. Half wore black scholar's robes with the edges trimmed in gold, red, or brown depending on their rank. They all also wore extremely annoyed expressions. He recognized Cressida's cousin among them.

The other group was dressed in the loose white linen of those with sickness-seeking and healing cards, though the badges on their shoulders displayed various animals. These must be veterinary specialists. Unlike the scowling scholars, they wore professional and expectant looks on their faces.

Valentina broke off from the man talking at her and gestured to Arthur. "Come quickly, boy. We have people here to look over the dragon."

He had not managed to cross the room before he found himself surrounded by the veterinary staff. Most of whom barked questions about the nature of his storage space, if he had seen any degradation of the dragon's health, and how long he had kept the dragon in there already.

Arthur finally got a word in to explain the basics of how his storage space worked. Some looked mollified, but not the oldest man, who had wild gray hair and a no-nonsense attitude that reminded him of Valentina.

"Well? Remove the dragon. It's doing no one any good moldering in your heart deck." He shot the leaders an annoyed look. "In fact, I very well think it might be doing the creature worse."

One of the scholars made a sharp squeak of protest. "Wait, you're going to have the beast here? Isn't it scourge-ridden?"

"You can't do that!" a scholarly woman protested, stepping back, alarmed. "What if it infects us?"

"Don't be a fool," Whitaker snapped. "No carded person has anything to fear from the scourge."

"I do, if the dragon has turned into a scourgling!" protested a third scholar.

The others murmured in agreement.

Arthur couldn't keep the derision out of his voice. "That can't happen."

"What a thing to hear from a supposed man of intellect," Whitaker scoffed. Behind him, the scholar went purple in anger. Whitaker continued, "Well? Remove the dragon, boy. Let's see what we're dealing with."

But the scholars were not finished. One particularly round man with gold edging to his robes pushed forward. "Gentleman, ladies, if you insist on this foolishness, then we shall take ourselves elsewhere."

Lightning cracked so close to the outside windows that several people flinched.

Valentina spoke in an icy voice. "You will stay. Not only because we require the scholars to give us a working theory of how a dragon could have possibly become infected with the scourge, but your people are our best shot to link the beast."

The man started to sputter.

Valentina raised her voice to override him. It was easy since she had command of the air. "If the dragon shows no interest in your cards, you are, of course, free to go."

Arthur decided he'd had enough sniping between the two groups.

With a thought, he removed the baby dragon from his Personal Storage space.

She appeared in the same position as when he had stored her, lying limp and flat on the floor. Perhaps it was the light, but the baby dragon looked smaller and paler than before.

Instantly, the healers and Sickness Seekers surrounded the dragon and began to cast their magics. Several of them murmured chants, others made arcane gestures in the air. Most just stared intently at the dragon as if they were looking inside her body.

Flickering lights played over the little dragon, who looked around with dull eyes.

Though he stood back, Arthur watched carefully, too.

His long-neglected **Nursecraft** skill twigged at him. Glancing around, he saw a low table where several pitchers of water had been set. He went over to pour a cup before returning to kneel by the dragon.

"Excellent thinking," the gray-haired healer said. "Yes, it does seem to be dehydrated."

"Among other issues," a woman murmured under her breath.

Several Sickness Seekers had broken off and clustered several feet away, talking to each other in low, worried voices.

Ignoring them, Arthur offered the cup to the dragon. She flinched back.

"It's only water," Arthur said. "It will make you feel better."

Carefully, he placed the half-tipped cup to her pink snout. The baby dragon swallowed reflexively. Then, once she got a taste, she sipped some more.

Arthur saw ominous black veins at the base of her throat. The healers hadn't managed to rid the dragon of the scourge.

In fact, most of the healers had stepped away from the dragon and were now gathered around Valentina and Whitaker, speaking in urgent tones.

Whatever was said made Whitaker's face darken. He looked over to the scholars.

"Line up and present your cards to the dragon."

The leader puffed up. "How dare you—"

Whitaker gestured, and the speaker along with two others were shoved forward by an invisible tug on their clothing to fall onto their knees in front of the dragon.

"I won't ask again," Whitaker said.

Arthur didn't know if there was an age limit to linking with the dragon, though judging by the mutinous but terrified looks from the scholars, it was the card that counted the most.

Still, they were cowed enough to keep quiet and allow the dragon to look them over. Indeed, she seemed briefly interested.

Then her head sank to the floor. "No."

The scholars scrambled up much faster than their ages suggested they were capable of. Whitaker gestured for the others to follow. One by one, the angry-looking scholars trooped past the dragon.

She occasionally twitched in interest, but never for long. After the last scholar, the baby dragon heaved a wheezy sigh. "I'm tired."

Arthur, who still kneeled by her head, looked at the leaders.

Valentina nodded once.

"We'll try again with a new group," Arthur suggested. "It will be just a moment for you."

Again, the baby dragon sighed but didn't resist as Arthur placed her back in his storage.

The scholars gusted a breath in relief.

The one in gold had regathered his courage enough to give Whitaker a scathing look. "I'll have you know I intend to lodge my complaint to the top."

"Oh, yes, the king," Whitaker said boredly. "He does have a *history* with scholars. Tell me, how is the shape of your library, Bartus?"

The man flushed. "I'll have you know our guild is on the cusp of several important discoveries that will benefit the kingdom. Meanwhile, I hear the king is unhappy with the numerous scourge-eruptions. You should look to your own hive."

"We're in a difficult cycle, which is why the king will not be happy with an unlinked Rare dragon."

"One who will likely never fight!" Bartus the scholar roared. "Linking that thing would be a waste of a perfectly good scholar."

Whitaker looked like he was about to reply with something nasty, but Valentina broke in. "Luckily for us all, the dragon showed no interest in you. Now get out of my sight."

"With pleasure," the man snarled. Turning, he gestured to the other scholars. They left, all throwing nasty looks over their shoulders at the hive leaders.

Arthur, meanwhile, took the opportunity to touch on his **Stealth** skill to stay quiet and unobtrusive. This was a potential gold mine of information, and he didn't want to risk being kicked out, too.

The moment the last scholar was gone, Whitaker turned to the healer.

"Well? What is your diagnosis?"

Several glanced at each other as if daring the others to speak. It was the gray-haired man who piped up.

"It's our general opinion that the young dragon's core card isn't fully formed. That is a risk with premature hatchings."

It took a beat for that to sink in.

Valentina groaned, head falling into her hands. Whitaker, however, looked angry.

"Premature? It was cracking shell!"

Several of the healers exchanged uncomfortable looks.

A young woman spoke up, delicately, "It may have been less of a crack and more of a . . . break."

"What is that supposed to mean?" Valentina asked.

"Scourge-corruption could have caused the shell to become brittle, so it broke early," said the gray-haired man. "The dragon was very close to hatching, so it looks formed on the outside, but on the inside . . . its lungs and heart are struggling to support the rest of its body. We don't see this often with dragons because the magical strength of cards overwrites defects. Frankly," he continued, "the dragon needs a full card. Historically, linking has been known to . . . to fill in the gaps, as it were. Only then would it be strong enough to fight the corruption."

"And you can't?" Whitaker demanded.

The man spread his hands. "We are of Common and Uncommon rank. Not a Rare between us, and for scourge to take hold . . ." He hesitated. "Sir, unless that poor dragon links up soon, it will need a Legendary-rank healer to have a chance."

"You're saying I need to appeal to the palace?" Whitaker growled. "Do you know the storm that will bring down on us?"

"I'm a healer, sir. Not a politician."

Valentina spoke up. "I notice you've neatly danced around how a dragon tucked safely in the middle of a hive managed to catch scourge-corruption in the first place."

"Scourge-born diseases often target the weak and sick first."

She frowned. "Yes, but there's been no indication of any scourge-born disease in or around our hive. No eruptions nearby, and certainly no trips to the borderland."

Arthur's heart felt like it froze in his chest.

He had been to the borderland a few weeks ago. And the children he'd brought to the orphanage had lived there for years.

Had he brought sickness into the hive?

Lost in his thoughts and self-recrimination, Arthur barely kept track of the conversation.

"Then the seeds of scourge-infection are somewhere," the healer said. "They would not spontaneously appear in a dragon. They are the antithesis of scourge."

Another spoke up. "Perhaps if someone has a pair of cards. The king forbids it—"

"That's an old wives' tale."

"All legends have elements of truth—"

Valentina's sharp tone broke through the bickering.

"I need you to spread the word among the Sickness Seekers. We need to know if there's any sign of scourge in our uncarded."

"That would be a mistake," Whitaker said. "Word will get out and cause panic. Next thing you know, people will hide their disease—"

Both leaders went very still. Then, as one, looked to the double doors.

A moment later, the bells began to ring. Not the excited high-pitched chimes whenever a Rare egg was laid, but the bone-rattling bong-bong-bong of alarm.

The hive was to muster for a scourge-eruption.

"Another one," Valentina said. "Damn."

Whitaker strode to the door. "It is what it is. You have the hive, Val. I'll take care of this."

Arthur caught a glimpse of frustration on Valentina's wrinkled face. He couldn't tell if she was annoyed with Whitaker or if she wanted to go out and fight, too. But as she was in her eighth decade, that wasn't a good idea.

Rumor said Valentina's dragon was so old it couldn't easily fly.

Mastering herself, Valentina nodded to the healers. "Scourge-protocol takes precedence . . . but keep an eye on the animal populations. If corruption is taking root, it may show there first."

The men and women bowed and left.

Finally, Valentina turned to snap her fingers at Arthur. "Follow me."

He had no choice but to obey her as she walked out.

Valentina did not walk fast. She was shorter than him and had such a stiff gait that he wondered why she didn't use the floating cloud trick to get around.

His silent question was answered when she led him to a luxuriant office, only two doors down from the ballroom. A roaring fireplace sat in the corner, and the whole room was stuffed with polished wood furniture, sitting couches, and one large desk that had a grand view of the hive city vista through floor-to-ceiling windows.

Valentina crossed the room and went to a small stand topped by fluted glassware. "Drink?"

"Uh, yes, please?" He was vaguely aware of some kind of protocol between nobles offering drinks and accepting them . . . but couldn't remember whether accepting or declining was polite. He went with the option that got him a taste of their expensive booze.

Maybe it would level up his **Sommelier** skill.

But the small drink she poured him was a brown liquor. Brandy. He took a sip and found it smoother than any he had tried before.

New enhancement gained: Alcohol Resistance (poison class)
Due to your previous experience and your card's bonus traits, you automatically start this enhancement at level 4.
This is an optional enhancement. Do you wish to activate Alcohol Resistance?

An optional enhancement. His Master of Skills card had never given him the ability to turn a skill off or on before. Was this strictly a function of his new Body Enhancement card, or because he had a pair of cards in the same set?

Either way, the prudent thing was to select yes. He needed to be as sharp as possible while dealing with Valentina.

She poured herself a more generous glass and then gestured for Arthur to sit down on a leather chair. She sat in the opposite chair and studied him for a long moment . . . so long he wondered if he was being scanned by some sort of seeking power.

After what felt like an age, she spoke. "I wanted to let you know that I acknowledge and appreciate your help with this delicate hive matter."

"Of course," Arthur said.

"To be frank, and I like to be frank, your behavior is already more than I would have expected, knowing what I do about your father."

Arthur choked.

She shrugged, obviously not caring that she had just insulted Baron Kane. Not that Arthur gave a damn either.

"I like to think I take after my mother," he said.

Her lip twitched in a smile. "Indeed. Well, I wanted to let you know that your continuing discretion is appreciated and expected. Don't think I have forgotten you're interested in the Legendary egg."

He perked up. "How is the egg?"

"We've had the veterinary healers look it over as best they could. As you heard, none are above the Uncommon rank, so there is a limit to what they can discover. However, they agree that if it hasn't died yet thanks to neglect, it's not likely to at this point." She sighed and took a rather large sip of her brandy. "The standard procedure is to introduce likely dragon riders to the egg at once. However, considering it may be in a delicate state, we're not going to rush the thing now. Especially considering this recent fiasco."

He tried to keep the disappointment off his face but knew from her look that he failed.

"Legendary eggs are not like Rares," Valentina continued. "There is a great risk. Not only from the egg but from your other *competitors*. And I use that word deliberately. I don't know if you've yet written to your father for a higher-tier card, but you may want to consider it carefully. This will be a cause you must be willing to put your life on the line for."

Death had been a constant companion growing up in the borderland village. Arthur couldn't say he didn't fear it, but it was at least a known phenomenon. He couldn't say the same for the other nobles.

"Will I have many other, uh, competitors?" he asked, then leaned into the lie of Ernest Kane. "I know the state of my noble house, but I have a hard time believing many others would be willing to sacrifice their sons and daughters."

"And you think the financial boon from the crown won't sway them?" she asked dryly. "How many noble houses wouldn't sell their firstborn sons off to be known by the king and rewarded with riches by him personally?"

Arthur had no idea what she was talking about, but she acted like this was common knowledge.

He nodded, playing along. "One other thing: the recruiter who brought me to the hive. I assume she will be compensated?"

"Of course." She smiled. "If you do become a Legendary rider, you'll learn that the best way to get people to work hard is to reward them when they do a good job."

The words were pleasant, but her smile was edging toward sarcasm. He had the feeling she spoke with a double meaning, but he had no idea what it could be.

"Is there anything else?" she asked.

"Can I see the egg?" he asked, deciding to press his luck.

Again, she looked at him for a long, long moment. "Yes, I do think you're eligible for a reward, considering. But you must not get too close. Even if I was to show an utterly shameless preference for you—and I'm still deciding if I should—you're carrying a precious package in your storage, Ernest. I can't risk it."

"Forgive me for asking—"

"Oh, just blurt it out," she snapped. "If you already know you need to be forgiven, then you know you're doing something wrong. Just say it."

He paused and then nodded. "Why is this Rare dragon so important to you? I know she's a high level and a shimmer, but . . . she's also a pink. She probably won't be able to fight the scourge like a red or an elemental-based dragon. Don't get me wrong," he added, "I want her to live, but I don't know why she's important to you."

Thankfully, she didn't take offense to his words. She just stared at him, and though her face was aged, her eyes were bright and fiery. "We need *all* dragons to create a healthy, functioning hive. Yes, some pinks are downright scholarly. But . . . ah, *she* could also be the next tactical genius. We have problems in this hive, and we need solutions. We need thinkers. We need scholars—actual scholars and not those lazy robed louts you saw earlier today. Furthermore, pink dragons are known as wild cards. They aren't strictly knowledge dragons. They are also meta dragons. And right now, we need that out-of-the-box thinking. We cannot continue forever in this stalemate with the scourge, always reacting and never doing." She sighed and stood, signaling an end to the conversation. "Now, do you want to see the Legendary egg or not?"

He wanted to question exactly what she meant by all that, but he wanted to see the egg more.

Once again, she led him down the hall a short way and then through a door that led to a grand balcony.

There, twenty feet away at the end of the balcony, placed in the full sun, sat the tiny dark egg. It was nestled in a woven straw nest, surrounded by braziers of roaring fire to keep the temperature warm. Several dragon-sized divots were carved into the cliff walls directly on either side. Sitting in them, within easy leaping range, were large dragons. Arthur recognized them as hive Rares, though he didn't know their names.

They were guarding the egg—a task important enough that they were excused from fighting the scourge-eruption.

Valentina stopped him and pointed to a chalk outline near his feet. "Stay on this side of the line."

He nodded absently, all his attention on the egg.

It was a spot of black, bracketed against the deep blue of a high-altitude sky. It seemed to suck in the light around it, and despite the many braziers set up around the balcony, Arthur could almost feel the warmth leaching into the black heart of the egg.

But . . . it wasn't entirely black, was it? Gazing straight at the egg, he caught a hint of a deep dark purple. Or perhaps that was a shimmer quality to the egg.

Arthur didn't realize he was swaying forward until Valentina caught his shoulder. The tiny woman was stronger than she looked.

"I might have to adjust the chalk line farther back," Valentina said. "It seems the egg is growing in strength. That's enough for today, I think."

He and Valentina walked back into the hive in silence. She was lost in her thoughts, and he was wondering what would happen if he broke away and made a sprint to the egg.

Nothing good, probably.

"Ernest."

It took a beat to realize Valentina meant him. With a mental shake, Arthur turned to her. "Yes?"

The leader looked straight at him. "You may have noticed I'm not fond of people shirking their duties to the kingdom by hiding away in their guilds. Especially when they have the means to help but won't."

She meant the scholars. He nodded, waiting for her to get to the point.

"You've already taken some steps to put yourself in my good favor. If you could think of some way . . ." She paused. " . . . to get the pink dragon linked, I would *appreciate* it." Another pause. "Do we understand each other?"

Arthur's heart began to beat fast. Was she saying what he thought she was saying?

Looking into her steely eyes, he knew that she was.

She had someone following him and likely knew that he had met up with Cressida, who was desperate to link with the dragon. The scholars were in disfavor, and she had just said in not so many words that she would be willing to overlook certain things.

"Yes," Arthur said, "I understand."

"Then you may go."

Valentina turned her back on him and started to walk away. As she did, a new miniature cloud formed under her feet. It carried her up the next set of stairs and out of sight.

Arthur turned and started his long, long trek back to the lower levels.

It all came down to finding the pink dragon's card match. Now he had the means, ability, and permission to do what needed to be done.

And then he could focus on the fact that he might have accidentally brought scourge-sickness into the hive.

CHAPTER 9

A few hours later found Arthur jogging another loop around the lower hive tunnels. This earned him a few looks from the stuffiest of the hive attendants and more than a few raised eyebrows from the nobles still hanging around, but he hardly cared.

His **Running** skill was at now at level 9, and he wanted to see what happened once he crossed the level 10 threshold.

It turned out that taking the many, many staircases down from nearly the top of the hive at a quick pace had been challenging enough to quickly level that skill.

And, as with his Master of Skills card, this new Body Enhancement skill came with additional knowledge. It was odd. Arthur had been running all of his life. But now he simply knew, without being able to put a finger on it, how to run better. Every step was more perfectly extended, he was more sure-footed, and his breathing came smoother than it ever had before.

And he had a feeling about reaching level ten.

But he was also a man on a mission. He wasn't simply running for the pure sake of running (though it was more fun than it had ever been before). No, he took this time to think about what Valentina had said—and carefully not said. More importantly, he took this time to plan.

Grinning to himself, he increased his speed, jinking right and left through some sharp tunnels. A young orange dragon standing just around the bend squealed as he came rushing around, and extended its wings in automatic defense.

Somehow Arthur managed to step to the side and slide right past it between the tip of its wing and the wall without losing his footing.

"Sorry!" he called over his shoulder.

The dragon threw a disgruntled grumble back at him, but Arthur was already well down the tunnel.

New skill level: Running (General)
Level 10
For reaching this threshold on a body-enhancing skill, you have gained a 5% bonus to all stamina while running. In addition, you gain a 10% speed bonus for the first fifteen seconds while sprinting.

"Yes!" Arthur leaped and punched the air in success. Several people milling around looked at him oddly, but he didn't care.

He was starting to love his new Legendary card. It was very much like his Master of Skills card, but subtly different in the effects with body-type skills.

He couldn't wait to see what else he could do with it.

However, that would have to wait. Now that he had stopped, he realized his jaunt around the hive had left him sweating. His clothes were rumpled, and he probably stank of sweat.

It was not proper for "Ernest Kane" to be seen in public in such a state. It was unacceptable to see Cressida like this.

Still grinning to himself, he headed to his small room to bathe and get changed.

Feeling fresh, Arthur started his next plan of action in the traditional way: with a bribe.

A few coins in the hands of the right hive attendants got him pointed to Cressida's rooms.

Rooms, plural.

Arthur knocked on the dark polished wooden door and was greeted by a man wearing her house colors of gray and white. He took a long moment to look Arthur up and down. By the sneer on his lip, he thought Arthur was no better than something scraped off the bottom of his shoe.

"Can I . . . help you?"

Thankfully, his Gentleperson's Charm kicked in. "Ernest Kane, here to see Cressida—"

"Do you have an appointment?"

That stopped him short. "Appointment?"

"Yes, the noble lady's time is valuable. She cannot simply stop her business for every suitor that comes along."

"Oh, I . . . uh . . ." Whatever charm Arthur thought he had melted away. He knew he was flushing red, and by the gleam in the man's eye, he was enjoying Arthur's discomfort. "It's not—I'm not—Cressida!" he called in relief, seeing her walk up from behind her attendant.

"He's fine, Karles," Cressida said. "Ernest Kane is a friend."

The man sniffed but backed out of the doorway and bowed him in.

Cressida's formal greeting room was larger than Arthur's old apartment. It also had giant windows to let in the light, several pieces of furniture for sitting and eating, and a collection of musical instruments tucked into one corner. It was every bit as richly appointed as the hive leaders' rooms up top. He'd had no idea these types of rooms even existed in the lower levels of the hive.

Cressida watched him with a worried expression. "What's wrong, Ernest? Has something happened to . . ." She glanced at Karles, who hovered nearby in case he was ordered to fetch a drink. "To . . . the dragon?"

That snapped him to the present. He glanced at Karles, too. "Can we speak alone?"

"Unchaperoned?" Karles said. "I think not!"

Arthur was getting tired of this guy's attitude and opened his mouth to tell him so. Cressida got there first.

"I haven't been properly chaperoned this entire trip, Karles, and we both know why. Please, do give us some privacy."

The man's lip curled, but he bowed stiffly and walked to one of the side rooms. Arthur had no illusion that he wouldn't be listening at the door.

He stepped close and kept his voice low. "How much do you want to link with the pink dragon?"

"That's a stupid question," Cressida said. "You know I've searched high and low for an appropriate card—"

"No," Arthur said more forcefully. "How much do you want it, Cressida, *really*? Enough to take risks? Enough to possibly bring shame to your family?"

Cressida's fingers twitched, and for a moment he wondered if she was about to summon one of her flame bears. "What exactly are you asking of me?"

"I have an idea, but it's risky, and if we're caught, well . . . it'll mean time in the dragon-soil pits." Valentina had given her tacit permission, but Arthur doubted she would stick her neck out for either of them if things went wrong. "And that's aside from the family shame. Oh, and I can't guarantee this will work."

"You aren't selling me on this," Cressida said, though her upper lip was ticking as if she was trying to keep down a smile.

"It gets worse," Arthur admitted.

"Worse than shame and failure?"

With a grave nod, Arthur reached into his storage space and pulled out one of the items he had procured earlier that day while jogging the hive levels.

It was a labor worker's uniform—drab and utterly shapeless. "You'll have to wear this."

Cressida looked a little ill. Then she steeled herself. With a visible shake, she looked Arthur in the eye. "What is this plan of yours?"

* * *

Arthur was feeling mighty pleased with himself. It had been a simple matter to obtain a hand-pulled rental cart along with a few boxes of produce for authenticity. He wore a standard worker's uniform, too. Unlike Cressida's, his was fit to size . . . which made sense, considering it was his clothing.

Not that she needed to know that.

"You're scowling too much," he said to her.

The noble lady, who had been pinching her drab, heavy fabric shirt, simply scowled some more. Her bright-red hair was tucked under a worker's cap, and her face was washed free of makeup. She certainly didn't look plain, but she also looked less like herself. She also looked unhappy.

"Why shouldn't I be scowling?" she asked. "I'm apparently a common worker doing . . . worker things. Why would I be smiling?"

"Because if you did actually work for a living, this would be just another day in your life?" Arthur suggested. "Look, it's a relatively warm evening, not a cloud in the sky. It'll be dark soon, so if we were delivery folk, this would be our last run for the day."

She rolled her eyes, but her expression lightened. "Do you think this plan will work?"

"I can get us in the scholar's guild," Arthur promised. "You said you know your way once we're inside?"

"Well enough."

"Then we have a chance," Arthur said. And because he was in a good mood—it wasn't every day he got to see a real noble in worker's clothing—he added, "And if we get caught . . . well, I'm certain the dragon-soil pits aren't that bad."

In answer, she flicked a bit of bear-shaped flame at him. It fizzled out well before reaching his skin.

Arthur chuckled but fell silent as he concentrated on pulling the cart. He half wondered if he was going to receive some sort of "hauling produce" skill, but another question plagued his mind.

"So, your manservant . . ."

She glanced at him. "Yes?"

"He mentioned a chaperone, and you said you haven't needed one? Uh . . ." Arthur had started out strong, but he faltered as Cressida looked at him. Why was it so hard to talk to girls sometimes? "What was that about?" he finished in a rush.

Again, Cressida rolled her eyes. "My father either expected me to link the Rare dragon or come home engaged. But that's hardly shocking—I'm sure most noble children were under a similar edict."

Arthur looked away. "Of course."

"Then again, few have family willing to give us a Legendary card to try for the other egg . . ." Cressida said, and although Arthur wasn't looking her way, he could feel her gaze on him. "That is extraordinary, if I might say, for a baron's son."

To this, Arthur could only shrug. Frustration, fear, and more than a little guilt was a noxious mixture inside him. His cover story was paper thin, despite all the help the **Acting** skill could give him.

Cressida didn't press the issue, and they made the rest of the short trip in silence.

The scholar's guild would have been considered a huge structure . . . if it wasn't literally in the shadow of the giant hive behind it. Still, for a human-made building, it was quite large. Five stories tall with four-point spires that reached to the sky. According to Cressida, there were four more levels downward.

As they were supposedly delivering produce, they made their way to a servant's entrance on the shadowed side: an alleyway that never seemed to get any sun, as it was coated with moss.

Since, of course, this delivery wasn't expected, Arthur had timed it deliberately an hour before dinner. That was when the kitchens would be the busiest, and the staff would be harried and not likely to ask questions . . . or keep a close eye on Arthur and Cressida.

At least, that was the plan, right up until the moment the kitchen door opened.

Arthur looked up at the familiar face and felt his heart sink.

The man who'd answered the door had the exact opposite reaction.

His face split into a wide smile. "Arthur!" he bellowed and clapped one ham hand heavily on the shoulder, just as he used to when Arthur had been a twelve-year-old brat. "It's been years, m'boy!"

"Hi, Barlow," Arthur said, trying not to grimace.

CHAPTER 10

Barlow let them in, all smiles, and completely unaware he had just blown Arthur's cover.

Arthur felt Cressida's eyes like a hot spot on the back of his neck. Considering her card's power, that might not be an exaggeration.

Still, she kept silent as they lugged boxes of produce through the door.

His **Acting** skill nudged him, and he thought that if he treated this as nothing special—nothing to be guilty about—perhaps Cressida would take his cue. She hadn't put up a fuss yet.

With that in mind, he looked to Barlow. "Why are you working at the guild? Nothing's happened to the restaurant, I hope?"

The restaurant where Arthur had first gotten his start was not far from his old orphanage. As such, he hadn't visited that part of town on a regular basis. But the city wasn't that large. He was certain he would have heard if Barlow had sold or shuttered it.

The big chef waved his concern away. "The restaurant's doing fine. I finally got a second-in-command who doesn't need constant oversight. The kids are a handful." He gave Arthur a direct look.

Arthur chuckled nervously, aware Cressida was still watching.

Barlow continued. "That freed me up to cook for special events. It's been a mighty lucrative side business if I say so myself."

"What special event?" Cressida asked.

Barlow shrugged. "Them scholars didn't tell me this time—only thing I know is it's short notice. Not planned like a retirement or a promotion. And they were willing to pay top coin. In fact"—his gaze turned shrewd—"it was so last minute that I wasn't able to hire the workers I needed. I don't suppose you'd be willing to step in for a bit?" He looked at Cressida. "That goes for you too, young miss. Many hands make light work, and I pay well."

Cressida looked offended that she would be asked to *work*.

Arthur stepped in to cover for her. "She doesn't, um, cook professionally. She works at Bob's as a server, and delivers on the side."

"Ah, yes. Cooking on your family's hearth fire is a bit different than a demanding restaurant. But you can help, right, Arthur? For old times' sake?"

"Yes, *Arthur*," Cressida jumped in, her voice sweet. Far from being vexed, she looked like she was enjoying catching Arthur out. "You do know how to cook, don't you?"

He shot a glare at her. Cressida smiled back.

Oh, why not?

"I can do vegetable prep," Arthur said. "But me and my friend *Tilly* here need to get back before we're missed . . ."

Barlow clapped his hands, and before either one of them could say otherwise, Arthur found himself in front of a mountain of vegetables needing to be sliced, diced, or minced. Cressida was left to unload the rest of the cart by herself.

Judging by her renewed sour expression, she hadn't counted on that half of the deal. Luckily, the boxes were light, and there wasn't much left to unload.

Barlow wasn't exaggerating about being shorthanded. Half of the people in the kitchens seemed to be new, which added to the chaos. It was no wonder that no one had questioned the surprise produce delivery.

Grinning to himself, Arthur focused on his **Knife Work** skill and fell into a rhythm he had developed years ago. Soon the vegetables were prepped, and he was asked to slide to a station to sauté some of them for a soup pot.

With expert practice, he shook and flipped the contents of the pan to make sure there was an even cook on all sides. He replaced it over the fire and looked up to see Cressida watching him in consternation.

"Is that your card, then? Your Rare?" she asked in a low undertone.

He blinked. "No, my Personal Space card is my Rare." Which wasn't entirely the truth. That was only one of his cards.

"But you do have a . . . a kitchen work card, don't you?" Her nose scrunched up. "Why?"

"There's nothing shameful about working for a living," Arthur said. "Maybe you should try it. You never know, you might like it."

"If it's not shameful, why don't these people know your real name?" she asked. Thankfully, she still kept her voice low enough so only he could hear.

That might have been a good point . . . except Arthur was his real name.

Arthur shook his head and decided not to correct her. "You got the rest of the cart unloaded?"

"Yes, why? I hope you don't intend to stay here all night . . ."

"No, just long enough not to raise any suspicions. A half-unloaded cart will make people wonder what's going on. Here," he said, "take that pan and toss some of those minced onions in there. Then add oil and do what I do."

She didn't move. "Why?"

"Because," he said patiently, "this kitchen is about to become frantically busy. You'll stand out if you're not doing something."

"No, I mean . . ." She looked around and reluctantly took up a clean pan, holding it gingerly like she was afraid it would bite her. "Why bother with this at all?"

"When would you rather wander around the scholar's guild? When there are people around, or when they've all sat down to eat this feast we're preparing?"

The light of understanding dawned in her eyes. She threw the onions and a scant handful of crushed garlic into her pan and awkwardly set it over the cook stove beside his.

"You are a sneaky man, Ernest."

"My friends call me Arthur," he said.

They slipped out as meat for the main meal was well on its way to cooking. Arthur caught Barlow's eye and made a motion with his head—not to the outdoor kitchen exit, but to the doorway leading deeper into the guild.

The man looked briefly confused, then glanced at Cressida and nodded.

With a slight feeling of shame, Arthur realized he thought he meant to sneak off with the girl.

Which he was doing . . . but not for those reasons.

Barlow, being Barlow, would go along with it because Arthur would know better than to ask for coins for his work, afterward. His silence would be payment.

Well . . . whatever it took.

Cressida looked relieved to be away from the stoves at last. She had managed to burn everything she'd touched. Only Arthur covering for her had ensured it didn't result in disaster.

Nevertheless, once they were out of the kitchens, the next part was up to her, as she had visited the scholar's guild before, thanks to her family connections.

She strode confidently ahead, causing Arthur to grab her arm and pull her up short. "Stop, you're walking like a noble."

She gave him a scandalized look, then visibly checked herself and glanced down at her simple laborer's clothing. "I don't know how to 'walk' any other way."

"Go slower. Keep your head down. Shoulders hunched," Arthur said, and proceeded to do just that.

"My mother would be having hysterics if she knew I was walking with hunched shoulders . . ." Cressida muttered. But she attempted to follow Arthur's lead, even though her steps were unusually graceful.

They walked past a loud dining area. From the looks of it, the first appetizers had been served along with generous glasses of wine. There wasn't an empty seat at the long tables, but the halls beyond were empty.

"What are they celebrating?" Arthur wondered.

"Oh, they never need much of a reason," Cressida said sourly. "Though usually it's when someone from the local guild impresses the king. Or when they feel they've scored a political point against the hive."

Arthur gave her a sharp look. "They're against the hive?"

"There's a rivalry," Cressida said. "Which the king encourages. The same pool of funds from the crown go to either the hives or the guilds, and he makes sure they know it. I've been told it's to encourage friendly competition."

Was that why the scholars were so against linking with the pink dragon?

Cressida went on. "The guild has long maintained they will be the ones to eliminate the scourge through research and scientific discovery. That sets them against the hive, too. Here we are," she added, pointing to a stairway that went downward.

Arthur made them stop at every landing on the way down to listen for the sounds of footsteps of a scholar late to dinner. He shouldn't have bothered. There was no one.

In fact, the candles that lit the way were nearly melted to the nubs. It seemed no one had been by to change them out all day.

And then there was the smell.

At first, Arthur noticed it as something in the air that reminded him of the cottage he had shared with his father. He thought it was the lack of light and the moisture beading in the cracks in the walls.

But as they went lower and the funk in the air grew stronger, he finally identified what it was.

With a thrill of equal parts relief and fear, he realized he didn't have to worry about regarding being the one to bring the scourge into the hive after all.

"Do you smell that?" he asked.

Cressida nodded, looking green. "What is that? Rot?"

"No," he said. "Scourge-dust."

Her head whipped around, and she stared at him. "You're joking."

"No," Arthur said grimly. "I'm from a border barony, remember? You get whiffs of that smell when the wind blows in over the dead lands."

"But . . . you aren't saying there . . . there are scourglings here?"

"No, just scourge. There's technically no scourglings in the dead lands either. What we call scourge-dust is just all . . . dead. It's death."

"Is it dangerous?" she asked.

"Not to the carded."

Cressida glanced down the dark stairwell, back to him, and then nodded. "Then we continue on."

The library was at the bottom level. The best Arthur could say about it was that at least it was better lit than the stairwell. There were eight rows of shelves absolutely stuffed with books, scrolls, and thick stacks of parchment. Interspersed here and there were small glass cases. And in those cases were cards.

Arthur took a candle to light the way and stepped to the first card he saw.

Herb Identification

Common

Knowledge/Meta

Upon physical contact with any edible herb, the wielder will instantly be able to accurately identify the name of the plant. This card does not use mana.

Not that impressive and somewhat niche considering it only worked with edible herbs, but he could see why it would have its uses to researchers.

Arthur picked up the glass case—not to take the card but to get a better look at the lock surrounding it. The moment he did, the card crumbled as if it were a structure of delicate ash.

He made an inarticulate sound of protest, hand jerking away. It was too late. That light touch was enough. In a moment, the card was nothing more than dust. It had rotted away.

The smell that came from it was death.

CHAPTER 11

Arthur went down the line of shelves. Most of it was stuffed with paperwork of all types: books, scrolls, and loose papers with scribbled notes. Here and there, set like markers between them, sat the cards in glass cases.

Every one of them was rotten and turned to dust at the slightest touch.

Cressida let out a happy cry and turned to Arthur in triumph. "This one is still good." She glanced at it and then sagged slightly. "It's only an Uncommon, though."

"The rank shouldn't matter. This is . . . this is criminal!" Arthur hadn't fully understood the term "spitting mad" before now. If he were a dragon, he felt like he would be able to breathe fire.

Cressida gave him an arch look. "Well, yes. If this gets out, the scholars will have to explain the waste of cards to the crown. Why are you so upset?"

"Why aren't you?" he demanded. "Do you know what these cards are worth?"

She sniffed. "They're only Commons."

"No, Cressida. I'm not talking about worth in coins. I mean safety, security, health . . ."

Cressida just looked at him like he had grown an extra head.

Arthur had to struggle not to growl. "You don't get it!" Turning, he shoved the glass case back on the shelf, the sad little pile of dust the only indication something magical had been locked within.

It occurred to him that if someone opened up the case and cleaned out the dust, there would be no evidence of what the scholars had done. If anything, that pissed him off even more. He had the urge to grab some of the books, start a fire, and burn this whole scourge-tainted place to the ground.

"Perhaps I don't understand because you are acting like a madman." Cressida cocked her hip, hand on her waist.

"No, you don't understand because you are a noble!"

"And you're not?"

"I may as well not have been." Arthur gestured vaguely. "I lived on the border. I smelled this smell, this rot, every single day of my life. Do you know what dust from the dead lands does to people? Do you have any uncarded people in your lands?"

"Of course," she said, though her expression was vaguely troubled. "Not everyone can afford a card. My father told me that some of his tenants out in the sticks outright refuse them for moral reasons."

"But you've seen them," he persisted. "They're shorter, less healthy. The women die in childbirth more often. They get sick—" His voice broke, and he looked away for a moment, swallowing before he continued. "That's when they don't live next to the dead lands. It's worse when they breathe this in every day."

A final glass-enhanced card sat on the end of the shelf. Arthur snatched it up. It disintegrated before he even had a chance to read it.

Frustrated, he shook it in Cressida's direction. "These may only be Commons to you, but having just *one* card can change someone's life. I've seen it."

Her expression remained unreadable, and he would have given a lot to be able to sense emotions as Kenzie did.

Cressida took two steps to cross the distance between them and carefully tugged the case out of his hand. Then she replaced it on the shelf.

"Is that why you go by a different name among the common folk?" she asked. "I've watched you. You don't see yourself as a noble at all, do you?"

"I don't," Arthur said with a frown. That was true for more reasons than one. "But I don't see how that matters right now."

She shrugged. "It matters." Though she didn't explain why. Her gaze returned to him, searching his face as if looking for her own answers. Then she shrugged again. "And you're right. I haven't seen . . . what you've described. I've been rather sheltered. But I'm also not responsible for this . . . neglect."

"Yeah." His shoulders slumped, some of the anger draining out of him in a rush. "I know that, Cressida."

"Good," she said. "Now, please get over your indignation and help me find the Rares. We might have some blackmail on the scholars if we're discovered . . . or they may just decide it would be easier to kill us and keep it quiet."

He blinked, a little surprised at her matter-of-fact tone. Then again, she was probably right.

He had practically been yelling out his impassioned speech there. They were lucky the scholars were feasting a few levels up.

And that no one bothered to come down to the library as they ought.

"The Rare cards. Right." He nodded and quickly walked down the next set of shelves.

Those held no joy, either. Some of the Uncommon cards also crumbled to dust upon being touched.

From what he understood, Commons took several months of inactivity to rot away like this. Uncommons were several times as long. That meant it might have been years since someone interacted with these cards.

How hard would it have been to stuff a card into a card anchor, use it once, and take it out again? The scholars could have paid someone to do it.

Lack of trust might have made finding a worker complicated, but not impossible.

Arthur suspected it was just laziness.

He seethed, though mindful of keeping quiet, he seethed silently.

Cressida, too, seemed more disturbed as they walked down one row after another. It was more than just the smell of the rotting cards. A feeling of wrongness saturated the air.

It felt like a desecration. As if he were walking over someone's grave. It grated at his nerves, and he wondered if this feeling was also responsible for his foul mood.

Truth to tell . . . none of the rotted cards he'd been able to read had been exceptional. He suspected anything of real value had been taken by the scholars long ago. What was left was incredibly niche: the ability to analyze existing wind patterns for types of pollen, fluency in a language Arthur had never heard of, the ability to instantly measure time, distance, and weight of objects. One of the few Common cards that hadn't crumbled away at a touch granted the ability to accurately add up the value of a pile of coins at a glance.

Not a stretch to guess that it had seen some use. He was tempted to take it himself, but automated counting and estimating powers easily tripped up anti-gambling powers.

"Arthur."

He turned at Cressida's hushed call, and then winced internally at automatically reacting to his real name. Should he lean into "Arthur" being his peasant name?

Although he liked the way she spoke his name.

She wasn't paying the slightest bit of attention to him anyway. She had walked on ahead to the final row set against the far wall.

Beyond it stood a thick steel door.

He had seen similarly heavy doors in card shops when the keepers wanted to guard their best cards.

He didn't think cards for identifying pollen on the wind were kept back there.

Cressida stared at the door, her hand raised as if half of her wanted to touch it and half wanted to cover her mouth over a scream.

Runes surrounded the frame of the door in an intricate lock. Normally brightly lit with a card's power, these were now dark and dead.

A creeping rot, looking a little like bread mold and a little like a rotten black mushroom, extended outward from the frame. The scourge—because that was all it could be—stretched to the edges of the runes. No doubt that was why they were dark and dead.

"How could they?" Cressida whispered. "Oh, this is . . . this is wrong. Don't you see?" she turned to Arthur. "They must have let a Rare go rotten. Maybe even a few Rares."

A rotten Common was unpleasant. A fart in the wind. The rotten Uncommons had probably been responsible for the scourge-smell that had permeated this floor and the ones right above it.

A Rare that had gone bad was several orders above that.

"I think we found the source of the pink's sickness," he heard himself say. He couldn't be a hundred percent sure, but he would rather any suspicious eyes fall on the scholars than the kids he'd brought in from the border. Unethical? Sure. But staring at the scourge-infection sitting in the middle of the hive made him feel ruthless. "We have to tell the hive leaders."

"Of course," Cressida agreed, voice distant. Then she seemed to shake herself. She continued, stronger. "But not until I rescue the cards still in there."

Arthur eyed the door speculatively. As card wielders, they were protected from the usual ravages of scourge-sickness. But whatever lay in the room beyond was not normal.

He wasn't worried for his own safety. This scourge-infection had been started by Rare-strength magic. He had two Legendary cards in his heart. If he wasn't safe, he doubted anyone would be.

"I'll go," he said.

"I'll be right back," she said at the same time.

They looked at one another.

Cressida smirked, and the air shimmered around her in a bubble. "You didn't think my flame bear was my only Rare card, did you?"

"You have a shield card?"

She nodded. "It will keep me safe, but it's mana hungry. I'll have to move fast."

"I . . . have something similar," Arthur said.

She just looked at him, doubt on her face.

"I'll be fine," he insisted. "You're not going alone."

And to prove his point, he strode forward, grabbed the door handle, and yanked. The runes surrounding the frame should have stopped him cold. But they were magically dead, and apparently, no one had bothered with a mechanical backup.

With the sound of something peeling off a sticky surface, the door opened.

Glowing scourgling eyes blinked back at him.

CHAPTER 12

Arthur slammed the door shut.

An instant later, something hit the other side of the door. The cracked runes around the frame lit, flickered, and went out again.

There was a rush of hot air behind him. Arthur turned to see Cressida had summoned her flame bear to her side. It was the full version, not the baby bears meant for warmth. It was a hulking figure next to her, its shoulders of equal height to her own, but on all fours.

"Watch the flames!" Arthur yelped. They stood next to the bookcases, and some loose pages sticking out of the shelves were starting to smolder.

"Who cares about— No! Down, boy!" Cressida hurriedly added in an aside to her summon.

Arthur had leaped forward to put out some of the smoking papers. The bear snarled at his approach, round ears pinned back. At Cressida's command, it shuffled slightly to the side to give Arthur room.

"You'll care plenty when we're trapped in a room full of burning books," he snapped, tearing free a page and stomping it down as the edge glowed orange.

Cressida seemed not to have heard. "There are scourglings in there! In the city!"

Another thump from the door, followed by a flash of cracked runes. The magical barrier seemed to be holding up for now, but who knew how long that would last?

Cressida flinched at the noise, but then stared at the door, one hand to her forehead in amazement. "This is way beyond a few rotted cards. Actual scourglings! How could this happen?"

Arthur stomped out the last scorched piece of parchment. "One or more of the Rare cards went rotten, and the magic was strong enough to fruit scourglings.

The only reason why this doesn't happen in the border is—" He stopped himself with a shake of his head.

She stared at him. "No, go on."

He hesitated. Long years of engrained habits of hiding his past warred with the building pressure to let Cressida see the real him.

This fact was harmless enough, however.

"That's why they call them the dead lands out beyond the kingdom. There's nothing left—nothing can grow even if you watered the soil and mixed good dirt in. The scourge has soured it all. Even to themselves. It takes dragon soil to rekindle life." He gestured to the door. "If a powerful card dies in an area where there's the building blocks of life—paper used to be trees, and vellum is made of animal hide—then that's a perfect mixture for scourge-spawn."

"But we're in the middle of a city!" Her fear had faded now that the shock had worn off. Now Cressida seemed scandalized. "Practically next door to a hive!"

"Eruptions happen in cities," Arthur said.

There was another thump at the door as if to punctuate his words. However, the impact was lighter, as if the scourgling were only making a half-hearted attack. Once more, the runes flared and held.

He and Cressida glanced at one another and then fell silent, guessing that the sound of their voices was provoking the creatures now that they'd been woken by the door opening.

After a moment, Cressida dismissed her flame bear. It evaporated into a wisp of harmless smoke.

Arthur took a sideways step closer to her and spoke in a low tone. "I'm worried about two things."

"Two? I counted at least eight pairs of eyes in there."

He was a little impressed she'd had the good sense to count their enemies. Arthur shook his head and continued. "The first is those runes around the door. They're cracked, but what are the chances they've broken in the exact right way to let someone open the door, but allowed nothing to come out?"

Cressida whipped her head around to look at the runes. After a moment, she shook her head. "Those runes are meant to keep something in."

"Which means either the scholars have created that as a trap to imprison anyone who tried to access their Rare cards, or . . ."

"Or they created it knowing they wanted whatever was in there to stay in there," Cressida finished. "And they added a measure so someone can open the door and . . . what?"

"Feed the scourglings," Arthur concluded grimly.

They exchanged a long look and then, as one, glanced back to the door.

"And the other thing you were concerned about?" Cressida asked.

"Scourglings eat cards."

"So, if there were any left when they spawned . . ."

"Yeah," Arthur confirmed grimly. "Those scourglings probably have Rare cards in their core."

Another beat of silence. Neither suggested they retreat or go for help. Surely the hive officials would be interested in a small infestation within the city.

And scholars who were possibly . . . what? Cultivating the scourglings? For what purpose?

Arthur didn't know. He only hoped his conclusions were wrong.

"I'll resummon Wicker," Cressida said after a moment.

Arthur barked out a laugh—slightly high-pitched due to stress. He coughed into his hand and choked out, "You named your summon?"

"Just the combat form. The miniature form is, ah—never mind." Cressida's face lit up red in a blush. She went on before Arthur could push her on it. "I'll send Wicker through the door, and we close it afterward. It's a contained area with plenty to ignite. I'll dismiss him when my mana runs low, and we mop up whatever is left."

"You . . . don't want to call for help?" Arthur asked. "If we report back, the dragon riders will descend on this place like stink on dragon soil. I think Valentina probably suspects something's wrong here. They'll believe us."

She looked at him, eyes steely. "I came here for Rare cards."

That was the crux of it.

Yes, once the infestation was exposed, the hive would happily melt this whole rotten guild to slag. The Rare cards inside the scourglings would be lost, or, more likely, harvested by the fighters.

And they would be back to square one with the pink dragon still fighting for her life.

"Are you certain about this?" Arthur asked.

Cressida drew herself up then looked at the door. She nodded. "You haven't seen fire in an enclosed area, have you? It doesn't just burn, it eats the air. Even scourglings need to breathe."

"And if we open the door and we're wrong about the barrier keeping the scourglings in?" he pressed.

Now the look she turned on him was tinged with derision. "I want to be a dragon rider, which means I'll be fighting scourglings someday. I'm not afraid to fight now. What about you?"

Her challenge stung. She also had a point.

If Arthur was going to put himself forward as a Legendary recruit, it meant he would be fighting the most powerful scourglings.

As he saw it, the risk was small. The rewards, including helping the little pink dragon, was large.

Arthur nodded. "I'll fight."

"Good," she said crisply. "What are your combat capabilities?"

Arthur was well grown for his age—especially considering the underfed pipsqueak he used to be—but at that moment, he felt very small.

"I . . . um . . ."

Damn it all, why hadn't he kept that Common stinging bubble card he'd stolen as a kid? Yes, it was a ridiculous power, but it was better than flat-out nothing.

But he didn't have nothing, did he? Yes, he was facing a room full of Rares, but Arthur had two Legendaries in his heart. They were utility-type cards, but if he couldn't make them work for him then he didn't deserve them.

"I need a moment," he said.

"Oh?" Her eyebrows lifted. "You have an armor card, then? I've heard those can be awkward to conjure in . . . What are you doing?"

Arthur had taken out several overripe tomatoes from a produce bin within his Personal Storage space that he'd placed there while unloading their vegetables earlier. Never could be too prepared. Stepping to the side, he concentrated on a map of the hive city tacked to a wall and started throwing.

The first tomato splatted just below the map. The second, a little above. He hadn't been this bad throwing stones at rats as a child. Was he out of practice or was it the card?

The third hit right on target, red juices spattering over the poorly drawn map.

New Skill Gained: Throwing (General Class)

Due to your previous experience and your card's bonus traits, you automatically start this skill at level 8.

That was a decent starting level. Then again, he had been throwing things all his life. He just hadn't bothered to practice with intent enough to make a skill out of it.

Next, he stepped to a likely looking stone statue. It was the figure of a half-naked man, posed with a chiseled chest. The stone base was equally impressive.

Arthur gripped it and, focusing on the muscles in his legs and not his back, tried to pick it up. It was heavy, and he only managed it a short way from the ground before he set it down. Then he tried again.

Yes, he had picked things up plenty of times since he gained his Master of Body Enhancement card, but as he learned from his Skills card, developing a new skill required deliberate practice, concentration, and repetition.

"What are you doing?" Cressida demanded for a second time.

"I have a new card," he grunted, putting the statue down before trying again. "I need practice before— Ah, there we go."

New Skill Gained: Lifting (Strength Class)
Due to your previous experience and your card's bonus traits, you automatically start this skill at level 5.

Hmm. The fact that strength was a whole class of its own was interesting for the future, but not helpful now.

With a sigh, Arthur reached once again into his Personal Space and grabbed a cleaver. It was his personal knife—perfectly balanced and meticulously sharpened.

He would be so annoyed if the fine razor edge got chipped tonight.

Cressida stared at him like he had grown an extra head. "You're using your cooking card to fight scourglings?"

"I used it to duel Mattew," he said. "Remember, I almost won."

"Everyone thought you were joking around!" she said. "You seriously don't have *any* combat cards?"

"I've always been able to defend myself," Arthur said. "And you never know. Maybe I'll end up with a Rare combat card after this."

He nodded to the door.

She hesitated, and he read doubt on her face. Then she visibly gathered her courage and nodded. "I can use my shield card if we get in trouble and need to retreat."

Arthur nodded and reached to grab a book from the nearest shelf. It was a large, heavy tome. He could throw it in a pinch but would rather use it as a shield . . . or beat a scourgling to death with it.

Holding it against his chest with his knife hand, he walked to the door and reached for the knob. "Ready?"

In answer, Cressida summoned Wicker. The bear summon lowered its head, ready to charge in.

Arthur opened the door and stepped to the side.

Ten seconds later, he regretted it.

He didn't know what they were facing, exactly. It would make sense if Rare scourglings could use the cards inside them. That meant they could be facing any type of attack. Thankfully, fire tended to cleanse and overpower mostly anything.

But he had let himself forget that the scholars didn't have combat cards. They had knowledge and meta-type cards.

The door opened, and Wicker barreled through. The runes flashed, and for a brief moment, a barrier was visible in the doorway. They were right: the runes were meant to keep things in, not out.

But the scourglings had not been idle. In that moment of disturbance when the flame bear charged in, three of the creatures used the disturbance in the barrier to squeeze out.

They were a little like bats, if bats had bodies the size of a ripe watermelon and coin-sized red eyes . . . and ragged dagger teeth in a mouth that stretched from one side of the head to the other.

With whistling shrieks, the scourge-bats dived down in an attack.

CHAPTER 13

One of the scourge-bats flew right at Arthur. He braced himself and swung the cleaver. His weapon passed right through the bat as if it were an illusion. Except the creature was all too real as it latched on to his forearm with claws like needles. Arthur flailed, switching the knife from one hand to the other to slash down.

But as he did, the bat's body seemed to dissolve through his arm, dropping down through the limb to catch itself on the fabric of his shirt. It brought its teeth down, and Arthur screamed as it latched on to his chest right below his collarbone.

It was as if the thing were trying to chew its way to his heart.

The knife clattered to the ground as Arthur struck at it—hands going right through the thing as if it didn't exist. It had a power to allow objects to pass right through.

It let go and started crawling up his shirt, clearly aiming for his neck.

Arthur did the only thing he could think of: He ran at the wall and hit it head on. Graceful? No. Effective? Also no. The bat simply phased through his body before it was squished.

But it came out turned the wrong way.

Anticipating this, Arthur spun around and threw a wild fist at the bat as it flapped to regain air. Either it hadn't expected this, it had a cooldown before it could phase through solid objects again, or he got lucky. Either way, his fist connected, and the scourge-bat hit the ground. It looked half stunned.

Arthur scooped up his cleaver and focused on his **Butchering** skill. A moment later, the bat was in chunks on the floor.

Only then did he look up to see where the other two had gone.

Cressida was doing better than him. She had retreated behind a dome shield. It sparkled with force every time the attacking scourge-bat touched it. And she had managed to summon a second flame bear. It was every bit as large as Wicker, but the fire that outlined its form was noticeably thinner, and Arthur didn't feel any heat pouring off it. The bear was chasing a bat, swiping futilely at it with giant flame paws. The bat seemed to have no problem dodging. In fact, it brushed up against the edge of Cressida's shield too often to be coincidence.

It was smart enough to know the shield cost mana—more when actively repelling something. That along with two flame bears must have been a terrible strain on Cressida. She looked pale, and her forehead was beaded with sweat.

But she would have to hold out. The third scourge-bat hadn't attacked them at all: it was busy scratching out the runes surrounding the doorway.

Arthur let out a wordless yell and charged at the bat. Even as he did, it fluttered to a rune at the top of the doorway. It had already scratched out several ones close together. In fact, it seemed to be picking its runes carefully.

They were intelligent enough to create a plan and send out two bats to distract them.

It was a trap, and he and Cressida had been arrogant enough to fall right in.

Arthur put this together in a flash. That, added to the twinge of foreboding, was enough to make him change his mind.

"Cressida! Reinforce your shield!" he shouted and dived to the side, away from the door.

He hit the ground hard and rolled behind a bookshelf just as the bat used one of its razor claws to slash the last rune.

The barrier between them and the room fell.

Back when Arthur had worked for Chef Barlow, one of the line cooks had been drunk, having an idiot moment, or both. For some inexplicable reason, he had taken a handful of flour and thrown it into one of the wood fire-ovens. The resulting explosion had knocked the man back, given him burns that had required the attention of a very expensive healer, and had charred that day's bread. That had been the day Barlow demonstrated he had some sort of strength card. He'd picked up the still-smoking man like he weighed no more than a kitten and literally threw him out onto the street.

All of this to say that Arthur understood the danger of a fire in a closed environment with a lot of fuel, despite what Cressida had said.

He wasn't disappointed.

A ball of flame roared out of the door as if from the throat of a red dragon. Scourglings whistled in fear and hate, and Arthur thought he heard the crackle of Wicker going wild inside the room.

Runes from a card anchor lit up under his hands. Abruptly, the main library was plunged into icy darkness. All the flames, including the candle flames, were extinguished. The warmth drained away.

The massive fire must have triggered a card anchor tied to a trap card. They were lucky it hadn't been triggered before, but he supposed there hadn't been enough fire spread around.

His relief lasted for a moment. Seconds later, the room was filled with scourglings shrieks and bat wings as the remaining bats escaped from the Rare room. Cressida's shield flashed several times as they ran into it.

Arthur pressed himself flat on the floor, covering his head. For a moment, he thought he felt something brush against his mind, like a cool breeze. The sound of notes . . .

He flinched, and it was gone.

The scourge-bats seemed to only want escape. With more whistles that sounded suspiciously like words, and the drift of song, the flapping sounds continued past him.

He imagined they were heading to the stairway and to the upper levels.

The scholar's feast would soon be interrupted.

"Arthur?" Cressida's voice echoed strangely in the sudden silence. "Are you okay?"

"Yeah. I'm over here. How about you?"

"I'm fine. The shield took the blast, but I'm out of mana. I had to recall Wicker to reinforce it."

He lifted his head and looked around.

Not all of the fire and light had been extinguished. The Rare room still glowed a sullen red. Arthur supposed that if there had been trap-card securities, it had been scratched out by the bats long ago. He rose to his feet.

Cressida had already strode to the next room and was looking in warily.

Wicker had been on a rampage. Though from the patches of still-unburned black scourge-rot, fire had probably improved the look of the place. He had been thorough, and several burned lumps glowed with unharvested cards.

Arthur made a snap decision. "Get those cards. We need to get out, fast."

But Cressida was staring at him in horror. "Is that blood?"

He looked down at himself. Fear and shock must have blocked the pain from his brain because he hadn't thought about his injuries until that moment. There were shallow slashes up and down his right arm. The bat had also bitten his chest under his collarbone, but his thick work shirt and undershirt had taken the brunt of the damage. The skin was only scratched. The arm, however, might need stitches or a healer.

"I'll be fine. Get the cards."

That reminded him of the bat he had downed and chopped.

Arthur glanced around and found it right away thanks to the soft glow over the biggest body part left.

He bent and gestured, lifting the card and three Rare shards from the body.

Phase In, Phase Out

Rare

Teleportation

This card grants the wielder the ability to temporarily make their body incorporeal to pass through objects or allow objects to pass through them. Limit is ten seconds of incorporeal time per hour, on a rolling basis. This card does not use mana.

Arthur had to resist the urge to shove the card in his heart. Instead, he tucked it away in his card anchor.

If the pink dragon didn't want this card, he intended on using it himself.

Cressida returned a moment later, flushed with success. "Got five full cards. One scourgling was just full of shards."

Arthur tried not to think about how many cards had flown by them tucked inside the bats. "It'll have to do. Let's get out of here."

He could already hear the faint sounds of shouting from the levels above.

CHAPTER 14

Arthur and Cressida ran up the stairs to find the scholar's guild in complete chaos. The scourge-bats had not made their escape quietly, and it seemed they were not used to flying outside of the confined space of the room. There were black marks wherever they had brushed the stone walls—patches of scourge-rot. Arthur hoped it would not take root before someone came to exterminate it.

A distant scream came from a level above. He and Cressida exchanged a grim look. The scholar's feast had been interrupted.

He supposed he should have felt guilty. Certainly, he didn't want anyone to get hurt.

But he didn't.

Instead, he felt seething anger.

He and Cressida weren't the ones responsible for neglecting Rare cards so badly that they had rotted away. Even then, he doubted that rot had instantly resulted in these scourge-beasts. No, that had taken time to appear. Then there was the damning presence of the runes meant to keep the worst locked in the Rare room.

For whatever reason, someone had cultivated a nest of scourglings.

No one could be held at fault for blundering over a carelessly laid trap card. The law pointed toward the wielder of that card.

Or in this case, the cultivators of the nest.

Arthur's main worry wasn't for the scholars, who were responsible. It was for the actual innocents. The servants, caretakers, and other staff. Including Barlow and his kitchen workers.

New skill gained: Rapid Stair-Climbing (Endurance Class)
Due to your previous experience and your card's bonus traits, you automatically start this skill at level 5.

Really? he thought with a mixture of amusement and frustration. *Now I get that skill?*

Much like **Running**, it wasn't as if his legs grew any stronger, he merely became aware of how to position his feet to make each push off the bottom step that much more efficient.

Suddenly, Arthur was taking steps two at a time. Not impossible even before, but now it felt exactly as easy as taking steps the normal way.

He surged past Cressida without realizing it. Turning back on the next landing, Arthur extended a hand to her. She waved it away.

"Go! Warn them!"

He intended to, if by "them" she meant the workers. As far as he was concerned, the scholars were on their own.

Arthur bolted up the next set of stairs.

Another scream alerted him to trouble at the next level.

A man in dark scholarly robes was facing off against a scourge-bat just down the hallway. Backed into a corner, the man swung a candlestick holder at the scourge—a *lit* candlestick holder.

One swing, and two of the three candles went sailing off their base. One snuffed out as it fell to the ground. The second rolled under a full-length window curtain where it started to smolder.

Clearly, the man didn't have a Common Sense card.

"Stop!" Arthur yelled, before the man could swing again and send the third candle flying.

Too late. The darting scourge-beast folded its wings and struck at him, aiming for the scholar's neck the same way Arthur had been bitten.

No . . . no, he was wrong. It wasn't aiming for his neck. It was aiming for his *heart*. The scourge-beast was trying to chew the cards out of his heart deck.

The man dropped the candlestick and tried to claw the scourge-beast off him. But it had a tight hold, and judging by the man's watery scream, a painful one.

Meanwhile, the curtain was aflame.

Arthur hesitated for a second, torn.

As disgusted and angry as he was against the guild, he didn't want to see the man die. And an out-of-control fire could kill many more.

He sprinted to the curtain, yanked it down, and used the thick fabric to smother the flaming hem. Then, gathering it up, still smoking in his arms, he turned to the scholar.

The man was on the ground, either dead or in a faint. The bat was latched to his chest, and there was blood everywhere.

Arthur used his new **Throwing** skill to toss the curtain over the bat. The smoldering fabric trapped its wings like a net, but he expected that to last a half second. Those teeth were like daggers.

So Arthur grabbed up a heavy tome—this was the scholar's guild, and heavy books lay on tables everywhere—and brought it down as hard as he could on the flailing lump. Then he did it again and again.

Cressida reached the top to the stairs just as the bat-sized lump stopped moving.

She took in the scene at a glance and then went over to the final candle, which had fallen and was flickering dangerously against a thick rug.

With dread, Arthur yanked the blanket away. The scourge-bat was dead, evidenced by the glow over its chest. The scholar was not. The thick robe must have helped protect him, and though there was blood, it seemed the bat hadn't bitten past the top layer of flesh.

As Arthur guessed, the man had fainted. He'd live.

Arthur turned to the scourge-bat and passed his hand over the glow to harvest its remains.

Meanwhile, Cressida had finished putting out the fire. To Arthur's surprise, she hadn't stomped it out but held her hand over the flame. Motes of energy floated up to her palm as the flames shrank in size. Within the space of a few breaths, it was out.

She looked at him. "Did the bat have anything?"

Not "Will the scholar live?" Cressida was either as card hungry or as disgusted with the scholars as him.

"Ten Rare shards," Arthur said, standing. He felt a twinge of disappointment at that, though ten Rare shards was a nice haul. One had even been an elusive corner piece. That was possibly why the scourge-bat had stayed behind the rest to attack the first scholar it saw. It had a hunger for full cards.

Together, they made their way back to the stairwell. They were one level from the main floor, and Arthur heard shouts, stomping feet, and grinding of furniture across the floor. He guessed people were barricading themselves in rooms. That was smart, as long as no one tipped over any more candles and risked starting an inferno.

The main floor was chaos. Scholars ran this way and that, some with their long robes up over their heads, as if worried the giant scourge-bats would get tangled in their hair. Tables were flipped over with more scholars hiding behind them.

From the whistling shrieks in the high rafters, a few of the scourge-bats were flitting among the ceiling.

One dived down to a group of older men hunched in the corner of a wall. One man gestured, and several pages tore themselves out of nearby books to wrap themselves against the bat. It staggered in midair, but the papers fell to ribbons a few moments later. With a piercing whistle, the bat flew back up with the others in the rafters.

Then, notes played down from above.

Arthur slowed. So did everyone else.

He didn't think much about it. He simply stopped and listened.

He couldn't not listen.

Worry drained away . . .

Dimly, he was aware of others listening to the addictive play of song. Lyrics teased at the edge of his mind, though he couldn't tell what they were.

It was as if the singer—or were they singers?—were infinitely talented, but unpracticed still.

A shatter of breaking glass brought him back to himself. One of the wide, obscenely expensive windows out to the gardens was broken. With a whirl of wings, the scourge-bats flew out and into the night air.

Around him, people were blinking and looking about as if having surfaced up from a dream.

Arthur, too, felt like he'd just been jolted awake.

He and Cressida stared in horror at one another. That . . . that had been mind magic.

They'd just been caught in a spell. It was only pure good fortune that the spell had been used as a distraction so the scourglings could get away, and not as an attack. Arthur had been utterly helpless.

People seemed to be coming to the same conclusions around him, judging by the angry shouts.

But Arthur didn't hear a lot of surprise—mostly indignation and yells to go "check the lower library."

Scholars, obviously, were not stupid. Once they got over their shock, they'd take note of the faces of the two unfamiliar workers among them.

Arthur caught Cressida's wrist and pulled her on, out to the back halls.

"Come on!"

She followed, her steps stiff as if she was too shocked to think about where she was going.

There was a racket ahead through the hallway that led straight back to the kitchens. It sounded like a half dozen people were banging every pot and pan in the kitchen with metal spoons. The doors to the kitchen were locked solid, as if barred on the inside. Arthur had to pound on the door with his fist for nearly a full minute before the door cracked open.

Barlow glanced out. He held a wicked black blade in one hand, the end dripping a vicious dark sap of a card power. His eyes widened upon seeing Arthur, and he all but pulled him in, Cressida following, before slamming the door shut and relocking it with a sturdy piece of wood through the handles.

Barlow bellowed something Arthur couldn't catch over the noise. The cooks all around were indeed banging pots and pans with grim determination, eyes darting to every shadow.

"What's going on?" Arthur had to shout at the top of his voice, gesturing to the crew.

Barlow gestured them to the back of the kitchen. It was slightly less noisy—they could hear each other if they yelled.

"I thought you were dead for sure!" Barlow said. "How'd you get past the rogue mind-mage?"

Arthur thought he didn't hear correctly. "Rogue mind-mage?"

Barlow nodded. "One of the servers caught the edge of the spell—heard singing—came to warn us, just in time. I was nearly caught up in it myself."

"You drowned out the noise?" Cressida yelled, though it was more of a statement than a question. She had snapped back to herself and even seemed impressed, as if not believing mere common workers would figure out a way to counteract mind magic on the fly.

Again, Barlow nodded. "How bad is it out there?"

"It's over with now," Arthur said and tried not to think of the chaos that must be going outside.

"It's no mind-mage," Cressida cut in. "It's a scourge-infestation."

Barlow went pale. "An eruption? Here?"

"No, an *infestation*," Cressida said with emphasis. "The scholars are working against the hive—against all living people. Keep the doors barred. Ern—" She caught herself. "Arthur and I must leave."

Barlow turned to him, eyebrows raised. He didn't believe her. Arthur didn't blame him. It was pretty unbelievable. He was also surprised at Cressida's truthfulness, and her accusation.

Almost as if . . . as if she expected Barlow to spread the word around the city. Knowing Barlow, he would do just that. He always had an ear for gossip.

Arthur wasn't entirely sure of Cressida's motivation, but he was sure they didn't want their names to be associated with what had happened here today.

"The scholars let cards rot right under our feet," Arthur said. "Rare cards that became a scourge-infestation."

Now Barlow looked a bit green. He took a step back and made a warding sign, as if speaking about it was unlucky. "Are we safe?"

"Keep the doors barred until the hive dragons arrive. They should be here anytime now." He couldn't imagine people hadn't escaped out of every exit once the chaos started. "Carded can't catch scourge-diseases. And Barlow." He reached into his Personal Space and withdrew every Rare shard he'd collected except for the corner piece. "We were never here."

Barlow took the bribe with a nod and unbarred the exit for them.

None of the workers followed. There was no telling how many of the scourglings had escaped into the night. While in the kitchens behind shut doors, the workers were safe.

Arthur and Cressida didn't have that luxury. They ran down the streets, and Arthur kept his ears sharp for the sounds of singing.

They barely made it down the block before the first of the dragon roars started. The hive had been alerted.

Cressida pulled Arthur to a stop. Her eyes were wild. "Do you think the scholars let Rare-tier mind-magic cards go rotten? Or . . ."

Arthur finished for her. "Did the scourglings grow the cards themselves? I don't know. I think . . ." He hesitated, then forged on. "I got the feeling the magic wasn't as strong as it could be, yet. It had us all dead to rights in the banquet hall. But it only held everyone in its sway long enough to escape. I don't think that would have happened if it started with full mind-magic cards. My guess is, it—or they—are still developing them."

Her eyes went wide. Then, just as fast, they narrowed again. "The dragons have been alerted. I hope whoever decided to grow a nest of scourglings *pays*. That can't have been the only breakout, not with the little pink dragon falling ill. That room must have been leaking for a while now."

Arthur suspected as much, too. But he was less hopeful about seeing justice. In his experience, people responsible for atrocities rarely suffered for them.

Cressida must have seen the doubt in his eyes, because she squared her shoulders and tossed her hair back. "I'll testify against them. The leadership will take my word as a noble and . . . as a Rare dragon rider. If I'm lucky." At once, her bravado melted away. "I only collected five Rare cards from ones Wicker killed."

"I got one," he said. It wasn't as many as they had hoped, but it was better than nothing. "Let's see if the pink likes the look of them."

They needed somewhere private, and he had just the spot.

CHAPTER 15

Whose apartment is this?" By Cressida's wary tone, she already knew the answer.

Arthur shrugged and stepped to cover a stain on the thin rug. He couldn't remember what made it. Likely a spilled drink, but it had dried into an unsightly brown splotch. And . . . there was a lot more dust than he remembered. It covered every surface.

He had never brought a girl back to his apartment before, and now he was remembering why.

Cressida's curious gaze fell on Horatio's old cot, which still sat tucked up against the opposite wall. Arthur had taken down the sheeted walls that separated their beds after Horatio left to give himself more room.

"That's . . . a friend's," Arthur said. "A boy friend. Not a boyfriend!" he said quickly, "I mean, he was my roommate but he's, uh, gone now." He didn't want to tell Cressida about Sams. She already knew a dangerous amount about him already.

"And you lived here," Cressida said slowly. "While, what, pretending to be a commoner?"

He shrugged again. "You know the Kane family's status. I'm not much of a noble. Look, do you want to do this or not?"

The sound of dragon roaring could be heard faintly through the cracked glass window. The hive dragons had mustered yet again, this time for a hunt for scourglings in their own home. The dark sky above was thick with the sounds of dragon wings.

Arthur didn't know what tipped them off about the breakout from the scholar's guild, but he fully intended to go to the hive leadership with the full story, including his part . . . Just not until Cressida had her chance to link with the pink dragon.

Cressida looked like she very much wanted to argue this point, but she glanced out the window and nodded. Then she deliberately shook out a thin, delicate purse hidden up her sleeve.

From it, she withdrew her five Rare cards. The purse was her card anchor.

Arthur removed the Rare Phase In, Phase Out card he'd taken from the bat scourgling and placed it on the cot. She did the same, fanning them out.

He knew what his card already said, so he eagerly read over hers.

Polyglot Tongue
Rare
Knowledge
The wielder of this card will be able to understand and repeat any spoken language, cant, dialect, or accent. This does not include written words.

Eidetic Imagery
Rare
Knowledge
This card grants its wielder the ability to recall images and visual concepts from memory with perfect precision. Sound, taste, and touch-based memories are recalled with a higher, though possibly imperfect, precision.

The Quest of Life
Rare
Meta
Warning: This card's features are only accessible in the heart deck. This card fundamentally changes the wielder's outlook to semi-gamify their life. Internal tasks and goals are outlined, and waypoints are rewarded with minor to moderate prizes depending on the difficulty of the task. Search for additional cards in this set to expand abilities.

Mental Bookshelf
Rare
Knowledge
This card grants the wielder the ability to organize learned knowledge into a mental bookshelf, and is able to find and retrieve that knowledge at will. If placed in the heart deck, the wielder may voluntarily display pages from the mental book to other parties. As memories fade, so do the pages inside the books.

All About Fish

Rare

Knowledge

This card grants the wielder the ability to instantly identify every species of fresh and ocean creatures in the class Osteichthyes, or bony fish. With the additional use of mana, this card will impart additional knowledge of the best filleting methods. This card unlocks mana.

Arthur stared with greed at the cards. He wanted all of them. Well, maybe not the Polyglot card. He'd never encountered anyone who spoke another language, though he heard it was possible. And the fish card only had limited uses, outside of cooking.

The rest made his fingers itch.

"How do I know which one the dragon will like?"

Cressida's words snapped him back to the present. She was biting at her lower lip, clearly worried.

Shame welled up within him for his self-centeredness. This wasn't about him. These were for the dragon.

"I suppose I shouldn't test them out?" Cressida continued doubtfully. "If they only touched my heart briefly, perhaps there wouldn't be damage . . ."

Arthur shook his head vigorously. "There would be. It's your heart—they'll *always* be a part of you. Especially this one." He pointed to the quest card. "It changes your entire outlook on life. You might not be . . . right afterwards."

Her shoulders slumped. "And using them all would be foolish."

She probably could. Everyone had a different upper limit before the number of cards began to weigh down on their heart, but ten was considered average. There were exceptions when it came to cards of the same deck. Arthur's two Legendary cards functioned as one, for example.

He guessed that three knowledge and two meta, including the Phase card, wouldn't work well with Cressida's existing deck. Hers seemed more combat-oriented with the Flame Bear Summon, the shield, and whatever power had allowed her to manipulate fire.

Adding one or two knowledge/meta-type cards might be a good idea to introduce balance, but all of them together risked introducing imbalance.

Also, it wasn't guaranteed to work.

"Why don't we ask the expert?" Arthur suggested and mentally reached for the pink dragon.

She appeared lying on the floor, blinking wet eyes.

"Where?" she gasped.

Cressida sank into a graceful kneel beside the hatchling. "I have some cards for you. Would you like to see them?"

The pink looked at her with something like hope in her eyes. "Please . . ."

One by one, Cressida brought the cards right before her muzzle. The baby dragon couldn't read, so Cressida described them.

"I don't . . . I don't know . . ." The pink waved her head back and forth, agitated. "They don't feel like anything . . . I can't . . ." She stopped and let out a chain of rattling coughs. By the end, she was wheezing, and her vivid pink hide had paled to a washed-out hue. It made the dark streaks stand out more vividly.

The dragon was dying. Fading right before their eyes.

Arthur stepped forward. "Let me put you back in my storage. Chances are, the hive leaders will strip the scholars of everything not nailed down. They might have more Rares available. Or we can look to other hives."

He could write to Horatio. He and Sams owed him. Maybe they had a line on local card shops. Valentina and Whitaker wouldn't like anyone reaching out to another hive, but surely the death of a hatchling Rare was worse.

Cressida shook her head. "No. She can't feel the cards because it's not inside of a heart. I have to choose."

She looked over the cards, plucked up the Quest of Life, and before Arthur could say anything, pulled down the collar of her shirt and stuck it in her heart.

Her reaction was immediate. She gasped, hunching over. The pink dragon, who was half slumped in her lap, fell back.

"Cressida?" Arthur gripped her shoulder. He'd never seen a poor reaction from adding a card, but the way Cressida was hunched over made her look like she was in agony.

Cressida straightened at his touch. She stared at him with eyes that burned an unnatural blue, and just for a moment, something else flashed within them—like floating text ripped out of a book.

Then she let out a gasp like someone who'd been underwater coming up for air at last. Her eyes faded back to normal, and she blinked at him.

"Are you all right?" Arthur asked.

She opened her mouth to reply, but before she could, the pink dragon surged to her feet, and with strength Arthur had no idea she had, pushed him away to stand before Cressida.

The dragon's legs shook, and though she tried to speak, she didn't have air to gasp out words. Instead, she brought out a dim, flickering image of her own card.

Charlatan Pair

_eta

Ra_e

When linked ____, matches and duplicates a ___ random card of the same set. Warning: Must use ___ of the ___ rank and tier.

There was something wrong with the hatchling's card. Parts of the description were blurred as if it had yet to be written. This was what the healers had meant when they said the card was undeveloped.

Arthur felt a twinge of fear for Cressida. Her card was potentially powerful on its own. Would the dragon's card drag hers down or enhance it?

Cressida didn't seem to care either way.

"Yes," she breathed. "I'll link with you."

Then she gestured out a projected copy of her own card and pressed it against the dragon's.

Arthur looked away from the newly created card, though he was intensely curious. It was a private moment, and Cressida was allowed to keep her secrets.

Arthur certainly had enough of his own.

He looked back at a squeak from the dragon. Her scales had returned to full vibrancy, an almost eye-watering pink. She stood up on newly strengthened legs and launched herself, front and back legs and wings, to capture Cressida in a tight hug.

"I can breathe!" the hatchling said, full throated and happy. "And the world looks so shiny and colorful. Where am I, anyway? Where is my eggshell? Oh! I'm Joyberry, by the way, but you can call me Joy. What's your name? And who is that?" She craned her head around to look at Arthur, wrinkling up her nose slightly at the end as if in distaste.

Cressida looked bowled over by Joy's . . . enthusiasm. "I'm Lady Cressida of Icehouse."

"That's a long name," Joy said. "Can I call you Cressida? Or just Cress? Oh! Can we go flying? I can make a quest for it right now."

"Not just yet. I'd rather get you looked over by a healer. And call me Cressida, please."

"Okay!" Again, Joy looked at Arthur. "Is he the one that really, really, really long quest is about?"

Arthur was hit with a sense of foreboding. "Long quest?"

But Cressida shook her head. She still looked overwhelmed, but she seemed to be getting her feet back under her. She gave Arthur a significant look that he interpreted as *We'll talk later.*

He had to bite the insides of his cheeks to keep from asking.

"What is this place?" Joy twisted her head to look all around the small apartment, going so far as to turn completely upside down so that Cressida had to hold her head so she didn't overbalance. "There is so much dirt everywhere. Is this what outside looks like?"

Arthur coughed. Yes, he could stand to use his **Tidying** skill a little more. Things had been hectic over the last few weeks, and he hadn't dusted.

"She looks healthy." Arthur stepped forward, extending his hand as he would a horse or a dog to sniff. Head turned upside down, Joy watched him. "It's nice to meet you."

"Your card wasn't right," she replied. "I mean, it was better than most but way, way, way too strong. It would have burned me up from the inside out. Cressida, do you hear that?" she asked excitedly, straightening. "All of those wings? Do you think they're dragons?"

Arthur couldn't hear anything. Joy's senses must have been sharper than his own.

"The full hive is mustering," Cressida said on a sigh. "I only hope no one was taken in by that terrible mind-singing scourgling."

"I'm not just talking about them," Joy said. "There's one really close, and it's huge."

"How do you know—" Arthur started.

And that was when the window blew in.

Thankfully, the glass was thick and badly blown enough to fall out in one piece with a clunk instead of shattering like a thinner pane.

Gale-force winds ripped through the room after it, blowing Arthur back a step, ripping down the curtain, and flinging loose dust and detritus everywhere.

Cressida shrieked in surprise, instinctively curling around Joy to protect her. Arthur saw a spurt of flame as she tried to summon Wicker, but the raging wind snuffed the bear out before it could fully form.

He looked at the window, which was now dominated by a single, slitted green eye. The tiny scales around it were a powdery blue.

It was a dragon. A dragon bigger than any he had ever seen, and by the way that eye narrowed, it was a very unhappy dragon.

"CRESSIDA ICEHOUSE. ERNEST KANE," a voice bellowed so loud that it vibrated the air around them. Arthur hunched over, and Cressida clapped her hands over the sides of Joy's head as if to protect her ears. "COME OUTSIDE RIGHT NOW. YOU HAVE EXPLAINING TO DO."

There was no way they could say no to the dragon. From the size alone, it could rip off the top of the apartment building as easily as Arthur opened a jar.

He suspected he knew which dragon this was. That suspicion was borne out when he and Cressida exited to ground level and got a better look at her.

Not an entire look of the dragon, because she was currently perched on a thunderhead. A thick, cloudy mist obscured most of the dragon's form. And as she was much too large to fit in the city streets, she stuck her head down from the bottom of the cloud to glare at them. She was an aged dragon, wrinkles running like cracks between her powder-blue scales.

She was also appropriately grumpy with them.

"HURRY UP. I DON'T HAVE ALL DAY."

She extended a clawed hand the size of a canal barge. Tentatively, Arthur stepped on the palm. Cressida, carrying Joy, did the same.

While the pink dragon clung onto Cressida, tail wrapped around the woman's waist, she didn't look frightened. "Ohhh . . ." she cooed to the big blue. "You look very scary. Will I grow as big as you someday?"

To Arthur's surprise, the giant dragon inclined her head to look down at Joy. With her aged face, she looked a little like a grandmother squinting to read a recipe. "YOU'RE THAT RARE HATCHLING WHO HAS BEEN VEXING MY VALENTINA, AREN'T YOU?"

"Yup! I'm Joy! Who are you?"

"Joy!" Cressida hissed, alarmed.

"YOU MAY CALL ME ELISSA. NOW, HOLD ON TIGHT. AND NO SCREAMING. I DO HATE THE SOUND OF SCREAMING," she grumbled, though loudly.

With that, the cloud she was perched on shot straight up into the air, faster than an arrow leaving its bow.

Arthur's stomach dropped to the floor. The dark city streets below were a glittering spread of lamp lights, like a reverse night sky. Looking at it made him feel so sick he thought he might topple over.

No wonder people screamed.

There was more. Though darkness had fallen, he was aware of dragon shapes darting back and forth in the air. Some were punctuated by card abilities, which highlighted a flash of scale or a rider conjuring a charm. Some dragons' magic made their eyes glow as they searched below.

They were searching for the escaped scourglings.

The ascending cloud didn't slow until they had nearly reached the top of the hive's cone. Curiously, Arthur's ears didn't pop, and the air was still at a comfortable temperature and easy to breathe. He suspected that was Elissa's doing.

Valentina stood at the end of a long open-air balcony that looked like a pathway out to the sky.

"I DARE SAY THE HATCHLING RARE WILL LIVE AFTER ALL," Elissa announced as if she had anything to do with it. Then she unceremoniously dumped her passengers on the balcony—causing Arthur to stumble close to the edge.

Valentina looked no more happy than her dragon had. She glowered at them like they had interrupted her night's sleep, even though the sun had just set.

"I hope for your sake you have cards worth all this trouble," she said to Cressida.

"We do," Cressida said, with a slightly awkward curtsey considering she was holding a baby dragon. "But I also come with dire news—"

"The scholars?" Valentina asked. "Save it. I know. Or at least, Seekers already put you two there. Come on." She turned, a miniature cloud forming under her feet to carry her back across the balcony and to the hive. "Let's get this over with."

"Are we in trouble?" Joy asked in a stage whisper.

Arthur wasn't sure how to answer. Judging by Cressida's silence, she didn't either.

CHAPTER 16

Valentina brought Arthur and Cressida into the same luxurious room Arthur had visited before. Which meant that the dark Legendary egg was somewhere on a nearby balcony. Arthur tried not to search around too obviously, but judging by Valentina's grumpy expression, he failed.

Meanwhile, Joy found the stuffed couches utterly fascinating and had abandoned Cressida's arms to leap on one . . . much to Cressida's horror.

"No, don't bother," Valentina snapped as Cressida went to collect her dragon. "It's only a three-hundred-year-old couch and completely priceless. At least the dragon is showing some life—not that pale, half-dead thing it was. Sit down next to her, she'll settle. Not you," she said, fixing Arthur with a stern look. "You stand over there and wait while I talk to our newest dragon rider."

Arthur didn't have much of a choice, as a gust of wind pushed him to stand by the far wall. That gust then turned into a rapid swirl around him, visible as a ghostly light fog. Abruptly, all noise cut off from the rest of the room.

Arthur saw Cressida's lips move but couldn't hear her voice. Valentina had set up a wind privacy shield.

It was a long conversation. Arthur didn't have much talent at lip reading, and though he watched closely whenever Valentina didn't glance his way, he didn't develop a skill.

From Cressida's expressions, he guessed she was recounting their evening in the scholar's library. At the end, Cressida pulled out the remaining cards they had harvested from the scourglings. She must have collected them before they were whisked out of the apartment. She handed them to Valentina, who looked them over carefully.

Finally, Valentina took a few minutes to examine the pink dragon. She extended her thin but vibrantly colored wings, checked the baby dragon's teeth, and felt down the length of her hide for anything unusual.

Then, with a curt gesture, Valentina gestured for Cressida and Joy to go.

Cressida stood and curtsied. She glanced at Arthur, concern etched on her face.

Valentina made a shooing motion for them to get going, and Cressida wasn't left with a choice.

Once they were out of the room, Valentina allowed the privacy shield to drop.

"Whatever Cressida said," Arthur began, "visiting the scholars was my idea. I dragged her along. I made her—"

Valentina snorted. "Do you take me for an idiot?"

"Of course not," Arthur said, sidestepping that easy trap. "But she shouldn't get into trouble for my mistakes. Don't send her away."

"Away?" Valentina rolled her eyes. "The card they made is a little unpredictable, but one of the more useful pink powers I've seen in some time. Plus, we didn't have to go begging to the other hives for their Rare recruits."

Arthur was still worried. This night had been morally dubious at best, and escaping without punishment felt too easy.

Valentina must have read the expression on his face. "Lady Icehouse is off to training, you dolt. If you're lucky, you may someday join her . . . though we both know you have your sights set on higher than a Rare."

She gestured to the couch. "Sit. Let's talk."

Cautiously, Arthur did.

She studied him for a few moments. Her visible irritation had faded, but it just made her unreadable.

Arthur tried not to fidget. Surrounded by such luxury and wealth, he felt like he ought to be doing something like serving tea. He was used to working for the rich, not to talking with them.

"I'm unsure if you should be commended for your actions tonight or thrown out on your ear," Valentina finally said. "I ask you to save the Rare and hinted that you should make the scholars look foolish. Instead, you revealed a deep-seated rot. But then you managed to let scourglings loose in the city! We still have dragon riders chasing them down."

"We didn't mean to—" Arthur began.

Valentina jumped on that at once. "Then please tell me your version. Don't spare the details."

Arthur felt like he was being led by the nose into a trap.

He did as she asked anyway. The only parts he kept to himself had to do with Barlow, not wanting to implicate his old friend in any way.

There came a knock at the door as he finished.

Valentina looked neither surprised nor frustrated at the interruption. "Come in."

A bald man in pure white robes glided in. He was thin with an overly large nose that didn't manage to distract from the shininess of his skull. He also wore the badge of a snow-white dragon pinned on his shoulder.

This was a mind-mage.

Arthur desperately tried not to think about all his secrets . . . which made him immediately think about all his secrets.

The mind-mage didn't so much as glance at him as he bowed a greeting to Valentina.

She waved at him in irritation. "Yes, yes. Did we get them or not?"

The mind-mage shot a look at Arthur but must have decided Valentina gave permission for him to hear the report.

"Unfortunately, no. Whitaker continues the search, though he is certain the scourglings are no longer within the city."

Pursing wrinkled lips, Valentina shook her head. "If they had knowledge cards, they're smart enough to leave and set up a colony somewhere else. And if one is a mind-singer . . ." She looked like she was on the verge of a headache. "Well, Ernest, we will need your official testimony."

"Testimony?" Arthur repeated.

"Yes, to the king. He takes special notice whenever scourge fester up, and we'll have to act quickly to ensure the scholars are fully to blame. Not the hive."

He sensed an opportunity here. If he were shown to be helpful, a team player for the hive, Valentina might be obliged to look more favorably on him. "You need me to write out a statement?"

"Hardly." Valentina looked to the mage. "Devi, show him your trick."

Devi the mind-mage reached into his robe and pulled out a thick sheet of cardstock. The size and shape with the rounded edges reminded him of magic cards, but this was simple, blank paper.

Or at least, it was for a few moments.

Devi pinched one blank card between his fingers. It filled with ink, which started to move before Arthur's amazed eyes. The image was a perfect representation of himself and Valentina sitting in the room. The last few moments of their back-and-forth conversation was represented by bubbles of speech that appeared and disappeared over their heads.

Devi let him absorb the sight for a few moments then tossed the card aside for a fresh one. "That's one ability. My secondary card allows me to see specific memories."

Which he then imprinted on the card with perfect accuracy.

Arthur recoiled, all intention of being helpful draining away. "You want to read my memories? What if I refuse?"

Devi's expression was oddly compassionate. "Ernest, every man entertains dark and unworthy thoughts. No experienced mind-mage will hold that against you. But if it makes you feel better, I will only see what you intentionally choose to show."

"Also, you don't have a choice," Valentina said bluntly. "You are a key witness, and I expect the king himself to take interest in the events today. If you don't provide voluntary testimony, he'll send one of his mind-mages to take what they need—and they won't be gentle."

Arthur looked back and forth. He wasn't sure he trusted the two of them . . . but he did believe her.

"I haven't forgotten your help with saving the hive's newest Rare," Valentina said. "Establishing what you saw will help you in the short and long run. Also, if the scholar's guild is dabbling with mind magic, we must know."

Arthur thought about it for a moment. "Let me see that card again."

Devi handed it over. Arthur looked at it carefully. The moving illustrations were only pictures. No inner monologue.

"You choose when the memory begins and ends," Devi said.

That meant if he was careful—if he was in control—he could shield Barlow's involvement as well as his own card's powers.

"All right," Arthur said. "What do I do?"

"Simply focus on the beginning of the event and go it through linearly." Devi reached out and touched two fingers to Arthur's temple. After a moment, he drew back. "Interesting."

"What?" Valentina said sharply.

"This boy has rudimentary mental shields."

His **Empathic Resistance** skill. Arthur's mouth went dry.

"A card?" Valentina asked.

"No, simply a natural resistance." Devi smiled down at Arthur. "It speaks of high discipline. But no matter, I can bypass them if I am prepared. Let us begin again."

Arthur went through the memory in surprisingly little time. The speed of thought was not just a saying.

Devi dutifully recorded the memories on three cards—apparently there was a limit to how much each could hold.

Since it was his testimony, he let Arthur see and approve of each. To his relief, there wasn't anything objectionable . . . though since the memory was from his eyes, he was embarrassed about how much was centered on Cressida.

"Will Cressida provide testimony as well?" he asked.

"No," Devi said. "Never on newly linked dragon pairs." He gathered the cards up. "I will transmit these to the crown at once."

"You do that," Valentina drawled. "Tell me if the king has anything interesting to say."

Devi smiled wryly at her, and Arthur had the impression the two were friends.

As he left, Valentina turned back to him.

"Now, let's talk about your reward."

"My . . . reward?" he asked, dumbstruck.

"You were key to getting that Rare linked with a rider. And though I would have preferred the scourglings not have gotten out to wreak havoc on the countryside . . . that guilt falls on the scholars who let the rot fester, not to the two idiots who tripped into their scheme." She fanned out the Rare cards Cressida handed over, then considered for a moment. "Pick two."

Arthur was not about to argue that he should be punished. He looked eagerly over the cards.

The Phase In, Phase out tempted him, but now that he had time to examine the cards in detail, the Eidetic Imagery and Mental Bookshelf had the same general look to them. A look that he knew from one of his own cards . . .

Could they be part of the same set?

Only one way to find out.

Valentina nodded in satisfaction as he made his decision. Then she tucked the remaining cards away. He supposed she intended to take her due.

"Excellent. Now, I suspect once this hullabaloo dies down, the hive will host a festival to celebrate our new Rare pairing."

Arthur nodded and, sensing he was being excused, rose.

Valentina's next words stopped him in his tracks.

"Afterwards, of course, we will introduce the Legendary egg to the world. Be ready."

PART 2

LEGENDARY RECRUIT

CHAPTER 17

Arthur made his way, deliberately and slowly, and with dignity he imagined befit a noble, down to the first few levels. No one offered him a dragon ride down. Not a big surprise—from the glances outside the windows, many of the hive dragons were still on the wing, seen as darting shadowed shapes in the night air.

This had already been a long, long night. And he still had quite the walk ahead of him.

But there were more important things to be done.

By the third level down, he was reasonably sure no one had followed him. He increased his pace to a jog and ducked into one of the side rooms marked with a servant's stamp over the doorframe. It was a storage closet about as big as his apartment. It even had its own lamp lit by card-anchor magic.

Touching it to illuminate the anchor stone, he sat down on a crate and drew out his new cards.

He had some decisions to make.

Back when he'd been a boy, he had no qualms about shoving cards in his heart without considering the consequences. He knew better now. Not only was there a general limit, plus or minus a few cards, anything tucked away in a heart became part of that person. It changed who they were on a fundamental level, so it was important that he choose wisely.

He looked at his new Eidetic Imagery and Mental Bookshelf cards.

Did he want these as useful tools, able to switch out at need? Or did he want them to become an intrinsic part of him?

Arthur weighed the pros and cons for a moment, but he had already come to his decision.

The scholars had likely used these cards on a temporary basis. Perhaps given to a favored disciple to memorize all books on a subject before they returned them to the library. And in the long run, they'd lost them.

He wouldn't make the same mistake.

But what really tipped the scales for him was that these cards were too much alike. They looked like they could be part of the same set, and they resembled one he already had. It was a risk, but a well-reasoned one.

He put the two cards in his heart.

Mental Bookshelf

Rare

Knowledge

This card grants the wielder the ability to organize learned knowledge into a mental bookshelf and is able to find and retrieve that knowledge at will. If placed in the heart deck, the wielder may voluntarily display pages from the mental book to other parties. As memories fade, so do the pages inside the books.

Eidetic Imagery

Rare

Knowledge

This card grants its wielder the ability to recall images and visual concepts from memory with perfect precision. Sound, taste, and touch-based memories are recalled with a higher, though possibly imperfect, precision.

There was a mental tug, and Arthur followed it.

Abruptly, he found himself standing in front of a basic wooden bookcase. Part of him was aware he could leave this area at any time—if he concentrated hard enough, he could go back to his physical body. It would be as easy as stepping from one door to another.

Instead, he concentrated on the bookcase.

It was of simple, almost amateurish design. Planks of rough, unvarnished pine wood nailed together to form three shelves. These shelves were sparsely filled with books.

An unexpected spike of shame stabbed through him. He . . . wasn't a big reader. In fact, he couldn't remember the last time he had leveled his **Reading** or **Writing** skill. There had been so much else to do, so many other skills and classes to explore.

Now that he was faced with his anemic bookshelf, he knew he had some work to do.

Stepping closer, he examined the books themselves. Leather bound with gold lettering on the spine, they were organized into differing subjects. *Cooking Recipes* was the fattest tome by far. *The Art of Gambling* was second. Third, oddly, was *Philosophies of Nobles and Their Relations to Commoners.*

Arthur grabbed that one and flipped through it. Unsurprisingly, the pages were filled with his own musings, deftly organized into subcategories. It was like reading a report he'd written back in his school days and hadn't quite forgotten.

He stopped on a chapter entitled: *How the system encourages nobles to gain wealth off the backs of oppressed laborers.* With memories forefront of Baron Kane's men underfeeding the border village folk, pocketing any profits, and the ways in which the oppressed were forced to stay . . .

Not exactly light or fun reading. Since it came from his head, none of it was a surprise, either.

Arthur reshelved the book.

Briefly flipping through the cookbook brought more joy. He didn't remember all the recipes he'd ever read—that would change thanks to his new card—but he could easily fill in the gaps in some of his half-remembered recipes. There was even a whole section dedicated to the time he had read through Barlow's family recipes.

Lastly, he took a look at the gambling book and was surprised to find charts with odds organized by game. There was an entire section on the odds of when to hit and when to fold according to a particular hand received when playing blackjack.

Again, none of it came as a surprise since it had been plucked out of his own head. But seeing these numbers laid out for him in a new light made him itch to sit down at a table.

Would Ernest Kane, the mildly respectable baron's son, be caught dead in a gambling hall? Arthur thought about it as he slid the book back into place.

Yes, he decided. His family had little to lose in terms of honor, and he personally had too much to gain to give up gambling.

With that thought in mind, he yawned, stretched, and was about to step back out of this mental space and back into his real body. Then something caught his attention.

Something lay beyond the simple bookshelf. The bare edge of an outlined door—like a wall cast in shadows within the darkness.

He gripped the bookcase and pushed. It slid aside as if it had wheels attached to the bottom.

A metal vault stood behind the bookshelf. A lock barred the way, but it fell open when Arthur brushed his fingers across it.

The door opened inward to a vast, dark room. One that Arthur knew well. Filled with an odd collection of produce, knickknacks he had found on seasonable sale, and a few extra card shards . . .

This was his Personal Space.

He was aware of it—even saw the items within itemized as a list. But how could he see it like this? Unless . . .

Arthur's eyes widened. Turning away from the space, he heard the vault door slam shut behind him as he "stepped" back into his normal body.

Back in the storage space, Arthur gasped and looked around, heart beating fast.

He had been so eager to look at the bookshelves, he hadn't gone through every notification in his heart deck.

Alert: Three of your cards share a set synergy.
Mental Bookshelf
Eidetic Imagery
Personal Space
These three cards have been combined into three of a kind.
Alert: Due to this Rare find, your basic Luck stat has been temporarily increased by +1.

His hunch had played out.

The hair on the back of Arthur's neck rose. He rubbed at it, and when that didn't calm him down, he started to pace the length of the small room.

By all rights, he should be jumping with glee. Finding a pair of cards within the same set was extraordinary luck and a big part of the reason why he'd picked the bookshelf and memory cards over Phase In, Phase Out.

The fact that they were the same set as his Personal Space was . . . unbelievable. Or it would be, had he just not spent the last two nights with a Rare meta dragon in his storage space.

Had Joy had something to do with this?

Metas twisted the fabric of the universe in strange ways. Joy had linked with Cressida's quest card, but before that, her existing card was partially unwritten.

No one knew exactly how sets came into being. It was a slow process guided by the world's magic. It was known that a set could take years to complete, if they ever did at all.

He thought that Joy's card had something to do with quests. But what if it was actually related to completing existing cards?

No wonder Valentina had sent Cressida off to train. Joy wasn't a dragon who could fight the scourge, but she was invaluable to the hive.

An old memory flashed across his mind: a pink dragon set upon by other hive dragons, its rider falling to his death. That was how Arthur had gained his Return to Start card.

Pinks were dragons with incredibly valuable cards who couldn't defend themselves.

He was glad Cressida had fire and shield cards to protect them both.

Meanwhile, whatever suspicions he had about their card, he'd keep to himself.

* * *

By the time Arthur made it back to his room within the hive, the beginning of dawn was visible along the edge of the horizon. His mind was still buzzing with revelations, but his body had hit a wall. Exhausted, he stumbled in, haphazardly tore off his clothing, and lay down on his bed.

Knocking at his door woke him what felt like five seconds later.

He stumbled across the room clad in only old trousers. When he cracked open the door, it was to see Kenzie glaring at him from the other side.

"Do you know what time it is?" she demanded.

He squinted at her. "I was about to ask you the same."

His groggy mind and body insisted he'd only been asleep for moments, but Kenzie was fully dressed and didn't look tired at all.

"It's well into the afternoon! I can't believe you're still sleeping." With a frustrated sound, Kenzie pushed open the door and made to walk right in. She paused mid-step and stared at him, horrified.

"You look like a scourgling chewed you up and spit you out."

He looked down at himself. Specifically his chest, which had scabs and hours-old streaks of blood thanks to the scourge-bat. His right forearm had its fair share of scratches, too. The wounds were red around the edges and sore, but he'd had worse as a child.

"That's not too far from the truth," he said, amused.

She gripped his arm—his good arm, thankfully—and stared at him, eyes wide. "Don't tell me you were mixed up in the scholar's guild mess."

"Okay," Arthur said.

"Okay, what?"

"Okay, I won't tell you."

Her mouth dropped open, and he grinned, pleased with himself.

That faded the next second when Kenzie stepped into his small room, grabbed a pillow from the bed, and whapped him hard. "You! Blasted! Idiot!" She punctuated each word with a pillowy smack. He raised his hands to fend her off, but then she tossed the pillow away with a frustrated growl. "Of *course* you were involved. And you didn't even bother to clean up your scourge-wounds! What's wrong with you?"

"Hey, I'm carded! I'm not an idiot."

The look she gave said she disagreed. "Rumor said those were Rare-tier scourglings!"

Now it was his turn to give her a *look*. She should know he didn't have to worry about Rare powers when he had Legendary in his heart deck.

"Right," she admitted. "Well, you should have at least put a bandage over them."

"What's that going to do that a scab couldn't?" he asked, bewildered. Even the lowliest Common card protected against infection and other sicknesses.

Kenzie gave another frustrated growl. "Scars, for one thing. And if you're going to play the fancy uptight noble, you can't be seen as scarred up like a commoner. Now, tell me you have some suitable outfits . . ."

She all but shoved him aside to head straight for his small closet.

"By all means, come on in," he muttered, rolling his eyes, but shut the door to give them privacy.

Kenzie was head deep inside the closest, pawing over the three outfits he'd managed to hang up. "Are all of your best shirts made for work?"

"Not all of them. There's . . . ah." He picked up the shirt he wore last night and shook it out. The front and sleeve were slashed and spotted with blood. His **Tidying** skill told him it was a lost cause. His common sense agreed. "Umm . . ."

"Fine. We're going shopping. Put on something decent. I'll wait." Kenzie turned her back to him with a false air of giving him privacy.

He was too tired for this. "Look, as you can imagine, I've had a long night—"

"Word's come down from the leaders up high. They'll be announcing the Legendary egg tonight."

"I know that," Arthur said, annoyed. "But I have things to do—"

"And," Kenzie continued, "all the silvers who managed to snag a recruit were given a stipend."

That stopped Arthur cold. "Stipend?"

Kenzie risked a glance over her shoulder. She was grinning. "A *generous* stipend. No commoners were hurt from last night, thank my dragon's scales. But the hive will want to hush it up with a big to-do. This is going to draw the cream of the crop from the kingdom, and the people in charge want to put their best foot forward."

While she spoke, Arthur shoved his feet into his boots and grabbed the first shirt he could reach. "What are we waiting for?"

In the scant hours Arthur had slept, the entire hive city had changed. Word from the leadership of Wolf Moon Hive had gone out that the new Rare had linked with a rider. It was time to celebrate.

Vendors took up the call and lined the streets with their wares; non-entertainment businesses closed and children's classes were let out. Dance squares were set up at every street corner. Some quick-acting folks had even strung banners across the road depicting pink dragons, in celebration of Joyberry. A few images were even card-charmed to walk across the banner's fabric. Arthur and Kenzie passed musicians tuning up their instruments in preparation for a busy night.

It looked like a festival, but it didn't feel much like a festival.

Conversations were kept to a low murmur, and despite the fact that all classes were supposed to be let out for celebrations, there wasn't a child to be seen.

Townsfolk risked constant glances up to the sky as if worried something would sweep down to snatch them.

Word of the scourglings with a mind-mage had made the rounds. People were worried.

"I'd like to walk by the scholar's guild," Arthur said.

Kenzie shook her head. New lines etched between her eyebrows—her card powers swung toward emotional empathy, so she had to be hyper aware of the tense atmosphere.

"There's no point. Whitaker ordered it slagged this morning."

Arthur stopped. "What does that mean?"

Again, she shrugged. "Slagged. You know . . . hotter than burning, but less than turning everything into pure lava. It was a scourge-infection. You can't let that grow— Hey, where're you going?"

Arthur turned and sprinted down the street.

He had worked for Barlow for years and knew the man wouldn't leave a job until the kitchen was as clean as when he'd found it. They had barricaded themselves in to hide from mind powers.

Had they been trapped inside?

Kenzie called after him, but Arthur ignored her, running full pelt through the city. He was on the wrong side of two canals, and it would take ages to get to Barlow's restaurant with the city in festival mode . . .

But the streets weren't as choked as they should be, on account of nerves. And the strength in Arthur's legs didn't flag. In fact, he ran sure-footed down alleyways slick with moss that grew in the shadows, leaped over small barrels that obstructed his way, and once turned neatly to avoid spooking an oncoming cart horse.

He gained two levels in **Running** and arrived at the Salt and Spoon, Barlow's restaurant, faster than he believed possible.

The restaurant was shut up tight. All lanterns dimmed.

Arthur pounded a fist on the door then turned down the next alleyway to the rear kitchen entrance. There should be a small crew in the back preparing dinner service.

That door was locked as well.

It looked as if no one had visited at all.

But Barlow spent all his waking hours there . . .

What had he done? He should have insisted Barlow and the other workers escape along with him. Instead, he'd been so concerned about keeping his identity secret, he'd left them behind. If he'd given it a moment's thought, he would have considered what the hive's reaction would be to a scourge-infection in the middle of the city . . .

"Arthur?"

Whipping around, Arthur made an inarticulate noise as he spotted the man he'd been looking for standing right behind him, holding a crate full of market-fresh vegetables.

Relief crashed over him with an intensity that was almost painful. The back end of the wave came with a heaping sense of guilt.

"You're alive," he said dumbly. "Why isn't the restaurant open? Why— I thought . . ." His throat tightened, and he had to stop talking for fear of shaming himself with tears.

The corners of Barlow's lips tightened. He reached forward, patting a heavy hand on Arthur's shoulder. "I gave the lads a day off. They deserve it after last night. Dragon riders got us out—one of Leader Whitaker's retinue riders, in fact. I should be *honored*."

Arthur heard heavy sarcasm in the last words but didn't understand why. He shook his head. "I should have guessed they wouldn't want any scourge-infection to spread. I knew how bad it was. I should have warned you."

"Arthur, you aren't a dragon rider. That's not your job. Though . . ." Barlow smiled. "I hear it might be soon. You tried for that Rare, didn't you? Well, maybe you'll have better luck next time." He patted his shoulder again in condolence.

His guilt wouldn't go away that easily. Barlow, the kitchen crew, and likely many of the workers had been caught up in last night's mess through no fault of their own. Yes, the room had likely been leaking scourge-rot, but the mass breakout wouldn't have happened if Arthur wasn't there.

He was working up an apology, but Barlow caught his attention.

Barlow glanced around as if to make sure no one was listening. Then he took a step forward and spoke in a low voice. "Dragon riders got us out, but it wasn't out of the kindness of their own hearts."

"What do you mean?"

"They swept the place for any . . . unclaimed cards."

From bodies, Barlow meant.

Arthur felt bile rise. "Did they find any?"

"No, judging by their sour expressions." Barlow shrugged. "But I thought you should know, before you go beating yourself up. Even our heroes aren't above harvesting from corpses. I know you're well grown, Arthur, but you watch yourself in the hive. And if you ever find any interesting cards . . . you best keep them to yourself."

Arthur found Kenzie, who had been searching the streets for him, a few minutes later.

"Where were you?" she asked, annoyed. "What got you so panicked?"

"Had to check on a friend," he said gruffly. "Kenzie, does that stipend only cover fancy clothes?"

"Covers a fancy room on a higher level, too," Kenzie said. "Something with a window. I was going to surprise you with it before you ran off." She eyed him. "Why?"

Arthur took a breath. "You know how competitive Rare recruits can be. Legendary is going to be ten times worse. I need a way to defend myself. I need a combat card."

CHAPTER 18

Like most businesses, the card shop was briskly busy for festival day. There were several around the hive city, but Kenzie and Arthur went to the one widely known as the largest and best stocked.

However, it didn't mean that the shops were well-stocked with what he wanted.

Arthur grimaced as he glanced over the shelves. All were of the Common variety—Uncommon cards were behind the counter, where one had to pass through the approval of the store clerks to get a closer look. And the ones set out for display were . . . frivolous.

"Oh, look. Here's one that charms long pieces of fabric to wave in the air, even when there isn't a wind." Kenzie helpfully held up a glass case with the Common card locked inside. "It doesn't require mana to work. That means no secondary card to unlock magic within you."

He glared at her, not appreciating the teasing. "How does that help?"

"It's one of those that levels up as you practice. Give it enough time, maybe you can wrap a scarf around someone's throat."

"Why is that even a thing?" Arthur grumbled, then reached to pull out another card from the shelf. "Why is *this* even a thing?"

Item Camouflage

Illusion

Common

Camouflage a single item no larger than one foot square to perfectly match its surroundings. This is an illusion-based charm and does not alter the object's size or weight. Illusion will fall if item is touched by a living person. Cooldown: 12 hours. This card requires mana.

Actually . . . now that he thought about it, he could see a few uses for that one. It would make an excellent thief's tool.

Arthur slid it back onto the shelf. "Why didn't we go to the hive's commissary again?"

"Because if it's a combat card you want, you'll need to keep it secret. That won't happen if we're using your stipend to pay in the hive. Besides," Kenzie added, picking up a card with the image of a scantily clad woman on it.

Because it was a Common, the image didn't move, but the image alone still painted . . . quite the picture. Her eyebrows rose at what she read, but then she returned it to the shelf. "All the real interesting stuff has already been picked over. You know how riders are. You're not going to find an 'Instant Sword Mastery' card there."

"Likely not going to find one here, either," he muttered.

There was a reason why he and Horatio had worked for literal years to gather enough shards to create cards of their own. Though card shops had more in them than a bumpkin from the borderland could ever imagine, the truth was, they were mostly the dregs the dragon riders had passed over, then the nobility, followed by the guilds, the merchants, the well-to-do middle class, the lower middle class, and the lower workers. Not to mention the professional card collectors and resellers who knew how to spot a diamond in the rough everyone else had missed.

Arthur picked up and set down a Rapid Dash card that allowed someone to skip every third step at a run when they used mana.

Actually, he could see a use for that, too. If he didn't have his Master of Body Enhancement card to assist with running. Someone who was looking to link with a Common purple dragon might find use of that card.

Abruptly, he realized he was being a twerp. All cards had their uses in the right hands. Even that risqué card Kenzie had picked up.

Arthur waited until she moved on to the next shelf, took a peek himself, and hurriedly put it back: A card which gave a mild seductive effect via belly dancing to the audience. The rest of the description was simple and intriguing: *This effect is a mood enhancement only and can be mentally dismissed by the unwilling.*

"That won't help you in combat, either," Kenzie called from the next shelf over. She must have known what he was looking at via his emotional aura. "But it might get you out of a fight if you use it right."

With a cough, Arthur went down the next row. He already knew better than to ask the price of any Rares—not only were they strictly locked away, they were available only to high-priority customers, and the markup was insane—but he might be able to afford an Uncommon card.

Why bother? asked a little voice in his mind. One that sounded a lot like his gloomy friend, Horatio. *You'll soon be surrounded by Legendary card wielders. You think you'll win any duels with an Uncommon card?*

No, Arthur thought at him. *But I'm a Legendary wielder, too.*

He needed something to play to his strengths.

With that in mind, Arthur moved to the Uncommon Utility shelves.

Here, he found several cards that granted individual skills.

Expert Hair Shaper
Uncommon
Utility
This card grants its wielder the ability to cut and shape specific hairstyles. This is a level-based card. With higher levels, the wielder will complete more complex hairstyles at a quicker rate.

Industrial Temperature Sense
Uncommon
Utility
The wielder will be able to read the temperature of any forge, glass glory hole, or oven. The wielder may adjust and refine these temperatures using mana.

Competent Tree Surgeon
Uncommon
Utility
Using mana, the wielder will instantly be informed of a living tree's health and grade of wood. 15% enhanced ease in pruning or limbing of a tree. This card will not work on non-living, already-harvested wood. This card does not unlock mana.

Interesting, but nothing that would help him in combat.

He was reaching the limit of what this card shop had to offer. With a sense of resignation, Arthur went to the last shelf in the corner of the store, the place where miscellaneous cards were kept.

These were a mix of Common and Uncommon cards. Everything from being able to instantly count the number of crayfish and snails in a small pond (the size of the body of water increased as the wielder leveled the skill) to enhanced flower arranging (a note on the bottom said higher levels were rumored to be able to send messages via flowers) to a Common partial tailoring skill—

Arthur did a double take at the last. Then he snatched it up and reread the card.

Kenzie joined him a few moments later, standing on tiptoes to read over his shoulder.

"Giving up the whole dragon-riding idea to join the tailoring guild?"

"No." Ideas flicked in Arthur's mind—dangerous, stupid, perfect ideas. "I just realized I don't need a combat card. Well, no, I still need a combat card," he amended, "but it needs to be the right card—not something I buy on a whim. This card, though . . . this will be perfect."

Kenzie looked hesitant until he gave the bare outline of his plan. Then she called him an idiot.

But the important thing was, she paid the overpriced fee for the card.

She still dragged him to a proper clothing shop afterward to get him a new wardrobe. That was, after all, what the stipend was supposed to cover. In addition, Arthur spoke to the shopkeeper and purchased two bolts of low-grade fabric. Kenzie refused to pay for those, even out of the stipend, so Arthur was forced to dip into his dwindling coins.

The new clothing would be delivered to the hive when it was completed. As for the bolts of fabric, Arthur simply placed those into his Personal Space.

His last purchase was for a candle with dyes worked into the wax to mark the time.

By the time he and Kenzie were done shopping, the city streets had taken on a properly festive atmosphere. Likely, this was helped by free-flowing alcohol and the up-tempo music kicked out by performers.

"The official announcement over the Legendary's supposed to go out tonight," Kenzie reminded him. "It's the worst-kept secret in the hive, but people will be happy to know the thing's alive. Are you staying around to watch?"

He shook his head. "I have things to do."

"Tailoring?" she asked dryly.

His response was a grin.

Back in his room at the hive later that night, Arthur rechecked the lock on the door. Then he lit the candle. It was high grade with a mark for every quarter hour. Even more accurate than an hourglass, the shopkeeper had promised.

Arthur hoped so.

After lighting it, he sat on his bed, closed his eyes, and reached for his Rare cards.

A moment later, he found himself mentally standing in front of the bookshelf. It was just as sparse as last time. That was fine. If this worked, he had a guaranteed way to fill it.

Turning from the shelf, he instead inspected the vault that represented his Personal Space.

He opened the door. Then, holding his breath, he stepped in.

Everything was there, exactly as he'd stored it: the bolt of cloth, the odds and ends, and a few of his sharpened knives.

He got to work. The new Common card in his card anchor gave him just the skill he needed:

The Perfect Snip
Common
Utility
The wielder of this card will have an enhanced ability to accurately and concisely cut fabric. This is a skill-level based effect with greater benefits the higher the level.

This was a Common card and didn't offer anything above basic benefits. His other cards took up the slack.

The moment he made his first cut, he received a skill notification for **Fabric Snipping** (Tailor Class) at Level 3.

Arthur kept going, hacking away at the bolts of fabric, at first randomly, but then with greater precision as his skill leveled up. After a bit, however, the knives felt . . . wrong, so he switched to scissors.

By the time he had thoroughly destroyed the first bolt, every snip felt like he was carving through butter.

He had reached level 9, which was a good night's work. And it felt like an entire night's work—though he was in a mental space, his fingers ached from snipping the scissors. And mental or not, the fabric was destroyed. He had been at this for hours.

Putting the scissors back, he left the vault and "stepped out" of his mental space.

He blinked awake back in his room, feeling like he had been in a trance. Clenching and unclenching his fingers, he swore he felt a ghostly twinge of soreness from working the scissors so long. But it faded away within a few moments.

His head, however, ached like he had spent hours intensely stuffing his mind full of new knowledge, like he was back in school.

The real test was the candle. Still blinking, it took a few moments for Arthur to focus on it.

The candle was still fresh and new. Nowhere near the first fifteen-minute mark.

Time did not pass within his Personal Space. He had just trained himself up to Level 9 **Fabric Snipping** in moments.

The downside, of course, was the headache.

At first, Arthur thought he could handle it. Then he stood to put the time-mark candle out. The pain in his head sharpened as he moved. It was as if someone had shoved a metal bar up through the bottom of his skull, just where head met neck, all the way through and out the top.

He staggered to the candle, unsure if the sudden vertigo was due to the pain or if it was all rolled into one. It took all of his concentration to snuff the candle out. After that, he fell to his bed, curling up with his hands cradling his throbbing head.

He had lived hours in the space of moments. The backlash made sense, though it wasn't pleasant.

Still, he couldn't keep a grim smile from stretching his lips.

What else could he improve, given all the time in the world?

Opening up his heart deck and scanning through his list of skills made his eyes water. So instead, he planned.

He didn't realize he was drifting off before he was already asleep.

Arthur woke the next morning to a reduced—though still present—headache. It wasn't severe enough to keep him from moving.

When he sat up and looked around, he found someone had slipped an envelope under his door.

The paper was pristine white, the sort of bleached he'd only seen the rich use. The note inside was on such thick creamy paper that for a moment he thought it was a card.

The moment Arthur's fingers brushed across it, he felt warm energy zip up to his heart. There was a small card-anchor mark on the corner used for identification. He must have passed because fine dark ink revealed itself across the page as if being written in front of him.

This was a formal invitation for all Legendary hopefuls to attend a dinner in the hive banquet hall tonight.

For a moment, he allowed himself to imagine it would be like the Rare promenade. Would he be allowed to get close to the Legendary egg tonight? Close enough to formally present himself to the hatchling inside?

No, he realized after a moment's consideration.

Considering the danger of unleashed Legendary magic, there was no way the hive leaders would allow noble scions to troop past the egg and hope for the best.

After another moment's consideration, Arthur revised that: Valentina might threaten to do it, if only to weed out people who weren't serious.

Nevertheless, he doubted this was going to be a simple dinner. The hive leaders might have something in mind to narrow the recruits. The recruits themselves would be fiercely competitive.

With that in mind, Arthur decided to conduct a little experiment.

He had hit **Fabric Snipping** Level 9 last night using the skill card. But would he keep the skill if he removed the card from his anchor deck?

Only one way to find out.

A moment later, the card was in his hand. A quick check to the status list in his heart deck confirmed that the skill itself remained, as it was still linked to his Master of Skills card.

But something felt . . . missing.

It wasn't nearly as bad as that time he removed the Return to Start card from his heart deck. He wasn't in danger of damaging himself or yanking out a piece of himself along with the card.

He simply felt, without being able to put his finger on it, that the card had more to offer him.

After a moment's thought, Arthur replaced it into his card-anchor deck. It wouldn't hurt to keep it there for now. He had the room. Plus, he could always switch it out later for other single skill-based cards. He'd seen a few smithing-type skills in the card shop yesterday. Learning quick skills from Common cards would be faster than apprenticing himself to the local crafters.

He had so much to do and so little time.

Speaking of time, the dinner was this evening. He knew Legendary recruits would be flooding into the hive. The beginning of the social pecking order would be established tonight.

Arthur wasn't interested in being at the top of the heap. He just needed to stay in the game: only the egg mattered.

He briefly considered returning to his Personal Space, but he needed to be at his best tonight, not crippled by a migraine.

With that in mind, he stayed in real time and simply withdrew the largest piece of plain fabric he had left, along with a pair of scissors.

Ignoring a warning bolt of pain through his head, he concentrated on the **Fabric Snipping** skill and got to work.

Generally, reaching the tenth level meant breaking through some sort of bottleneck. With some skills, breaking through was a breeze. Others, like **Stealth**, had him stymied for a good period of time before he figured out a new approach and broke through.

He got lucky this time. His revelation came only an hour later.

It happened when he stopped cutting up the fabric like he was trying to make expensive confetti and actively tried to create shapes. This was part of a tailor class, after all. He was meant to design clothing.

Arthur didn't know the first thing about tailoring, but he figured trying to cut out the rough shape of a shirt couldn't hurt. Once it was complete, he was awarded with the tenth level.

Perhaps it was in conjunction with his Master of Skills card, but the new level came with a touch of wisdom. He started his next cut thinking about how to roll up the fabric to make a sleeve. It would be sort of like a tube, though he would have to make sure the edges overlapped for later sewing . . .

He made his next cut quickly and with new precision.

With it came a notification.

Alert: Your skill, **Fabric Snipping**, now has a new benefit. Future snips now have a 5% chance of being symmetrically duplicated along the same project. Continue to level up this skill for added benefits.

Arthur leaned back for a moment, pleased. He had hoped for something like this. He'd seen guild-level crafters work, and the most advanced had card abilities to duplicate their products.

So far, none of his skills from his Legendary cards had shown that type of hidden benefit. But he had been haphazardly leveling them, focusing more on classes and survival. Now that he had use of his Personal Space, he would have time to focus on leveling his existing skills.

In any case, a 5% chance of duplicating a cut wasn't high enough. He would have to increase it.

That meant leveling.

Arthur resumed his cuts.

He finally took a break at level fifteen. Though he received no new benefits, his chance to copy a snip increased by 2% every level.

Now, whenever he tried to make a shape—say, a star—an identical cut would inconsistently appear to complete that shape.

He could see how, under the practice of weeks or months in the craft, those small, inconsistent time savings would add up. Plus, it meant less wear on his tools.

He would have leveled more, but it was time he got ready for the supper.

Arthur changed into the new clothing Kenzie had bought for him. He spent entirely too much time making sure his hair sat exactly right. Finally, he slipped a small knife into his pocket. Not a knife for dueling or even butchering, but one meant for thread snipping.

He was as prepared for tonight as he could be.

With a mix of anticipation flavored with anxiety, he made his way out of the room and walked down to the first level.

He barely rounded the first corner before he nearly ran into Cressida.

She looked . . . different.

Dressed in sturdy clothing that was meant to take heavy wear rather than noble finery, there were actual dirt stains on her elbows and knees. Her red hair looked like it had been pinned up into a bun earlier in the morning, and then completely forgotten about. There were so many errant wisps that it created a mini halo around her head. Her fair skin, too, was reddened as if she had spent an unusual amount of time out in the sun. The mild burn made her freckles stand out all the more.

All of that, and Arthur's mouth still went dry at the sight of her.

He simultaneously tried to say, "I'm glad to see you" and "What are you doing here?"

It came out as: "Cressida, I'm glad you're doing here?"

Thankfully, she seemed too busy taking him in to notice. Her eyes narrowed.

"You intend to be seen in public . . . like that?"

"What?" He looked down at himself and checked to make sure all buttons were secured, especially around his pants. All was well. "Is something wrong with what I'm wearing?"

"Other than it's from at least three seasons ago? I can see why Joy said I was needed."

"What?" The mention of her dragon kick-started his mind back into action. The little pink was nowhere around. "How is she? Where is she?"

Are you all right? he wanted to ask, but that felt like too personal of a question.

Cressida's sharp gaze softened. "She's wonderful. Taking a nap, actually. The hive trainers have her on an exercise regimen to strengthen her lungs. But she sent me to you with an odd quest." She held out her arm, and Arthur realized she was carrying folded dark fabric. He took it, shaking out a blue shirt so dark that it was almost black.

"It's not the most recent in men's fashion," Cressida said apologetically, "but it should fit. And it's better than . . . that."

"This is new!" All the pride in his new clothing had drained away.

"And which tailor's shop did you buy it from? Wait, don't tell me. Something close to the hive?" Cressida rolled her eyes. "You buy for the shop name, not for the location. Anyway, try it on."

It was only a shirt, though he felt a little strange changing in front of a girl. At least there was no one else in the tunnel to see.

He felt the difference the moment the shirt slipped over his shoulders. It was a much tighter fit than the last one, though by design, as it cinched in the middle. The fabric was breathable, and there wasn't a bunch or pull. He still didn't know much about tailoring, but he could tell the fabric was, well, a cut above.

"Where did you get this?" Arthur asked.

"From one of my servants." She waved away his dark look. "They work for me, so they're impeccably dressed. Now, tell me you'll accept it."

"But I . . ." He felt bad possibly taking the shirt from someone else. Especially something as nice as this.

"Go on," she insisted. "*Accept* it."

Oh well. Cressida had likely compensated the staff member. "Fine. I'll accept the shirt."

There was a brief flash of light, and Cressida plucked a glimmering jeweled hairpin out of the air. She examined it with an air of satisfaction.

Arthur could only stare. "What?" He felt like he'd been saying that a lot recently.

"I get rewards for every quest I complete. So far, it's just small things," Cressida said as she casually slipped the jeweled pin worth more money than some families made in a month into her pocket. "But I'm certain that will improve as Joy's power grows."

"Huh. Maybe I should try to link with a pink dragon," Arthur said. "Meta powers are amazing."

"They are. She is. Joy, I mean." Cressida looked down and bit her lip. She looked like she was coming to a decision. "I never properly thanked you for helping me. You went above and beyond to help me link with Joy and . . . thank you, Ernest."

To his utter shock, she leaned in and brushed her lips across the side of his cheek. When she pulled back, he knew he was flushing beet red.

Mind stuttered to a stop, the only thing he could think to say was, "I said to call me Arthur, didn't I?"

"Arthur, then." She smiled. "You wouldn't be the first to hate your given family name."

"I . . . uh . . . yeah." He wanted to scream at himself, but it was as if all intelligent thought had evaporated away.

Somehow Cressida looked at him as if he wasn't an idiot. "I mean it. I owe you, and if you're ever in need of my or Joy's help . . . call on us."

The favor of a powerful meta dragon rider was no small thing. Arthur nodded.

Cressida said her goodbyes, wanting to return to her hatchling dragon. Arthur watched her go, still a little poleaxed.

Something she said drifted around his thoughts:

You wouldn't be the first to hate your given family name.

Huh. That gave him an idea . . .

CHAPTER 19

Arthur had to show his formal invitation at no less than three checkpoints on the way. Each was staffed by professional-looking hive guards Arthur had never seen before—likely men and women who worked exclusively in the upper levels. At each waypoint, the invitation was carefully examined as if they were looking for a forgery.

Surely a forgery would be quickly discovered once someone presented themselves to the Legendary egg. But Arthur supposed some people might take the chance just for the opportunity to get close to the hive's elite.

The last checkpoint was the strictest. The guard looked over Arthur and then, pointedly, behind him. "And your . . . attendants, sir?"

"I have none. I've always been independently minded," he said smoothly.

The guard's face remained professionally blank as he handed back the invitation. "Very good, sir."

Arthur walked on and double-checked his deck. Charming Gentleperson card for extra charisma was in full effect. He kept his Return to Start card nullified for now, as he was certain there would be intrusive scans. Perhaps even duels.

But that could change at a moment's notice, so he had preemptively dropped a pebble he used as an anchor point outside the hive in an alleyway close to Barlow's restaurant. That card was a useful escape hatch.

Adjusting the cuffs on his new shirt one last time, Arthur strode in.

The room itself was much changed since the last Rare promenade. Every inch of the floors and walls had been scrubbed. Someone had affixed a massive chandelier to the ceiling. It had been enchanted with card illusions. The ghostly images of dragons flew in mock battles around flickering candle lights. It made for an impressive sight.

But that paled in comparison to the people.

Cressida might have had a point about being seen with this crowd. The dress code was a few steps above that of the people who'd vied for a Rare. Most of the men wore long tails and stiff-necked collars that looked incredibly uncomfortable. The women had come in full-on ball gowns.

The room wasn't as crowded as it had been before. Made sense, considering there were far fewer Legendary cards in the world than Rare. However, there were many more servants running around with platters of small snacks and fluted glasses on trays. Above it all, the stage sat empty, with the egg nowhere in sight.

Making his way in, Arthur tried to get a feel for the crowd. Had he grown up as a proper noble, he likely would have known these people by sight if not by reputation. Most of the crowd was gathered around a few individuals. One bearded man was holding the biggest court. The crowd around him laughed whenever he did, and every female eye was fixed his way as if he were the light in a dark room. Some of the males, too.

Arthur found himself . . . drawn to that crowd. He took a few steps closer just to hear what everyone found so interesting. Catching himself, he shook his head and stepped back, deliberately focusing up on the chandelier to drown out the noise.

New skill level: Basic Empathic Resistance (Shield Class)
Level 5

He started in alarm, then checked to see if anyone had noticed. They hadn't. All attention around him was focused on the bearded speaker.

Arthur had originally gained that skill when Kenzie had used her aura-manipulation cards on him. That meant whatever that guy was doing, he was messing with emotions.

He didn't know if this was the same thing—surely the leaders wouldn't allow a Legendary-rank mind-mage in among the recruits—but he decided to step away.

The other side of the room was quieter, darker, and sparse.

A few sat at tables, talking. Arthur spotted one where a lone boy about his age sat, reading a book. The fact he seemed set on ignoring everyone else was the most interesting thing about him. Nicely, though not extravagantly, dressed with mid-brown hair and an average face, he seemed harmless enough.

Arthur took the empty chair near him, ignoring the pointed looks from his servants. He didn't plan on interrupting the boy's book. He just wanted a moment to gather himself.

But the moment he sat, the boy said, "Ah, finally. Someone with true conviction."

"Excuse me?" Arthur asked.

The boy didn't look up from his book. "Just an accident, then. Well, you're stuck here now. Look at your invitation."

Arthur had carried the card in his hand and automatically set it on the table as he'd sat. Glancing at it, he saw the card had sunk into the table. A stone place setting with the name "Ernest Kane" had risen in its place.

Arthur reached out to see if he could wiggle it free.

"Don't bother," the boy said, still not looking up. "It's immovable by design. It's to keep people from jockeying for position all night. You see?"

"Oh." Arthur decided to make the best of it. At least his table mate seemed willing to talk. He eyed the thick book. There was no title on the cover. "What are you—"

"It's a series of essays on the evolving relationship between the monarchy and the hives. Terribly boring, but necessary."

As far as Arthur could tell, the boy had still not lifted his eyes from the page.

He started to get a bad feeling. "How do you—"

"Know what I'm going to say?" the boy finished. He flipped the page. "You really don't know?"

In shock, Arthur started to ask, "You're not a—"

"Mind reader? Of course not. Huh." Finally, the boy lifted his eyes and studied Arthur. After a moment, he shrugged and came to a decision, reaching into his pocket and pulling out a card.

One of the attendants stepped forward. "You must not—"

"I'm in public. Yes, yes. Save it. I know the risks. Besides, you're here to save me, aren't you?" The boy slipped the card into an elaborate anchor tattoo on the inside of his left wrist.

He blinked, and some underlying tension seemed to drain away from his face. "What's your name?"

"Ernest Kane," he said slowly, expecting to be interrupted at any moment. But the other boy let him go on. "I go by Arthur."

"Well, Arthur, you happen to have chosen a seat by Marion Amberlion." He paused for effect.

An effect that was completely lost on Arthur.

"*Prince* Marion Amberlion," one of the attendants snapped, offended at Arthur's lack of reaction.

"Prince?" Arthur glanced from the two attendants to Marion and back again. None of them looked like they were joking, though Marion's lips were curled in a smile.

"If that was the case," Arthur continued, "why aren't you surrounded by, ah . . ."

"Sycophants?" Marion filled in. Not like he had done before, when he'd blurted out the words a moment before Arthur had said them. Now it was an actual guess. He even nodded to the adoring crowd around the bearded man. "Like my brother's group?"

Arthur's voice was a bit weak. "Brother?" There were *two* princes in this room? He was competing for the egg against actual royalty?

For the first time, he wasn't certain of his chances. Subconsciously, Arthur had assumed he was meant for that egg, but who knew what amazing cards the sons of the king had in their heart deck.

Marion waved a hand. "He's not that great. It's just his Charisma card at work. As for me, I'm seventh in line to the throne, and my card annoys people." He flashed a grin at Arthur, but it was brittle at the edges. "Usually I only get the desperate sycophants."

Arthur straightened. "I'm not—only unlucky."

The servant's eyes widened. Marion barked out a startled laugh. It seemed he wasn't used to people taking jabs at him.

He regarded Arthur for a moment. "I'm not familiar with the Kane family, and you don't have the look of a wealthy merchant . . ."

"Minor noble," Arthur filled in. "My father has a barony out at the border."

"And now you've dived right into the deep end." Marion chuckled.

The other boy seemed to be in a good mood, so Arthur decided to press his luck. "You said your brother has a Charisma card?"

"That's right."

"Most people keep that information to themselves," Arthur observed. You never revealed information about heart-deck cards if you could possibly help it.

Marion waved his concern away. "We're royalty. The cards we're bequeathed are public knowledge, but what you really want to know—and are too polite to ask—is about my card."

"The card you should not have blocked," one of the servants cut in. "My prince, I must insist . . ."

Marion heaved a great sigh but with a flick, removed the card from his anchor. He flashed it to the servants as if to prove he had done so before he slipped it back in his pocket.

When he turned back to Arthur, that subtle strain was back on his face. It made him look older.

"The answer is time. I see several seconds ahead, which is great for avoiding assassinations but tedious for everything else. And before you ask, yes, I can turn it off in my card anchor, but my minders insist on proof."

That sounded like it had a story to it. Arthur leaned forward, interested. How often did he get to speak to a chatty prince?

Suddenly, Marion's eyebrows shot up. "This should be fun."

Before Arthur could respond, he heard a voice.

"Kane? What are you doing here?"

Arthur turned, and his blood went cold as he spotted the speaker. Pennrow Rowantree. His cousin. Though, of course, Penn didn't know that.

Their gazes locked, and Arthur saw a cascade of emotions cross Penn's face. Shock, disbelief, realization that Arthur had a Legendary card.

Then, of course, rage.

Penn's family had just had a Legendary card stolen from him. And here was "Ernest Kane," a baron's son, who by all rights shouldn't have a Legendary card, among the group.

He was, of course, right. Arthur had stolen the card. And he suspected Penn had a Legendary of his own.

Without another word, Penn grabbed a fork off the nearby table and lunged straight at Arthur's face.

Arthur mentally retreated into his timeless Personal Space.

CHAPTER 20

The very next instant, Arthur found himself standing, whole, in his Personal Space.

He looked around wildly. It took him a few moments to realize he had come immediately here. He hadn't even gone through the extra step of standing in front of the bookshelf first. Apparently, panic was a good way to discover a shortcut.

That was great and all, but it didn't distract him from the fact that while his mind was suspended in timeless space, his body was under attack.

"Well . . . this isn't good," he muttered.

He began to pace the length of his Personal Space from one end to another. He had all the time in the world to decide what to do, but only a fraction of a second in which to act it out in the real world.

What skill could help him out?

Reluctantly, he decided that none linked to his Master of Skills card could help him. He had a **Butchering** skill, and there had been a butter knife on the table within easy reach. However, it took a few moments to get into the right frame of mind.

He wasn't sure he would even be able to activate **Butchering** on a human being.

That left his Master of Body Enhancement.

He could . . . grab the knife and use it to block Penn's fork? There was a certain poetry in that, but Arthur didn't think he had the time. The fork had been plunging down right at his face.

No. He couldn't fight back, and he couldn't reliably block the danger. That left escape.

Except . . . he got a sense from the two cards humming in his heart that "dodge" or "escape" would qualify as a combative skill. He wouldn't gain those unless he somehow found that card.

Okay, so he didn't have to escape completely. He could dive off the side of his chair, land on the floor, and try to roll away?

Surely one recruit attacking another out of the blue wouldn't be tolerated. He was surrounded by people with Legendary cards.

Aside from perhaps his father, Arthur had never expected anyone to jump in and save him from danger. Not when he'd traveled in the traders' caravan with Red, not when he lived in the orphanage, and not now.

No. His only true chance at escape would be to deactivate the Nullify on his Return to Start card. Penn was likely using his card's power to attack. That would be enough to transport Arthur away . . .

. . . And he'd likely miss out on the rest of the night. His invitation had been locked into the table, and he doubted those vigilant guards would let him in again.

He might even lose a chance at the egg, if it was presented tonight.

That was unacceptable.

Suddenly, Arthur recalled that Prince Marion had a card which allowed him to see several seconds in the future.

Why hadn't he warned Arthur he was about to be attacked? Had it been casual cruelty? Maybe he just wanted to see a show. Arthur had only just met the guy, but he didn't think so.

What else, then?

A new idea struck him.

Fighting wasn't an option. Escape was either risky or unpalatable.

But there was a third option.

For the first time, Arthur started to really consider Penn's motivations. He'd assumed that it was just a moment of rage.

But what if Penn suspected Arthur had stolen his card—which was fair, because he had—and fully expected Arthur to use it by reflex?

Marion had already seen the future. One which he hadn't seen fit to warn Arthur about.

That left one choice: to do nothing at all.

Penn expected Arthur to use his Master of Body Enhancement card. So . . . he wouldn't.

This was perhaps the riskiest choice of all. Still pacing, Arthur took one deep breath after another in an effort to calm his racing heart.

That was odd, because his body wasn't even here. Still, he worked on calming his mind, readying himself for what he knew would come next, and hoping he wasn't about to make a big mistake.

Penn hadn't struck him as the type to casually murder someone. He hoped.

When he felt he was ready, he mentally stepped out of the space.

In the next instant, he found himself once again sitting in the chair.

He thought he would have to actively stop himself from reacting. The truth was, Penn was so fast the choice was taken away from him. He didn't have time to flinch.

The fork stopped a hair from his right eye.

For a frozen moment, Arthur looked past the fork to meet Penn's eyes and found his cousin staring back, his own steely gaze already melting.

Chagrin flashed over Penn's face.

"Penn," Arthur croaked. "What are you doing?"

Abruptly, Penn smiled. "Easy to startle as ever, Kane," he said, letting the hand with the fork drop.

"Move aside, I can't see." Across the table, Marion shoved irritably at his two assistants. They had jumped in front of him—protecting their prince and letting Arthur fight on his own. He knew he couldn't count on anyone to save him.

Arthur, meanwhile, leaned hard on his **Acting** skill. He whooped in a deep breath and raised his hand as if to check his face for a scratch. "You nearly scared the piss out of me!" he complained, as if thinking this was part of a joke.

Penn's grin broadened. "Just checking your reflexes. I didn't know you had a Legendary card." He grabbed one of the nearby chairs and straddled it, sitting down at the table.

"Father's been saving up." Arthur added a sour edge to his voice. "He'll probably rip it out of my heart again if I don't link with this dragon."

Penn winced. Arthur doubted he was completely out of suspicion, but there was something obscene about the thought of taking a card out of a still-living heart.

One of Marion's assistants cleared his throat. "Your Highness, I strongly advise you not to allow this troublemaker a seat at your table."

That drew Penn's attention. He twisted in his seat, caught a look at Marion, and nodded. "Sorry for the scare, Prince Marion. I caught sight of my friend here. Couldn't help but rib him a little." He slapped Arthur on the back. Hard.

Marion watched the two of them, eyebrows raised. He seemed to sense the energy but wasn't sure what to make of it. Still, he nodded. "Not at all. It was the most interesting thing I've seen all night."

"Then I hope you don't mind letting this troublemaker sit . . . oops." Penn made a very bad show of fumbling his invitation just so that it fell onto the table. A moment later, his name was locked in right next to Arthur.

Arthur tried not to sigh in exasperation.

The next few minutes passed easily enough.

Penn and Marion seemed to know each other distantly, which wasn't a big surprise considering Penn was a high noble's son. The two spoke about places that they visited at one of the big cities, Amberlion, which was Marion's last name.

"My father, Lional, was named for that city," Penn said. "The story is, he was conceived there, and my grandparents were inspired."

That startled a snort of laughter from Arthur.

Marion, however, looked like he was a few seconds away from picking up his book. Apparently, he was uninterested in small talk.

Penn turned back to Arthur.

"So, tell me about this new card of yours."

Arthur stared. That was an incredibly rude question. "Excuse me?"

"I'll show you mine if you show me yours." Penn waggled his eyebrows. "Oh, come on, Kane. We all know the prince's secrets—"

"Because he's royalty! That's public knowledge." Arthur huffed. Inside, he was pleased. He just had to make sure Penn didn't see it.

Arthur made a show of thinking about it, then looking around as if watching for spectators. No one paid attention. Not only was most of the room still gathered around the bearded prince, Penn's stunt earlier had been so quick it hadn't caused a stir.

Arthur leaned forward conspiratorially. "You'll tell me about yours? You swear?"

"Would I lie in front of the son of our sovereign?" Penn asked, gesturing dramatically at Marion, who'd gone back to his book.

Arthur had the feeling the other boy was listening, though.

Again, Arthur hesitated. Then he nodded once. "It's a little embarrassing, actually. You know my family's . . . situation. I wasn't kidding when I said we'd saved for this. We had to purchase the card for the rank, not for the ability."

Penn leaned forward.

"Ultimate Crafting," Arthur said. He wasn't going to show Penn the card and would use the excuse of being in public in case he was questioned. He only hoped his sincerity won out.

"Crafting?" Penn repeated, expression inscrutable.

"It has skill-based advancement," Arthur continued, "and additional bonuses if, say, I learned tailoring or cooking. I would kill it in a guild hall."

"Your father expects you to link a dragon with that?" Marion demanded. He had set the book down and stared at Arthur with pity.

"Baron Kane's never been known for his reasonable expectations." This time Arthur didn't have to fake his bitterness. "Besides, the hive just hatched a pink meta—"

"What are the chances of two metas in a row?" Marion snorted. "Besides, pinks are just as likely to have knowledge-based powers. Sorry ol' chap, you're screwed."

Arthur barked a laugh and turned back to see Penn watching him carefully.

Abruptly, Penn rolled his shoulder in a shrug. "That's hard luck. I'm afraid you'll hate me when you hear of mine."

"That bad?" Arthur asked, grinning. He tried not to show he was holding his breath. He fully expected Penn to either lie or weasel out of his agreement.

"Mine is called Master of Combat."

It took every bit of **Acting** skill for Arthur to look only politely interested.

Inside, he was reeling.

He had half-guessed it was something like that, but to have it confirmed meant Lional had intentionally sold the second card out of a Legendary set. That was a huge advantage to give up. Were they that financially bad off?

Or were they that afraid of the king's wrath?

Still keeping his expression politely interested, Arthur said, "Sounds impressive. What does your card do?"

Penn started to reply when a general hubbub drew their attention to the front of the room. The hive leaders, Whitaker and Valentina, strode across the raised stage. The little dark egg was still nowhere in sight.

The leaders were dressed resplendently in a more formal version of the dragon rider's uniform. The fabric was primarily gray and white with brown edging. Both also sported colorful medals across the right sides of their chest.

Whitaker looked full of energy and enthusiasm. Valentina took her time. She didn't have the cloud under her feet, and every step looked halting.

Though she walked slower, Valentina was full of her usual fire. Looking over the crowd, she snapped, "What are you all standing around here for? We provided tables, didn't we? Find a seat. Immediately!"

What followed was low-key chaos as people tried to grab the best seats—especially those around the bearded prince.

Several scuffles broke out, and Arthur caught a few flashes of power let loose from someone's temper. Nothing as spectacular as the duel during the Rare hatching, however.

Their table still had one free seat. A tiny girl with drops of pearls beaded into her dark hair sat down. She looked hardly old enough to have a card of her own, and her delicate lace dress didn't help. She looked nervously at Marion, who nodded at her and smiled in reassurance.

Before long, most everyone found a seat with their invitations locked in . . . except for an unlucky few who were either too slow or too picky for a specific location. Whitaker gestured for them to stand at the back of the room.

Valentina nodded once sharply. "We've gathered you here today for what may be a once-in-a-lifetime chance. Whomever is linked to the Legendary egg will find his or herself automatically separated from their peers. Though you will be training with other new pairs, when you graduate, you will be promoted to the top of the hive leadership."

Marion snorted, and Arthur glanced his way in time to see him roll his eyes.

Valentina continued, "This is not a commitment any of you should take lightly. Those who are ultimately brought before the egg do so at the risk of their lives. Make no mistake: a Legendary's power is not to be underestimated. If your personal cards clash with the hatchling's, there will be harsh consequences."

She paused as if to take a breath. In that moment, Whitaker spoke boldly. "We cannot guarantee your safety."

Several people shifted in their seats.

Valentina shot the other leader a look for interrupting her, but then nodded sharply before she turned back to the crowd with a withering eye. "Furthermore, I'd wager most of you aren't worthy of the egg. It's not good enough to hold a Legendary card in your heart. You must use those powers to add value to the hive."

Again, Whitaker broke in. "That ultimately means protecting the world from scourge."

"Ugh, here he goes," Marion muttered a moment before the bearded prince's voice drawled out.

"We are all ready and eager to prove ourselves."

Arthur would have bet money that Valentina would take a strip out of him for interrupting. But she simply looked at him and said, "We'll be putting that to the test. Remember you said that. Meanwhile, anyone who finds this . . . unpalatable should leave. By my count, we still have five people waiting for a seat at a table."

Thick silence fell over the room.

Valentina and Whitaker simply stood there, waiting for someone to take them up on their offer.

Eventually, the silence grew awkward, and several people glanced at one another.

"No takers?" Whitaker said. "Perhaps this will change your mind?"

He gestured to the edge of the stage. From out of the shadows floated a box—no doubt summoned via his telekinesis. The box was etched with glowing runes as if they were an elaborate decoration.

Or a powerful protection.

Arthur felt his heart pick up the pace. He knew what was in that box.

So did a few others, judging by the murmurs. Marion leaned forward, eyebrows raised. Then he leaned over and spoke quietly to the little girl. Arthur couldn't tell what he said, but it sounded like reassurance.

"We will unshield the egg here and now," Valentina said. "Anyone who reacts poorly—you're out."

Several people at the front table leaned back, which Arthur thought was poor showing. But no one got up to leave.

Valentina nodded to Whitaker. Both of the leaders took several steps back from the box, which spoke of the egg's danger. Whitaker then made a twisting motion with his hands. The runes dimmed, and the sides of the box fell away.

It was as if all of the energy in the room was sucked in toward the egg. Floating in air under Whitaker's power, it seemed to glimmer darkly in the lamplight. Arthur found himself balanced at the very edge of his seat as if pulled in.

Several people let out audible gasps.

One laughed.

"That's it? I've seen chicken eggs bigger—"

A blur of motion crossed the room, from one of the back tables to the stage. It resolved into a young man of about twenty who fell on his knees in front of the egg.

He's trying to hatch it! Arthur thought, terror and rage erasing all caution.

Marion's hand fell on his shoulder hard, shoving him back down in his chair just as he twitched to stand.

"Calm down," the prince said. "There's still plenty of time to make an idiot of yourself—"

"But—"

One hand outstretched to the egg, the boy started to scream. He looked like he was trying to pull himself back, free hand locked around his own elbow, but the egg had a lock on him and was dragging him closer.

Whitaker grabbed the boy with his power, clothes going tight around the boy's frame as Whitaker took a mental grip and hauled him back. The arm made a loud snap like a dried twig as a bone broke, followed by a wet pop as his shoulder was wrenched out of its socket . . . but Whitaker's power was stronger. The boy was flung across the stage where he collapsed, arm hanging strangely, moaning.

"Get him out of here!" Valentina ordered. "Take him at least three floors away. He's too susceptible to the egg."

Servants who'd hung off to the side rushed in to hustle the boy away.

Whitaker, too, turned to the crowd. "Well? What are you waiting for? Someone take his seat immediately. Who else?"

"She's choking!" a girl cried out, standing to hover—literally—over another girl at her table who was bent over double. "Help her!"

Whitaker snapped his fingers, and more servants rushed to lead her away. Arthur heard the girl take a wheezing gasp as she neared the exit.

The ones who hadn't found a table quickly moved to take the girl's seat . . . though the boy who sat looked nervous, as if the chair were unlucky.

Within a minute, another girl broke out in hives. Whether it be from stress or another bad reaction to the egg, Arthur didn't know. She looked relieved as she excused herself.

Valentina swept a cold gaze over them all. "That's three. We have two more people meant to take seats."

Silence.

"This is the easy part, kids," Whitaker rumbled.

One boy toward the back of the room stood from his seat and walked out. Arthur did him the courtesy of not staring. His seat was taken by a determined-looking man.

That left one final woman standing awkwardly at the back.

The two leaders exchanged looks.

"Well," Valentina drawled, "there will be openings after we're done. Until then, for the rest of you, the people sitting at your table will be your team members for tonight."

At her command, the air suddenly became bitterly cold. The moisture crystalized into numbers that hung over everyone's table like a decoration.

A perfectly formed *4* stood over Arthur's table.

He glanced around with more interest. Was there to be a team elimination? If that was the case, he could do worse than a prince who could see seconds into the future and a Master of Combat.

And that meant Penn may be less inclined to kill Arthur. At least for tonight.

"You may be asking yourself why you've been shoved into teams," Whitaker said, voice silencing the beginnings of murmurs through the room. "And why we know by this time tomorrow, those with useless cards and overall cowards will have packed up and gone home."

His smile was as wolfish as the hive he served.

"Our seers have called for a scourge-eruption, and by all reports, it'll be a *festive* one." He paused. "We'll need volunteers on the front line."

The uproar was instant.

CHAPTER 21

Valentina closed her fist. For one heart-stopping moment, all of the air in the room . . . evacuated. Arthur's ears popped painfully, and when he tried to breathe in, he only received a wisp.

Instinct made him glance up. A dense fog had collected at the ceiling of the room—everything but a bare hint of air, densely packed into a miniature cloud.

All sound stopped.

Valentina let the moment linger for the space of three heartbeats. Her fist relaxed, and the air whooshed down again.

People gasped all around him as if they had been strangled for minutes instead of a handful of seconds.

Arthur's gaze snapped to the black egg, which still hovered under Whitaker's power. He hoped that the momentary lack of air hadn't hurt it.

It glittered darkly. And he thought, perhaps, it seemed a little amused.

Whitaker's voice boomed out over the still-shocked room.

"You think leading other dragon riders is a stroll in the sunshine? I'd wager most of you have never seen a scourge-eruption. Now it is time for you to truly see what the hive fights against."

Give it to the young nobles: most of them were not cowed so easily.

"But I'm not dressed for battle!" one girl called, gesturing to her lacy dress.

"You don't think I've gone out in a fancy ball gown?" Valentina asked. "When a call that there has been a scourge-eruption comes in, you answer."

Again, Marion snorted.

This time, Arthur looked at him with eyebrows raised.

The prince raised them back as if to say: "What do you expect?"

Looking across the table, Arthur looked at the little girl. She stared up at the stage, and the egg, trembling.

Penn must have noticed the same. "Don't worry," he said. "No matter what happens out there, stick by me. I'll protect you."

Arthur thought it was a sweet offer, and much better than what he was going to say, which would have been a version of, *I've seen a scourge-eruption, and I'm certain they'll keep us well away from the front.*

Far from being reassured, the girl gave Penn an affronted look.

Seeing a glimpse of the future, Marion chuckled softly.

"Maybe I'll be the one to protect *you*," the girl said, glaring daggers at Penn. Her features blurred. She gained at least two feet in height, and her shoulders broadened. Her clothing switched color and shape, from a girlish dress to a pressed dark shirt and pants.

Within seconds, she was Penn's exact double. Though she still wore the glare.

Marion gestured broadly.

"May I introduce my sister, Princess—"

"You're the Echo," Penn interrupted, looking like someone had hit him over the head.

"Maybe you're the echo," she shot back. She looked down at her hands. "I think I like this. You have . . . some sort of fighting card?"

A stable shape-shifting card definitely rated as a Rare. But to copy someone else's card while taking their form? That was a Legendary power.

That was problematic. Arthur resolved to be as uninteresting as possible to the girl.

The moment he had that thought, the girl turned to him. "You have a problem with me, too?"

"I never said I had a problem . . ." Penn objected weakly.

Arthur shook his head. "No, Princess. Allow me to introduce myself: I'm Ernest Kane, though my friends call me Arthur."

As he'd hoped, she returned the gesture.

"I'm Princess Echo, not *The* Echo." Another dark glare for Penn.

He couldn't help his next question. "Was your name a coincidence?"

Now her derisive look was turned firmly on him. Her features melted, and the next thing Arthur knew, he stared at a copy of himself, down to flyaway hairs that had escaped the oil he'd tried to slick his blond hair down with.

"You don't feel like an idiot," she said with his voice. Then she frowned. "But . . . what's with your cards? I don't feel any combat abilities at all."

Feel. Not see.

Arthur felt a small bit of tension ease. He decided to play it like it didn't bother him. "I'm utility focused, but my Legendary is based on leveled crafting skills."

"Your mana's not even unlocked?" Now she looked at him like he was a weakling.

Marion jumped in. "Arthur's a baron's son, from the outer reaches. It's rather extraordinary he has a seat at our table at all." The words might have stung, but Arthur didn't sense any ill intent from them.

"Oh. That's boring." Echo let his image go, and she melted back to her own.

"Don't be rude," Marion said lightly.

She huffed out a sigh but turned to Arthur. "To answer your question, my card was assigned from birth. All of ours were." She gestured to Marion, likely indicating all the royal children. "My mother thought naming me after my card's power would be cute. So now I'm stuck as Echo Spyglass."

Arthur glanced at Penn, who had turned away from them all, looking to the stage. Several more of the nobles had been shouting objections, which the hive leaders had coldly shut down.

At least Valentina hadn't pulled the air out of the room again. They likely expected some level of pushback, though no one had relinquished their seat, either.

Arthur turned back to the princess. "If you'll forgive another question: Why do you and your brother have different last names?"

Marion's eyes glinted in amusement. "Because we have different mothers, of course. Royal children take on the paternal last name only if we ascend to the throne."

Penn clearly had been listening. He turned at the last part of the conversation. "From what I understand of the king, I'm surprised he would let any potential heir lead a hive. Wouldn't that give his children too much power?"

Echo looked sour, though it didn't seem to be at Penn's question.

Marion shrugged. "It's only a temporary step for us."

"What is?" Arthur asked.

"Bonding." He shrugged again. "It's only meant to be a temporary step up to the big seat."

Arthur stared. He couldn't mean what he thought he meant . . .

Echo blew air out from her cheeks. "The king is a Mythic card holder linked to a Mythic dragon. Whoever ascends takes on that link. That's how it works. You knew that much, right?"

Penn nodded, looking grave. Arthur nodded as if he did, too. Though inside, he was stunned and more than a little sickened.

That meant the ruler of their kingdom was someone who was willing and able to break a link to their own dragon and trade up for a higher tier.

What kind of a person sat on the throne?

"Enough!" Whitaker abruptly barked out, and the floors trembled with the strength of his voice. The arguing voices fell silent, though many still looked mutinous.

Whitaker went on. "The seers have called for a scourge-eruption tonight. I suggest instead of whining, you use this time to prepare yourself—including dressing appropriately." He looked to the girl who had spoken of gowns before. "When the call comes, I expect you to gather back up in your teams here. Until then, you're dismissed."

"Excellent," Marion drawled. "More waiting."

Arthur stood. "I suggest we take him seriously."

"I hardly care if these clothes get ruined . . ."

Penn stared at Arthur, eyes narrowed. "What do you have in mind?"

"I have a personal storage space—part of my utility set." He didn't see a reason to keep that quiet. He'd been open about it when it came to the Rare, and rumor was bound to get around. "I can pack whatever we need in there. Supplies, weapons, anything we can think of in case of an emergency."

Marion had already been digging around in his pocket while Arthur spoke, likely already having seen this conversation play out.

He thunked a coin bag on the table.

"I have no idea what to bring out in the wilds, but you seem like a knowledgeable fellow. Whatever this team needs, buy it."

"And not only boy stuff," Echo said. "If you get clothes, make sure they look good."

Penn rose and scooped up the bag. "Come on, Kane. Let's go to the hive stores and make this quick."

CHAPTER 22

Arthur couldn't quite figure Penn out.

When he'd first met his cousin, he was gregarious and outgoing—no, that wasn't true. The first time he'd met his cousin, Penn had helped ruin Arthur's behind-the-bar juggling act. But of course, he'd been too drunk to link a random bartender with "Ernest Kane."

Now, though Penn no longer acted overtly suspicious, Arthur sensed a new distance between them as they walked the halls toward the commissary. Penn kept calling him Kane and remained unusually silent.

That was fair, considering Arthur *had* robbed him blind.

He didn't feel bad about it, either. Penn's father had no doubt done far worse by Arthur than he ever could in return. Penn, in fact, stood in place for Arthur's old rank.

He was struck by a sudden thought: Had Calvan never lost his duchy, would Arthur now have the Master of Combat card?

Perhaps, though it made him feel oddly squeamish, as if the cards in his heart rebelled at that thought.

In any case, the silence between them was growing pointed. Arthur decided to break it. "I suppose this means we're competitors again," he said, though he kept his voice light. "First for the Rare egg, and now for this Legendary."

Penn gave him an odd look. "We're not competitors, Kane. We're on the same team. Take this right here. It's a shortcut to the store. Here, if I'm navigator, then you're the pack mule." He tossed the bag of coins at Arthur like it meant nothing to him.

Within moments, they walked into the commissary. Arthur glanced at the pouch of coins Marion had given him . . . and nearly staggered in pure shock.

"What is it?" Penn must have been watching him like a hawk, because he was instantly at Arthur's side. He glanced in the bag and whistled. "Huh. I didn't think he'd actually fill it with gold. You think he'll let us spend it all?"

There was an odd tone in Penn's voice. It made Arthur feel like this was a test of character.

"I think we could buy out this whole shop and still not spend all of it," Arthur said dryly, then pulled the top of the bag tight. He shoved it into Penn's hands. "You take it."

"Why?"

Arthur stared at him as if he were an idiot. "Because you're the Master of Combat. I'm the craft-skills guy. I'd dare any pickpockets to take it from you."

It was the best cover he could think of to cover his real reason: He didn't want to be a part of any test of character.

His Ernest Kane backstory already had more holes than a block of cheese to anyone who cared to look. Best to throw Penn off the scent if he possibly could.

Penn gave him an odd look, then shrugged and slipped the bag in his shirt pocket. "Should we go up to a higher level? There would be better goods there."

"No time. I don't want to risk being left behind when the call comes." Arthur moved past him to the inner store, already browsing.

It seemed giving Penn the ludicrously rich bag of coins was taken as an act of trust. While his cousin wasn't as friendly as he'd been before, the atmosphere had thawed noticeably.

Or maybe it was the fact Arthur swept through the small store like a hurricane, buying everything he thought might be remotely useable . . . and quite a few items that were edge cases.

"The folded knives, I understand," Penn said. "But why are you buying blankets . . . and are these cooking pans?" He held up a cast iron pan by the tips of his fingers as if he was afraid it was going to bite him. "Surely, you don't intend to stay in a commoner village long term . . ."

"I have no idea what we'll be getting into." Arthur glanced at the center table where several cards were on display. Typical for the lower levels of the hive, they were Common and pointless. What was an origami crane, and why would someone dedicate an entire card to it? "Besides, not all of this is for us."

"Who, then? You don't intend to help out other teams—"

Arthur waved that away. "Of course not. But there will be evacuees. Many families will have lost everything."

Penn looked a little taken aback. Then he glanced around with new eyes. "Say, how much can you put in that extra space card, anyway?"

"Personal Space."

"Whatever."

* * *

They returned a half hour later, the store much emptier, Marion's bag only a little reduced, and Arthur grateful there wasn't a weight limit to his Personal Space.

They found Marion dressed in still fancy, though more practical clothing. He sat next to a ridiculously burly man with shoulders so broad it looked like he would have to turn sideways to fit into doors . . . and who was currently chomping on a beaded necklace. The exact nervous gesture a little girl would do.

"Prince Marion," Penn greeted, sitting down at the table. "And . . . Princess Echo." His voice carried a lingering "I hope" at the end.

"My minders said I have to be in my battle shape," Echo rumbled, still biting on the necklace. She accidentally got a few wisps of beard in there, too.

Marion casually picked under his perfect nails. "I don't foresee battle."

"Only because you 'foresee' three seconds ahead," she snapped.

"How long can you hold that, ah, shape?" Arthur asked, looking at her curiously. Most active charms used mana. As a Legendary, perhaps it used a lot less or leveled up the way his own did to bypass that requirement.

She glared across the table at him. "None of your beeswax."

"Actually, it is our business as part of your team." Penn gazed across the table sternly at her. "There's no point activating your card if you're burning through your mana."

She wrinkled her nose at him, which looked ridiculous on a full-grown man.

Marion sighed. "To forestall a tedious back and forth, she's fine. Our family gives supplemental cards to cover those types of weaknesses."

Which meant that she had one, or possibly several, higher-tiered mana-boost, mana-regeneration, or mana-supplement cards . . . or all three.

Arthur wondered how many cards the little girl had already shoved in her heart . . . but he'd likely had more at her age.

Just then, the bells began to ring. Not the joyous sounds of announcing a high-tiered egg laid, but the sounds of a scourge-eruption.

The seers had been correct.

Whitaker and Valentina arrived as if teleported.

"It's time. Stand up and follow us through this door. Transport dragons will be waiting on the balconies—"

"But the rest of my team hasn't gotten back yet!" one girl cried out.

She found no sympathy from Whitaker. "They were warned to make ready and be back here. If they want to prove themselves as viable recruits, they'll find their way there. Now, move!"

Latecomers streamed in through the front door, and Arthur was certain any noble who could afford a Legendary could afford to bribe a dragon rider to take them to the eruption. He didn't spare them any pity, either.

Everyone at their table stood and got in line for the balcony. It went fast. It seemed the leaders had already planned well in advance.

A small cloud of purples buzzed, hovered, or simply flew in tight circles in the night sky, according to their preference.

Arthur searched the dark sky for a familiar face, but she found him first.

"Tess found boy!" A moment later, a four-winged purple swooped down to hover to a stop just over their heads. All drew back except Arthur, who tried not to cringe.

Rider Johanna craned over to look down at him. "Heya, Arthur, surprised to see you here."

What are you doing mixing with Legendary noble recruits? her expression silently asked.

Arthur shrugged and tried to plead with his eyes to keep quiet about it. The problem was, while Johanna might get it . . . Tess, not so much.

"Tess fly boy!" the purple crowed to everyone within hearing range. "We flied far, far, far . . ."

Thankfully, Johanna stepped in. "Land, Tess. We'll carry Arthur again."

"Yay!" The dragon did just that.

Arthur decided to make the most of it. From his time at the hive, he'd seen a lot of dragon saddle configurations. Tess was rigged up for two additional passengers aside from her rider.

Johanna stuck her fingers in her mouth and whistled. A moment later, another purple, quieter than Tess but similarly saddled up, landed beside them.

Arthur turned to his team. "I guess we're line jumping. Who wants to ride with me?"

CHAPTER 23

Tess and her passengers emerged out of the rip in the sky into blazing afternoon sunshine.

Echo, who sat behind Arthur, let out a girlish scream. She had briefly returned to her natural twelve-year-old form at Johanna's request. It meant less weight for Tess to carry.

Arthur twisted around in his saddle to make sure she was still secure. Her eyes were wide as she gazed around. Catching his look, she pointed straight ahead.

Arthur nodded.

The wind blew too fiercely to allow any conversation, but words weren't needed. A sharp cone of scourge-eruption was growing right in the middle of lush farmland.

And that farmland stood at the edge of a small city.

Dragons appeared out of rips in the sky from all directions. Half went to deal with the scourglings clawing their way free from the top of the cone. The other half headed for the city to help with the evacuation.

Naturally, that was where Tess went. Folding all four of her wings, she fell into a dive . . . leaving Arthur's stomach hovering somewhere above him. It wasn't just the quick fall, but Tess used her tail as a rudder in the air and managed to twist around other dragons as she fell.

Arthur had spent an entire day on a frantic ride across the kingdom on Tess's back. He was at least used to her antics.

He yelled over his shoulder to Echo, "Lean with her turns."

The girl yelled something back that Arthur didn't catch. It was likely snotty anyway.

The closer they came to the edge of the city, the sharper and clearer the panic.

The outer edges of the city on the erution side were in chaos. People ran from the direction of the farmland. Some pulled carts loaded with goods and what looked like some harvest they could save. Some carried children. Some had nothing at all.

All rushed toward the center of the city, whose narrow roads were already being choked. Once they were jammed, panic was sure to set in.

Meanwhile, the scourge-eruption was growing by the moment. Though dragons poured in from different hives, many scourglings had already taken to the sky.

"Get ready to dismount the moment Tess is down." Johanna had to bellow to be heard over the growing shouts of people as well as the wind. "Then get clear. Tess and I have to help with the evacuation."

"What are we supposed to do now?" Echo asked. "They never told us."

She was right. Arthur didn't reply because he had no idea. The Wolf Moon Hive leaders were nowhere in sight. Tess was only among the first of a wave of purples who were setting down Legendary recruits.

The moment Tess's claws touched the cobblestone road, Arthur slid off her side. It was an easy drop. Just like riding a donkey.

Echo followed, looking anxiously up at the sky. She pointed out the dragon carrying Marion and Penn, and they met them when they landed.

The moment the passengers were gone, the purples took off again.

Penn stared around at the chaos. "Any idea what we're supposed to do here?"

They all looked to Marion, who was already rolling his eyes.

"I see three seconds into the future. If I find out anything in addition ahead of time, I'll let you know."

"Signal us or something," Penn suggested.

Arthur glanced about. Most of the Legendary recruits had clustered together, looking around for direction.

"It's a test."

He didn't realize he had spoken until he felt the weight of the others' gazes on him.

"Go on," Penn said in what sounded too much like an order.

Arthur let it go and shrugged. "They want us to show how useful we can be to the hive, right? So, they drop us here." He remembered the feeling of being watched when he'd carried Joy in his Personal Space. The hive leaders hadn't let him go to trotting around the city without keeping careful tabs on him.

He suspected that some person—or people—could easily slip into this chaos and do the same here.

"We're not going to get any specific orders," Arthur said. "We have to find a way to show our mettle here."

Marion muttered, "Ah, dragon soil. Too late."

A second later, the bearded prince jumped up onto the edge of a decorative fountain. He clapped his hands once, and Arthur felt the force of his personality sweep over the immediate area.

Instinctively, he reached for his own Charming Gentleperson card and activated it. That provided a temporary boost to his own charisma.

He suddenly noticed that the prince's face was . . . rather lumpy. Like he had gotten the worst in a few bar fights that had left his nose the wrong shape.

Still, the man easily acquired everyone's attention. He smiled with teeth that were crooked. Odd. Arthur had the impression at first that they'd been sparkling.

"These people need our help, and we need to prove ourselves to the leadership. I suggest we separate ourselves into groups. This city will need a wall to defend themselves against the scourglings. Anyone with earth, rock, or building-type cards meet over there." He gestured to the right. "Next we need defenders to protect people and property until the dragons get control of this eruption. Everyone who can fight, stay here." He pointed directly in front of himself to the fountain. "Lastly, support. Those who don't fit in the first two categories—well, you know your cards. Help out where you can. And if you have any ideas, I'm all ears."

It was a good plan, and Arthur couldn't find immediate fault . . . other than who in the world made him the leader? He tried and failed not to resent the man, or the fact that no one else called him out for taking command. Damn Charisma card.

Penn and Echo seemed to be caught in the thrall of the plan. They'd already moved away toward the combat teams.

Marion heaved a sigh and spoke before Arthur could ask. "Yes, I'm going with them."

"With . . . the combat group?"

He shrugged again and pulled a pocket-sized book out of his coat. "Sure, why not?"

Well, he knew his card better than anyone. Arthur gave a lingering look and let out a sigh of his own. "I'm support. I guess I'll . . . find a way to make myself useful."

But that wouldn't be good enough. He had to make himself stand out.

Marion gave him a sympathetic look as if he understood, but then turned to follow Penn and his half sister.

With the greatest reluctance, Arthur turned toward the snow-white tent, which showed all signs of being hurriedly built.

Sickness Seekers walked quickly in and out. People were carried in on stretchers, on carts, and hobbled in on the shoulders of loved ones.

The ghost of Arthur's long-dead friend, Ernie, echoed in his mind. Being a nurse was women's work.

Well . . . Ernie had been twelve at the time, and Arthur would like to think that he'd matured a little.

Besides, helping out with the sick had to be better than volunteering in the kitchens and cooking for the masses, right?

"I really need a combat card," he muttered.

Then he mentally stepped into his Personal Space.

It was a large area, but he and Penn had gone wild with shopping. In addition, Arthur had supplies of his own.

He grabbed an hourglass and flipped it. He couldn't afford to be debilitated by a headache.

Only . . . the sand didn't fall. It hung there, suspended as if frozen in place.

Arthur frowned. "How does that work? I can move things around. I can alter objects, but time doesn't flow by itself?" Something seemed off about the logic there. Then again, a card's power had rules of its own.

Okay, so he couldn't time himself. He just had to step back out in the real world before he went too far leveling his skills. Should be easy. Right?

. . . Right?

Arthur bee-lined for one of the medical kits he'd purchased from the hive's store. It was wrapped in leather and was meant to be tucked away in a pack. It held a small roll of white bandages, a tiny bottle with a wax seal filled with a salve that was meant to aid healing, a needle, and a spool of gut-thread for stitches.

He took out the needle and thread.

Then he went to one of the three cured hams that sat on a shelf that he swore hadn't existed the last time he was there.

Using a knife, he sliced into the side. Then he threaded the needle and got to work stitching it up again.

In an effort not to get an obscure version of a **Taxidermy** skill, he focused his will on making each stitch neat and on the skin only. Like he was trying to close a living wound.

Either because ham was food and not a living person, or the Master of Skills card sensed his dubious mood, it took five repetitions to get the skill.

New skill gained: Wound Stitching (First Aid, Nurse Class)

Due to your card's bonus traits, you automatically start this skill at level 3.

"Nurse," he repeated sorely, hearing the echo of Ernie's laughter. The corner of Arthur's mouth twitched up. Years on, and he missed his friend . . . but if Ernie were here, Arthur would be laughing along with him.

Besides, helping people out wasn't so bad. Due to his card's benefits, he started at level 3. That should make him useful enough to help out inside the tent.

Not enough to impress the hive leaders, though.

Maybe . . . he'd done enough already? Ernest Kane had certainly developed a high profile recently with the mess at the scholar's guild and helping to save the pink dragon. Not to mention, he and Kenzie had been the ones to find the dark Legendary egg in the first place.

Just this once, it might be wise to let someone else have attention. The egg was the one who would ultimately choose the winner.

Though every time he thought of the bearded prince—or anyone else—standing in front of the dark egg, his blood wanted to boil.

No matter. It was time to leave this space and return to the world.

The last thing Arthur did was to ensure the Nullify card was on, canceling his Return to Start. The anchor point for that card was back in his room in Wolf Moon Hive. He would never be able to live it down if he was sent back because of a healer's aggressive scan.

An eye blink later, Arthur was back in the real world. He felt a slight sense of strain behind his eyes as if he had been up studying the night before, but it was manageable. And he had a new skill to level.

Arthur headed for the tent.

CHAPTER 24

Arthur imagined his newly learned skill would be put to good use. He didn't quite count on the pure chaos he'd find inside the tent.

Either the weaver guild had stitched some silencing runes in the tent's fabric or someone was using a powerful dampening card, because the sight of injured people, one of whom was holding his own finger in his bloody hand, the smell of vomit and blood and all sorts of unspeakable fluids, and unvarnished sounds of agony nearly sent Arthur back out of the tent again.

But he was a hale young man with no visible injuries. Before Arthur could do more than start to turn away, someone yelled that they needed help with a lift.

Arthur was pressed into service by grabbing the other end of a sheet and helping to lift a stricken man onto a table. Then someone else called for water, and, well, the jug was right there.

He did eventually practice his new **Wound Stitching** skill. On the man who had the severed finger, no less.

It turned out he was a woodcutter with the very bad fortune of having an accident just as the scourge-eruption started. The initial alarm was enough to make his saw go sideways at the wrong moment.

The very good news was his Common card, which he calmly told Arthur about as Arthur stitched his finger back on and quietly tried not to pass out from stress. Apparently, it was a self-healing card. Though as it was a Common card, the healing took a bit.

"This ain't the first time I lost that damn finger," the woodcutter said. "Though it is the most inconvenient. I'll be right as rain in a couple days—assuming no scourglings get to me first."

"Dragon riders will see to that," Arthur said as he tied the last stitch. That little stunt had bumped him two more levels to 5.

The woodcutter opened his mouth to reply. He was interrupted by a blood-curdling scream coming from the other side of the tent—the side where the scourge-stricken were taken. Those who had tangled with scourge-beasts, lived, but caught the infection.

The woodsman pulled a face. "If the dragon riders want to help, they'd donate cards to those wretches. They're rich in cards, aren't they?"

Arthur said nothing. Yes, dragon riders were rich in cards. He was, too. Especially compared to these folk. He'd seen more uncarded people over the last couple of hours than he had the whole last year in the hive.

Not counting his side trip to his old border village, of course.

Arthur tried not to think about the cards he'd seen for sale in the hive's store. How he had discounted them as Common and useless. Once again, he had lost touch with his roots. Those cards would have been life or death for some of the people in the next room.

I can't help everyone, he thought, but it felt sour.

"So, what do you say, doc?" the woodsman asked with forced light-heartedness. "Think I'll live?"

Arthur opened his mouth to tell the man he wasn't a healer, just a volunteer. However, his **General Nursecraft** skill and a few old memories from the first day in the hive whispered in his mind. "You've still lost a lot of blood. You need to replenish it—orange juice would be best, and red meat. As much as you can get."

The man blinked at him, then smiled as if thinking Arthur was making a joke. "Juice and meat? You think I'm rich—"

Something big hit the top of the tent, nearly right over Arthur's head. He threw himself to the side as a big something crashed in, whistling in agony. A scourgling.

Arthur had the quick-flash impression of a fat body and wings before it hit and burst open like an overripe fruit.

He didn't have time to be satisfied the scourgling was dead. Dozens of tiny scourglings flew out of the burst corpse and straight at the screaming, injured people.

They were each as long as Arthur's hand, like naked weasels with beating wings and long fangs that jutted from their jaws.

Once again, Arthur stepped into his Personal Space.

"This is becoming a habit," he muttered and went to the wall to grab an axe and a shovel.

He returned a moment later and shoved the axe in the woodcutter's good hand.

Then he whipped around and brought the head of the shovel on one of the baby scourge-weasels.

Arthur didn't have a skill for this—and wouldn't receive one because Master of Combat belonged to Penn—but he was strong and full of frustration and rage.

The woodcutter still ended up doing the bulk of the work. He cut them from the air as if the axe were an extension of his arm.

Others rushed in to help. One girl screamed. The air warped in front of her mouth, and a scourgling exploded in front of her from the force of her card's power. Arthur's ears rang afterward.

It was over quickly, and Arthur stumbled to the main corpse.

The creature had fallen from a great height—no doubt from a battle with a dragon, and it was so burned it would have been hard to tell what it was, except he'd seen the babies.

Arthur located the glowing chest and harvested the Common card inside.

"Charm Weasels?" he muttered, looking at it. Not a card he wanted, but he caught the looks from others in the tent. It represented more than what the card's charm could do.

Others were already collecting from the little ones, but Arthur doubted they'd have more than Common shards.

Some of the healers had come out at the noise. Arthur turned and extended his hand with the card out to them. "Here," he said gruffly. "Use this to save one of them."

The healer took it. "Thank you."

Arthur had already turned away. He didn't want to be thanked for that. A real leader, he was sure, would have strode in the other room himself and bestowed the card personally. Made sure whoever got that card was worthy of living.

He didn't want the weight of that choice on his heart.

And the truth was . . . he could be doing so much more with his skills. Two Legendary cards in his heart and he was stitching wounds by hand.

He had to do better.

He had to make himself worthy of being a companion to a Legendary dragon.

An idea hit him.

"Wait," he said to the healer.

The man turned back.

"Are . . . any of them in their right mind?" Arthur asked. "I have a storage space card that may give them time, but they need to agree—"

He stopped at the healer's sad expression.

"It's a nice thought, but once the scourge-sickness sets in and they're beyond our healing, reason has long flown out the window. All but the worst will take a card—they crave cards. But I doubt you'll be able to get through to them."

Nodding, Arthur turned to the entrance. He needed a moment of fresh air to clear his disappointment.

The front of the tent flap opened just as Arthur was about to step through. He nearly came face-to-face with Penn.

"Whoa." His cousin looked past Arthur, eyes wide. "Looks like you've seen more excitement than the rest of our team."

"What do you want?" Arthur asked.

Penn gave him a look for his abrupt tone, then tilted his head outside. "The rest of the team's tired of sitting on our thumbs. We're going hunting."

"Hunting?" Arthur repeated.

Penn's smile was sharp. "What if the leaders weren't looking for us to play nice with the locals? What if they want us to bring back proof we're scourge-killers?"

In the form of cards, Arthur thought. He carefully didn't look back toward the healers in case that one he'd just given the Common card to was still there.

He didn't want Penn to know in case he was tempted to take it back as a trophy.

Instead, he looked up at his cousin. "I'm in."

CHAPTER 25

Arthur had only spent a couple hours in the tent, but the landscape outside had drastically changed. With the silencing magic placed around the area, Arthur hadn't suspected a thing. The Legendary recruits had been busy.

He stared at a twenty-foot-high stone wall which encircled the outer edges of the city. The scourge-volcano had grown in size, too, but the wall represented an impressive bulwark. A deep moat had been dredged up to the edge of the wall and filled with a venomous green liquid. If any scourglings happened to get over the wall and fall, they'd get a nasty surprise.

Penn saw him looking and grimaced.

"Yeah, we've been going all out trying to impress each other. I heard there's some kind of life-sucking spikes covering the other side. And watch." He picked up a rock and hurled it over the top of the wall. The rock smacked a shimmering barrier, which extended out over the top and into the sky, only visible when activated.

"That explains why no one is manning the top," Arthur noted, though his throat felt tight with intense bitterness. All his skills and he couldn't do anything like that.

"Yup. Some earl's daughter from the south put it in place. It's self-sustaining—feeds off of sunlight somehow, so it'll keep until the sun sets," Penn confirmed, his voice growing sourer with every word. "She couldn't make it too high on account of the dragon riders, but it's made the rest of us defenders useless."

Arthur nodded. That flying scourge-weasel had likely been knocked out of the sky from a dragon rider.

Protecting the city at large was a good thing, but . . . they were here to prove themselves. It was frustrating not being able to do so.

A burning sense of uselessness ate at him. He could practically feel it like a hot coal inside his heart deck.

Yes, he had helped some people back in the healing tent, but he was a Legendary user two times over. He was meant to do more.

He had to be better—show he was the best possible choice to link cards with that egg.

Just by glancing around, he could tell he wasn't the only one feeling that way. Most of the townsfolk who could get away from the eruption had been shuttled to the inner city, leaving the Legendary recruits. And there were half as many as there were before. All wore looks of sullen frustration, unhappy about being held back.

Penn led him on. Soon, they came to Marion and Echo, who had returned to her twelve-year-old-girl form. Likely to save on mana. That was a good thing, as her pouting sulk fit her face perfectly.

"What took so long?" Echo said.

"Two more teams just left now, through the gate," Marion added, pointing to the single break in the wall.

Echo stomped her foot. "They got a head start on us. I told you we shouldn't have waited for them." She threw a dismissive glance at Arthur, who had to clench his fist to keep from throwing a rude sign back.

You've dealt with plenty of brats in the orphanage, he reminded himself. Though none of them had been in direct competition with him before.

So instead of dipping down to her level and snapping back directly, he attacked her from another angle. "Have you ever hunted anything in your life? It's not going to be roses and daisies out there."

"Of course I have," she snapped. "I go bow hunting all the time with my attendants."

He made a show of looking around. "And where are your attendants now, Princess?"

Marion was the one who answered. "Back at the hive." There was a definite sparkle in his eye. "This is the first time without them that I can remember. I want to take full advantage of it."

"Let's go, then," Penn said. "Arthur, if you have any combat cards at all, this is the time to bring them out."

He could not, under any circumstance, show anything from his Body Enhancement card. But he still had a few things up his sleeve. "I have an Uncommon stealth card," he lied. What he actually had was a nicely leveled **Stealth** skill. "I could help scout the forest ahead."

Echo changed shape back to the brutish man, though her long beard was now elaborately braided. She struck one fist into an open palm. "You show us where they are, and we'll smash them."

Penn casually unsheathed his sword. "Sounds like a plan to me."

Marion shrugged. "I'll do what I always do."

"Which is?" Arthur asked.

"See ahead."

"All right," Penn said. "Let's move out."

True doubt only began to hit Arthur once he was out of sight of the wall. The scourge-volcano seemed to loom much, much closer. The erupting scourglings were visibly rolling out from the sharp top. Some dragons hovered nearby to snatch the scourglings before they could do damage, but many more escaped their grasp.

The farmland was separated from the city by a winding river and thick trees. Those trees shook with so many bodies passing by, and the whistling shrieks were so thick in the air that it all came together to form a white noise.

Riders with barrier or large area-of-effect cards were likely doing their best to reroute the flood of scourglings away from the city. Or else even that impressive wall wouldn't hold them back.

More doubt crept in. What was he doing? He was a utility expert. His position was of support. And he had walked away from it into the heart of the battle.

Marion had slowed, too. "Do any of you guys have a bad feeling about this?"

Echo stopped and blinked. She looked toward the river and the shivering trees and paled. "It didn't seem so bad back in the city."

Only Penn continued striding forward. He looked back over his shoulder at them. "What are you guys waiting for?"

"No, wait, what . . . what are we doing?" Arthur asked, looking down at his hands. He had just strode out of the city, bare-handed. Hurriedly, he grabbed a pickax from his Personal Storage. He'd left the shovel back in the tent.

"I've never been this far in the wilderness without protection." All the bluster had left Echo, and though she kept her brutish shape, it was easy to see the little girl within.

Penn turned and scowled at him. "We're all the protection you need, kid. Don't wimp out now."

Arthur and Marion exchanged a look.

"I can provide a distraction," Marion said, "but I'm not good at the actual . . . fighting part."

"That's good enough," Penn said. "Come on, we're losing daylight."

Arthur became more and more certain by the moment that something was wrong.

"Penn, slow down. Ask yourself why you're charging out here like this."

"What are you talking about? We need to get cards because . . . because . . ." Trailing off, Penn looked down at his own hands. He clenched and unclenched his fingers. "Wait right here."

Then, turning, he shoved past Arthur and Marion to head back the way they'd come.

He slowed about twenty feet back, shook his head again, and turned to glare at them. "No, this is stupid. We have to be out there. We *have* to prove ourselves."

"That's what I thought," Marion said. "Come over here, big guy."

Penn stomped over to join them. As he did, his expression melted from determined to more complex. "Uh . . . wait . . ."

Marion sighed. "There's a mind-mage in the city."

Arthur stared at him, shocked he could deliver that so casually.

"Maybe a dark-emotion tinkerer," Marion corrected.

"I was under a spell?" Echo squeaked in her manly voice.

Penn paled, but his jaw was set and determined. "Are you sure? What exactly did you see?"

The prince's eyebrows rose. "See? This isn't about seeing the future, it's about noticing a pattern. Your mind changed from walking over there to over here. That indicates there's a spell with a large area of effect—one with a border."

It wasn't that Arthur didn't believe him, it was just that the implications were horrific. "If that's the case . . . we were sent out here. No," he said at once, realization dawning. "Not just us. All of the other teams, too."

He'd felt so useless in the city and was convinced the only way to fix it—to succeed—was to go out.

"Yup." Marion stuck his hands in his pocket, looking around with curiosity. "I suspect we've been led into a trap. And right on cue . . ."

It was as if the clouds fell out of the sky on top of them. Instantly, they were shrouded in fog so thick Arthur could not see the length of his outstretched hand.

For a heart-freezing moment, he was certain this was a direct attack. That they were about to be set upon.

Distant shouts, distorted by the fog, told him they weren't the only ones.

"What's happening?!" Echo yelled. Then, just as quickly, "We have to go back!"

Arthur saw a huge shadowy figure pass him by. He reached out and grabbed her giant ham-hock shoulder. "No, wait, if you go back and that spell's still in effect, you'll come right back out here again."

"We can't stay here," Marion said. "This fog is perfect cover for assassins."

Echo whimpered.

"They don't need assassins." Penn's voice was dark. "They just have to sit back and let the scourglings deal with us."

"The dragon riders will see something is wrong," Arthur said. "We just have to stay together and stay alive." He didn't waste time asking if anyone had a Nullify area-of-effect card. If they did, they would have used it.

"Penn, do your thing." Casually, Marion hooked Arthur's elbow with his own and pulled him two steps to the right. It was done so smoothly that at first Arthur didn't register the rush of air passing by.

A scourge-wolf landed, jaws snapping, exactly where he'd been a moment before.

Penn brought down his sword in one easy motion. The wolf's head came off, and the body crumpled.

Letting go of Arthur, Marion reached up to cover Echo's mouth before she screamed. "You don't want to attract more, do you?"

Two feet away, the wolf's jaws continued to snap at air. Arthur stared at it, frozen, and only came back to himself when he saw Penn reach for the glow above the body.

"Two Common shards, one Uncommon," Penn announced, straightening.

"You keep them for now." Arthur recognized the need to extend an olive branch while he could. "You're the team leader, right?"

Even through the dense fog, Penn looked pleased. Though he waited for Echo and Marion to nod their agreement before he stuck the shards in his pocket.

"I want to go home," Echo whimpered.

"Uh." Penn looked around. With his free hand, he scratched the back of his neck. "Anyone know which direction we go to get back?"

Arthur started to point, but then paused. It was more than being disoriented from the attack. The small patch of ground he could see before the world turned gray and blank looked utterly unfamiliar. "I think there's a disorienting aspect to this fog."

"Hmm. A wide-ranging area of effect with added bonuses," Marion said. "Sounds like a Legendary card to me. I think someone's got the idea to pick off their competition."

Penn gave him a look. "You don't sound worried about it."

"I know for a fact I'll be alive three seconds from now. It's hard to be worried when you're never surprised."

Echo broke in. "What do we do? How do we get back?"

"Pick a direction, I guess," Arthur said. He pointed to where he thought might be the way to the city. The fog distorted all sounds, and he couldn't tell where the whistles from the scourge came from, but he thought there were fewer of them to the right. "I think it's that way."

The others looked at each other. Then with a mutual shrug, they moved.

They kept close together. Echo held on to Marion's arm, but the other three were too proud to touch.

Arthur frowned down at the ground, trying to determine if it looked different from before or not. Shouldn't they have reached the city by now? Or at least felt the urge to go back on a suicidal scourge-hunt?

And if they did reach the city, could they power through their own impulses to go back outside again?

"Wait," Marion said suddenly. "I think something's wrong—"

Arthur's next step hit empty air. He tipped forward with a shout and started falling.

And falling. And falling.

It was as if he had fallen down a deep well or mine shaft, only everything around him continued to be gray fog. He shouted, reached for a handhold, but there was nothing.

He fell and fell and *fell.*

It took a few seconds that felt like years for Arthur to realize he hadn't hit the bottom of the endless fall.

It wasn't an endless bad dream. He was trapped in an illusion.

Which meant he was likely standing in the middle of the fog, surrounded by scourglings, assassins, or both.

"This isn't real!" he yelled out loud, voice shaking. It didn't seem to help. "This isn't real. I'm not falling . . ."

Why hadn't the dragon riders done anything yet? Surely they would have come to investigate an unusual bank of fog. Someone had to be watching the Legendary recruits, if only to see how they performed in the field test.

Unless this was part of the field test?

He dismissed that thought immediately.

Valentina and Whitaker had strict requirements for the egg, but they were hosting the sons and daughters of nobles. They wouldn't want them killed. That was one of the reasons they were preemptively trying to eliminate unworthy people.

So why hadn't anyone investigated?

Maybe because they couldn't see the fog.

An illusion inside an illusion? That felt like a Legendary-level ability.

This isn't real, he thought again and spoke aloud to reinforce it. "This isn't real."

Squeezing his eyes shut, he clenched his fists and willed himself to believe it.

His mind flashed to his brief training with Kenzie. Using aura manipulation, she could alter emotions. Eventually, he was able to push her back.

He wasn't quite sure how—it was like a particular twist in his thoughts, projecting them outward. Solidifying them. Making them as strong as a shield.

"This isn't real!"

His outward shield struck something that was remarkably delicate and brittle, like spun glass. The glass shattered around him.

Suddenly, Arthur was no longer falling. He stood on steady ground. The day was bright around him. The fog was gone.

His team's wanderings had taken them parallel to the wall. They stood in the middle of a churned-up wheat field. Penn, Marion, and Echo stood stock still around him, staring blankly out to the middle distance.

And three flying scourglings had taken off from the high trees and were headed their way.

Arthur's immediate instinct was to grab everyone and run. He reached to touch Echo and tried to store her in his Personal Space. He'd apologize later.

Echo didn't budge. After a frantic moment, he remembered why: He needed her permission.

"Echo, can you hear me? You're not falling. It's an illusion! Let me take you out of there."

Nothing.

Arthur looked to the sky. The three scourglings were close enough to identify as more of those naked flying weasel things. Though the outsized fangs gave them the look of moles.

In desperation, Arthur grabbed Echo's arm and Marion's, who stood right next to his sister. He pulled them forward.

They stepped forward like dolls, eyes blank. But they moved too slow. They were in the middle of an open field with no chance for cover. And that still left Penn.

Arthur looked back at his cousin and at the oncoming scourglings.

A terrible thought struck him.

Penn had the Master of Combat card. With it, Arthur could finally fill in the missing piece to his set.

Arthur's pickaxe lay a few feet away. He'd dropped it when he fell into the illusion. One swing at the throat ought to do it. Then he would grab the card and use it to save the prince and princess. Simple and easy.

Instead, Arthur mentally slotted Thief into his class slot, turned to Marion, and started rifling through his pockets for a card-anchor bag. Instead, he found two more bags of coins in addition to the one he'd already shown Arthur and Penn. Had he brought all his money?

New Skill Gained: Pickpocketing (Thief Class)

Due to your card's bonus traits, you automatically start this skill at level 3.

Would you like to add this skill to your existing Thief class?

Arthur dismissed that. The oncoming scourglings whistled in excitement. They were so close Arthur could hear the snap of their fleshy wing-sails.

Then Arthur remembered: He'd seen Marion's card-anchor tattoo on the inside of his left wrist.

Hopefully the prince had hidden something good up his sleeve.

Arthur pressed his pinched fingers to it and activated his **Card Shuffling** skill.

He removed a single card and shoved it into his own anchor bag.

Instant Tool and Weapon Competence
Rare
Combat
The wielder of this card will be able to pick up and use any tool or weapon with the ease and ability of someone with level 10 general experience. The user may gain more ability while using the weapon.
Warning: *Competence boost will end once card is removed from the wielder's deck. Any additional experience or levels gained will reset back to base ten once the tool or weapon leaves the wielder's hands.*

The scourglings were almost upon them. Arthur grabbed the pickaxe.

New skill gained: Pickaxe Proficiency (Miner Class)
Due to your card's bonus traits, you automatically start this skill at level 13. (+3 Master of Skills, +10 Tool Competence)

And if the scourglings were made of rock, maybe he could do something with that. Arthur pulled his arms back and threw it end over end at the oncoming scourglings.

It was enough to send two of them into a quick, scattering turn. The third didn't so much as flinch. It came on straight and true, aimed directly at Penn.

Arthur ran back for Penn, too. He snatched the sword out of his cousin's hands.

New skill gained: Saber Proficiency (Swordsman Class)
Due to your card's bonus traits, you automatically start this skill at level 10.

No bonus from his Master of Skills card, of course. It didn't matter. He knew exactly how to set his feet, how to best grip it under the pommel that combined flexibility and strength. This wasn't an ideal weapon—he intuitively knew it was best to use this sort of sword from the back of a horse. Or a dragon.

But the scourgling was in a dive, and it was all Arthur had.

He slashed it in a back cut, rather than an instinctive stab to let the edge do most of the work. The cut hit home and parted flesh down its neck and hide to the wing joint. Arthur stepped back before the blade could hit bone and stick.

Good thing because, with a whistling shriek, the scourgling turned in midair to bite at him. It missed his wrist by a hair. Arthur turned away as it struck ground in a tangle of limbs. Bone snapped.

Kicking the body, Arthur turned. The other two scourglings had used those few seconds to swoop into their own dives. They aimed themselves at Marion and Echo.

Echo was blinking long and confused blinks, as if coming out of a trance. But she wasn't yet focused on the scourglings.

"Echo, duck!" Arthur yelled.

She blinked slowly at him and didn't move.

Arthur stepped in front of them both, slashing wildly in a way his new skill said was horribly inefficient but would hopefully look intimidating.

The tip of his weapon caught the shoulder of one of the diving scourglings. The creature chittered out and jerked away. That motion knocked the sword to the side for one crucial second.

The second creature plowed into Arthur.

Arthur fell to the ground with the scourgling on top of him. Foul, rotten breath washed into his face.

In a flash, he mentally retreated into his Personal Space, grabbed an extra shirt to wrap around his arm, a scarf he wound to protect his neck, a knife—

New skill gained: Dagger Proficiency (Swordsman Class/Thief Class)
Due to your card's bonus traits, you automatically start this skill at level 10.

Correction, a *dagger*, and stepped back into reality. He shoved the dagger into the creature's open maw. The teeth sliced through the cloth around his arm like tissue paper, his skin even worse than that.

Arthur screamed but jammed the dagger up through the top of the mouth and into the brain. The scourgling shuddered and twitched, drawing new agony from his arm in its mouth and the claws against his body. Then it went limp.

There was still another scourgling.

Arthur rolled the dead scourgling off him and tried to rise, but he only made it to his knees before a wave of dizziness made him sit again. His arm was covered in red, and there were . . . strips of flesh hanging off his hand and wrist. He'd lost the dagger somewhere, couldn't feel anything past his elbow at all. Not a good sign.

The scourgling had hit the ground in a controlled fall. Spreading its wings wide, it chittered angrily before it charged—four additional limbs making it just as dangerous on land as in the air. Sort of like a dragon.

Arthur braced himself.

Echo stomped into the scourgling's path, picked the beast up by the back of the neck, and slammed it down again. Her battle cry was as fierce as any dragon. The scourgling twisted to bite, but she kicked it with one solid boot, making its head snap to the side unnaturally. It fell into a heap.

"Gross! I hate these things!" She gave a full-body shudder and turned. "Are there any more? Where's Penn?"

Penn stood less than ten feet away, still caught in the illusion. Judging by the way Echo looked around, she was still caught in the fog.

Arthur shook his head, and the entire world seemed to wobble along with the motion. The next moment, he was on the ground.

"Oh no, hold still." Echo knelt by his side and reached into her leather vest to withdraw a glittery silver handbag edged with pink gems. A very appropriate accessory for a twelve-year-old girl. It looked ridiculous in the hands of her current huge form.

She pulled a bottle that . . . well, either Arthur's eyes were playing tricks on him or the green wax-sealed bottle was bigger than the tiny bag.

"Here . . . oh no, your arm. I'll get it. Drink." She popped the wax and pressed it to his lips. "Don't tell anyone I gave you this. I'm only supposed to use it for myself."

He had a momentary thought that he was surprised she wasn't squeamish about his blood. Then the warm peppermint liquid hit his lips.

It was an instant infusion of energy and clarity. He gulped it down, using his working hand to steady the bottle and tip it back.

Sensation returned to his damaged arm, and it itched, but in a distant not-unpleasant way. He looked down to see the wounds sealing themselves off. The blood obscured much of the mess, but he saw either tendon or bone reknit and covered by new skin. The old hanging skin dropped off, unneeded.

It was kind of gross, but he was too fascinated to care.

Little wounds he wasn't even aware of resealed themselves, and within a few moments he was entirely whole and felt as fresh as if he'd gotten a good night's sleep.

"Was that alchemy?" he asked, stunned. "A real potion?"

There were no card alchemists in Wolf Moon Hive, as it was one of the smaller hives. Arthur had heard stories of their potion abilities but discounted them as exaggeration. Now he was a believer.

"Don't tell," Echo said again. She started to worry her bottom lip with her teeth, but then made a disgusted look as she encountered the beard. "I'm not supposed to, but you protected me and Marion. Is Penn . . . Is he gone?"

Arthur stood. "No, he's standing to your right. The fog's an illusion, too."

"I have a dispel-illusion card." Echo's haughty voice lost its edge as realization hit her. "But if this was done by a Legendary power . . . it'll be too strong for me to fully dispel."

"Yeah."

He looked out. More scourglings had broken off from the trees but were intercepted by a pair of red dragons who turned them to ash before swooping to snap up the falling card shards.

It was far from safe out here.

"We have to get Penn and Marion away from here. Can you carry your brother? I'll see what I can do with Penn."

"He's my half brother," she corrected, then paused, again biting her lip despite the beard. "Marion has a camouflage card. I don't think he knows I know he has it, but he could hide us all."

"Where?" Arthur asked sharply. "In his anchor tattoo?"

"No, his heart deck. Why?"

Drat. He couldn't grab it, then.

He didn't think they could easily walk out of here—not if Echo was still caught in the fog illusion. And if they made it back, then what? The mind-mage would be waiting.

That camouflage card would come in handy. Somehow, Arthur had to wake Marion.

His **Empathic Resistance** was part of a shield class.

Could that mental shield be expanded and strengthened?

CHAPTER 26

More scourglings were breaking off from the aerial fights with the dragons and flying on a beeline toward the city. They'd be spotted soon.

Those were the ones Arthur could see. There could be others in the brush waiting in ambush he couldn't. If they stayed in place, their luck would soon run out.

Arthur's own mental shield protected him, but . . . what if he could expand it? Extend it around others?

He had no idea if this would work or not, but he had to try.

Arthur concentrated on the mental image of extending that skill outward. To encompass Echo, Marion, and Penn.

This illusion isn't real, he thought fiercely. *It's not real. It's—*

He felt like his skill brushed up against something solid, like a barrier. Arthur couldn't tell if it was a barrier he could break past or not. But maybe—

"All right, fine! But you can't tell my minders about this."

Echo's petulant voice snapped him out of his near trance. Blinking, Arthur focused on her. Then he blinked again, this time in confusion.

In his moment of inattention, she had returned to her usual, childish form. Now she glared up at Arthur with her arms crossed over her chest.

"What are you doing? It's dangerous out here—" he started.

"I told you that Marion has a camouflage card. Duh."

"What? Oh." Arthur stepped back, looking around to make sure the area was still clear. "Anything I can do to help?"

The girl shook her head. Her cheeks were rosy red, as if she had been running straight out. She took three deep breaths like a diver about to plunge underwater. "I hate being Marion," she muttered.

Then her body blurred, growing taller.

Hopefully being Marion meant she kept her own dispel-illusion card. But Arthur figured she knew the pros and cons of her deck and wouldn't appreciate him questioning her.

A moment later, a double of Marion stood beside the real copy. She staggered in place as if struck by a dizzy spell.

Before Arthur could even raise a hand to steady her, she flicked her own arm as if to knock it away. "I'm fine, don't touch me! Ugh, I *hate* this. It's like seeing double of everything—Where?" She twisted around to look sharply to the right.

At the edge of the churned-up field emerged a pack of six scourglings. They had the shape of weasels and flowed over the ground like a living wave.

Arthur backed up a step in alarm, then looked around. Where had he dropped that saber?

"Bring Penn over here," Echo commanded, for once sounding older than her twelve years. Her face still scrunched in distaste, she started making arcane gestures with her hands as if she were weaving something in the air.

Arthur had to fight the urge to watch. This must be an actual spell—not a charm done on command. He didn't know much about complex spell work, as those who had access to those cards weren't hive workers or dragon riders, generally.

Also, Echo's ability to copy card powers was frightening.

All this flashed through his mind as he ran toward Penn, scooping up the fallen saber as he did.

He got another notification that he had picked up the **Saber Proficiency** skill again. So, he had lost it when he let go of the weapon because his Master of Skills and Master of Body Enhancement didn't have the ability to keep it. That was a disappointment.

Reaching Penn, he grabbed his cousin's wrist and pulled him toward Echo and Marion. Penn walked along slowly, utterly passive, like someone in a daze.

Arthur held mixed feelings toward his cousin, but he hoped he hadn't been trapped in the falling illusion all this time.

Echo and Marion were starting to fade from view by the time he reached them. As he stepped close, a tingling sensation washed over him, as if he had stepped under a waterfall. It was over a moment later, and the two royals became easy to see.

Echo finished her arcane gestures. A sheen of sweat covered her forehead. "It's done."

"What—"

"Look for yourself," she said impatiently, gesturing to the other side of the field.

The scourge-weasels had split into two groups and flowed around them like they were a boulder stuck out of a river. They converged back into one group after they passed. All this was done without hesitation, as if the scourglings hadn't realized what they'd done.

"I'll be fine," Echo said. "But you should catch me." Then her legs gave out from under her.

Arthur barely caught her in time—Marion's body was heavier than he looked—and eased her to the ground. "What's wr—"

"It's too much. I can't deactivate his time card, and I have mine working to echo him, and this camouflage card . . ." She drew up her knees, head hanging down as if she was nauseous. "I can't keep it up."

"Is it your mana?"

She shook her head. "It's just too much at once here." She tapped her heart, indicating her heart deck. "You have to do something."

He waited a beat, fully expecting her to preemptively interrupt him as she was seeing the future. "Do what?"

"I don't know! Something!" she snapped.

The best, quickest solution would be to break Marion and Penn out of the illusion.

Arthur pulled back his hand and punched Penn in the jaw.

Penn's head snapped to the side. Arthur, meanwhile, felt like he had just hit a brick wall.

He hissed and shook out his hand, looking from his cousin, who remained oblivious, to Echo who, still sitting with her face against her bent knees, was shaking with laughter.

With Marion's time card, she would have known that wouldn't work.

"Why did you let me do—"

"Because it was funny!"

"Well, it didn't break him out of the illusion." Arthur sighed. "I have something else I can try."

Once again, he reached for his **Mental Resistance** and imagined that shield extending outward. It was easier this time. And again, he encountered that barrier.

He gritted his teeth and pushed past it.

New skill gained: Mental Resistance (Area of Effect)
Due to your card's bonus traits, you automatically start this skill at level 3.

Then he saw a message he'd never seen before:

Warning: The use of this skill requires mana.

It felt as if something was being ripped from him. Something he could ill afford to lose.

Arthur collapsed, barely aware he was clutching at his own chest. He caught a flash of Marion and Penn blinking rapidly, coming awake before Arthur's own vision dimmed.

Funny. He'd thought that tunnel vision was just a saying until now.

Despite everything, he kept a hold on the skill. The moment he let it go, Marion and Penn would be vulnerable to the illusion again.

He heard voices over his head, distant words Arthur couldn't understand.

Someone slapped him upside the head and pressed another bottle to his lips.

More healing?

He drank eagerly. The liquid tasted of sunshine, like pure energy.

His sight returned in a flash, and that terrible sense of something vital being sucked away . . . stopped. It simply stopped.

His heart deck bloomed in his vision. There was a new icon: an image of a radiant sun with a swirl in its center.

Temporary Mana Boost
100/100

Then, a moment later:
99/100
98/100

Arthur blinked the image away and looked up to see Penn tucking the half-drunken bottle away in his pack.

"Hasn't anyone told you not to use a charmed card when your mana's not unlocked?" Penn asked, lips curling grimly. "It'll start eating into your life force."

"I . . . er . . . thanks." Arthur's head pounded, and his thoughts spun. He wasn't about to tell Penn the truth—it wasn't a card, but a skill. He had just developed a skill on his own . . . and one that was still incompatible with his other cards.

How was that possible?

Marion stood by Echo, who still wore his form and didn't look much better than Arthur had.

The fact he and Penn weren't demanding to know what was going on told Arthur he'd been out for some minutes.

"I can put up another camouflage spell," Marion said, "but not until Echo drops hers, and it will take a minute or two."

"Meaning we'll be visible to every scourgling that's looking to eat a card," Penn said grimly. "And we still need to harvest those bodies I see you two managed to kill."

"My mana boost is draining fast," Arthur warned. He was already at 78/100.

"Stop using that card," Marion said. Arthur started to speak, but he waved him off. "You're going to say Penn and I will get trapped again. But I think we'll only get lost in the fog. Something as strong as a falling illusion is usually tied to a trap card. And thanks to you, we've broken out."

Arthur nodded. He didn't have much of a choice. His mana boost was fading quickly.

"All right," Penn said. He absently touched the side of his jaw with a finger as if trying to figure out why it hurt. "On my mark, Echo drops the camouflage and returns to her battle form."

"That'll take a few seconds," Echo said. "I have to return to my body first."

He nodded. "Until then, Arthur's and my job will be to keep the scourglings off you two." He paused, looked at his belt, and then at Arthur. "Why do you have my saber?"

Sheepishly, Arthur stood and handed it back. He checked his list of skills and mentally sighed when he found the **Saber** skill still listed, but dead and gray. Inaccessible.

So he grabbed one of his old reliable butcher knives from his Personal Space. It had never felt so natural in his hands.

"I'm ready."

Penn nodded to Echo. "Drop the camouflage."

CHAPTER 27

It was clear the scourge-weasels could sense the presence of humans nearby. Thanks to Echo's arcane camouflage spell, they couldn't pinpoint them. More small packs had joined the others. Together, they ranged across the mud-churned field.

With a relieved breath, Echo dropped her hold on the camouflage spell.

As one, the scourge-weasels looked their way. Some stood up on hind legs, long teeth clacking.

Penn placed himself between the royals and the bulk of the weasels. Arthur took the other side.

Echo started to shrink back to her regular form. By her side, Marion started his own arcane gestures to replace the camouflage spell. However, that would take some time.

With a butchering cleaver in hand, Arthur faced the oncoming scourglings, for once brimming with confidence. Thanks to the competency boost, his **Knife Work** skill had gone from level 35 to 45.

It was easier than ever to imagine the disgusting, half-rotted scourglings as pieces of real meat to be butchered.

His cleaver slashed down on the first weasel to reach him, effortlessly parting skin from flesh in a perfect fillet. The next strike took the head off the weasel. After all, butchering meant dispatching the animal.

The pack of scourge-weasels coming at him hadn't had time to group up, so he was able to take them on as they leaped one at a time.

He killed three in a handful of seconds. The fourth was a hair too quick for him and bit down at his pants leg. Its teeth caught mostly fabric, and Arthur sliced down at it before he kicked it away.

He caught a glimpse of Echo out of the corner of his eye. She'd returned to her original form, though she looked pale with dark circles under her eyes. Changing from one form to another was obviously taxing.

The girl wasn't letting that stop her. She was sprouting a beard even as Arthur turned back.

He took on another weasel before two more jumped at him at once. Arthur threw his forearm up to block, chopping down on one and preparing himself to take the hit from the other. Hopefully it wouldn't injure him as bad as last time . . .

A gleaming silver arrow struck the attacking weasel, pinning it to the ground.

Arthur finished his chop on the second weasel and turned to see Echo was fully returned to her battle form. She held a delicate bow and arrow in her giant hands. Gleaming silver, it was decorated with pink flowers up the bow's length and looked utterly ridiculous with her battle body. But he couldn't complain about the results.

"Almost done," Marion said. "Gather close to me."

His hands had not stopped flashing the arcane signs for a moment.

Arthur glanced at Penn. His ego popped like an overfilled bladder as he saw the small mound of scourge-weasels in front of him.

Arthur had only battled off scraps of the attack—the bulk of the scourglings had attacked Penn. All were dead, and Penn didn't even look winded.

He needed a combat card. A good one.

He could have had one had he been willing to ignore his morals.

The fight had gone faster than he'd expected. Still, Arthur checked his heart-deck dashboard and was surprised to see he had less than ten mana points left.

"Almost out of mana," he warned.

This was the test. Once his area-of-effect shield ended, would Marion and Penn drop back into the falling illusion?

Everyone clustered around Marion, who was finishing up the last of his spell.

Arthur counted his mana down. "Three . . . two . . . one . . ." He let go of his hold on the skill.

Marion's fingers faltered, but he continued on doggedly. Penn sucked in a breath, then let it out again.

"Well, I'm not falling. But the fog's back. I can't see a thing."

"And now, neither can they," Marion said, finally dropping his hands.

As he did, Arthur again felt magical power rush over him. Like a flash of a rainstorm falling over his head and shoulders before rolling on.

"I can still see," Echo said smugly.

Dropping the area-of-effect portion hadn't disrupted Arthur's own internal **Mental Resistance** shields. The land looked clear to him as well.

"How long can you keep this camouflage spell up?" Penn asked Marion.

"An hour or two before I have to take a mana potion. Most of the power is used in the casting." Marion glanced at Echo. "It's easier when you're not running three cards at once."

Echo flashed him a hand sign no twelve-year-old princess should know.

Penn turned his frown to the rest of the field. "Since Marion and I can't see, we're going to depend on you two to keep watch. One of you should go harvest from our fights before someone else does."

"I thought proving ourselves with loot was a subliminal suggestion?" Marion asked.

Arthur shrugged. "Collecting what we can is still a good idea. I'll do it."

No one had objections—it was either him or Echo, and anyone with eyes could see the girl needed a break.

Arthur exited the camouflage zone, paused to pile up a couple sticks to mark the spot or else he wouldn't find his way back, then quickly went about harvesting from the myriad scourglings.

All had card shards from Common to Uncommon. But there were several corner pieces. If someone else had some corners, they might have enough to make a new card.

He found the sticks and stepped back into the camouflaged zone.

Penn and Echo immediately demanded to see the loot. Marion, however, was frowning and glancing at the card-anchor tattoo on his wrist.

He must have realized one of his cards was missing. It wouldn't have been immediately obvious as if one had been removed from his heart, but all he had to do was check his anchor inventory.

Arthur struggled with himself for a moment. Should he keep the card? Admit to the theft? He'd done it out of need, but that might raise Penn's suspicions even more.

He should have known better. Marion was a few seconds ahead of everyone else. Before Arthur could do more than consider the question, Marion looked at the way Arthur gripped the knife.

He shot him a very significant look. "You and I are talking later."

Echo glanced up from where she was counting a small pile of shards. "About what?"

Neither replied. Marion held Arthur's gaze until he nodded. He could only be grateful Marion wasn't throwing a fit right now.

Knowing nobles, it meant Marion wanted something.

"Kane, you didn't see any other active scourglings out there, did you?" Penn asked.

"They're everywhere," Arthur said. "We're still at the edge of the eruption, but none close in the field. Why?"

Penn frowned and turned to stare off in the distance. "I have a Common danger-sense card. It's screaming at me."

Instantly, everyone was on full alert.

"Can you tell where it's coming from?" Arthur asked.

"No, it's only a Common. The best it can do is tell me there's danger nearby. Not where or from whom."

"There are scourglings everywhere," Echo said. "It's probably alerting you to that."

"No, it's more . . . distinct. It's something else." He shook his head, frustrated.

Arthur caught movement toward the distant tree line. And by movement, it was two trees parting as something larger than a horse blasted through.

It was another scourge-weasel. A massive one. And it was heading directly their way.

Echo saw it too. She would have to have been blind not to. With a gasp, her silver-and-pink flower bow appeared in her hands, an arrow on the string.

"Don't shoot," Arthur said. "That might show it exactly where we are." He turned to Marion, about to ask a question. Of course, the prince preempted him.

"The camouflage spell is strong but inflexible. Something powerful enough might be able to see through it."

"What is it?" Penn peered in the direction they were looking, but to him it would have been a wall of fog. "What's out there?"

"The scourge-weasels' mother," Arthur muttered.

Penn's eyes lit. "If it's strong enough, it'll have a card. Maybe two."

"That is not a good thing," Arthur snapped. "If it has cards, it can use those cards—"

Abruptly, the mother weasel stopped a hundred yards away. It lifted to its hind legs, belly marred by patches of rot, and then slammed back down to all fours again.

A blast of wind hit them like a focused hurricane. Arthur lost his footing and was blown like a leaf in the wind. They all were scattered in every direction.

He felt something indefinite shatter and suspected it was the camouflage spell.

They might have been well hidden, but it didn't matter if they could be knocked out of their hiding place.

The blast of wind was mercifully short. Arthur scrambled up to his knees, fingers still around his butcher's cleaver.

The mother weasel was headed straight for Marion.

CHAPTER 28

Once again, Arthur was torn by a choice.

Marion knew, or at least strongly suspected, Arthur had stolen his card. And it was a very good card.

He didn't have to stand back. He just had to be a few steps too slow.

But then the mother weasel would have access to a Legendary time card.

More importantly, Arthur thought Marion could be a good friend if he let him get close. Cressida was great, but he missed having a guy friend, and he thought Marion could be that . . . if he didn't blow up at Arthur for stealing his card.

Plus, Arthur wasn't going to sit back and allow someone to die on his watch. He'd already made that choice when he saved Penn.

But even with all of Arthur's good intentions, he had no hope of taking on the mother weasel by himself.

All of this flashed in his mind in a moment. It felt like he was standing still, like he had accessed the frozen time in his Personal Space. But it was only adrenaline.

Marion suddenly jerked around to face the oncoming scourgling, even though he had no hope of seeing it through the illusionary fog.

Arthur knew what he had to do.

"Marion, it's coming at you from the left!" he yelled, knowing Marion had already heard his voice in the future. He was already acting before Arthur finished speaking.

Then Arthur pelted to Penn, who had picked himself up and was looking frantically around in all directions with his hand on his sword. Arthur was the only one who could see through the fog. He would have to guide him.

Even as he raced to Penn, he saw he would be too slow.

The mother weasel had barreled forward and was only a few strides away. It opened its jaws in anticipation, teeth sticking out at all angles from its muzzle like a hedgehog's quills. These weren't jaws for chewing and swallowing. The scourglings weren't real animals—they killed, and they "ate" cards.

Marion stepped to the side, unprompted. The scourgling barreled past several steps before it turned to whip around. Marion followed its movements to keep behind its flank. The scourgling twisted, and he did as well, moving along with it as if they were part of the same choreographed dance.

As if he could see what the scourgling was about to do a moment before it did it.

Seeing the future bought Marion time to dodge the creature, but it was a stalling tactic at best. Arthur had taken his combat card.

Arthur reached Penn, who visibly startled at his "appearance."

"Come on." Forgoing all dignity, Arthur grabbed Penn's free hand and dragged his cousin behind him. He wasn't going to risk Penn getting lost in the fog. "Follow me. It's after Marion."

"Where's Echo? Doesn't she have a bow?" Penn demanded but followed Arthur. In fact, if not for Arthur's **Running** enhancement boost, Penn's longer legs would have allowed him to overtake him.

"She hasn't gotten up. I think she was knocked out." At least, he hoped that was only it. Everyone had tumbled end over end in that blast of wind. It was possible she hit her head on something.

Speaking of wind, the mother weasel had quickly become frustrated with Marion's antics. It aimed a blast of wind in Marion's direction, but the prince leaped away out of the direct cone of destruction.

The wind blast seemed to be a range-focused spell. It missed Marion completely and was angled wrong to threaten Arthur and Penn, but it was enough to knock over three trees standing at the edge of the field. It must have gotten stronger the farther it was cast.

As the trees toppled over, Arthur spared a glance up to the sky. Surely some dragons or their riders had seen that?

The skies directly above were completely empty. Not a dragon wing or a claw to be seen. No aerial scourglings either, but considering they were in the middle of an eruption, it was eerie.

He didn't have time to think about it. Arthur and Penn were nearly at the battle.

He knew the moment they were close enough for Penn to see through the fog because he sped up, overtaking Arthur's stride. With a kick off the ground, he jumped higher than Arthur would have thought possible—was that a combat skill, or was the man that athletic?—and brought his sword down to slice deep across the scourgling's haunch.

The scourgling whistled a sound that made Arthur's ears want to bleed. It whipped around to face the new threat, swiping a claw.

Penn flicked his blade. Sparks flew as the sword met claws, and the scourgling's paw was knocked aside. Penn followed it up with a kick to its face, which forced it back a step.

Arthur stepped to Marion, who had bent to rest his hands on his knees.

"That was close," Marion said. "Another few seconds and . . ."

"It's not over yet," Arthur said grimly.

Marion waved toward the battle. "Really?"

Penn was standing on top of the scourgling, somehow maintaining his balance and stabbing down while the creature flung itself back and forth to try to shake him off. And since it had modeled itself after a weasel, it was extremely flexible.

In desperation, it threw its head back and tried to wind-blast Penn off. Penn slashed a quick backhand swipe at it, nearly taking off the end of its nose. The blast went wild.

"You might have a point," Arthur conceded.

Marion frowned. "Where's my sis— Oh. Never mind."

A moment later, a silver arrow erupted out of the scourgling's eye and out the other side. It dropped like a stone, finally pitching Penn off.

Echo stood not far away with her bow raised, looking dirty and bloody. She had clearly gotten the worst of the first wind blast.

"Hey!" Penn complained. "I had it. I didn't need help."

"That thing made me get blood in my beard!" The girl stomped over and kicked the dead scourgling. One of her eyes was half shut, caked with blood that tricked down.

"What does it matter?" Marion asked. "It'll heal once you return to your body."

"I don't have the mana to switch back and forth again. That means I have to stay like this, all gross!" She kicked the body again, rather viciously.

Penn rolled his eyes but returned to business. "Kane, do you see anything else about to come at us?"

"No. Nothing." Arthur frowned. "Nothing in the skies, either. I don't see any dragon riders nearby."

There were some in the distance, clustered around the still-erupting cone. But . . . not as many as he would have expected.

He looked at the others, who frowned or shrugged back at him.

Penn bent to harvest from the dead scourgling. He stood up, grinning. "Two cards."

"Ohhh." Echo clapped her hands in delight. "Are they good?"

"Decent. They're Uncommon. One is a plant-growth power—I bet it got that from a farmer," Penn said without a trace of sympathy. "Second is that ranged wind attack." He frowned, and then to Arthur's complete shock, extended the card out to him. "You ought to have it."

"Me? Why?"

Was this some sort of a trick?

Echo seemed to have the same thought. "Why him? I thought we were keeping the loot to show we're a good team."

"He's the only one without a strong offensive card. Plus," Penn added, "it unlocks mana."

Marion didn't say anything but watched the byplay with narrowed eyes.

He thinks this is suspicious too, Arthur thought but reached to take the card anyway.

Wind Release

Uncommon

Charm

The wielder of this card will be able to direct a powerful blast of wind at will. Blast strength is dependent on heart-deck mana usage. This card unlocks mana only when added to the wielder's heart deck.

Ah, there was the catch.

"I'd have to add this to my heart deck," Arthur said.

Penn shrugged. "An Uncommon or two shouldn't be a problem. It's not a bad power." He paused. "You have *plenty* of room in your heart deck, right?"

Like Arthur was going to rise to the bait that easily. "That's not the point."

"You should think carefully before adding anything to your heart," Marion said. "But that's not a bad card to have up your sleeve."

Arthur frowned down at the card, wondering if he was being stupid. He did need a good combat card. Yes, this was unlike any of his others, but that didn't mean it was a bad thing. Did he really expect the Legendary dragon hatchling to be impressed by a budding utility specialist?

Especially when there was someone like Penn who could effortlessly win every fight?

After a moment of consideration, Arthur placed the Wind Release card in his card anchor instead of his heart deck.

"That's not going to do you any good," Echo said, and for good measure added, "Dummy."

"Uh, it needs to go in your heart to unlock the mana," Marion added, slightly kinder.

"Not unless you want that spell to eat away at your life force every time you use it," Penn added, smirking.

Arthur looked at him. "What does that mean, exactly? My life force?"

"What?" Echo asked. "It's your life. Duh."

Arthur forcefully reminded himself that she was a twelve-year-old girl, and a princess. It was not appropriate to snap back at her.

"If I do this—"

"Aim toward the bushes!" Marion yelped, seeing what Arthur was about to do.

Arthur held out his palm away from the others, toward the bushes, and concentrated a small amount onto his palm.

At least, he thought it was a small amount.

It felt like the air was punched out of him. At the same time, something invisible yet indefinable shot out of his palm. A bush a half dozen yards away bent over sideways before springing back, minus a few loose leaves.

Penn and Marion both yelled, voices overlapping with one another.

Marion wanted him to be careful of damaging the bounds of the arcane spell. Penn just called him an idiot.

Shaking his hand out, Arthur ignored them. He felt out of breath, like he had just run up three flights of stairs. A cold sensation on his forehead and his pits told him he had worked up an instant sweat, too.

Other than that, he wasn't worse for wear.

"So?" His voice had a bit of a pant to it as he turned back to the others. "Did that just shorten my overall life by a few minutes?"

Penn slapped him upside the head. "How are you this dumb?"

"No . . . I think he has a point." Marion frowned at Arthur. "I've never thought about it before. Is life force a single well someone can draw from, or is it temporary and renewable?"

"Why does it matter?" Echo asked. "Everyone *important* has a card to unlock mana so you don't have to worry about that." She wrinkled her nose at Arthur. "What kind of a household lets their scions leave their estates without one?"

Penn answered that for her. "Kane's from a small border barony. Gets most of his wealth off the backs of condemned families. It's a miracle they could even afford one Legendary card, much less two."

"Two?" Marion asked.

Arthur froze, then he understood what Penn was talking about. "My family had an incident some years back—bandits stole a Legendary card from my father. Trust me, the one I have now came at a price." He darkened his voice and hoped no one would ask further.

"Oh, you're *that* Kane . . . uh, ahem." Marion hastily cleared his throat and then shook his head. "In any case, how do you feel now?"

Arthur paused a second to check himself. "Fine."

"I suspect using that card is a temporary draw from your vitality, rather than you . . . uh . . . borrowing time from your future," Marion said. "But best not to push it."

"Or you can just stick it in your heart," Penn said. "What's the problem?"

"It doesn't fit with any of my other cards," Arthur said. "I can use it as a temporary surprise. Then when I get to the hive, I can trade it for something better." A real mana card, or better yet, a combat card.

"When are we going back?" Echo asked.

Arthur looked to the sky. The only dragons in sight were small, far-off silhouettes flying around the other side of the eruption point.

Weren't there usually hundreds in the sky during an eruption? Then again, he wasn't seeing new scourglings thrown from the top of the cone. Perhaps the excitement was dying down and the remaining dragons were flying low on mop-up duty.

But that didn't feel right.

Where were the rips in the sky? He looked up and realized for the first time that they, and the high-shimmer dragons who manned them, were gone.

"Where are the dragons?" he asked, interrupting Penn and Marion, who were batting back and forth the idea of returning to the city or not.

Everyone looked at him, and he pointed upward. "Right, I forgot you guys only see the fog. The hives have stopped bringing dragons in. No, wait . . ." He turned and peered back to the cone.

The dragons he thought were darting around the sharp top of the cone had even smaller silhouettes to his eye.

They were flying away. Directly away.

"They're fleeing," Arthur said. "They've all gone."

"No, that can't be right. If the dragons were gone, we'd be drowning in scourglings," Penn said.

"Uh, we just fought a whole bunch of them a few minutes ago," Echo said.

Arthur shook his head. "Those were just the dregs of what's left. I've seen more at one time before, at a different eruption. I thought they were just the ones that escaped the dragons, but . . . there's more. The eruption has stopped."

Penn stared toward the direction of the cone, one hand clutching his sword hilt. "When does a scourge-eruption just . . . stop? They aren't supposed to do that, are they?"

Everyone looked to Arthur, who shrugged. "I didn't stick around for the last one."

Echo spoke up. "What if the scourglings are hiding?"

Penn huffed a dismissive laugh, and Arthur half smiled. That smile faded as he thought more about it. Marion looked disturbed, too.

"Something's wrong," Arthur said.

"We knew that already, Kane," Penn snapped.

"I mean really, really wrong."

"Yes," he growled. "The only thing half of us can see is fog, and either you're under some new delusion or the dragons have left us. Something is wrong, but whining about it isn't going to help!"

Arthur opened his mouth to object he wasn't whining.

Echo interrupted him by striding over and touching Marion's arm. "Could you . . . ?"

Marion rubbed his mouth. "I don't know if it's a good idea. I'll be useless afterward."

"What are you two talking about?" Penn demanded.

Marion and Echo exchanged a glance that seemed to contain an entire conversation. They might only be half siblings, and possibly rivals to the throne, but they were close.

Finally, Marion sighed. "I have a card that might be useful."

He paused.

Everyone stared at him.

"And?" Penn demanded.

"It . . . enhances other cards to the power of five," Marion said. "It's a once-a-day Rare, but I'll be dead on my feet afterward. The headache is abominable," he added. "You might have to literally carry me."

"I can do that, with your permission," Arthur said. "It's a storage power. But what is the point . . ." He trailed off. "You are going to use it on your Legendary, right? You've said you see three seconds ahead . . . Marion, is that exact?" There was no reason to give out frank details about their cards to competitors. Arthur certainly hadn't been honest about his cards.

Marion smiled, though it came out a little sickly looking. "I always knew you were smart. It's true. I can see about five seconds ahead."

Echo yelped. "You cheat! You've always told me it was three when we play games . . ."

Arthur ignored her. "Five to the power of five . . ." He bent, grabbed a stick, and started working the math. "Five times five, times five, times five, times five . . . that's 3,125 seconds. Divide by 60 . . . About 52 minutes ahead. Roughly. Wow." He looked at Marion. "You can see a little under an hour ahead if you use this?"

Only then did he realize everyone was staring at him. "What?"

"Tell me you have a math card," Echo muttered.

He had an **Arithmetic** skill. One that didn't even level for that easy work. "I like math," Arthur said defensively.

Marion snorted. "Yeah, you're right. It'll give me an hour to look ahead. But I can't promise I'll see anything interesting. We might just be standing here for the next hour under this camouflage charm. And . . . the further away I move from the future, the less stable it is."

"What do you mean?" Arthur asked.

"The future splits every time there's a choice," Marion said. "Most of the time, what I see is accurate. I'm only a few seconds ahead, so when there's a split, I pick the most likely choice. But I can be wrong. An hour ahead? That's a lot of choices." He shrugged. "The future isn't set in stone."

"Huh." Arthur eyed him. "Normally, I'd say that's a good thing. I don't like the idea of a future set in stone—"

Penn made a chopping gesture between them as if to physically cut the conversation. "You two can talk about time philosophy later. Marion, use the card. Anything is better than sitting here navel gazing. Kane will take care of you if you faint afterward."

"Who made you leader?" Echo demanded.

Penn glared at the girl. "Anyone have a better idea?"

They looked at each other, but no one offered up anything. Arthur didn't appreciate Penn's high-handedness, but he didn't disagree.

He also didn't want to order Marion around. It was his card in his deck. He should be the one to know when to use it.

"Fine." Marion took a deep breath, then another, closing his eyes.

Arthur half expected . . . something. More arcane gestures, glittering lights, or for Marion to whip a card dramatically out of his anchor tattoo and yell out its power . . .

But since both cards were apparently in his heart deck, Marion could access them with a thought.

So he stood there, and the only indication something was happening was that his eyes tracked back and forth under his lids.

"Oh shit," Marion said, shocking them. "Oh SHIT." He threw his arm up as if to stop something.

"What?" Penn demanded. "What is it?"

"Bad split. But I don't think it's likely. Let me try. Oh . . . GAH!"

His eyes flew open. He seemed to stare at them and past them at the same time. "We need to run. We need to go. Now! And don't listen to it!" He slapped his hands over his ears. "Lalalalala!"

"He's gone mad," Penn breathed.

But Arthur had a very bad feeling about this.

Barlow and his cooks had kept the mind-singer from their minds by doing something very similar.

"He's not mad, he's still in the future." Echo stepped up to her brother. "Marion! Marion, come back!" She shook him, which had quite the effect considering she was still in her fighting form.

Marion stopped. "That was a bad split . . ."

"Are there any more?" Arthur asked anxiously. "Do you see batlike scourglings?"

Marion didn't answer. "The third . . . but it's brightening by the second." His skin looked paler by the second. Arthur couldn't tell if it was fear or usage of the card catching up to him. "It's my father, the king. If he comes . . . he'll raze this whole place to the ground."

CHAPTER 29

Arthur's stomach felt like it turned to ice. "Why would he do that?" he said, but his words were lost over Penn and Echo's exclamations of horror.

"The king?"

"He's coming?" Echo's face paled. "No . . . no, he wouldn't. Not for this!"

Penn turned to her. "What do you mean?"

Arthur was just glad that Penn seemed out of the loop for once, and it wasn't just him.

Marion didn't answer. His eyes were still unfocused—still nearly an hour into the future. Hopefully, he was seeing some better ones.

Echo looked around. "It . . . it's not that bad. He wouldn't come for this little city. It's not lost!"

"Lost?" Arthur repeated. He and Penn exchanged a look and a mutual shrug. Neither one knew exactly what she was talking about.

"Yes, lost," Echo snapped. She backed a step away from Marion and wrung her hands anxiously. She looked far more upset now than she had during battle. "It's the king's duty—his onus and responsibility—to raze the land when it's fallen to the scourge. To keep it from spreading and taking over the kingdom like a living rot." Her words were monotone, like she was repeating something learned in a lesson.

That ice in Arthur's stomach extended into his veins. Again, he and Penn exchanged a look. Penn didn't look as surprised—he'd clearly heard of this before—but he did seem confused.

"This land hasn't been overrun. We're sitting in the middle of a field." He turned to Arthur. "Can you see the city walls? They haven't been breached, have they?"

"I would have mentioned it." Arthur could see walls in distant flashes between the trees. They looked whole.

Marion gasped like a man surfacing from underwater. His eyes were wild, white around the edges, but focused on them. "The king's coming," he said hoarsely, "but only if the white dragons fail . . ."

The white dragons. Then they *were* dealing with mind-mages.

Several separate puzzle pieces clicked in Arthur's head. He reached out and caught Marion as the prince's knees began to buckle under him.

"Let me store you."

Marion gasped an affirmative.

With a thought, Arthur stored him in his Personal Space. Then, mentally, Arthur followed.

He wasn't exactly sure what he would find—would he be able to talk to Marion? After all, Arthur had practiced his skills without a problem.

Time seemed to be a wishy-washy concept inside his Personal Space.

Marion was there, utterly frozen in the same half-crumpled position he'd been in moments ago, outside. He didn't move. He didn't blink. He only existed.

It was eerie, and Arthur edged to the side to be out of his line of sight.

Then he reached for what he'd been meaning to grab—several metal cooking pans and spoons.

Incidentally, he received notifications of a **Spoon Proficiency** skill from Marion's card. What a shame he didn't have time to discover what that meant.

He returned less than an eye blink later to Echo's and Penn's verbal shock at seeing Marion disappear in front of their eyes.

"He's in my storage," Arthur reminded them. "And if you don't want to hide out there, too, I suggest you take these." He shoved the pots and spoons at them.

Echo took a set out of reflex, but Penn didn't move. "Have you lost your mind—"

"Just before the call for the Legendary egg was announced, Wolf Moon Hive had a scourge-infection break out." Arthur spoke quickly, half his attention to the sky. If he was right—and he feared he was—they were on borrowed time. "The local scholar's guild let some of the Rare cards go rotten. Scourglings grew like mold, but when they broke out, they weren't using knowledge or even meta powers. They used mind magic. Some of the people involved mentioned mind-singing."

"What does that mean?" Echo demanded.

"How do you know this?" Penn asked.

Arthur decided to answer Echo. "I think the scholar's guild was studying mind cards. I don't know why or how they could have let one rot. It doesn't matter—" Though he suspected it very much did. Just not at that moment. "The point is the hive wasn't able to find and kill the scourglings. They reportedly got away. But . . . what if they didn't?"

"Kane . . ." Penn looked at him like he very much hoped Arthur had a screw loose.

Arthur plowed on. "We all agree we were sent out here on false pretenses. An idea that we needed to prove ourselves forced into our heads. Then there were the illusions that we only broke out of due to luck."

"You're not saying one of our number is actually a scourgling," Penn said.

"No, the hive leaders would have sniffed that out. The scholars' cards were only Rares." At least, he hoped. If they were Legendaries, they were doomed. "I think it's more likely someone's working with implanted commands. Or the scourglings followed us all through the rips in the sky. The dragons have fled." He pointed up. "Even this eruption has gone dormant. They're lying quiet. And now the king might be coming to raze the whole area." He fixed Penn with a look. "You tell me why."

Penn's jaw tightened, and he looked like he very much wanted to argue but couldn't find the words.

"What do we do?" Echo asked quietly. Somewhere in Arthur's monologue, she had reverted back to her usual form. Now she held the pot and spoon in limp arms and looked very tiny and very scared.

Arthur took a breath. "The way I see it, we have two options. The people who survived the attack in the scholar's guild . . . well, it's silly, but they banged pots and pans together. They made so much racket that they couldn't hear the mind-singer."

"That actually worked?" Penn still sounded skeptical, but not like Arthur was crazy.

He shrugged. "Or they got lucky, or they didn't have the cards the mind-singer wanted . . . They were cooks and serving staff."

Penn looked like he wanted to ask Arthur how he knew so much.

Echo said, "What's your other idea?" while looking at the pot and spoon doubtfully.

Arthur took a breath. This was a risk and a test of bravery on both sides.

"I'll store you in my Personal Space, and I'll make my way out. I have some resistance to mental attacks, but if things go wrong, I have a trap card that's set to return me to the hive."

Penn's eyebrows went up. "How come you haven't used it already? Things have gotten pretty dire."

Arthur stared at him. Wasn't it obvious?

"Because that's as good as giving up. I'm here for that dragon egg, and I won't show I'm worthy of it by running away."

"Why can't we all go away now?" Echo asked, sounding every year of her age.

"Because the trap card only works for one person. You'd have to be in my Personal Space and . . . well . . . I might be wrong." He shrugged and resisted the urge to rub the back of his neck. "This is all a guess, and I hope I'm wrong, because if I'm right . . ."

"What if you *are* wrong?" Penn asked. "Or this is a plot to disappear us in your storage space?"

Arthur couldn't blame him for his paranoia. He held out his hands. "If you don't believe me, you have the pot and spoon."

"Yeah." Penn jutted out his chin aggressively. "So we make enough noise to attract every damn scourgling within a mile! Marion's camouflage spell isn't going to last long now that he's stored—"

Echo screamed. Arthur and Penn turned to see her pointing up.

There was a new rip in the sky followed in short order by another and another.

White dragons poured out: the type never seen in public, as they were marked as too dangerous.

Arthur was right about one thing. And if Marion's visions were correct . . . the king would follow.

He turned to the others. "It's your choice. If you have a better idea, I'm listening."

"I . . . I don't know," Echo said weakly.

By now Penn's jaw was clenched so tightly he looked like he was ready to break a molar.

"What happens to us if we're in your Personal Space and you're killed?"

"I don't know," Arthur admitted. "I guess that's up to whoever harvests my card next."

"You can't fight, and putting your Wind Release in your card anchor is an awful idea," Penn said. Then, to Arthur's flat shock, he reached for his own chest.

Was . . . was he about to give him a card out of his heart deck? *The* card? A brother to Arthur's own?

Instead, Penn pulled out a fine leather bag from a pocket tucked under his shirt. It had a card-anchor mark. From that, he pulled out a card.

"I expect this back, Kane."

Arthur took it.

Steel Fists

Rare

Combat

The wielder of this card will have unbreakable skin and bone from the tips of their fingers to elbow joints. Any strikes using a closed fist will deliver injury compatible with twice the wielder's base strength.

Arthur almost wanted to ask "Are you sure?" but he didn't want to give Penn the chance to take it back.

So he moved to stick it in his card anchor.

Quick as a striking snake, Penn caught his wrist before he could complete the movement.

Their eyes locked. Penn's gaze was hard.

"Tell me you're not crossing us."

"If I were," Arthur said evenly, not looking away, not even daring to blink, "I wouldn't have told you about my escape card."

Penn held him there for another moment, clearly at war with himself. Then he nodded once and released Arthur's wrist.

Arthur added the Steel Fists card to his temporary card-anchor deck.

At once, his hands felt . . . different. Like he was wearing invisible gloves that coated his skin up to his elbows. Yet when he rubbed the tips of his fingers together, there was no loss of sensation. That must be the card's mana protecting him.

Above, one of the white dragons roared out a command to the others. They turned on a wing, falling into an arrow formation.

An indefinable something passed over Arthur's mind like the brush of winter wind. It left him with the feeling of being searched and found . . . not good enough.

Penn shuddered, and Echo let out a squeaky breath of surprise. The princess stepped forward, holding out a dipped hand to Arthur.

"You have my permission to . . . to store me. And be assured, if I am saved, the Kane barony will be rewarded."

That was not the incentive she thought it was.

Nevertheless, Arthur took her hand, and she vanished into his Personal Space.

Penn grumbled "I can't believe I'm doing this," under his breath but held out his hand as if to shake with Arthur.

A moment later, he, too, was stored.

Arthur took a deep breath and turned in place so that he faced directly west to the setting sun—the direction between the town walls and the distant eruption cone.

Then he ran.

After his **Running** enhancement skill hit level 10, he had received a 5% bonus to all stamina and a 10% speed bonus to the first fifteen seconds of a sprint.

His feet dug into the soil, and the wind rushed past his face as he ran flat out.

The skill was at level 12, and since he was fleeing for all he was worth to put distance between himself and the scourge-eruption, he wanted to level it as much as possible.

He'd leap over anything, climb a tree, balance on the edge of a rock—anything he could do to level up his skills, because if this mess had taught him one thing, it was that he needed to get stronger.

Arthur knew he was taking a risk, but not a dire one. He kept a firm mental hand on his Nullify card, ready to deactivate it the moment he met something he couldn't handle.

Then the next magical attack, whatever it was, would send him back home to the hive.

He'd have to explain how he returned there, but he doubted many of the noble scions stayed within the town once the dragons started leaving. Likely, they'd bribed their way out too.

Arthur kept to the flat fields, which both allowed him to avoid obstacles and kept him at a decent speed. His **Running** skill hit 13 in short order. With it came an extra boost of stamina. It was as if he had just come off a twenty-minute breather and drank from a refreshing waterskin at the same time.

His **Running** skill wasn't the only thing getting a workout.

Skill level gained: Mental Resistance (Area of Effect)
Level 4

It seemed he got the area-of-effect bonus even when he was just protecting himself. Still . . . why?

He slowed and looked around. The field he'd been running through was bare, with churned mud and the remains of sprouts all stomped down from fleeing people and scourglings.

It was incredibly ordinary. But it would be impenetrable to someone still lost in the fog.

Had he run through another illusionary trap? One minor enough he hadn't even noticed?

Arthur closed his eyes and looked inward, trying to see if he sensed anything out of the ordinary.

It was a little like waking up and hearing the songs of chirping robins—a sound he'd only been dimly aware of while asleep.

There was a feeling in the air. A suggestion to turn and walk to the north end of the field, which was closer to the scourge-eruption. The farmers had diverted a small stream there, and the area around it was thick with vegetation.

Arthur started following the suggested path. Not because he was caught up in its net, but because he wanted to see where it led.

It turned out he was not the first to stumble across the trap.

A team of four people lay unmoving by the canal's edge, their bodies hidden from easy view by tall grass.

Arthur vaguely recognized them as hopefuls for the Legendary egg, though none of them had made a strong impression on him. Well, not until now.

All of them had gaping holes in their chests. Like something had chewed out their hearts.

Hot bile rose up in his throat, and he had to turn away and breathe deeply to keep from throwing up.

These were people his age. Innocents. And he, Marion, Echo, and Penn would have likely shared in their fate if they hadn't been able to break free from the illusion in time.

Now these people were dead and . . . wait, where were their cards?

Arthur's head snapped back, and he stared in renewed horror at the corpses. None of the ruined chests had the glow of unharvested cards. On the contrary, they were scooped out as if something wasn't satisfied with what they found and had wanted every last drop.

The scourglings had Legendary cards.

Arthur turned to the sky. The white dragons had arranged themselves into several arrow formations and seemed to be doing a search in a gridlike pattern.

Were any of them of Legendary rank? Arthur doubted it.

If they were slaughtered, that would be proof the king would need to raze part of the land.

Arthur cupped his hands around his mouth and yelled, "The scourglings have Legendary cards!"

New skill gained: Voice Projection (Leadership/Politician/Merchant Class)

Due to your card's bonus traits, you automatically start this skill at level 3.

The white dragons were too high up to hear. Likely, too high up to see him clearly. He'd be like an ant waving its forelimbs to get the attention of a man.

White dragons, stupid! he thought. *They're mind-mages. They aren't searching the area with their eyes.*

He focused on the closest arrow formation and thought as hard as he could at them, projecting the danger they were in, the images of the dead Legendary recruits, Marion's warning.

His thoughts hit a brick wall.

It was a sensation Arthur had never felt before. He staggered back in place as if he had been physically struck.

Did the dragons have a mental shield up? Or—

The notes of a song, half forgotten and much treasured, drifted into his mind. Arthur couldn't help but listen. It was like being called in for a warm dinner at the end of a long day. The sound of festival bells. Of someone finally telling him, "You've done enough, Arthur. I'll take over from here. Let go."

Arthur knew it was a lie—knew from the first note it was the mind-singer.

At the speed of thought, he went to deactivate the Nullify card. The moment it was off, his Return to Start would whisk him away . . .

And the white dragons would never be warned.

Arthur hesitated.

In that split-second pause, the mind-singer snared him.

CHAPTER 30

Arthur walked.

His awareness came and went in vivid flashes.

One moment, he was crossing through the canal, soaked from the chest down. The next he was on the other side, halfway through the next churned field. Another blink of an eye and he stood with others his age, all together at the foot of the scourge cone. This close, he had to crane his head to look up and up, and he still couldn't see the top. Wait . . . why was he here? Why was . . . ?

The song invaded his head, and Arthur drifted.

Each moment of dim awareness came with notifications passing in front of his eyes.

New skill level: Basic Empathic Resistance (Shield Class)
Level 7
New skill level: Basic Empathic Resistance (Shield Class)
Level 8
New skill level: Basic Empathic Resistance (Shield Class)
Level 9
New skill level: Basic Empathic Resistance (Shield Class)
Level 10
You have reached Apprentice in Empathic Resistance.

New skill gained: Basic Telepathic Resistance
Due to your previous experience and your card's bonus traits, you automatically start this skill at level 6.

Arthur blinked.

The sweetly seductive notes played through his head, but he was aware of other noises. Roars. The booms of explosions. Some of them were close.

Slowly, he turned his head from where he had stared expectantly toward the cone—they were all staring expectantly. He stood in the middle of a vast crowd of people. Townsfolk, farmers, evacuees, old, young . . .

Instead of the cone, Arthur looked to the sky.

The arrows of white dragons had fallen into disarray. Small dark pinpricks flew among them. And from those dark points—scourge-bats—came immense explosions.

One of the cards the scourglings had harvested from the Legendary recruits must be combustive.

And that didn't count the living tornado he saw in the near distance, winding ever closer. Someone had either a wind or special tornado card.

New skill level: Basic Telepathic Resistance (Shield Class)
Level 7

His mind cleared just that little bit more, and he realized he was actively pushing on something in his mind. His thoughts built an ever-crumbling shield, but the more skilled he became in the method, the less likely it was to disintegrate.

The white dragons dodged, some diving straight down to avoid the concussive blasts. Arthur got the impression they were fighting back in their own way. The edges of his weak mental shields were battered by stinging pressures. The mind-mages were trying to fight back.

Perhaps the battle was what kept Arthur's own fight from being noticed.

Unfortunately, the people around him weren't shielded. Some flinched, others let out low moans of pain, and one or two collapsed, foaming at the mouth. They all stared toward the cone, however.

Why?

What were they waiting for? Why had the mind-singer gathered all these people together? They could have harvested their cards, like what had happened to the Legendary team, and been done with it.

New skill level: Basic Telepathic Resistance (Shield Class)
Level 8

With the new strength to his shield came a touch more distance and clarity.

The mind-singer had sung in his mind to gather here and wait. For what, Arthur didn't know.

What he did know was the singer surely had a Rare card. That's what gave Arthur, with his Legendary skill, a slight edge. It also meant it likely had to strain to keep so many people under control.

Arthur had been caught alone. No reason to think he had a Legendary card unless the singer had looked closely. And it had the white dragons to contend with.

Another rapid series of explosions blasted around one dragon that had fallen behind the others. It fell from the sky in pieces.

Two of the dragons doubled back and snatched at the remains—Arthur hoped it was to keep any more mind-mage cards away from the enemy rather than greed for themselves.

Half of the dragons were in pure flight back to the rip in the sky. They'd report a failure, that the land was lost.

Then the king would come.

Arthur knew he should leave. He had regained enough mental control to access his heart deck. A flick of thought, and he could turn off the Nullify.

An instant later, he'd be away.

And these people would be left to their fate.

He might have done it, but some of the white dragons weren't fleeing outright.

They headed toward the rip in the sky but kept low just to the clouds. One let out a piercing note, low and sad, and Arthur took an involuntary step toward it before he caught himself. He wasn't the only one.

The dragon was calling for the lost. Searching for survivors.

We're here! he thought fiercely at it.

Unfortunately, his resistance skills did nothing to enhance the strength of his thoughts.

The dragon flew so low Arthur could see the rider scanning desperately along the ground. Behind them, the battle raged on, but they wouldn't have much time to act.

Why didn't he see them? The crowd was several hundred people strong, and they were out in the open. Were they blind?

Oh. Or the crowd was hidden under an illusion.

New skill level: Basic Telepathic Resistance (Shield Class)
Level 9

Arthur turned and found who he half expected all along, standing in the crowd a few rows away.

The bearded prince.

His Charisma effect was either nullified or targeting someone else. He looked painfully average standing there in the crowd. Arthur suspected part of his subtle charm had been woven into an illusion surrounding himself. From his blank-eyed gaze, he was just as much of a victim as the rest. At least, Arthur hoped so.

This . . . was going to hurt.

Arthur stepped out of his row and weaved past several others toward the prince.

He knew the moment the mind-singer noticed because the notes in his mind—which had been steadily fading—grew sharply louder.

Invisible teeth clamped onto the shield in his mind and started to rip and tear.

Arthur stumbled to his knees, shook his head with his hands over his ears—it didn't help—and forced himself to stand. But he couldn't remember what he was doing or why he was bothering to resist.

They were coming, and he needed to be there to greet their arrival.

New skill level: Basic Telepathic Resistance (Shield Class)
Level 10
You have reached Apprentice in Telepathic Resistance.

New skill level: Apprentice Telepathic Resistance (Shield Class)
Level 11

The levels brought fresh clarity. He staggered the last couple of steps and nearly fell against the blank prince.

Arthur focused on his **Mental Resistance (Area of Effect)** skill.

A sense of weakness brought him down to the ground again. He couldn't keep this up for long. The mind-singer was so strong that his own life force was flowing out of him like a river.

The prince blinked. So did several other people around him.

A woman screamed, perhaps realizing where she was and what had happened to her.

That seemed to shock a couple others half awake.

Arthur made an inarticulate noise and reached up to grab the prince's arm, shaking him.

"What?" the prince said vaguely, and looked around with horror dawning on his face.

The illusion around them shattered.

Arthur didn't see the effect since his skill had already resisted it.

Instead he felt the mind-singer's rage. Her mind was battering at his own. There was no way she could hide that from him.

Or the command she sent to her sisters to tear Arthur's heart out.

Overhead, white dragons roared anew—both in surprise and in triumph as the lost people were found.

His attention was drawn by two dark streaks diving at him from the trees above.

Eat his heart, hissed a voiceless voice in his mind. *Eat his cards*.

Wheezing, Arthur raised his hand and activated Wind Release.

A sharp gust of wind caught one of the diving scourge-bats—the same one's he'd glimpsed in the scholar's guild—and flung it to the side.

Arthur collapsed flat to the ground. His heart labored in his chest, and it felt like the air itself was too thin to fill his lungs.

Which was unfortunate, as the second scourge-bat descended on him, razor jaws wide.

Arthur released his **Mental Resistance (Area of Effect)** skill. The drain cut off completely, but he was too weak to send out another gust of wind.

All he could do was throw his hands up—hands that stopped the jaws. The teeth were like razors, but his hands and forearms were like steel.

In an eye blink, Arthur reached into his Personal Space and withdrew a tiny knife. Awful for combat but perfect for snipping threads.

His Instant Tool and Weapon Competence card kicked in.

New skill gained: Small Knife Proficiency (Swordsman Class/Thief Class)

Due to your card's bonus traits, you automatically start this skill at level 10.

Holding it, he focused on his **Fabric Snipping** skill.

He had no strength, no dexterity. No time except to maybe make one cut.

His new proficiency in small knives combined with his **Fabric Snipping** skill, which was in turn boosted by his The Perfect Snip card.

One cut became a dozen, deep and perfect, as though by a skilled tailor. It destroyed the fabric that was the creature in front of him.

A third of the pressure on his mind lessened as the scourge-bat fell to pieces in his hands.

The mind-singer's scream rang through his skull—so loud and fierce that Arthur was on the verge of blacking out from it. Or maybe that was his dwindled life force. The world had started to darken around the edges again.

His grasp on his skills slipped, and the mental shield crumbled like a child's sandcastle.

He felt the mind-singer's mental crow of triumph—her need for revenge was like a hot brand against his mind.

I'm here, said a calm voice in his mind. Its presence helped soothe the burn, and, he slowly realized, the damage.

Three white dragons, one of them shimmering like diamonds in the sun, landed in the clearing.

An invisible field pulsed out from them. Abruptly, the mind-singer's presence vanished to a whisper.

Around him, people woke as if from a dream. They looked around, murmuring, confused but not alarmed.

New skill level: Apprentice Empathic Resistance (Shield Class)
Level 13

The white dragons are keeping the people calm, Arthur thought. But he didn't mind. Slowly, he climbed back to his feet. He was far from recovered, but the shimmering white dragon's presence buoyed him.

As he stood, he stored the remains of the scourgling in his Personal Space. He didn't have the time or mental energy to deal with harvesting its card.

The white shimmer's rider cupped her hands around her mouth and called out, "Everything will be all right. Please line up, and my riders will evacuate you to a safe area."

People immediately moved to do as she told them. No questions. No hesitation.

Arthur stood in place, looking around. Perhaps he was still damaged from the mental battle with the mind-singer, because it didn't occur to him to move with the rest of the crowd until he felt the weight of a gaze on him.

The white shimmer dragon had crystalline-blue eyes. Arthur had to focus not to feel like he was falling into them.

Her rider had white-blonde hair, so bone straight it didn't look real. She noticed her dragon's attention and smiled down at Arthur. "Are you resisting us, young man? We mean no harm."

"I . . ." The word felt thick in his mouth, his tongue like a piece of cotton. Either the mental damage from the mind-singer, the life-force drain, or both. Slowly, Arthur shook his head. "You're lying," he said calmly. "We're not safe."

He looked behind himself. Some of the braver dragons were still fighting the Legendary-rank scourglings—though the tornado seemed to have stalled out a few miles away. Small mercy.

There weren't enough dragons there to take anyone by a long shot. What was the plan? And where had the mind-singer gone?

As if in answer, he heard a hiss in his mind.

This isn't over yet.

The ground started to shake.

Arthur had felt this before, during his first scourge-eruption when he'd been a boy. But that shaking was like a warm summer's breeze next to the earthquake now.

Everyone was thrown off their feet, including the landed dragons. Trees cracked and fell, and some of the enforced peace over the crowd lightened.

People screamed and pointed up to the cone they'd all been fixedly staring at before.

Arthur still couldn't see to the very top, but he had a good view of the sudden bulge growing out of the narrow neck of the cone. It was to the side, leaving the mountain distended and pregnant looking.

Another sickening lurch of the earth, and a giant fist, larger than any dragon, punched its way out of the cone.

The earth fell away in a landslide, thankfully away from them.

Mind-mage voices echoed in Arthur's mind, snapping orders at one another. Some loud, some quiet. All of them, he suspected, he wasn't supposed to hear.

It was too much. He again sank to his knees, hands over his ears. His palms were hot and wet with blood.

It did nothing to stop the voices, but one—the white shimmer, though he wasn't sure how he knew that—echoed above them all.

Call the hive leaders. This is a Legendary-rank scourgling and far beyond us. Save as many civilians as you can.

Glittering white claws closed around him.

"No," Arthur protested, voice slurred. "Got my own way home . . ." But he couldn't remember how he'd get there.

His hands fell away from his bleeding ears as darkness closed around him.

PART 3

THE DARK EGG

CHAPTER 31

Arthur woke up.

He wasn't entirely sure what was going on, other than something was terribly wrong.

Notifications from his heart deck flashed in front of his face. Though he saw the words and recognized them to some degree, he was unable to piece them together. It was as if someone was screaming gibberish in his head. A constant noise he was unable to block out, and he was much too scatterbrained to understand.

But he wasn't frightened. Not even particularly upset. Perhaps that should have been the most alarming thing of all, but he found himself almost completely disconnected from his own emotions.

A face swam into focus over him. Though he knew those features and there was nothing wrong with his eyes, it still took Arthur a few moments to recognize him.

"You cut your hair," Arthur croaked.

Horatio smiled, though there were lines of strain on his severe face. His dark hair was cut short to his scalp, which sharpened his features and emphasized his nose. He looked like the bully's evil toady Arthur had seen in plays.

More than that, he looked both worried for Arthur and anxious about something else. He kept stealing glances across the room.

"Arthur, you're blocking the healing."

"I . . . what?"

Again, Horatio glanced across the room as if for confirmation over what he was about to say. "You need to release your mind skills."

Words and understanding still felt slippery. Arthur blinked at him, replayed what he had just heard, and then wondered how Horatio had such a firm grasp on his abilities.

Only then did he realize he had been unconsciously holding on to his **Empathetic** and **Telepathic Blocking** skills.

Horatio had known Arthur for years and must have seen the stubbornness on his face. "Please. They know what they're doing. Trust me."

It was the worry in Horatio's eyes that made Arthur waver. The moment he did, it was as if a cottony cloud swept into his mind.

He didn't think he passed out, exactly. He just wasn't present in his own body anymore.

The next thing he knew, he was sitting up in a massive bed, leaning against half a dozen feathered pillows. The room was large and well-appointed with oil paintings of dragon riders posing with their beasts up on one wall, double doors leading out to a sweeping balcony large enough for a dragon to land on, and several expensive-looking pieces of furniture meant for sitting or lounging.

Sitting next to his bed was the rider of the white shimmer dragon.

Up close, she wasn't as young as Arthur thought. Crow's feet pinched the corners of her eyes, but her bone-white hair was straight and perfect as ever.

She has to have a card for that, he mused and realized it was the first clear thought he'd had in . . . he didn't know.

The rider smiled at him. "Hello, Arthur. How are you feeling?"

She knew his name.

He looked around cautiously for a clue of how deep in trouble he was. He found nothing in the unfamiliar room to reassure him. No sign of Horatio, either.

"Was my friend even here?" he asked instead of answering. "Or was that a vision placed in my head?"

"Junior Rider Horatio was here," she said. "I had hoped a familiar face would set you at ease. You had extensive psychic damage, and your skill blocks prevented me from healing them."

Swiftly, Arthur checked the notifications he had been too muddled to read earlier.

New skill level: Apprentice Empathic Resistance (Shield Class)
Level 13
New skill level: Apprentice Empathic Resistance (Shield Class)
Level 14
New skill level: Apprentice Empathic Resistance (Shield Class)
Level 15
New skill level: Apprentice Telepathic Resistance (Shield Class)
Level 13
New skill level: Apprentice Telepathic Resistance (Shield Class)
Level 14

New skill level: Apprentice Telepathic Resistance (Shield Class)
Level 15

It seemed the more she tried to access his mind, the stronger he became.

She'd succeeded in the end, and that worried him.

"My name is Agatha," she continued. "Here is my card."

To his shock, she gestured to her chest, and a projection of her card flashed into view.

Mind Healer
Rare
Healing/Mind
The wielder of this card has the ability to repair physical, mental, and emotional trauma. This healing is limited to the mind, physical brain matter, emotional state including aura, and subconscious. Deep and/or extensive healing sessions may require the use of mana. The wielder must be within physical touching distance of their patient in order to heal.

Arthur read it swiftly and flicked his gaze back to her. This could be a trick, but to what end?

His thoughts had been so muddled he couldn't function before. Now he felt good as new.

There may still be an unpleasant surprise in store, but he felt the healing was legitimate at least.

"Uh, thanks," he said, feeling awkward. "How bad was it?"

A look of annoyance crossed her face, though it wasn't aimed at him. "That blasted scourgling injured you far more than you were aware. Then you went and exacerbated the psychic tears by using skills that required mana, which you don't have." She gave him a sharp look. "As your healer, I strongly urge you to purchase a card capable of unlocking mana."

He nodded, unnerved that she knew so much about his abilities.

"Then there's the usual damage," Agatha said. "There is usually some scarring from trauma. I patched that up while I was at it. Think back to the events around the eruption. How do you feel?"

Arthur frowned. He remembered everything perfectly, but . . . "It feels like I'm . . . not there? It's like it happened to someone else?"

She nodded. "Standard practice in these cases is to separate the emotions from the events. This is temporary, and the full emotions linked to the memories will return. You may have nightmares. This is normal," she stressed. "It is your mind's way of processing."

"Uh, okay." He hesitated and blurted, "About my skills . . . when you went through my mind . . ." He took a breath and looked her in the eyes, searching for any sign of deception. "Have you read my cards?"

Agatha didn't flinch or look away from the question. It looked like she anticipated it. "I had to scan through your recent memories to fix the trauma, and to understand what was blocking my own card. That isn't unusual for a Legendary card user. The fact you have two of the same set is—" She paused, searching for the word. "Rare. But you are my patient first. You are allowed a level of confidentiality."

He wasn't certain he fully believed her about the last part. It had been something in her eyes. But he had been healed, and he had other questions.

"What happened after I . . . uh . . ."

"Went into psychic shock?" she asked instead of the word he was about to use, which was "fainted."

"Yes," he agreed quickly.

"I could show you. We have a memory-keeper on staff who witnessed nearly the whole incident."

Arthur's eyebrows rose in surprise, and he nodded.

She reached to him, then paused. "Please don't block me. This won't work otherwise."

He nodded again, and she touched the tips of her fingers to his temple.

Arthur was high in the sky, wings stretched to catch a balloon of warm air to keep him safely aloft. Far below, he saw the top of the scourge-created crater.

The memory-keeper was a dragon. Arthur was in his memory, but also far enough away from it so he wasn't confused about who he was or what he was seeing.

And he only vaguely felt the memory-keeper's alarm as the top of the crater fell away and the Legendary-ranked demi-scourgling climbed out. Below, the rest of the white dragons dived to collect as many of the villagers as possible. Some stayed behind in a final sacrifice to head off the Legendary card-wielding scourge as long as possible. Others risked flying close to the emerging demi-scourgling to land and collect people.

Some of the effort was in vain.

The memory-keeper felt a pulse of mental energy. At least a quarter of the villagers and farmers turned to sprint flat out toward the demi-scourgling.

Some of the dragons snatched them up, but they struggled, kicked, and wriggled to get free. There were too many people with their minds still intact to save and too few dragons to fly them away. Most of the strugglers were let free again.

They ran, clawing up the sides of the cone, slipping and falling down unsteady ground.

The demi-scourgling reached down and snapped them up by the handful, popping them in its mouth like popcorn. Then it tipped its head back and roared. A rainbow of magic flooded out of its mouth.

The grim certainty of the memory-keeper's thoughts told Arthur the demi-scourgling had absorbed the villagers' cards and added their power to its own. That was the reason why the mind-singer had brought them in the first place: They were to be sacrificed.

Those poor people, the memory-keeper thought.

Meanwhile, the white dragons had lifted off and flew at a flat sprint toward the rips in the sky. Some were so visibly weighed down with passengers, they were slow and lagged behind.

The demi-scourgling emerged. It was a mountain-sized, six-limbed lizard with oversized shoulders that had humanlike arms. Orange-and-red lava flowed out from the cracks it made from the cone.

Arthur had enough time to think *It has volcano powers!* before lava shot out of the cone and toward the fleeing white dragons.

Most were able to dodge. Two of the slowest were engulfed. They and their passengers went down in flames.

The demi-scourgling scooped up a handful of lava the size of a house and flung it at more of the dragons.

Just then, the sky ripped open, and an icy-blue dragon nearly the size of the demi-scourgling started to emerge. Its head was only just through, but it saw the impending disaster and reacted, blasting the oncoming lava out of the air with a freezing breath.

More rips cut through the air, and other giant dragons began to come through. At least a dozen of them.

Two of them, Arthur saw, were Whitaker's giant orange beast and Valentina's dragon, who rode, as always, on her living thundercloud.

The white dragons with their passengers escaped, but the memory-keeper stayed to watch the battle.

The Legendary-rank dragons launched their attacks, and the power seemed to warp the air. Between that and the now-fully-erupting volcano, Arthur only caught the battle in flashes: lightning bolts as thick as trees peppering the scourgling, the wind forming into living dragon-headed whips to flail and bite, the earth reforming under the scourglings to lock it in only to erupt into spines of razor-sharp rock around it. One monstrous green dragon, which looked ninety-nine percent muscle, attacked the scourgling with claws and teeth. Everywhere it touched, dark rot grew on the scourgling's scales.

But the demi-scourgling was hardly helpless. Lava flowed up around it, scouring any diseased wound clean and repairing minor injuries. It threw gobbets of lava as big as a dragon's head, forcing the dragons to dive and weave so they weren't knocked out of the air completely.

The demi-scourgling followed up by roaring a multicolored light of dozens of card powers. It struck a dirty gray Legendary dead on.

Terrible growths erupted up and down her skin, and it was all she could do to limp to the rip in the sky and retreat.

And the city and the once-viable land all around was utterly obliterated.

No need for the king to come. The fight between all of the titans reshaped the earth down to the bedrock. That was before the new lava splashed in.

The demi-scourgling put up quite the fight, but it was still outnumbered more than ten to one.

The memory-keeper turned to leave, and Arthur missed which dragon made the final blow.

The memory ended, and Arthur found himself back in his body, breathing hard and clutching the sheets under him as if for stability.

Agatha drew her hand away. "You accepted that memory quite well. If you ever come across a memory-type card, consider taking it. You have the knack."

That meant she didn't know about the bookshelf. He was glad he still had a few secrets.

"Who got the Legendary card?" Arthur asked. "I assume the demi-scourgling was harvested."

Agatha snorted. "Of course. And Harvest Moon: Neddy, the ice dragon. Likely, they'll present that card to the king for favors, as usual." Her voice turned wry at the end.

Arthur wasn't certain what to say. He had so many questions.

"You may ask, Arthur," Agatha said gently. "No, I'm not reading your thoughts, but it's clear on your face something is troubling you."

Well, better to show his ignorance here. She'd already been in his mind, so she couldn't be too surprised. "That . . . demi-scourgling," he said, remembering the word the memory-keeper had used, "does that happen every eruption?"

She shook her head, and her lips drew down at the corners. "No, scourge-eruptions are much like natural eruptions: some are minor and some . . . some are utter devastation."

"What about the mind-singer?" Arthur asked.

"There was no sign of it. Most of our white dragons are Common or Uncommon. A Rare mind-mage could easily hide. We think it slipped away when the fight turned against the demi-scourgling. But had it been able to feed more people to it . . . Well, you saw what happened to the grayling. She was lucky to live."

She paused and looked hard at Arthur. "You should know there have been serious questions raised whether Wolf Moon Hive should keep their Legendary egg after this fiasco. Valentina and Whitaker were not able to hide the fact they let a scourgling with mind powers slip through their fingers. Half the nobles who lost children are baying for their blood."

"Half?" Arthur asked.

Agatha's smile had a touch of darkness to it. "Well, there is an inherent risk in trying to link with a Legendary dragon. The king isn't happy either, though I doubt he'd met the children we lost."

Arthur didn't have time to react to that before she leaned closer. "My question to you, Arthur, is are you willing to go back to that hive? Knowing what you now know of what being a Legendary rider requires."

Because, of course, those Legendary dragons had not been alone. The memory-keeper had been too far away to see the riders who were with them.

If Arthur linked with a Legendary, his duty would be to fight scourglings with the strength of an angry volcano.

Arthur opened his mouth to answer, then paused. "Back?"

"Ah." Agatha shook her head. "Forgive me, I forgot. You're not in Wolf Moon Hive. You're at Buck Moon."

That explained how he'd seen Horatio.

"Yes," Arthur said, answering her previous question. "I still want to try to link with the egg. Why does it matter?"

"Because, dear boy, you're a hero."

He stared at her. "Me?"

In answer, she flicked her fingers around. "You don't think we give sickrooms like this to everyone, do you? No, several dragons felt you break the illusion that allowed us to save what people we could. Not to mention you"—she poked at his chest—"personally sheltered one of the king's sons and daughters, and the son of a prominent duke."

An unpleasant chill went down his spine at the reminder of his uncle. Agatha didn't react other than to watch him for his reaction.

"Why are you telling me this?" Arthur asked.

She smiled. "Because your star is rising, and that will only increase if you do happen to link with the new Legendary hatchling. And . . ." She hesitated, for once looking unsure. "You may someday find yourself in a position of power. If you do, I hope you remember that we mind-mages are not the enemy." She rose. "Now, tomorrow, you should expect to be interviewed by the king's inquisitors on the events of the town's destruction. They are only interested in what you saw. Do not volunteer anything else. Do not offer up your opinion."

He still wasn't sure how much he should trust her, if at all, but this seemed like good sense.

"I recommend you bring out the prince and princess before that," she continued. "That will at least build good will. And Arthur—"

Here it was, at last. The whole reason she had been kind to him. He steeled himself.

Agatha's smile was kind. "Do seek any of us out in the future, should you wish for more mind-strength training."

Then with that, she glided out, leaving Arthur flummoxed.

CHAPTER 32

Arthur barely had time to collect his wits before he heard the distinctive snap of dragon wings at the balcony. Now he was looking closer, he realized there weren't any doors leading to the outside. It was open air, shielded by gauzy curtains.

He pushed his covers back and stepped out, pausing when he saw he was clad in a white linen shirt and loose tan pants. Someone had changed his clothing? How long had he been out?

It was full night outside, but the moon was three quarters full and cast enough of a glow to see by.

Arthur's balcony was at least twenty levels high. And yet, looking out at the expansive and unfamiliar city, many of the buildings were higher. Lights blazed in the windows from illumination card magic, and though he couldn't pick out details thanks to the night, there seemed to be no end to the city.

He'd heard time and time again that Wolf Moon Hive was a small, inconsequential place. Now he was starting to understand what people meant.

He only had a few seconds to gawk. The sound of flapping wings grew louder. Arthur stepped back as a large dragon alighted on the balcony.

It was Sams, but there was something different about the dragon—

"Arthur!" Horatio slid off of Sams's neck with a practiced movement, landing easily on the ground to come up to him. "How bad did the scourglings scramble your brain?"

"Who are you again?" Arthur asked, grinning, and made himself take the friendly fist to his shoulder in reply.

Grinning, Arthur turned to Sams. "You look different."

It had been hard to pin down at first, but Sams's face looked subtly chubbier, as if he had gained weight that he had lost. He had new muscle definition under his scales and his belly . . . Was his belly darker?

"Come closer into the light so he can see you, Sams," Horatio coached.

The dragon shifted around, and the soft illumination from the candles inside fell over the dragon. The scales on his sides and legs were a richer shade of sunshine yellow, almost having taken on a burnished quality.

His belly scales had an iridescent sheen to them. From the right angle, they flashed purple.

"I have linked my core card to a new rider with a new power," Sams said. "Why shouldn't I be a bit different?"

"That and they're working us half to death in training. Like Sams doesn't know how to fly and fight already," Horatio grumbled, but there was a smile on his face as he patted Sams's foreleg. Then he sobered up, turning to Arthur.

"We saw a little of that last eruption, before we got word to scatter thanks to that mind-mage."

"You're in training and they had you fight in the eruption?"

Horatio's face briefly darkened, making him look much more like the boy Arthur used to know. "Yeah, but I had Sams to protect me. I can't believe the leaders sent you there without a dragon to back you up."

"I think they meant to keep us in the city—you know, to give the nobles a taste of what that life was really like." Arthur shrugged. With his emotions separated from the stark facts of the memories, he couldn't find it in himself to care.

Horatio eyed him skeptically. "Well, they got their taste and more. From what I heard, you made yourself a hero."

Arthur lifted a shoulder in a limp shrug. He didn't feel like a hero. When it came to the eruption, he didn't feel like much of anything. Likely, it was due to his emotions being stripped from the memories, but he couldn't bring himself to care much about that either.

Instead, he looked out over the strange city vista. "So, this is Buck Moon, huh?"

"Yeah." Horatio's grin was sharp. "You haven't seen nothing yet. It's so good to be back in civilization."

"I liked what I saw of Wolf Moon," Sams said. "It was quaint."

"Try living there for years," Horatio shot back.

Arthur, though, continued staring out toward the large buildings. How many of those twinkling lights were lit up in shops?

"You think I could find a mana card out there?"

"What, now? Aren't you supposed to be resting or something?"

"The mind healer said I've got an interview with the king's inquisitors tomorrow," Arthur said. Maybe a vestige of emotion still lingered from the last few days' memories after all, because he didn't want to be caught unprepared ever again.

Horatio's shocked reaction was enough to tell him he had the right to be wary.

Sams rumbled something deep in his chest and dipped his head down to look squarely at Arthur. "If the king's inquisitors have taken an interest in you . . ." He trailed off for a moment. "This is either a very good thing or a very bad thing."

"It's bad," Horatio said predictably.

"I have been under the scrutiny of the king's dragon once." Sams shuddered so hard the scales around his folded wings clattered. "I was never more grateful to be only a Rare and beneath usual notice."

"You're not 'only a Rare dragon,'" Horatio said loyally.

"A Rare to a Mythic is a mouse to a man," said Sams gravely.

Should he run for it? Arthur considered and then dismissed the thought immediately. No, he had come too far to turn away now. Plus, the king's attention might be a good thing considering he was seen as a hero.

But what if he learns I'm Calvan Rowantree's son? What if he's looking to place the blame on someone for the disaster around the demi-scourgling? What if he learns Cressida and I set loose those scourglings?

That had been an accident, and he certainly wasn't at fault for the Rare cards that spawned the mind-singer to begin with.

But would it matter if the king was looking to place blame?

Despite his fears and doubts, Arthur couldn't entertain the idea of fleeing. Not when he'd come so far and the Legendary egg was nearly within his grasp.

"All the more reason I need a mana card." He looked to Sams. "Would you be willing to give me a ride to a shop, or know a dragon who would?"

"Your brain's still scrambled." Horatio sighed. "You're in a *hive*, Arthur. We have commissary shops. Though," he said, "I'll have to do the actual shopping. The rules around who can shop at hive stores are stricter in civilized places."

"Why do you need a mana card?" Sams asked. "Surely you don't intend to fight the king's inquisitors."

"They might have a mind-mage with them—someone with a thought-sensing card." Habit had Arthur speak as generally as possible. "I can protect myself, but I've brought along some friends"—he touched his chest meaningfully—"who might need some cover."

"That Personal Space of yours has come in handy." Horatio grinned. "Are they townsfolk you rescued or something?"

Arthur winced. "Remember Penn Rowantree?"

"That's the noble you . . ." Horatio looked around and didn't finish. Smart. Who knew how many ears might be listening.

"Yeah," Arthur said awkwardly. "And Prince Marion and Princess Echo."

"You stuffed *royalty* in your chest?!"

After that, Horatio dragged Arthur farther back into the room—which wasn't just any absurdly luxurious sickroom. This was apparently Arthur's guestroom as a Legendary dragon recruit.

Then Horatio showed him the flag system. There was a pole attached to the end of the balcony, and several different-colored flags one could attach to the end using a pulley system.

"Blue is if you have a nonurgent request—if you want to send messages to staff who might be on lower levels. White is for emergencies—mostly medical, but the VIPs abuse it because they think *every* request is an emergency." Horatio rolled his eyes. "Purple is for personal transport, and green"—he deftly clipped that flag on and pulled the cord, so it shot to the end of the pole—"is for meal requests. Sams, if you would?"

Sams gestured with a lazy claw, and an invisible light source from nowhere illuminated the flag, as bright as if it waved at noon.

"I'd do it using my own card, but ultraviolet has funny effects on cloth," Horatio explained.

"Okay, but why are we putting up a flag?" Arthur asked. "I could eat, but we can just pick up something on our way to the hive commissary . . ."

Horatio turned incredulous eyes on him. "Look, I know things were a little small-minded at Wolf Moon, but you're not going to pull the next possible king or queen from a live eruption zone into safety and not offer them something to eat! Wait. Do they need healers?"

"Uh," Arthur said, "Marion might?"

Horatio actually facepalmed. Before he could properly yell at Arthur, there was a buzzing of wings at the balcony.

A graceful purple dragon with not the usual four but six wings moving so fast they were separate blurs, alighted in the small area Sams wasn't taking up.

"Hiya, Sams," she chirped.

"Eloise," Sams replied with an indulgent bob of his head.

The purple turned her sharp muzzle toward the room. "How can Eloise serve?"

"Tell the kitchens to send up good-quality food—enough for five people, two of which are royal."

"Five people, two royals, much food," Eloise replied amiably.

"And a top-grade healing potion, please," Sams added.

"Healing potion, aye! Bye, Sams!" Rather than a dignified launch into the air, Eloise backflipped off the edge of the balcony. She was briefly visible buzzing away before the darkness swallowed her.

Arthur turned to Horatio. "I can't afford this! Do you know how much healing potions cost?"

"Are you saying a prince can't afford it?" Horatio shot back, amused.

Arthur thought about how casually Marion had handed him a large sack of coins. He fell silent.

"You're in the VIP rooms. Very Important Pain in the hive's neck," Horatio said. "It would be a crime not to enjoy the benefits."

"I noticed you ordered for five people."

Horatio's grin reminded him that they'd both grown up knowing Kenzie. "As your friend, it would be a crime for me not to enjoy the benefits too."

A knock came at the front door not long after. When Arthur answered, he was greeted by a team of people who came to set up an extravagant feast on the long wooden table standing next to the balcony. Presumedly to catch the pleasant breezes.

None of them gave the fact there were only two of them so much as a glance. Arthur supposed they were used to eccentric requests from VIPs.

A tiny vial that was the healing potion was set up on its own table.

Once the staff left, Horatio gleefully started picking out his favorite foods and piling them up on a plate. "Be a pal and store this for me for later?" he asked. "I want to be out of here before the royals arrive."

"Where are you going?"

"Shopping. I told you I'd have to purchase a mana card at the commissary, didn't I?" He held up his hand before Arthur could object. "You know I owe you big time for my Rare card."

"You helped me with . . . uh, *getting* it," Arthur said, still not wanting to admit to the crime aloud.

"That doesn't equal up, and you know it. Besides, you got explaining to do, right?" Horatio was already on his way toward the balcony. "I'll be back later, with cards."

"Cards?" Arthur repeated.

Horatio just laughed, and with a leap, alighted on Sams's neck. The dragon turned and illuminated a path in the dark sky ahead before he leaped from the balcony.

Arthur returned back in the room, absently grabbed a candied fruit from the table, and then set it down again. He didn't have an appetite. There were too many things to be done.

Marion first, he thought and walked over to grab the small vial that was the healing potion.

Then he concentrated and unstowed the prince from his Personal Space.

He barely caught Marion as he crumpled to the ground, white around the lips and looking seconds from passing out.

"Here, drink this." Arthur flicked open the top of the vial and shoved it at him.

Marion looked too dazed to understand what was going on. His eyes had taken on that distant gaze he got when he was focused on the future and not the present.

Arthur's **Nursecraft** skill twinged, and he pushed the vial at Marion's slack mouth to practically pour it down his throat.

Marion grimaced, but it was only a small amount, and within seconds his eyes cleared, and color returned to his cheeks. Wiping his mouth with his sleeve, he looked up at Arthur.

"Where did you get a mana–health combination potion?"

"Was that what this is?" Arthur looked at the vial. There was no label. "Well, you're paying me back for it." He reached down to help Marion to his feet. "How are you?"

"Surprised not to be dead." He looked around. "The timelines I saw didn't include this place. Where's Echo?"

"She's—"

"Good idea storing her away too," Marion said, seeing his answer in the future. His interest turned to the food. "Do they have the candied— Ohh, they do!" He walked over to take one of the candied plums Arthur had seen earlier. "No, don't bring her here yet. She's not hurt? And Penn made it?"

Arthur nodded.

Distracted again, Marion made his way to a short bookshelf set in the corner. He bent to examine the spines. "You and I need to talk."

His stomach sank. He had a feeling he knew, but he still had to ask. "About?"

Marion picked out a book and turned back to Arthur, casually opening it as he spoke. "The card you stole from me."

CHAPTER 33

In the next moment, Arthur found himself inside his Personal Space.

Penn and Echo stood like living dolls in the middle of the room. Arthur turned away from them and instead went to the pile where he kept his tools.

Though he shoved everything into the Personal Space, the items were sorted more or less according to a category. He had not been thrifty during the impromptu shopping trip, and he'd gathered everything he could think of, from extra utensils to basic tools he thought would be useful for roughing it out in the wilderness.

New skill gained: Fork Proficiency (General Class)
Due to your card's bonus traits, you automatically start this skill at level 13. (+3 Master of Skills, +10 Tool Competence)

New skill gained: Fire Poker Proficiency (General Class)
Due to your card's bonus traits, you automatically start this skill at level 13. (+3 Master of Skills, +10 Tool Competence)

He had no idea what a **Fork** and **Fire Poker** competency would grant him, why he hadn't gained these before, or even if any of these skills would stay with him once he gave up the card. He hoped his Master of Skills card would take over from there.

Plates offered no competency skill, neither did the bowls or glassware. Apparently, those items didn't count as tools.

He moved on to more traditional items.

New skill gained: Garden Shear Proficiency (Herbalist/Alchemy Class)
Due to your card's bonus traits, you automatically start this skill at level 13. (+3 Master of Skills, +10 Tool Competence)

New skill gained: Shovel Proficiency (General/Miner Class)
Due to your card's bonus traits, you automatically start this skill at level 13. (+3 Master of Skills, +10 Tool Competence)

New skill gained: Trowel Proficiency (Herbalist/Alchemy Class)
Due to your card's bonus traits, you automatically start this skill at level 13. (+3 Master of Skills, +10 Tool Competence)

New skill gained: Letter Opener Proficiency (Scholar Class)
Due to your card's bonus traits, you automatically start this skill at level 13. (+3 Master of Skills, +10 Tool Competence)

New skill gained: Rope Proficiency (General/Sailor Class)
Due to your card's bonus traits, you automatically start this skill at level 13. (+3 Master of Skills, +10 Tool Competence)

New skill gained: Needle and Thread Proficiency (Tailor Class)
Due to your card's bonus traits, you automatically start this skill at level 13. (+3 Master of Skills, +10 Tool Competence)

New skill gained: Quill Proficiency (Scholar Class)
Due to your card's bonus traits, you automatically start this skill at level 13. (+3 Master of Skills, +10 Tool Competence)

And a half dozen more.

Sadly, picking up items stuffed into a traditional first-aid kit yielded nothing. He'd hoped to get some alchemy skills out of the salves, but again, that didn't count as a tool.

Hopefully, the skills had a chance of sticking. The **Sword** and **Dagger** skills had gone gray and inaccessible once he dropped those items.

Penn had the combat card. Arthur was the one with the general skills card.

Lastly, he turned to the still and silent visitors in his space.

They were utterly frozen in time. Penn was in the middle of blinking, which gave him a strange sleepy-eyed look. Echo was even more disheveled and worn out than Arthur remembered.

Arthur was severely tempted to go through their pockets. He wouldn't take any cards—the one he truly wanted was in Penn's heart anyway—but what if they had some money, some tools or surprises up their sleeves to help them?

Arthur wavered, shame, greed, and cold calculation warring through him.

He turned away.

No. He'd promised to keep them safe. He wasn't going to steal from them when they were at his mercy.

Even if they were fabulously wealthy by his standards.

In a blink of time, he stood back in front of Marion. And, with great reluctance, he reached to his card anchor to give back the card.

"Of course, Marion. It was a huge help—"

Marion held up his hand. "Stop."

Arthur froze with his fingers a half inch from the card anchor.

Marion sighed and tucked the small book he'd found on Arthur's shelf in a vest pocket. Apparently, he had no qualms about simply taking something he wanted to read.

"I want to know how you took it in the first place. Do you have a thief card?"

"A thief card?" he repeated with a half laugh. "Do they exist?"

Marion didn't laugh with him. "Almost any magic you can imagine exists. It's just a matter of finding it." He studied Arthur for a moment. "That's another thing—you don't add up."

Arthur did not like where this was going. He reached to his anchor and withdrew the card, holding it out to Marion. "Here. I'm sorry I took it, but I needed to do something to save our lives."

An emotion crossed Marion's face that Arthur couldn't quite catch. He didn't reach for the card. Instead, he looked away. "I'm aware, and I know I ought to owe you my thanks, but . . . it's vexing."

Slowly, Arthur lowered his arm. "What is?"

"People! Me! Everything!" He huffed in frustration and rubbed at his temple. "I'm not an idiot. One second we're in dire straits, and the next I'm back in luxury. This was your doing, and you saved my sister's life . . . you saved our whole team. You're a baron's son, and I'm a prince with power over time. Yes, only a few seconds of time—don't say it—and I'm sorry this is brash of me to ask, considering how much I already owe, but I need another favor."

"First of all, saving your life wasn't a favor. We all saved each other out there. You warned us that the king was coming."

"So he came after all?"

"Well, no." Arthur grimaced. The emotion was still separated from the memories, but it didn't make them all pleasant. "Let's wait for Penn and Echo. I don't want to tell the story twice."

"That's fair. You know," Marion said, "most people would leap at the chance to be in good graces with a prince. Even me."

"I'm a backwoods baron's son," Arthur said dryly. "I don't have the usual manners. What's your favor?"

Marion, knowing the question was coming, was already grimacing before Arthur was done. He reflexively grabbed another candied plum and bit into it.

"My Legendary card was chosen for me at my birth—though obviously I didn't receive it until much later, when I was Echo's age."

Arthur nodded. He supposed he was supposed to feel sympathy for Marion—and perhaps a tiny part of him did—but he wondered what it would be like growing up in luxury, being prepared for the powerful card you would one day receive.

That he'd gained his own had been through pure, dumb luck.

"Not only was my Legendary prechosen, my entire heart deck and the cards I carry in my secondary anchor tattoo have been carefully curated for me by the king's advisors. The Instant Tool and Weapon Competence card is meant to cover for my lack of martial or offensive cards. That way I can pick up any tool and make it a weapon." Again, Marion made a face. "It's the only card like it I will ever have."

"Wait, you can't add to your heart deck?"

"Not without express approval from the king. Or more realistically, his advisors. I doubt he troubles himself. As such, I . . ." Marion paused, swallowed, and got the rest out in a rush. "I was hoping for your Wind Release card. I know I have nothing but coins to trade, and I do need the Instant Tool and Weapon Competence card back as well. My minders—my babysitters—will grow suspicious if I don't have it."

Arthur reached for his card anchor.

"I know it doesn't fit with my current deck at all," Marion continued, still in that rush. "Which is perfect. My minders won't know, which means enemies won't either—"

He stopped and stared at Arthur, who held the cards out to him.

He could see a few seconds into the future, but he still had to pay attention outside his own angst to look.

"You've got a big sack of coins, right?" Arthur said. "That'll do."

It almost physically hurt to give up the Instant Tool and Weapon Competence card, as it synergized so well with his own deck, but if Marion couldn't give it up without raising suspicion, it wouldn't be right for Arthur to keep it.

The Wind Release was useful but not vital to his current decks. Besides, with the coins, he could pay Horatio for the mana card and possibly buy himself something better.

Marion carefully took the cards as if he expected a trick. Then, reaching into his jacket, he withdrew the coins. "That was easier than I expected."

"People aren't that hard, really," Arthur said. "And how's this for another trade: You don't worry about how I got my hands on your card, and I won't tell your minders about the Wind Release."

Marion smiled shakily. "Are you sure you're not the one who sees the future? That's what I was going to suggest."

"People really aren't that hard to figure out," Arthur repeated. "Once you start focusing on the present. Now, I think it's time Penn and Echo joined us. I gotta tell you what happened—and figure out what we're going to do next."

"Fortunately," Marion said as he tucked both cards away in his anchor, "I'm rather good at predicting the future."

Penn and Echo had much less dramatic arrivals than Marion.

Once they were assured they were out of danger and were, in fact, in Buck Moon Hive, Penn immediately demanded his Steel Fists card back. Then he went for the feast. Echo headed for the closets, which were stocked with generic clothing in different sizes for men and women. Arthur's room was luxurious but meant for guests of all types.

She joined them a few minutes later with hair brushed and in a pretty green dress.

No one asked how Arthur came by so much food. All seemed to accept it as natural they'd be presented with a table groaning with plates.

Ugh. Nobles.

Arthur was hungry too. Between bites of perfectly seared beef, greens so fresh they had to have been picked from the gardens hours ago, and a delicate fish hand-pie, Arthur told them the broad strokes of what happened. He left out the details of his skills, of course.

Luckily, Echo and Penn were much more interested in the demi-scourge-eruption, and the aftermath.

"Harvest Moon got the new Legendary card?" Penn asked. "That will annoy the other hives. They've got, what, the last three of those?" He looked around the table for confirmation.

"Four, I believe. Of course, they gave the cards directly to the king," Marion said. He smiled sarcastically at Echo. "More future heirs for us to worry about."

She rolled her eyes. "Who cares? Future babies have to wait twelve years to receive them anyway."

"I doubt the king has any plans to abdicate within twelve years," Marion shot back.

Arthur listened to the two of them, interested to get this glimpse of upper noble politics. He idly twined the fork he held through his fingers.

New skill level: Fork Proficiency (General Class)
Level: 14

Arthur hurriedly swallowed the bite and reached for a thin glass of bubbling fruit juice to cover the moment. He checked his skill list.

Every skill he'd added using the Tool Competency card—with the exception of the combat-based tools such as the dagger—was still there.

It really was a shame he had to give back the Tool Competency card, but he'd certainly received a boost while he had it.

Eventually the bickering wound down, and Arthur told them the news he dreaded the most: the upcoming interview with the king's inquisitors.

"That's not good," Penn said, echoing Sams's earlier statement.

Echo's face had taken on a pale cast. "You don't think they'll blame us, will they?" she asked Marion. "For not stopping that terrible mind-singing scourgling? I know we're royalty, but we don't even have dragons yet . . ."

"I believe that will depend on the king's mood," Marion said. "Also, as he currently thinks two of his possible heirs are dead, his mood won't be good. If he remembers who we are at all," he finished with a grumble.

Arthur got the impression the man was an absent parent.

Penn rose from the table. "I need to send a message to my father, in case news has reached his estate." He headed for the pole near the balcony to change the flags.

Echo rose as well. "We should do the same."

Marion sighed. "The moment we do, they'll send our minders to watch over us."

"So?" Echo asked. "You want to hide forever?"

"No, but I would like one night where I'm not being watched like a toddler around breakable glassware," Marion said, gaze flicking to Arthur. "But go on, this will be good."

"You can't say things like that!" Echo said. "You can't even think it. The king's inquisitors will likely have thought-sensors—"

"Actually," Arthur said, "I . . . had a plan for them, too."

Echo and Penn stopped what they were doing and turned to look at him.

Marion just raised his glass in a silent salute. "Arthur, you are full of surprises."

CHAPTER 34

A knock came at the door just as the last tones from the sixth-hour morning bell faded into the distance.

Arthur was already dressed and waiting, as was Marion, Penn, and Echo. They had expected the summons to come in the early morning, as it was an easy way to throw someone off.

After exchanging a look with everyone else and receiving nods in reply, Arthur rose to answer the door.

A severe-looking man dressed in fancy robes stood on the other side. His badge was emblazoned with the crest of the silver dragon: the royal house.

The man's gaze flicked over him. If he seemed surprised Arthur had answered his own door and not the servant that the hive leaders sent—the one Arthur had dismissed without allowing him inside—he didn't say anything.

"Ernest Kane? Your presence has been requested by the king's inquisitors."

Arthur pretended an air of surprise. "What? Now?"

"Indeed. If you could come with me." The man's tone was not a question at all as he extended a hand down the hall.

"What is this about, Kane?" came Marion's voice, behind Arthur.

Turning back to the room, Arthur made a show of bowing to Marion. "Forgive me, my prince," he said in his most formal, and hopefully not overdone, voice. His **Acting** skill would be receiving a workout today. "I have been told—"

"Prince?" The man roughly shoved Arthur aside, which neatly revealed Marion standing there, less than amused.

Penn and Echo stood off to the side: Penn made a show of resting a hand on the hilt of his sword.

The man made a choked sound and fell to one knee, head dipped in a full bow. "Forgive me, Prince Marion, Princess Echo. I had no idea you were . . ." He seemed to catch himself before he said *alive*. "Here."

That answered one question. With the exception of Horatio using word of VIPs for good food and a free potion, all had done their best to keep quiet about the royal presence in the room—including sending well-meaning servants away—but no one knew if Agatha the mind-mage had spread the information, or if word had leaked from the general kitchen staff to the hive's upper crust. Apparently, the news had not fully spread.

Marion looked down at the man, top lip curling. He was in full-on prince mode. "Why are you taking away my security guard?"

"Your . . . guard, my prince?"

Marion made an impatient gesture. "You don't see my attendants anywhere, do you?"

"Well . . . no. Forgive me, my prince, but—"

Marion gestured to Arthur and to Penn. "These two men kept myself and my sister alive in the wilderness during an active scourge-eruption. Now you wish to remove one of them from my presence?"

The man was obviously awed by Marion, but the king—and therefore his inquisitors—ranked higher than a mere prince. Lifting his head, his shoulders straightened, though he didn't rise from his kneel.

"I'm sorry, sir, but Ernest Kane has been requested by name." He hesitated. "We would be happy to send the elite hive guards to you, now we know you are here—"

"Out of the question," Echo said, speaking up for the first time. "I refuse to allow my person to be protected by mere guards."

"The solution is obvious," Marion continued where his sister left off. "We shall all go."

"Sir—"

"Ernest, Pennrow," Marion said over the objecting man. Though his face was completely devoid of humor, there was a twinkle in his eye he couldn't quite hide. "Be on your guard. There's no telling what awaits us in this hive."

The man tried again. "My prince—"

"And before you tell me there is no need, I assure you there is. It is my duty to report unusual activity to the royal inquisitors. As my sister and I suffered an assassination attempt from rogue illusionists, I say that qualifies."

"You . . . what?"

Echo let out a long sigh. "Why do you think we kept our presence here a secret? Honestly."

The derision of a twelve-year-old finally broke through the man's objections. Reluctantly, he stood. "Very well, then."

There were three others similarly dressed men waiting for them out in the corridor. Arthur suspected he would have been surrounded like a prisoner had he gone alone.

Instead, the man who came in to fetch him quickly walked to another and spoke in his ear. That man nodded quickly and bolted down the corridor. No doubt to warn the inquisitors of the royal surprise.

Arthur let Marion lead, just as Penn stood a step behind Echo, as if the two of them were really functioning as short-term guards.

They had planned during the night, and it was the simplest way not only to ensure they weren't split up, but to silently show the inquisitors their loyalty to the crown.

They were led up a few levels, which gave Arthur a few more sights to compare the two hives. Buck Moon's long hallways were a uniform lighter tan, as if it were made of a different rock. The outer walls were a latticework of large arched windows to the open sky. Only a few of those—located near important inner doors—had any type of covering, which could be swung shut against driving rainstorms.

Though the sun was only beginning to rise at this early hour, the air had a heavy weight to it. Filled with moisture and thick with scented flowers. The glimpses of the vast city outside showed foliage everywhere—huge blooms in riots of colors, which helped explain the scent. Birdsong was even louder than dragon calls.

Arthur knew Buck Moon bordered a desert. Water-based cards must be popular here.

As they ascended the levels, the way was made clear. People glanced at the flanking group and turned to press their backs against the nearest wall to let them pass, eyes turned away. They didn't even seem to notice Marion or Echo. The royal-badged men were more than enough.

As they came to the final junction, Arthur's **Telepathic Resistance** skill activated.

That meant the king's inquisitors had a thought-sensor with them. He only hoped it was the type and strength Arthur could resist.

Silently, he activated his **Mental Resistance (Area of Effect)** skill. That in turn fed off the new card Horatio had purchased for him last night.

Horatio had been as good as his word and had visited the hive commissaries on several levels in search of an appropriate card. He brought two cards for Arthur to choose from, saying he would return the one he didn't want and get his money back from it.

Arthur tried to pay him, but Horatio was insistent.

"I owe you," Horatio had hissed, glancing nervously over his shoulder at Penn.

Marion and Echo had been on the other side of the room, trying to eavesdrop on the Rare rider without looking like they were. Meanwhile, Penn was frowning as if he thought he recognized Horatio but was unsure where from.

"I won't take a single coin from you," Horatio continued. "Now pick a card so I can get out of here. That noble is giving me the evil eye."

"That's just Penn's normal face," Arthur said and heard Echo's giggle before he had turned his attention to the two cards.

They were both Uncommon mana unlockers, though with important differences.

Fire and Mana
Uncommon
Utility
This card unlocks its wielder's mana for the duration the card is in their heart deck. In addition, the wielder is granted a minor affinity to the element of fire. The wielder will be able to manipulate flame to a lesser degree and adjust his or her body temperature by several degrees with no ill effect. The wielder can gather mana from any flame, from direct sunlight, or an object hot enough to burn.

Mana Vault
Uncommon
Utility
This card unlocks the ability to passively gather mana from all ambient forms of free-floating magic. Mana total, usage log, and remaining mana is visible within the wielder's heart deck, labeled as the "Mana vault." This is a skill-based card. The wielder will be able to gather and store progressively larger amounts of mana as the vault levels up. This card can be stored in either the heart or an existing card-anchor deck.

The fire was tempting, especially as Arthur still needed a proper combat card. But considering his most powerful cards were skill-based, the more straightforward Mana Vault was an easy choice.

He had tested his new mana card with **Mental Resistance (Area of Effect)** late last night and found the skill itself was only a light drain on his mana. However, when that skill actively shielded others, the drain was faster.

He could get perhaps twenty minutes of usage out of it, if he was lucky. Likely, he would need every minute.

Marion, and even little Echo, had confirmed that the king's inquisitors mostly worked to confirm their own agenda. They were not a real investigative force. Their job was to simply lend weight to whatever the king's objectives already were.

They were dangerous men. No one wanted a thought-sensor to dig up something that could be used against them.

"Won't they be a little suspicious if they know you're hiding our thoughts?" Penn had asked when they were talking out their plan last night.

"I doubt any thought-sensor will be able to tell which one of us is doing it," Marion said. "That's a problem with those types—they get so used to being able to shortcut and read everyone's thoughts, they go blind everywhere else."

"They'll know it's not you or me," Echo pointed out. "Our cards are assigned."

"Which is why it's important both Arthur and Penn accompany us," Marion said to her. "It'll be more suspects to choose from."

Arthur only hoped it would not be seen as too suspicious. It wasn't illegal to hide one's thoughts, but perhaps the inquisitors wouldn't care.

They came to the final room at last: a large table with three stern men sitting on one side. Several chairs had been placed on the other.

Word must have spread that the royals had insisted on coming.

The inquisitors rose at their arrival and bowed at the waist to Marion and Echo. It was a short motion. Not nearly so reverent as the ones before.

The large double doors closed behind them, sealing the group in with the inquisitors.

The man in the middle smiled, thin-lipped. "We are pleased to find you two alive and well. Word has been sent to your father—he was quite annoyed at the thought of your loss."

"I do hate to annoy him," Marion said.

Echo simply murmured a quiet, "Thank you."

"Considering our security concerns, you don't mind if we conduct this little questionnaire as a group?" Marion asked, looking from one man to another.

Again, the thin-lipped man smiled. The other two shrugged. "Of course not. It's mostly procedure at this point."

Arthur didn't believe that for a moment, but he pulled out a chair and sat when indicated to do so.

The man in the middle nodded to one at the end, who made a show of tapping papers straight.

"Ernest Kane, son of Baron Mace Kane, isn't that correct?"

Arthur straightened. "Yes, sir."

"Interesting. You aren't labeled as Mace's designated heir. That would be your sister, Eleanor. Aged . . . eight." He looked up at Arthur. "Care to explain?"

Had Arthur not had any guidance, he would have surely frozen. That would have been a dead giveaway he was hiding something.

He had already been leaning hard on his **Acting** skill, and he reacted as naturally as an improv artist given a line. Squarely meeting the inquisitor's gaze, he kept his own posture alert and interested, but not defensive.

Though no one else dared to move, every jot of attention in the room was on him.

"My father believes my sister has shown promise, even at her young age," Arthur said evenly. "Meanwhile, I was sent to the hive to gain some knowledge of the real world and link a dragon if I could. Linking a Rare or a Legendary would bring prestige to the barony."

The two men on the right and left jotted down notes as he spoke. The one in the middle kept his gaze on Arthur.

"And you feel it's appropriate for the mere disfavored son of a backwoods baron to place himself at the same level of a prince?"

That caught Arthur off guard. "I'm afraid I don't understand."

"Our reports indicated during the Legendary recruit introduction, you approached Prince Marion and dared to sit at the same table." The inquisitor's flinty gaze never left him. "And now you have set yourself up as an equal?"

That's what got their pants in a twist? Not the fact that "Ernest Kane" wasn't the heir, despite being older and male. Or that there was likely no official mention of him at all. Not even that someone—a fifty-fifty shot being himself—was running a **Mental Resistance** skill?

No, they wanted to know why he was friendly with a prince?

It was almost harder to keep the incredulity out of his voice than it had been his earlier shock. "I didn't know who Prince Marion was at the time." He couldn't help himself. "As you said, I'm from a backwoods barony. I'm certainly not his equal, sir."

The man didn't so much as crack a smile. He turned to Marion.

"I understand you didn't immediately alert the king of your survival due to security concerns?"

"That's correct." Marion didn't volunteer any further information. He looked utterly relaxed—even bored. Arthur tried to take that as a good sign.

"Any current injuries? Any reason why you are unable to answer questions?" the inquisitor asked Marion. When he replied no, the inquisitor turned to Echo to repeat the same questions.

Meanwhile, the two men beside the inquisitor scribbled down notes as if trying to speed-write a novel.

Arthur glanced at their pages—his **Reading** skill was advanced enough that he could easily read upside-down text without much effort. But the lines on the page looked blurred to his eyes.

One of the men was using a minor illusion card to obscure what they were writing. Neat trick. Arthur wasn't foolish enough to push to see past the illusion—he counted it lucky no one had asked who was blocking a thought-sensor to begin with.

As soon as Echo gave her short answers, affirming who she was and that she was not currently injured or impaired, the inquisitor turned to Penn.

"Pennrow Rowantree?"

"Yes, sir."

More marks on the page. Then, "Please describe the events surrounding the eruption, starting from the moment you arrived."

Penn looked mildly surprised to be asked—and by default to be the speaker of their tale. Though on second thought, the king's inquisitors would want to be deferential toward the prince and princess. As a duke's son and heir, Penn outranked a mere baron's unfavored son.

Penn began with a credible accounting of the events. He wasn't a great storyteller, but his dry recital meant nothing was embellished.

The two inquisitors on either end kept writing at the same pace as before. The third in the middle merely laced his fingers and watched.

Meanwhile, Arthur's mana steadily trickled down.

Penn only hesitated at the end. He flicked a glance at Arthur, apology in his eyes, before finishing his story, "Kane offered to transport us in his space-storage card. Since we were facing limited mana resources, and we had seen the prince taken to safety within the storage, the princess and I agreed."

The inquisitor's eyes fell on Arthur. "What happened after?"

Arthur focused on his own dry explanation of the events. He didn't want to paint himself as a hero—partially because he didn't feel like one and partially because he wanted to underplay his card's powers. He insinuated that his Legendary card had minor disillusion aspects.

No one interrupted to ask how a so-called craft-type card would have such a feature.

The inquisitor's expression remained bland up until the end.

"And would you say you received no support from the Wolf Moon Hive leaders regarding this tragedy?"

That's his question? Arthur wondered. He had maybe a quarter of his mana left: Perhaps enough for five minutes.

"No, none," Marion answered.

"They put us in danger," Echo said, though she didn't seem happy to say it.

Penn and Arthur remained silent, but the inquisitors didn't seem to care about their opinion.

"Would it be accurate to say you have lost faith in the Wolf Moon Hive leaders?"

"Yes," Marion answered at once.

"Yes," Echo said.

The inquisitor turned to Penn and Arthur, eyebrows raised in expectation.

Penn hesitated, brows drawing together a moment in confusion. "Yes," he concluded.

"No." Arthur surprised himself with the answer.

For the first time, there was a real interest from the inquisitors. The two writing to each side paused and looked at him. The third's gaze was piercing.

"Explain."

Three minutes of mana left, if he was lucky.

"The original idea to give Legendary recruits a taste of what a scourge-eruption is like was a sound one. When it went south, any of the hive leaders could have stepped in. Instead, they sent their riders with mind-mage abilities. But the white dragons were helpless against scourglings with traditional Legendary-level magical attacks." Arthur heard heat enter his voice. "Someone should have guessed that could have happened with so many people with Legendary cards out in the field. Finally, when the hive leaders arrived to fight the demi-scourgling, Wolf Moon was among them. Valentina is elderly, but she fought with the rest."

"Interesting," the inquisitor said. "So, it is your position that the Wolf Moon Hive leadership attempted to avoid the pending danger, despite ordering Legendary recruits to the point of a scourge-eruption? That they only arrived when the demi-scourgling erupted?"

Under the table, Marion pressed the toe of his boot hard against Arthur's ankle.

It was obvious what the inquisitors wanted to hear. That was a warning to play it smart, not heroic. Even little Echo had understood.

Arthur swallowed his bile, and a lump he felt might be a sliver of his own honor. "Yes."

Immediately, the two inquisitors to the side bent their heads and resumed scribbling.

Castigating the Wolf Moon Hive leaders had been the point of this interview. Not catching Arthur out. Not even discovering the truth. They didn't care who was blocking their thought-sensor. Judging by their non-reactions, such a blocking skill might be expected. It didn't matter: This outcome had already been decided.

The middle inquisitor addressed them all. "Thank you for your time. Prince Marion, Princess Echo, we will, of course, relay the joyous news to your father." He could not have sounded more bored or less joyous. "You should expect proper security shortly. Now, I assume you all still wish to attempt to link with the Legendary egg?"

Everyone nodded, though Marion's motion was slight.

"Which hive will receive the egg is currently being discussed by the current leaders. Your testimony here will, of course, help." Another thin smile.

Arthur felt a mix of muted anger and exasperation. This was all politicking for the excuse to move the new Legendary hatchling to another hive.

Perhaps to Harvest Moon Hive, which had been providing the king with Legendary-rank cards from demi-scourglings.

"For now, you will consider yourself recruits of this hive. Carry these chips as verification."

The man pulled out four square silver pieces and pushed them across the table. Arthur took his piece and examined it. One side held the image of a six-pointed stag against a circle that represented the full moon. The other side was stamped with the image of a magnificent dragon: likely the senior hive leader.

As he touched the chip, a jot of his rapidly dwindling mana flowed into it, and the lines glowed briefly before dimming out again.

"You should expect to be presented to the egg in three days," the inquisitor said. "Do you have any questions?"

No one spoke. Arthur's mana was a bare trickle.

"Very well, then." The man flicked his hand in clear dismissal.

He hadn't even give them his name.

Arthur rose, stuffing the chip in his pocket. No one spoke.

The moment the door closed behind them, he broke into a jog. The mana in his new vault was down to the dregs. Any moment, his **Mental Resistance (Area of Effect)** skill would start eating into his life force.

Penn snapped at Arthur to slow down. Running wasn't dignified, and they had to stay around him to continue to be shielded.

Arthur only stopped when he was a level down and several corridors away. He would have run farther, but the last of the mana drained away. Arthur's chest tightened, and it felt like he sucked down his next breath through a pinhole. He let go of his grip on the **Mental Resistance (Area of Effect)** and turned to the others.

They were all puffing and out of breath. Arthur felt like he'd been going at a reasonable jog, but the glares he received said otherwise.

"That was close," Arthur said, and made a show of resting his hands on his knees as if he were winded.

Marion shook his head. "Something to remember . . ." he said between breaths, "when a disaster happens . . . don't be the person everyone else can blame."

"That's not very fair," Arthur said.

"That's politics."

Echo looked down at the chip in her hand. "Three days until we see the egg."

They all fell silent. Arthur's stomach twisted with a mix of emotion: lingering dissatisfaction and relief about the inquisitors' interview and escaping relatively unscathed. Anticipation and a bit of fear over finally being presented in front of the egg . . . and, most surprisingly, wistful sadness.

He, Marion, Echo, and Penn had stuck together to survive. But they weren't a true team. They were competitors, all reaching for a goal only one of them could have.

Three days. He had three days to prepare himself the best he could for the dragon egg. He still had a scourgling in his storage space to harvest and the depths of his Master of Body Enhancement card to be explored.

The others must have had their own plans. Marion gave Arthur a grimace that was meant as a smile. "Echo and I should meet our new minders. We'll see you later, yeah?"

"Yeah," Arthur agreed.

He turned to say his goodbyes to Penn, only to find his cousin already walking down the hall in the other direction. He didn't look back.

Arthur tried not to let himself be hurt by that. He didn't have time for it. He only had three more days to make himself the best possible prospect for the new Legendary dragon.

CHAPTER 35

The first thing Arthur did was to dip into his Personal Space.

He stood in the middle of the large room. All the tools and supplies he had purchased from the Wolf Moon Hive commissary were there, stacked neatly as possible.

"I should add shelves," he muttered to himself. "But I have no idea how I would attach them to a wall. . . ."

Perhaps a skill or two in woodworking would do him some good.

He was stalling, and he knew it. He turned, half expecting to see the frozen visages of Penn, Marion, and Echo standing there.

Of course, they were gone.

All that was left were bits and bobs of supplies he had purchased, stacked crates of produce . . . and of course, the corpse of the scourgling.

He had not let himself think much about the mind scourgling or wonder what cards it could be hiding. He couldn't be entirely sure his **Mental Resistance** skills would entirely block the mind-mage. In fact, it was possible that some thoughts did leak out—another reason why none of the inquisitors had put up a fuss.

Plus, if the thought-sensor had been Legendary level, he likely could have blasted through Arthur's skills without him knowing it.

Or the inquisitors had only been interested in placing blame on the Wolf Moon Hive leadership, the thought-sensing had been a passive card, and Arthur was overthinking things.

Stalling again.

He had all the time he wanted in his Personal Space, but he had run out of excuses.

"Just because I harvest the cards doesn't mean I have to use them," he muttered to himself.

His hands, he realized, were shaking.

Mind magic frightened him. It was a fear he had silently carried with him before the scourge-eruption. It was a fear linked to his Thief class.

He told himself over and over again that just because he had a class, and many skills in thieving, he didn't have to use it.

Yet, he found himself using them anyway.

And he couldn't make himself regret them. He had gotten his Master of Body Enhancement card by stealing from his own cousin.

Though Arthur liked Penn more than he thought he would, he still didn't feel bad for stealing from him and likely causing his family a lot of trouble.

If he had a mind-mage card—sooner or later, he would find himself using it.

"It might not be a good card," he said aloud, the better to try to convince himself. "The mind-singer likely had two sisters. When I killed this one, its power had gone down by at least a third. It had spawned from a library with Rares. Whatever I get, it won't be a Legendary rank. Maybe. Hopefully."

He wasn't sure he could resist the lure of a Legendary-rank card, no matter what it was.

Enough stalling. It was time to act.

The remains of the chest were glowing.

Holding his breath, Arthur reached over and gestured upward through the glow. Several shards and a whole card floated into view. He gathered them in his hand and examined them.

Five Rare shards, including one of the valued corner pieces. That was handy.

The whole card, however, took his attention.

Subconscious Injection

Rare

Mind

The wielder of this card will be able to implant a subconscious thought or suggestion into the mind of another. This action may be blocked by anti-mind-magic cards, skills, or items. Warning: complicated suggestions or thoughts that are repellent against the nature of the recipient's mind may be discarded. The subconscious may suggest, but it is the conscious which acts.

This card requires mana.

Arthur read through the description twice, frown deepening by the moment.

This was probably the card that had been behind convincing the Legendary Illusionist to set those traps outside the town. Possibly the card which had convinced him and his team to go out to prove themselves to begin with.

Was it possible there were other subconscious suggestions lurking in his mind?

No way to know for certain, but several things reassured him. If this scourgling had slipped in a subconscious order to, say, assassinate one of the hive leaders . . . Arthur doubted he would want to follow it.

But if the thought were more insidious. Something that dovetailed along with his own thoughts. Say: Steal a card from your cousin . . .

Well. He'd have a hard time saying no.

Arthur sighed.

He wasn't fool enough to dispose of the card or try to sell it. Especially as he was in a new hive and had no connections to a black market.

Best that he keep this safe in his Personal Space. At least no Treasure Seeker under Legendary rank had a chance of spotting it there.

Buck Moon Hive was larger and more extensive than Wolf Moon. He'd heard this many times, but he truly felt it when he tried to navigate through what felt like a vast, unending complex of tunnels, junctions, and byways.

Finally conceding defeat, Arthur approached a maintenance worker.

"Could you point me in the direction of the training hall?"

"Training hall?" the man had a bushy mustache and took a moment to look Arthur up and down. "That's for dragon riders only, son."

Oh. Right.

Arthur dug in his pocket for the identification chip the inquisitors had given him. He held it out, and on a whim, pushed a bit of his newly recovered mana through it.

The etched lines that made up the image of the stag lit up in brilliant blue. The power collected and shot out a foot above the chip in scattered light to form the words: *Legendary Recruit.*

It was . . . a bit much. Arthur felt his face grow hot.

The man jerked back in shock and then completed a hasty bow. "Forgive me, sir! I didn't think—" Again, his gaze flicked over Arthur, and he swallowed, "That is to say, you were unaccompanied and . . ."

And Arthur was wearing basic, though well-kept, borrowed clothing clearly not tailored to his body. His look didn't scream "Rich man who can afford a Legendary card."

He held up a hand. "It's fine—"

The maintenance worker turned and bellowed down the hall. "Carley! Get over here, quick."

A girl of fourteen or so in overalls splattered with masonry concrete jogged up. "What's going on, Pa?"

"This here Legendary-rank recruit needs to be shown to the training hall."

The girl turned wide eyes on Arthur and then visibly recoiled on seeing his reddened face. She likely thought it was anger, not embarrassment.

"Yes, sir! Of course. If you'll follow me, sir!"

Arthur followed. The girl was small—too small for her age. And why would she have work stains on her clothing? Most occupational card powers were clean.

Unless . . .

Arthur took another look at the girl and realized she wasn't carded.

Odd. Everyone working in Wolf Moon Hive was carded. He didn't think it was a rule, but there were several hive-funded programs—including the one that founded Arthur's orphanage—to get children a card as soon as possible.

Maybe Carley was like Red and didn't agree with card magics, or she was saving for a higher rank card.

Still, something about it unsettled him, and he made a note to take a closer look at other workers in the future to see if they were carded or not.

Either the girl was as good as her word or too intimidated to slack off. In less than ten minutes, Arthur found himself standing in front of the entrance to the training hall.

It was a huge curved room, making him suspect it may have originally served as a lair for a creature as big as the demi-scourgling. Though there were both torches and card-anchor-lit stones to provide illumination, he couldn't see to the top of the curved ceiling.

He paused to tip a surprised Carley five coppers for her effort and then walked in.

There were no windows to the outside. His sense of direction said he was near the core of the hive. One wall had been carved out for climbing handholds—a half dozen people stood at the bottom holding ropes for others who were ascending to the top.

There were hanging bars, sideways ladders to swing across over an open mud pit, a deep pond in which to do laps, and poles of varying height to jump over or balance on. One quarter of the room was dedicated to strength exercises with boulders of different sizes to lift. And surrounding it all lay a dug-out dirt track to run on.

This was perfect.

He wasn't sure what the Legendary-rank dragonet would be looking for, exactly, but developing his Master of Body Enhancement card couldn't hurt.

He decided to hit the track and work on his **Running** skills.

Hitting level 10 in Running had gained him a 5% bonus to all stamina and a 10% percent speed boost to the first fifteen seconds of a sprint.

He had hoped for more bonuses once he hit level 15. An hour of circling the track again and again, and he wasn't disappointed.

New skill level: Running (General)
Level 15
For reaching this threshold on a body-enhancing skill, you have gained a 7% bonus to stamina while running. In addition, gain a 15% speed bonus for the first twenty seconds while sprinting.

Arthur wanted more. His legs burned from the hour run, but he had been taking the laps at an easy jog. He had more to give.

He forced himself to lengthen his stride. Move faster, run to his limit.

By the time he hit level 18, his once-fine shirt was soaked to the skin with sweat. He shucked it off, leaving on his nice pants. The fine shoes he'd taken from the room still fit his feet with no discomfort. He suspected there was some card magic sewn in or else he would be suffering massive blisters.

His lungs and throat burned, and he longed to stop for a drink of water.

But he was only two levels from twenty. He wanted—needed—to explore the limits of his card.

Arthur pushed himself.

New skill level: Running (General)
Level 19

He hadn't activated his Charming Gentleperson card, and a lone person running the track didn't garner much interest.

Not until that person kept it up for two hours straight.

Some people glanced up from their training, sending him confused looks, hollering encouragement, or jeering jokes. Arthur paid them no mind. Perhaps it was exhaustion kicking in, but he felt like he was floating above his body—separated from aches and pains.

He'd always been fit through the need for survival, but he could have never run for hours straight before adding the card to his deck.

New skill level: Running (General)
Level 20
For reaching this threshold on a body-enhancement skill, you have gained a 10% bonus to all stamina while running. In addition, gain a 20% bonus for the first thirty seconds while sprinting.
For hitting level twenty in a body-enhancement skill, you have earned 3 attribute points.

CHAPTER 36

Attribute points?

Arthur slowed down to a stop as he read through the message. That was a mistake.

He hadn't realized how much sheer momentum and stubbornness had been carrying his body forward. The moment he let himself pause and become distracted, abused muscles protested all at once.

Arthur crumpled ungracefully to the dirt track to the sounds of "ohhhs" from watchers all around.

When had he gathered watchers?

He could barely think about that. Every long muscle from the soles of his feet to the tops of his legs decided to cramp up all at once.

Arthur half sat up, lips pulled back from clenched teeth. He'd had these cramps before—they used to hit a lot when he was a child with too little food and too much work to do—and knew he had to ride them out. But it was excruciatingly unpleasant.

"Sir? Sir? Drink this. It'll help."

Someone shoved a small tankard in front of his face. He could barely think through the pain, but his nose caught the metallic scent of water.

Raging thirst hit him like a hammer. He grabbed the mug in both hands and drank. Only common sense kept him rapidly sipping instead of trying to suck it down at once.

The water was flavored lightly with salt and herbs. His stomach protested against water after so long without food, and he slowed again to keep from cramping his gut, too.

He could have retreated into his Personal Space, but time wouldn't move outside. It wouldn't do him any good other than to delay the inevitable.

He managed to pull himself away from the water long enough to look up.

"Carley, wasn't it?" he rasped. "What are you doing here?"

"Heard the commotion and wanted to see it for myself, sir," she said cheekily. "Were you really running all night?"

"No, I . . . night?" It had only been a couple of hours, hadn't it?

With a bad feeling in the pit of his stomach, he glanced to the side to see a small crowd dispersing. He had attracted a lot of attention.

Penn wasn't among them, but if word spread what he had just done, and if Penn linked that to his missing Master of Body Enhancement card, he might be in trouble.

Had he been running all night?

"Hasn't anyone ever warned you not to play with new cards out in public?" asked a cheery voice.

Somehow, Arthur was unsurprised when he saw Marion step through the crowd with a book in hand. The prince was dressed in pristine clothing that looked starched and new. It even included a cape.

Arthur's answer was a pained grunt.

Rolling his eyes, Marion tucked the book he'd been reading away. He walked over and looked down at Arthur.

"Let me guess: You went out and bought yourself some sort of stamina-enhancement card, couldn't resist trying it out, and let it *run* away with you."

Marion's voice was pitched a little too loud for comfort—just enough to carry.

Arthur may be worn to the bone with exhaustion, but he wasn't stupid.

"Isn't it rude . . . to ask about other people's cards?" he shot back, forcing a grin.

"And that's a yes," Marion said, again loud enough for the lingering bits of crowd to hear. "You there." He snapped his fingers at Carley. "Help my minders pull him off this track." He waved toward two men who had stood off to the side and seemed less than pleased to be put into service.

"Prince Marion, we are here to serve you, not—"

"You don't want me to be seen getting my hands dirty in public, do you? Oh, and do hurry up." He nodded down the track where a group of runners were coming fast. "I suspect someone intends to 'accidentally' step on the newcomer to show off."

Arthur's legs were too cramped and his arms too weak to help himself. He had to suffer the indignity of being pulled bodily off to the side by a fourteen-year-old and two men who looked like they wanted to be doing anything else.

"Thanks," he said through gritted teeth.

"Don't thank me yet." Marion sighed. "I've come with news you're not going to like."

His stomach dropped. "What's wrong now?"

"All Legendary recruits are to gather for a dragon orientation and class"—he cocked his head—"an hour from now. I went to your room only to find no servants and an unopened notice on your table. Don't tell me you haven't hired any personal servants?"

"An hour?"

Arthur lay flat on his back, not able to sit up, much less stand. He had been through the rigors of being a Rare egg recruit. Though that would be shadow boxing compared to this.

His clothes were a sweaty mess. He could smell himself, and it wasn't pleasant.

Arthur glanced over at Carley, who was edging away from the prince.

"I'll pay you two Rare shards to be my assistant until the egg hatches."

The girl froze.

Marion sighed. "That is not how you hire help . . . but oh, I see you're going to do it anyway. Why do I bother?"

"Four Rare shards," Carley said boldly, even though one Rare shard for two days of work was outrageous.

Arthur forced a grin. "Three."

"Done!" She pointed to Marion. "And the prince witnesses."

"Yes, yes, I've witnessed his stupidity. It's official." Marion sighed.

Arthur ignored that. "Go to my room. It's on the seventh level, number five three six. I need fresh clothing—" He was about to add "Just get something clean from the closet" but was interrupted.

"No, no, no!" Marion said, uncharacteristically sharp. "Fetch the most formal clothing you can find, as well as a cape and matching boots."

"Boots? In this weather?" Arthur asked.

"Who is the prince, and who is the baron's son?" Marion said, still snippy. He looked back to Carley. "Be quick. We'll likely need you to send for a healing potion too, if we can't get your new employer on his feet."

Carley nodded and was off like a shot.

Marion flipped a hand at his minders. "Go away now. No, a few steps further. Honestly, I don't have a flight card. I'm not leaving your sight." Only when the men stepped back a reluctant twenty feet did Marion kneel by Arthur's side. "If you can't actually defend yourself, you'd better look like you can."

That was why he was so worried about clothing. Arthur would have been touched, but he was still in a lot of pain.

The cramps had eased but had been replaced by a deep sense of lethargy. Standing was impossible. Walking to wherever they were meant to go was equally so.

Arthur had one trick up his sleeve, and if that didn't work . . . well, he'd be likely emptying his newly acquired coin bag for a healing potion.

He accessed his Personal Space.

It only took a moment, and once he was inside, he let out a groan of pure relief. It wasn't really his body, but it was good to be able to "stand" and shake out his legs.

"Yeah," he said to himself. "Pushing myself to level twenty all at once was stupid. Might be worth it, though."

Time to see what those attribute points were about.

When he had first placed his Master of Body Enhancement card into his heart deck, he'd been able to view his overall body attributes.

Base Attribute Points
(20 = Average)
Strength: 18
Stamina: 16
Dexterity: 16
Perception: 14
Charisma: 17
Intelligence: 22
Wisdom: 25
Luck: 21 (1 temporary point increase)

Oh, right. He had a temporary +1 to luck. He'd probably used his fair share of that during the eruption.

He felt instinctively that all he had to do was to will the points into the stat.

His perception was the lowest and seemed important. But there were more pressing issues.

He had to be strong enough to face whatever was to come.

"One point in strength, two in stamina," he said.

The numbers changed before his eyes.

Arthur looked down at himself but didn't feel any different. Then again, time didn't pass here.

He returned to his body.

A rolling warm power flowed from the core of his heart deck through the rest of his body. It washed away fatigue and exhaustion. Arthur took a deep breath, feeling like he had just woken from a refreshing nap.

He rose and stretched. His muscles were still tight, and he suspected they'd be aching tomorrow—refreshing his attributes didn't erase any damage he had done—but he felt wholly rejuvenated.

Marion watched him, eyebrows raised. "That's some card."

Arthur grinned back. "It really is."

Marion guided Arthur to a room to the side of the gym he claimed was a sauna. Thick clouds of steam wafted out. The moment he and Marion stepped inside, they were greeted by a servant in a hive uniform.

"Do you need any assistance, sirs?"

"Full scrub down for my friend, top to bottom," Marion said before Arthur could reply.

"Very good, sir."

"Now wait—" Arthur started.

The man gestured, and the thick steam coalesced around him into a warm, syrupy cloak. Arthur didn't have time to be startled or worried about holding his breath before the steam abruptly vanished.

He felt . . . clean. His hair was messed up and his clothes were damp—even the inside of his boots—but the sweat and bits of dust he'd picked up were gone.

"That will be one silver, sir," the man said.

An expensive service, but probably worth it.

"I could have just taken a bath," he muttered as he pretended to draw out a coin from his pocket. In reality, he removed it from his Personal Space before handing it over.

"Baths are for people whose time is not valuable." Marion's voice was light, but he nodded deeper into the room. The whole thing was so obscured by steam that details were hard to make out. Arthur thought he caught shadows here and there. It reminded him uncomfortably of scourglings in the fog, but he knew the truth: they were other people who could very well be listening in.

As he was no longer an insult to the nose, he and Marion decided to walk outside the sauna and wait for Carley's return. Well, Marion walked. Arthur squelched.

Carley was not long in returning. "Here you are, Mr. Kane."

"Arthur's fine." He gratefully took the bundle of folded clothing, glad to see she had included new soft boots.

Marion gave an unimpressed sniff. "Don't tell me you're going to let your new servant—"

"Assistant," Carley piped up. "I'm not serving him, I'm assisting him."

"Yes, a proper servant would know to be quiet unless spoken to." Marion rolled his eyes. "Arthur, your assistant needs better clothing. She can't be seen in . . . are those overalls?"

Carley, who had been scowling at Marion, changed her tune and broke into a smile. "Proper assistants to important people always look the part," she agreed, then paused. "You are an important person, right?"

"Baron's son," Marion answered. "They're a dime a dozen, but your new master here is also one of the Legendary recruits."

"Yeah, yeah, I know." Then Carley's eyes widened. "Wait, if you get eaten by the egg, I'll still get paid, right?"

"This is getting more expensive by the minute," Arthur grumbled. He withdrew two silver coins from his Personal Space. Then on second thought—because he wasn't sure what would happen to his extradimensional storage if he died—he removed a Rare card shard. The normal one, not one of the corner pieces. He held the piece between thumb and forefinger. "This is payment in advance. Now, take these coins and buy an appropriate uniform. After that, return to my room and . . . take any messages for me."

She eagerly took the money. "Can I get something to eat, too?"

"Of course," he said, surprised she felt the need to ask. "Order whatever you want."

She grinned, and he wondered if he had just made a mistake.

"You know," Marion said as Carley skipped off, "people are going to think she is your little sister."

"Fat chance of that happening." That would be the same as if someone assumed Carley was his real sister, who died as a young child, or "Ernest Kane's" make-believe sister. Either way, he didn't want to explain. Fortunately, Arthur had the perfect way to derail him. "Why have you nullified your Legendary card?"

Marion actually flinched in surprise and cast a guilty glare at his ever-present minders, who stood not far away. "What makes you say that?"

"Because when you have it on, you don't let anyone get a word in edgewise."

"I don't! . . . Do I?"

Arthur gave him a look.

"Go change your clothes, you look like a Common egg recruit," Marion muttered. He wouldn't quite meet Arthur's gaze.

Marion didn't want to talk about it. Arthur could respect that. So he took his clothing into the sauna and got changed.

As promised, Carley had indeed brought down a cape.

When Arthur walked out, he felt like a complete idiot in his fine clothing, boots so new the leather actually squeaked, and a flowing fur-lined cape even though he was in a tropical location.

But if he looked like a fool, at least he had company. With a nod of approval, Marion joined him.

Arthur had no idea where he was to go, but Marion's silent and intimidating minders led the way, one in front and one in back.

While they walked, Marion shot Arthur a sidelong glance. "That's a mean game face."

Arthur checked his own expression. "That's just my face."

"What I mean is, you really want this, don't you? The dragon egg?"

"Of course I do." Arthur shot him a look. "Don't you?"

Marion shrugged. "When you're a prince, one of your first lessons is to separate duty from desire."

He wasn't sure what to say to that. "I'm sorry."

"No, no." Marion flipped a hand at him. "I don't say that to sound like a sad sack. I'm simply aware there is a chance this egg could kill us both. Granted," he added after a moment, "I'm counting on my ability to see ahead to do everything I can to avoid that."

Arthur nodded. "Must be nice to see the future."

"It's really not," Marion said. "It's boring, waiting for people to catch up to the part of a conversation you've already heard. Worse, it's only a few seconds ahead. Not enough to actually see anything important. But I'm expected to make the best showing that I can. Duty, you know?"

Arthur nodded, though he didn't know. As far as he could tell, "duty" was an excuse nobles used to give themselves more privileges.

Marion's mouth turned down at the corners. "I had a sister who died trying for a Legendary."

Arthur was so surprised he stumbled on his next step. Marion didn't seem to notice. His eyes were distant, somewhere else. "She'd just gotten her card. Had it maybe a few weeks before the Legendary egg was laid."

"I . . . I'm sorry."

Marion nodded. "Echo reminds me of her."

Once again, Arthur wasn't sure how to answer that. It seemed Marion was done speaking too. They made the rest of their way in silence.

The gathering was to be held in an auditorium with raised seating with the main stage at the bottom. Arthur was grateful it meant he could sit down. His stamina and strength had been refreshed, but he was growing sore after having run literally all night. Hungry too.

After he sat, he took out a plate of dinner rolls he'd saved from last night's feast.

"Want one?" he asked Marion.

Marion eyed him. "Is that strawberry jam on those rolls?"

"There's blackberry, too."

"That, I'll take."

The nobles sitting in the same row eyed them with contempt. One sniffed.

Arthur couldn't have cared less. He had something good to eat and was likely going to learn something valuable today. It was a good day.

Other Legendary recruits filed in. They were dressed just as nicely as Arthur and Marion—or even more extravagantly in some cases, with the women wearing gowns glittering with jewels.

That reminded him of the Rare promenade, which reminded him of Cressida.

He wondered what she was doing now. Had she heard of the disastrous scourge-eruption? Joy would be too young to fight, but would Cressida have any time from her training to think about Arthur, too?

A hush fell over the room as one of the doors to the side of the stage opened. A man in his late thirties walked in. He had slick black hair and a swarthy look. Stopping mid-stage, he clasped his hands behind his back and looked up at them.

"Good afternoon. I am Leader Ismael. I'm sure many of you are familiar with my dragon, Marv."

A susurrus of noise went through the crowd. Marion sighed.

Apparently this "Marv" was semi-famous. Arthur had never heard of him.

Ismael smiled tightly. "Let me be the first to welcome you all to Buck Moon Hive. Now, to get some immediate questions out of the way: The hive leaders have convened and decided since most of the Legendary recruits were evacuated here, it makes more sense to bring the egg to you than transport you all back to Wolf Moon."

Arthur's eyebrows went up. That sounded like pure politics to him.

"Make no mistake," Ismael continued, "linking a Legendary dragon will automatically propel you to one of the most important positions in the kingdom. It comes with a great deal of responsibility, but there is also a great deal of personal risk. You likely have been warned of this, and now I will warn you again. People have already died in the . . . *badly handled* scourge-eruption," he said with sly emphasis. "Chances are good that even more of you will perish attempting the link. As such, you are allowed to back out at any time for any reason. It will not impugn your honor."

Marion snorted. Apparently that wasn't the case for royalty.

Ismael went on. "Some of you may ask what makes a Legendary dragon so different from the lower ranks. After all, a sweet purple Common hatchling wouldn't hurt a fly. It's quite unusual to have any risk with a Rare hatching. The difference, ladies and gentlemen, is a matter of scope and power.

"A Common card has a fraction of the potential power of an Uncommon. The gap is even wider between Uncommon and Rare. And the gap between a Rare and a Legendary is the difference between a lake and an ocean.

"A newly hatched dragon has no control over its powers at first. When it kills people, it is usually by accident." He paused for a moment to let that sink in before he added lightly, "Not that it will matter: You'll be just as dead."

A titter of nervous laughter went through the audience. Ismael didn't crack a smile.

"Now, most of you will already know the things I'm about to discuss. Bear with me. It is imperative we do not link a powerful dragon with someone who is unaware of basic facts.

"Dragons are magical creatures. They are born with cards in their core. While they may have secondary or tertiary decks as they grow—the equivalent to a card-anchor bag or tattoo—their core card cannot be removed while alive. It is the center of their being.

"As such, an Uncommon dragon will always be an Uncommon dragon. Adding a more powerful card, such as a Rare, to the secondary deck will magically poison or outright kill them. This will not be something a Legendary-rank rider will have to worry about. But as a future leader, it is your duty to ensure no ambitious Common rider is trying to talk his beast into taking on a more powerful card. Remember: equal rank or lower only.

"Now, let's stamp out the usual myths: Dragons do not always link riders of the same gender. One thing you'll quickly learn about dragonkind is there are rarely any hard and fast rules. While most dragons link male to male or female to female, some happily choose the opposite sex. That means," he said, giving them a stern look, "if that Legendary pops out as female, I do not want to see you men turning away."

Another low chuckle.

"Another myth," he continued, "is you can reliably tell a dragon's card type by its color. This is not the case. I once knew a wine-colored Common with fast-attack fire powers. I thought it was a damn lightning bolt. Who here can tell me what colors make up purple?" he barked suddenly.

There was a moment of silence, and then several people called out "Red and blue."

"That's right," Ismael said. "Which means a purple very well may be comfortable with aspects of water or fire. The dragon I'm talking about had a swift attack card—you'll see versions of that with purples—and linked with a rider with a fire card. It made a potent combination.

"Now I'll go over dragon colors. Again, these are generalities—the shade can make a difference, as well as whether they have any shimmer qualities. Finally, linking with a rider can further distort the effects of the core card. Then you'll have the weirdos who don't seem to fit in anywhere.

"Now, purples, since I brought them up, tend to have physicality or enhancement-type cards. They are the acrobats, the quick couriers, and if you've ever dealt with one, you'll know they generally aren't the big thinkers."

He smiled.

"The dam who laid the egg you all are here for was a purple. We don't know who the sire was. Dragons can have offspring of any color, and will occasionally lay eggs of a greater rank. Your Legendary can be anything, ladies and gentlemen, so do not set your heart on a color.

"Moving on, we generally group the rest of the colors into loose family types. First is the elementals. The blues, which usually have water or occasionally wind-type cards, and all the combinations you can imagine those generate: ice, mist, steam, and so on. Green dragons usually run toward living nature powers. But that's not just growing pretty trees: Shimmer greens can pull apart the fabric of reality itself to create our portals. Many greens also have powers over soil, which is a living thing. Whereas your standard brown dragon usually has powers over rock, minerals, and all manner of earth but can't touch living soil.

"Rounding out the elemental types are yellows, which are light-based dragons, including light you cannot perceive. You'll see a lot of esoteric powers in there—we have a few yellows who don't deal with light, but sound.

"Our next family are the reds and oranges, which are generally not grouped with the elementals. Reds, as you guessed, usually deal with fire and energy. Orange dragons generally work on adapting that energy into some form. However, these two are set in their own family because they tend to interchange. We have a bright Common red in our hive whose power is to turn water into a mild acid, which she then sets on fire.

"Silver, white, and pink make up the final family group, with silvers edging toward pure magical-based attacks. Whites, of course, specialize in mind magic. Pinks are another esoteric catch-all color, with many having meta or knowledge-based power. Scholars have tried to define the boundaries of 'meta' for generations, and as far as I'm aware, none have succeeded."

He looked around at the audience.

"What does this all mean for you? Well, if you were a Common recruit, you would look for a dragon of roughly the same card type as your own. You have a card to smash rocks or draw water from the air, you look for a brown or blue hatchling. You're a smarty pants with a memory card? Go for a pink. But you aren't Common, are you?

"That's the final—and for you right now, the most important—difference of a Legendary versus the lower ranks." A pause. "Legendary hatchlings traditionally pick off-type combinations.

"Now, what do I mean by off-type cards?" Ismael said over the murmurs of people all around them.

Arthur leaned forward, fascinated.

He couldn't help but think about Joy's hatching and how she had nearly died because she couldn't link with an appropriate card.

Did that mean, on top of everything else, Legendary hatchlings were less likely to die than lower ranks?

"Let me make an example of myself and my dragon." Ismael smiled up at them, and to Arthur it felt like a practiced, showman's smile. A smile he had used himself while trying to bluff at the poker table. "I was a humble son of a master scholar. My father had done well for himself, and I was the first in my family to receive a Legendary card—knowledge based, of course."

Arthur glanced around the room to check reactions. Nobody seemed outraged that someone not noble born had linked with a Legendary. They didn't even seem surprised. This was likely a known story in their circles. As usual, Arthur was out of the loop.

Ismael continued, "I wasn't an official Legendary recruit, either. Oh, I had my daydreams of linking with a powerful dragon—I am only human—but on that day, I was simply there along with other high-ranking members of the scholar's guild to witness the hatching. I wasn't even standing close to the egg. We were kept away for safety purposes, you see.

"It didn't matter. The first true recruits stepped up and were rejected rather forcefully." The dark shadow in his expression made Arthur guess whatever had happened had not been pleasant. "Then the egg cracked, and the next thing I knew, a little green dragon was galloping my way."

His face softened at this last bit. The smile turned more real.

"It's no secret that Marv's portal power is the best of its type in the world. He's a Legendary dragon, so that ought to be the case. But linking with my specific card allows him a deep well of knowledge and insight he wouldn't have otherwise. As a result, he can now extend his portals back through time."

Arthur couldn't help himself. He shot a glance at Marion. The other boy simply sat back in his chair, looking bored.

Most people had similar expressions, as if none of this information was new.

Taking their cue, Arthur schooled his own expression into polite, interested boredom.

But not before he caught a flash of eyes looking his way. Penn was sitting a few rows down from him and had turned almost completely in his seat to see Arthur's reaction.

Determinedly, Arthur caught his gaze and nodded once as if in acknowledgment.

A frown flashed over Penn's face. He nodded in reply and then turned in his seat.

"Once again," Ismael continued, "these are all generalities. Some Legendary hatchlings prefer to reinforce their card with something of a similar kind.

"That leads us to our final myth I would like to quash for the day: Dragons know best. Legendary dragons are often strong-willed and can have their own, specific idea of what is best. It's up to their linked riders to encourage them to wield that power for the good of the kingdom, rather than the good of themselves."

Ismael turned and gestured to the side. Another man walked up. He was heavyset with a snow-white beard. At Ismael's direction, the man turned to make a broad gesture to the front of the audience.

Light projected out from his fingers and formed a list—though the characters were too blurry for Arthur to read.

"In a moment, we will reveal a list of the Legendary recruits' current standings. Those at the top will be allowed to approach the egg first, while those lower down must wait their turn. In the event that we cycle through the entire list without the egg hatching, we will wait a week, then try again with the survivors."

For the first time, Ismael received a question. A young lady at the front center raised her hand.

He acknowledged her with a nod. "Go on."

"Are the names on that list fixed?"

"Certainly not. The hive leaders and the rest of the high-ranking administration will be watching you as a group and as individuals. We anticipate movement within the list as people put themselves forward and others fall short of expectations."

Arthur could read between the lines. The names on the list would move up and down depending on who won and lost duels. Perhaps those who sucked up to the hive leaders, too.

Considering this a competition for a Legendary dragon, the duels would be fierce. Valentina and Whitaker had chosen to whittle down their recruits using the scourge-eruption. It seemed Leader Ismael would do so with duels.

With that, Ismael nodded to the other man again.

The fuzzy words sharpened to readable detail.

1. Francis Orchardtree
2. Echo Spyglass
3. Ernest "Arthur" Kane

He stopped reading after that.

Third from the top? Had his actions during the eruption impressed that many people?

Or was he being fed to the scourge-wolves?

Also, how much attention was he under that people here now knew he preferred to be called "Arthur"?

He half expected Marion to pat him on the back and joke something like, "Well, it was nice knowing you . . ."

But that was something the darker humored Horatio would do. And one look at Marion's face told him he found nothing funny about this. There was only sympathy in his eyes.

Arthur heard his own name being whispered about. Most were looking around, trying to identify him. He supposed that, being high nobles, they ran in the same circles.

He was mostly unknown, which made it easier for him to be picked out.

Ismael spoke up again, saying that he would stay back for any additional one-on-one questions, and that communication would be sent when they were to try to link with the egg.

Until then, they were dismissed.

"Come on," Marion said tightly. "We might be able to get out of here without being challenged if we hurry . . ."

"We?"

Arthur shot another quick look at the list and saw that Marion Amberlion was number four. People would be aiming for him, too.

They rose and filed out, though there was a bit of a jam at the door. Arthur heard commotion as some people were shoved aside.

"Hey! Ernest Kane! Or Arthur Kane—whatever you call yourself —" one yelled over the crowd.

Arthur pretended not to hear him and ducked through the door.

He pulled Marion to the side and focused on his **Stealth** skill. He knew he was just putting off the inevitable. There wasn't anywhere to hide, and someone with a Legendary card likely had other ways to find him.

"Isn't that your assistant?" Marion asked. He had his head down and was fiddling with his card-anchor tattoo—likely removing the Nullify card so he'd have access to the near future.

Sure enough, Carley stood at the end of the hall, looking both anxious and impatient.

Arthur raised his hand and signaled for her to come to him. He knew the moment he moved, it was a mistake. It broke the thin veneer of **Stealth** he'd attained.

Marion groaned. "Sorry, Arthur. You're not going to be able to avoid this."

"Avoid what—"

With a whoosh of wind, a tall dark-skinned man stood in front of Arthur, glaring down. "You're Ernest Kane?"

Arthur sighed. "Call me Arthur."

The man straightened and said in a formal, clipped voice, "Arthur Kane, I, Hart Caddel, son of Viscount Caddel formally challenge you—"

"Kane, I challenge you to a duel," spat a voice right behind him.

Arthur turned to see Penn. His cousin had a half smile on his face. "Sorry, Hart, you're too slow."

Hart Caddel jutted out his jaw aggressively. "Then I demanded the right to fight the winner."

"That would be me," Penn said smoothly. Then he winked at Arthur.

Was he helping him or mocking him? Arthur honestly wasn't sure. He wasn't a fool: He hadn't won in the Rare duel, and he had zero chance against Legendary opponents.

But the alternative was bowing out. That was unacceptable.

Marion nudged Arthur's back, which reminded him he had a role to play. "I accept your challenge, Penn. But . . . uh, my assistant is waving at me."

He left just as a young woman in a shockingly tight leather dress marched up to Marion to challenge him to a duel. Marion looked equal parts intimidated and intrigued.

Carley ran up to him and pressed a tightly rolled scroll in his hands. "Sir! Come quickly, you've got important visitors—hive leaders sitting in your room waiting for you."

"Hive leaders? Which ones?"

"I don't know. A guy and some old lady. Maybe she's his grandmother? Great-great-grandmother?"

Valentina and Whitaker.

He didn't know them well, but he doubted they would like to be kept waiting. Thanking Carley, he told her to return to his room and let the leaders know that he would be along momentarily.

Then he turned back to Penn. It looked like he'd have to schedule getting ritualistically beaten up until after the meeting.

CHAPTER 37

Arthur stopped in front of the door to his room, tugged down his shirt, and then smoothed it out again. He was already dressed as nicely as he could be, but when faced with the prospect of a private meeting with the leaders, he felt it wasn't enough.

Lastly, before he stepped in, he activated his Charming Gentleperson card.

Valentina and Whitaker stood near the balcony. They faced each other and looked like they were in the middle of an intense, angry conversation. They broke off whatever they were talking about when Arthur arrived. However, a dark mist looking like an angry rain cloud floated over Valentina's head.

Carley stood off to the side, looking more than a little intimidated. When Arthur nodded for her to go, she didn't hesitate to scuttle out the door.

Should he bow or something?

Arthur settled for standing at attention until Carley closed the door behind him.

"Leader Valentina, Leader Whitaker," he said with a nod to both. "I understand you wanted to speak to me."

Whitaker strode forward and made a point of looking Arthur up and down. "I can't decide if you are the cause of all this recent chaos or our savior from it."

"I don't understand what you mean."

His eyebrows lifted. "You don't? You just happen to be one of the two to find the blasted egg in the first place. And don't think I've forgotten about the scholar's guild or that business with our new Rare hatchling. And now it's come out you're the one who had a hand in saving most of the Legendary recruits. The real hero of the day—"

Valentina cut in. "You think that a mere baron's son arranged all that, Whitaker?"

"I think once is fine, twice is a coincidence. Three or *four* times . . ." Whitaker trailed off with a glower at Arthur. "Well? What do you have to say for yourself?"

"That I've been lucky," Arthur said. "And . . ." He wasn't sure if he should say what was on his mind.

Whitaker jumped on it at once. "And?"

Taking a breath, he decided to plunge in. "I feel like I'm the one for this egg. Everything I've done isn't for the rank or to impress the king. I want to link with that dragon. Perhaps it's made me more willing to take chances that others wouldn't."

His words sounded corny to his ears, but the two leaders exchanged a look.

Whitaker snorted, and some of the tension seemed to fade from the air.

"Keep that attitude, kid. You'll need it when the egg tests you to decide whether to eat you alive or not."

"You are too old to be this dramatic," Valentina said, then added, "But you're not wrong. Now, Ernest . . . oh, you wish to be called Arthur, isn't that right?"

"Yes, please."

"Then sit. We three should have a chat." She gestured to the sitting table outside on the balcony. It was a pleasant temperature outside with a warm sun beaming down. As Arthur gazed out, he saw a sort of shell made of wind in the air. Valentina's doing, likely. He didn't doubt it would be hard to be observed out here.

Valentina folded age-stiffened hands together. "You may have heard that the egg is no longer in Wolf Moon Hive's possession."

"It's to be hatched here," Arthur confirmed, "but no one mentioned where the new hatchling would go afterward."

"That is still to be determined."

Whitaker snorted. "The other hives have used this catastrophe to take the egg out from under us on the pretense it's easier to move the egg here than all the recruits back to Wolf Moon Hive where 'it may not be safe.' It's transparent, ugly politics if you ask me."

"No one did," Valentina snipped, but then sighed. "Though you're not wrong."

"We need that egg," Whitaker growled. "It was laid at *our* hive, and we need another Legendary rider. We're understaffed—dangerously so."

Arthur was a little shocked they'd speak so bluntly. They were almost treating him as if he were one of them.

"I've heard there has been an increase in scourge-eruptions. Is it that bad?" he asked.

"It could be," Whitaker said.

Valentina hastened to add, "There have been increases before. These things come in waves, and the scholars have dozens of theories why. But you may have noticed that our local scholar's guild is quite . . . decimated."

Arthur winced, remembering the remains of the building.

"The short of it is the quorum of hive leaders has come to the conclusion that it will be up to the new rider and hatchling which hive they want to go to. To be blunt, Arthur, if it's you, we want you at Wolf Moon."

"It is your home," Valentina added.

Deep in his heart, Arthur still thought of his old border-town village as his home. But he kept silent, waiting for the leaders to get to the punchline.

He was a little annoyed when Whitaker went the complimentary route.

"I hear you're number three on the recruit list. That's good standing."

He couldn't let that pass. "It isn't. I've been thrown to the wolves."

Whitaker cocked his head. "Explain."

Arthur hesitated but decided it wouldn't hurt. "Yes, I acquitted myself well during the eruption, but I'm just a baron's son with no real backing of my own. Now people will make a point of eliminating me to climb the list."

Valentina and Whitaker exchanged a look.

"It's not that dramatic," Whitaker said. "The quorum of hive leaders made such a stink about a few deaths that Buck Moon will make a point to ensure there won't be any more. They'll have healers on hand during the duels."

Relief must have shown on Arthur's face because Valentina smiled. "You should be aware that other hive leaders will be backing their favorites to entice them to their hive, should they link that dragon."

Whitaker rolled his eyes. "Oh, just tell the boy straight out: Other leaders will be bribing their favorites, and we are too." He looked at Arthur directly. "So, what we're asking is what you want to come back home to Wolf Moon . . . and what you feel you need to succeed."

Arthur sat back. There was every chance he would be visited by other hive leaders, but he'd been here for quite some time. No one had approached him.

And the fact of the matter was that if he did have a choice, he would choose Wolf Moon. He had roots there.

"A combat card," he said. "My Legendary is utility focused, and I need something so I don't embarrass myself in duels."

Again, the two exchanged a look, and Arthur's stomach sank. He knew it wouldn't be good news before Whitaker opened his mouth.

"It's not like we have extra Legendary cards floating around. The best we can do is load you up with a Rare—maybe two—and unless you played it smart or got lucky, it wouldn't be enough power to overcome a Legendary card. Plus, you still have to practice with the damn thing to learn how to best use it. All cards have a learning curve. You have your mana unlocked, at least?"

"I do," he said sourly. He should have expected that answer. One of the first things his father told him about cards was that it often took practice to master them. Especially if he was going to go in underpowered in a duel.

"Let's come back to that," Valentina said impatiently. "What else do you need?"

What else? Arthur didn't want much in life except for good shelter, semi-regular meals, and the time to grow his skills.

The things he truly wanted weren't for himself.

"My original recruiter, Kenzie," he said, and saw Valentina nod, "I want her to get the full reward if I link the dragon here." Some of the hive systems could be bureaucratic enough to deny her due if he went somewhere else.

"That can be done," Valentina said, confirming his fears.

"If I link the dragon, will I become one of the hive leaders?" Arthur asked.

Whitaker's eyes narrowed. "In training, yes."

"Then as a leader, I want a say in how the hive gives out funds to the city's orphanages. They have several programs that do a good job getting kids their first cards, but I think we can do better." Arthur continued, on a roll now. "I want a regular stipend, and I want—I *need*—time in addition to my regular dragon-rider training to level up my cards. They're skill based, and I've only scratched the surface of what they can do."

"They?" Whitaker asked.

Arthur realized his mistake at once. He shrugged as if it wasn't a big deal. "I'm building my deck around a utility specialty. It makes sense with my Legendary."

Valentina made a sound deep in her throat, but he couldn't tell if it was disbelief or agreement. But then she said, "What else?"

He couldn't for the life of him think of anything. Thanks to Marion's coin bag, he could buy what he needed. "That's it."

"Nothing for your family?" Valentina pressed.

Arthur barked a surprised laugh. "No, I don't want *any* compensation going back to Baron Kane."

Whitaker opened his mouth and looked almost offended on the baron's behalf. Valentina cut him off.

"Well, those are reasonable . . . demands. Let's talk about cards."

Whitaker sat back, annoyed. "Utility deck," he muttered. "You got nothing at least elemental, boy? Valentina, don't you have one of those Rare elemental enhancements?"

"As much as I appreciate Arthur, I am not giving him something from my heart," she said waspishly.

"We can't . . . go to a card shop and buy one?" Arthur asked. "I understand if the hive won't sell us something here, but you have dragons, and surely one of the cities . . ." He trailed off as he caught the hive leaders' expressions.

Whitaker looked chagrined. Valentina seemed quietly furious, though the anger wasn't at him.

"We have dragons, yes," she said, "but portal use is approved through the hive leaders."

"If I know Ismael, he'll let us go through to one of the kingdom's center cities and then shut the thing behind us again," Whitaker said bluntly. "He's a snake."

"It would take us days to fly back here the long way," Valentina admitted. "By which point, the egg would have hatched."

Tess had flown Arthur from the borderland town back up to Wolf Moon in one arduous day. But Tess was a purple dragon with speed and stamina and likely some quickening cards. Valentina's dragon was elderly, and Whitaker's wasn't built for speed either.

Interesting that in this case a Common outshone a Legendary.

"We'll have to make do from our personal decks." She pulled out a delicate coin purse from her pocket. He realized it was a card anchor when she pulled a card out of it.

Whitaker beat her to it. He reached for a tattoo on his forearm and flicked a card at Arthur.

"Here. I've been meaning to upgrade it anyway."

Moderate Self-Repair
Uncommon
Healing
The wielder of this card will be granted the ability to repair minor to moderate wounds and injuries. Severe, crippling, complex, or mortal wounds may be only partially healed. This is an active effect and requires the use of mana.

"Won't fix losing a limb or mortal wounds," Whitaker said. "Also, you have to concentrate to keep the card active, so you're out of luck if you pass out. But it might save your hide if the healers take their time getting to you."

It certainly wasn't the solution to all his problems, but any healing card was a valuable find.

"Thank you," he said honestly.

"I have one I think you'll like," Valentina said, then hesitated to look at Arthur as if studying him for a hidden quality before she drew out a second from her purse anchor.

"Use these two together."

Arthur looked and inhaled sharply. He recognized the first.

Phase In, Phase Out
Rare
Teleportation

This card grants the wielder the ability to temporarily make their body incorporeal to pass through objects or allow objects to pass through them. Limit is ten seconds of incorporeal time per hour, on a rolling basis. This card does not use mana.

The second card was intriguing.

Mana Amendment
Rare
Meta
This card has the ability to amend the abilities of any targeted Rare-tier card to enable it to use mana. This may change the fine details of the card, though it will not alter the target card's rank.

He wanted to find out what effect the Mana Amendment card would have right now, but one blaring fact held him back.

"I'm grateful for the use of these cards," he said carefully. Cards from the personal decks of hive leaders was no small thing. "But I don't think I can win duels with these."

They were hive leaders. Didn't they have anything more powerful?

Then again, why would they have powerful secondary cards? Their own Legendary cards and their linked dragons were more than enough power.

"I don't expect you to win duels with these," Valentina said. "You said you want that little egg? Well, if it wants you, it doesn't matter how many royal brats are put before it first. Don't fight to win, Arthur. Fight to survive."

CHAPTER 38

After the meeting with the hive leaders ended, Arthur opened the door to his room and was unsurprised to find two large men dressed in hive colors waiting for him just outside.

They had the air of guards come to march a prisoner to his execution, though they were polite when they greeted him. Arthur had no doubt they had some card magic up their sleeves if he refused to go along quietly.

However, he was resigned to his fate.

As they walked down the hall, the two men flanking him on either side, Arthur turned his attention inward to his card anchor and the three new cards waiting for him.

He had upgraded his secondary card-anchor deck on several occasions since he first purchased one—a simple bag at the time—as a child. But now, it felt like his anchor deck was reaching its limit. If he had not given the Wind Release card to Marion and returned Steel Fists to Penn, he doubted he'd be able to fit in three more cards. If he wanted to add any in the future, he would have to remove cards or upgrade again.

Just one more thing to do after the egg's hatching. If he survived.

I will survive, he promised himself.

He hadn't come all this way for nothing.

And he ignored the fact that other Legendary recruits were likely telling themselves the same thing.

The guards led him down twelve levels. That meant the dueling arenas were located within the sublevels, underground.

That would likely affect some of the pure wind or air elemental cards. Maybe not enough to really impede a Legendary card user, but it might be an advantage if he could find a way to use it.

He focused on these details rather than the giant crowd that had formed around the dueling arena.

It felt as if the entire hive had come to watch the show. Somebody with earth-building cards had constructed tiered seating that went from the floor all the way up to the high ceiling, where it was so shadowed it was hard to see the top.

Some dragons small enough to fit in the tunnels had even joined in and sat in their own area, occasionally flapping up high into the air to see something particularly interesting.

The crowd was rowdy, too. Swearing and catcalling and having a great time watching the elite—and people they would one day have to obey if they linked with the dragon—beat each other to a pulp.

As Arthur passed by, he heard an announcer calling out the odds of the next fight. A twinge of regret shot through him. He'd loved betting on card duels during the Wolf Moon Hive festival. A not-insignificant part of him wished he were among the crowd rather than one of the ones they bet on.

I am either going to win somebody a lot of money or be cursed for losing, he thought regretfully.

The arena itself was separated into four quadrants, all reinforced by semi-translucent magical shields. The shields stretched all the way to the dome ceiling. There was a reason for this, as one of the quadrants was currently filled with bubbling lava.

Somebody had a card with magma powers. Their opponent was well matched and seemed to be able to fly using the updrafts of incredibly hot air. The flyer peppered the magma user with silver, metallic-looking bolts. At a glance, Arthur doubted those bolts were Legendary rank. Likely Uncommon strength. But from the frustrated howls coming out from the one gap in the lava, they were effective.

That's what partially made a good deck. Legendary cards set the stage and the terms of the engagement. But only a fool relied on them exclusively. Other cards weren't as powerful, but they provided neat tricks that could turn a fight on its head.

Surrounding the perimeter of the dueling arena were men and women in healer's garb.

There were so many of them, Arthur was mildly alarmed. Who was running the clinics in and around the hive?

The recruits' safety was all well and good, but it would be at the cost of ill-timed broken legs and illnesses.

Arthur heard his name being called. He turned and saw Penn walking up to him. His cousin's pose was confident, with just a bit of swagger.

Penn clearly knew he was going to win this next bout.

Arthur tried not to feel bitter about that.

"Kane, right on time," Penn said, nodding to Arthur's two helpers as if to say that he had this.

"Penn," Arthur said neutrally. He glanced around. "So, do we wait for one of the quarters to open up or . . . ?"

"It seems Marion will be done shortly. I've booked our little duel afterward." He slapped Arthur on the shoulder, and although Penn had always been a handsy sort of guy, the slap felt harder than usual.

Arthur's internal alarm rose.

Penn had plenty of reasons to hate him, especially if he had guessed what Arthur had done.

But it wasn't like Arthur could run. Keeping his composure, he followed Penn around to the other side of the arena. Sure enough, Marion was facing off against the young lady with the leather dress.

He wasn't doing very well.

Marion could see several seconds into the future, which made him tricky to pin down. Unfortunately, his opponent seemed to have some sort of webbing power. Threads made of strands of air and moisture shot toward Marion, who dodged with uncanny accuracy.

Until she managed to finally back him into a corner, where every move in the future resulted in her victory.

Strands of the netting wrapped around one of Marion's arms and crawled up to his throat.

Use Wind Release, Arthur silently urged.

A focus blast of wind would handily disrupt the strands. It might even blow his opponent back across the arena. That would give Marion time to collect himself and strike back.

The other boy was bare-handed. He had a card that allowed him to become instantly competent with any tool. It wasn't as good as a sword, but his opponent didn't carry a visible weapon either.

Marion could even cut the strands with a high enough skill with a dagger.

The prince, however, struggled, his face growing purple as he was cut off from air. Finally, he ceased his struggle and raised his hand to signal a defeat, but his opponent had a point to prove. She didn't let up.

"He's conceded!" Arthur yelled. "Let him go!"

Marion's opponent didn't react.

Choking, Marion's eyes rolled up, and he fell onto his knees. Several of the healers moved in with concerned expressions.

Only when they breached the barrier—Arthur saw that each healer wore a strip of fabric emblazoned with a rune tied to their upper arm that allowed them within—was Marion released.

The watching crowd groaned or cheered, depending on their bets.

Light flashed above, and Arthur realized a running account of the Legendary recruit list was displayed high above.

Marion had just sunk several places.

Arthur's name had as well. Just by virtue of not dueling.

Seeing that, his resolve firmed. His chances against Penn weren't good, but he had gotten out of sticky situations before. If he managed to win, that was one step closer to the egg.

The healers worked their magic, and Marion was soon back on his feet. The translucent shielding dropped, and he and his opponent cleared out.

Arthur caught Marion's eye and wished he had time to commiserate, but he had to get his head in the game. It was time to duel.

When he had slotted his new cards into his secondary anchor deck, the Self-Repair card and Phase In, Phase Out card had gone in without any fanfare.

Mana Amendment required a little more attention.

Please choose a card to link with Mana Amendment.

In his mind's eye, he saw the available cards. He picked Phase In, Phase Out.

The two cards briefly merged with each other. As they separated again, Phase In, Phase Out was altered.

Phase In, Phase Out
Rare
Teleportation
This card grants the wielder the ability to temporarily make their body incorporeal to pass through objects, or to allow objects to pass through them. Limit is 10 seconds of incorporeal time per hour, on a rolling basis.
(Temporary Mana Amendment effect)
When using mana, the limit is extended to 30 seconds of incorporeal time per hour, on a rolling basis.

That was a straightforward, but useful, boost.

The question was, could he find a way to beat Penn before his boost ran out? If he timed it right, each phase should only count as a fraction of a second. He could stretch thirty seconds into many uses.

As he walked into the arena, Arthur reached into his Personal Space and drew out a hammer. He had purchased it back when buying supplies—what felt like years ago instead of only a few days. After that, he had used the Instant Competence card to boost his hammer skills to level 14.

He and Penn reached the middle of the floor and turned to face each other. The semitranslucent shield went up behind them. Instantly, all sound from outside was cut off.

Come to think of it, Arthur hadn't heard any noise from the duelists while outside. He had chalked that up to the noisy, enthusiastic crowd. But it seemed there was a sound dampener in effect.

Penn glanced at Arthur's hammer and smirked. His hands were empty. In fact, he wasn't wearing a sword sheath on his belt, and no daggers were visible.

However, Arthur wouldn't bet against him having something up his sleeve.

And a moment later, he was proven right. Only Penn's weapon of choice was psychological.

"I heard you put on quite a show last night, Arthur Kane," he said, slightly mocking. "You ran for hours. I didn't think you had it in you."

So, it seemed he had heard.

Arthur tried to pass it off. "New stamina card," he said, twirling the hammer in an expert way he hadn't known how to do a few days ago. "That means I can outlast whatever you have in store."

His attempts to get Penn to refocus on the duel didn't work. "We both know that's no simple stamina card." Penn's gaze was focused and icy. "You're trying to play in the big leagues, Kane. But I saw you during the eruption—you might have a crafting card, but I didn't see anything close to a Legendary power."

Arthur was honestly insulted. "I saved your life like three times!"

"Using cute tricks—something any Rare or Uncommon card could pull off. But you have something powerful in your heart now, don't you? Something that *enhances* your body."

Oh no.

Arthur pulled what he hoped was an affronted and confused look. "What are you getting at? Are we going to talk or are we going to fight?"

"I want you to tell me who sold you the card. You know the one I mean."

Yeah, he wasn't going to do that.

Arthur's plan had been to wait for Penn to attack, phase through it, and surprise him with a counterattack.

But fear and desperation to change the subject made Arthur desperate enough to attack instead.

He ran at Penn, bringing down the hammer, which Penn easily sidestepped. With a fluid motion Arthur couldn't follow, Penn used Arthur's own momentum to spin him around. His fist struck the back of Arthur's head hard enough to briefly ring his bell. A second hit his left kidney.

Grimacing, Arthur fell to his knees. Penn grabbed the back of his shirt and hauled him back up again, spinning him around. "I'll make this easy," he said.

"Tell me who sold you your Master of Body Enhancement card, or I'll beat it out of you."

"I don't know what you're talking about." Arthur said, still playing shocked. Though he had taken a hit to the head, he felt his thoughts clear up quickly. The self-healing card kicking in. "Penn, this is a duel. What are you doing?"

Penn shoved him away. "This is one of the few places in this forsaken hive no one can hear us speak. I know where your card came from. I don't blame you too much—you're poor, and you're the unwanted son of a borderland baron. I get it."

Hot, undiluted anger washed through him. For a moment, Arthur wasn't standing in an arena. He stood before his cabin back home, watching the baron's men destroy his and his father's meager possessions. Several dozen feet away, two graves sat marking his mother and his sister.

Arthur screamed at his cousin. "You don't understand a damn thing!"

He didn't expect Penn's anger to rise in turn. "You don't get what that card meant to my father—what it means for my family. Tell me who stole it so I can get justice. *I know it wasn't you.* Tell me and I'll end this duel easily for you." His voice darkened. "Or we can do it the hard way. Your choice."

"You know where I came from, Penn," Arthur said, lifting the hammer. The talk had given his Self-Repair card time to do its work. He felt fresh and ready to battle. "We don't do things easy on the border."

Penn's expression was hard. "For what it's worth, I didn't want to do this."

Then Penn came at him, still bare-handed. But with his Master of Combat, he didn't need a weapon to defeat Arthur.

Arthur swung his hammer again. This time, Penn raised an arm to block.

Arthur phased through Penn's arm—a motion that took a fraction of a second—and continued his swing right at the side of Penn's head. Something he would have never considered if there weren't a covey of healers surrounding them.

Penn, however, had a card focused on combat. And Arthur . . . simply wasn't practiced.

Penn's foot hooked around Arthur's ankle, and his swing went wide at the last second as he lost his footing. Arthur staggered back, arms thrown out instinctively for balance. In that unguarded moment, Penn jabbed his diaphragm, which knocked the air out of him. He followed that up by punching Arthur in the face.

Arthur went down, wheezing for breath. He scrambled backward, throwing up a hand to defend against Penn . . . but the final blow didn't land.

Penn had not followed up to finish the duel.

In fact, he stood back, waiting for Arthur to collect himself.

Confused, Arthur stood up again, feeling a trickle of blood coming out his nose.

"This ends when you tell me what I want to hear," Penn said grimly.

Arthur understood.

Penn was going to beat Arthur down again and again until Arthur told him what he needed to know. Public humiliation and not a little bit of pain.

Well, Arthur wasn't going to give in that easily.

He rushed at Penn again, this time, switching the hammer for a shovel from his Personal Space mid-swing. He hoped the surprise would be enough to land a hit.

Penn easily caught his wrist, and with a twist, disarmed him.

Then he hit Arthur again on the other side of the face. Arthur phased through the next punch, but the moment he solidified again, Penn kneed him in the stomach.

Ugh, he thought. He had to watch Penn's feet.

Arthur doubled over and took the punch straight in the eye. Light exploded in his vision like he was staring briefly at the sun.

The next moment, he found himself sitting on the ground. Penn stood a few feet away, waiting for him to stand back up and take another beating.

Then something else flashed in front of Arthur's eyes.

New body enhancement gained: Toughened Skin (Body)
Due to your card's bonus traits, you automatically start this skill at level 3.

New body enhancement gained: Blunt Force Damage Resistance (Body)
Due to your card's bonus traits, you automatically start this skill at level 3.

Arthur's eyes widened, and though there was blood running down his nose into his mouth, he smiled.

Time to change his perspective. This wasn't a beatdown. This . . . this was training.

CHAPTER 39

By the time Arthur's **Blunt Force Damage Resistance** hit level 10, he received a welcome notification.

For reaching this threshold on a body-enhancement skill, you have gained an additional 5% quickened healing bonus from all blunt force damage. In addition, your bones, organs, and soft tissues are 10% more resistant to blunt force injuries.

He also noticed a marked uptick in attention from the audience.

He could not hear them, of course. Only see their reactions.

The seated crowd was no longer craning their heads to look at other fights. More and more were gesturing to his and Penn's quadrant.

He supposed he and Penn were putting on quite the odd show. One boy who had the clear advantage, punching down another who occasionally dodged but more often took the hit, then kept getting up over and over.

I hope no one bet on me, he thought as he climbed to his feet once more.

Arthur wasn't passively letting himself get beat up. This was training, and he had a wealth of tools in his Personal Space. As he stood, he took out one of his butcher knives, concentrated on his **Butchering** skill, and went at Penn again.

Penn disarmed him ridiculously easily and slugged him hard enough to knock him down again.

At this point, Penn's knuckles were bloodied. Hitting someone over and over split the skin, apparently.

"You can end this at any time," Penn reminded him.

Arthur sniffed back a trickle of blood. That last hit had clipped his nose. "I don't have your stupid card," he lied for the dozenth time.

* * *

By the time his **Blunt Force Damage Resistance** had reached level 14, Penn was starting to look tired. And more than a little annoyed.

"What is wrong with you?" he asked. "Do you like this sort of thing or something?"

Arthur grinned at him through a broken front tooth. If his Self-Repair card didn't fix dental issues, he hoped one of the healers would.

"I told you, I have a stamina card. This is like a walk in the park."

"You think I'm an idiot? We've been at this for over an hour, Kane! No one can take this kind of a beating with a stupid stamina card. Just tell me where you got your Body Enhancement card."

"Can't tell you what I don't know," Arthur said lightly, and completely at odds with how he was currently leaning to one side. The last hit had messed with his balance, but his Self-Repair card should fix it soon. He put up his fists. "Now, you want to fight? Or do you want to give up?"

Penn's face twisted. He threw a quick punch, which Arthur phased through—he used that card sparingly to keep Penn off balance. Plus, if he wasn't getting hit, then he couldn't build up his resistances.

Arthur punched back, and though he had no skill for it, he managed, for the first time, to strike Penn across the face.

He wasn't sure who was more shocked—himself or Penn.

What he should have done was immediately follow up with another strike, but landing a punch for once had made him hesitate. In that moment, Penn's fist took on a slight metallic sheen: an indicator he was using his Steel Fists card. He hadn't bothered to do that up until now. No, until now he'd been treating Arthur lightly.

He hit Arthur in the ribs, driving him back and down.

On the ground, Arthur wheezed out a laugh, curling one arm around his middle. *Ow. Probably cracked a rib there.* He could already feel his Self-Repair card getting to work.

"This isn't funny!" Penn yelled. "I don't want to do this, Arthur, but you have no idea what that card means to my family. Just tell me! I don't want to hurt you anymore."

Painfully, Arthur stood and told him the truth. "I don't care what that card means to your family."

When **Blunt Force Damage Resistance** hit level 15, he received another welcomed notice:

For reaching this threshold on a body-enhancement skill, you have gained an additional 7% quickened healing bonus from all blunt force damage.

In addition, your bones, organs, and soft tissues are 15% more resistant to blunt force injuries.

Arthur, of course, celebrated this by getting punched in the head.

By the time his **Blunt Force Damage Resistance** hit level 17, the punches hurt less, and it was taking two of them in quick succession or landing one in a bad spot to knock him down.

Penn heaved for breath, red-faced, angry, his eyes burning. He was still the much better fighter, however.

Arthur wiped some blood off his face—though he suspected he only smeared it around.

That was for the best. His skin had stopped tearing unless it was a truly vicious hit. The blood covered that fact up.

When Arthur's **Blunt Force Damage Resistance** hit level 18, Penn's steps had become heavy, and he grimaced when he threw a wide punch, as if he had pulled a muscle. Arthur was tiring, too. But for being the one on the wrong side of the fight . . . he wasn't feeling too bad.

Now, he judged, was the time to strike back.

He came at Penn again, this time with a pair of scissors.

"Oh, come on," Penn groaned, and made to disarm him.

But Arthur had been watching closely all this time. Penn's disarming move, a grab at the wrist and a twist—was exactly the same every time. As if completed by a skill he had not bothered to level in a while.

Arthur phased his arm through the grab, still lunging forward.

Of course, he was up against someone with the Master of Combat card. Also, Penn wasn't a dummy. He was ready for Arthur's move, his other hand flashing up to jab at the crook of Arthur's elbow the moment it phased back into existence. Arthur's strike with the scissors went wild.

But Arthur wasn't aiming to stab.

The edge of the scissors caught Penn's sleeve. Arthur focused on his **Perfect Snip** card.

It was a sloppy cut—one that instantly duplicated again and again all over Penn's shirt, including several thin gashes along his torso.

Penn shouted in surprise and reeled back. His shirt was in ribbons, and blood seeped out in a half dozen places.

"You cut me!" Penn said, sounding outraged, as if he had not been beating Arthur down for the last few hours.

Arthur grinned at him. "Told you I got a crafting card, didn't I?"

He thought he saw a flash of true doubt in Penn's eyes. It was swallowed a moment later by sheer frustrated rage.

Penn came at him, and this time Arthur knew he wasn't just going to knock him down and let him get back up.

Arthur phased through the initial charge, but Penn spun on his heel and was ready when Arthur solidified.

He hit Arthur again and again, driving him back step by step until Arthur's back hit the translucent shield. He was pinned. Every move Arthur made was countered by an expert block, a slap across the face for his insolence that split his lip anew, and another hit against his body.

New Body Enhancement level: Toughened Skin Resistance (Body)
Level 9

"Who stole the card?" Penn screamed right in his face. "Who was in on it? Give me a name! Tedrah? Calvan? Ceeseal? Tell me!"

Hearing his father's name shocked Arthur into a rash reaction. He grabbed a simple nail from his Personal Space and jabbed it at Penn's eye.

Penn, of course, caught the motion. This time he didn't simply disarm Arthur.

With a vicious snap, he broke his wrist.

Arthur screamed, and on instinct, retreated to his Personal Space.

He sank to the floor, breathing hard and cradling his broken wrist. He wasn't physically there in his own storage space. This was a mental visit. Also, as time didn't pass inside, Self-Repair wouldn't heal him.

But he needed a few seconds to collect himself and reassess.

He could end this at any time. Simply remove the nullify effect off his Return to Start card.

The keyed-in point was still linked to the Wolf Moon Hive. He had not changed it in case he needed a true escape.

As tempting as it was, this duel didn't count.

His second option was to lie. Confess that he had the Master of Body Enhancement card and invent a story—perhaps something about a black market where he had found the card for cheap. He could include one of the names Penn had just thrown out.

But not his father. He would never implicate Calvan.

How did Penn know that name, anyway? Why did he suspect Arthur's father?

The answer came to him, and he groaned, rubbing his face with his good hand.

The card casing had a blood lock. Arthur had been able to bypass it because he and Penn were cousins. He was a Rowantree.

But it also meant anybody who had access to the card was part of the family.

The other two names, Tedrah and Ceeseal, meant nothing to Arthur . . . Could they be other cousins?

He almost wanted to go down that route just to find out more about Penn's—and his own—family tree.

But Arthur wasn't going to open that door. His made-up story was sure to have holes, and if Penn launched an official investigation . . . the *entire* truth might come out.

Besides, he wasn't going to risk his standing as a Legendary recruit if he admitted having a stolen card, much less a pair of Legendaries.

He couldn't escape, and he couldn't lie his way out of this. That left one option: Arthur had to win.

Still holding his broken wrist, he stood and looked around. What could he use?

His searching gaze fell on the Subconscious Injection card. The one he had taken from the mind scourgling.

He had seen that flash of true doubt in Penn's eyes. Perhaps he could play on that. Insert a thought into Penn's subconscious—not to let Arthur win, but to insinuate he was beating up a lesser opponent for no reason.

Arthur was tempted. So tempted.

But he had just promised himself he wouldn't use this card. He wasn't going to break that promise within half a day of making it.

So, what else did he have?

Tearing his gaze from the card, he looked around the room and realized it was starting to look a lot like what Freyja had called the junk drawer back in the orphanage.

Arthur had made a wide range of purchases using Marion's money back at Wolf Moon. In addition, he had decided he wasn't going to get caught without an outfit on hand again. After the hive leaders left, and before Arthur stepped out to join the duels, he had gone through the room and cleaned it out of anything useful.

He had utensils, every item of clothing that had been in his closet, a letter opener, nice sheets of paper, supplies of all sorts for camping and general use. He even had extra vegetables and fruit stacked in crates in one corner.

And he had level 19 in **Blunt Force Damage Resistance**.

His **Toughened Skin Resistance** was at level 9, as not every one of Penn's punches broke skin. But that wasn't nothing.

A plan formed in Arthur's mind. Nodding to himself, he stepped to the crates.

It had been too long since he had used his cooking skills.

* * *

When Arthur reemerged from his Personal Space, he immediately received a punch to the side of the head.

Gritting his teeth, he put both arms up to protect his face and just tried to endure the onslaught.

Penn was clearly at the end of his rope, screaming at Arthur to tell him—just tell him what he needed to know!

It wasn't enough. Arthur needed him to truly tire himself out. He needed Penn's reactions to be slowed as much as possible.

"Okay! Okay!" Arthur yelped. "I'll tell you how I got my card."

Penn grabbed a hank of Arthur's hair, pinning him against the wall. "Finally! Well?"

Arthur looked into his cousin's eyes. "I was having dinner with your mother the other day . . ."

That's as far as he got. Penn roared, and all Arthur could do was endure the next vicious round of strikes.

New Body Enhancement level: Blunt Force Damage Resistance (Body)
Level 20
For reaching this threshold on a body-enhancement skill, you have gained an additional 10% quickened healing bonus from all blunt force damage. In addition, your bones, organs, and soft tissues are 20% more resistant to blunt force injuries.
For hitting level twenty in a body-enhancement skill, you have earned 3 attribute points.

Arthur again threw one point into strength, bringing the base up to 20. The other two he tossed into stamina, bringing that to a healthy 20 as well.

More importantly, adding those points refreshed those attributes.

Arthur was invigorated. New vitality returned to his limbs—even his broken wrist didn't hurt nearly as much as it had before.

Penn hesitated for a moment, as if he sensed a change.

Arthur didn't give him time to react. He reached into his Personal Space, grabbed the cup of lemon juice, vinegar, and salt he had prepared, and splashed it right in Penn's face.

Penn screamed in surprise and backed up a few steps, clawing at his own face. He didn't know what Arthur had done. For all he knew, it could have been acid instead of a harmless marinade.

"Sorry, Penn," Arthur said as he grabbed a letter opener from his Personal Space. He whipped the sharp edge at Penn's throat.

Even half blinded, exhausted, and in pain, Penn raised his elbow, stopping the blade an inch from his skin.

His expression was of pure murder.

Grabbing the letter opener from Arthur, Penn reversed the grip and shoved it into Arthur's stomach.

It felt like the world had stopped.

Penn backed away, his reddened eyes wide with horror. "Healer!" he yelled over his shoulder.

All Arthur could do was stare down at his stomach.

He felt the pain, though it was distant. Mostly he felt frustration.

He had been so close to winning, but at the end of the day, all his little tricks couldn't defeat Penn's combat-focused card. Brother to the cards in his own heart.

"Healer!" Penn yelled again, frantic, turning to the healers who stood on the wrong side of the barrier. "He's bleeding out. He's—why are you all just standing there?"

There was a lot of blood. Not, Arthur thought, as much as there should be. He had butchered the meat off plenty of animals. Some were so freshly killed that the blood hadn't fully drained. This was nowhere near that much.

And now that he was truly looking, the letter opener had only sunk in about an inch. Penn had put the full force of his stab into it, but Arthur now had **Toughened Skin** and more resistance to blunt force damage. The letter opener's blade was sharp, and there was a tiny hook just short of the top made to catch the edge of a piece of paper. Otherwise, the point was quite blunt.

That's why the fight hadn't officially been called. Someone probably had a card to monitor the health of the combatants.

Arthur wasn't mortally wounded. He could rip the letter opener out and keep going.

Penn, who'd lived a sheltered life despite his combat card, didn't know that.

"For the sake of the first card!" Penn's voice was high in panic. "Why are you standing there?! You want him to bleed to death?"

Penn turned back to Arthur, apology and shame etched on his face.

His **Acting** skill kicked in. Arthur, slumped as if he were dizzy from the blood loss, looked up at his cousin and said in a weakened voice, "I don't have your card, Penn . . . I really don't."

Penn's face crumpled. It looked like he was about to cry. Nodding once, he turned back to the waiting healers. "I concede!"

With those words, the translucent shield fell, and the healers rushed in. As did the sound of the roaring crowd.

Green energy washed over Arthur, pushing the letter opener out as the wound sealed in an instant. He drew in a full breath without pain and tried to straighten. One of the healers pushed him back.

"Hm, better condition than I thought," she said, eyeing Arthur.

"Stamina card," Arthur croaked, loud enough for Penn to hear.

The healer nodded and reached into her pocket to draw out a vial. "Well, it seems to be doing the trick, but you best take this in case."

"What is it?"

"It will restore your blood, and it has some vitamins that couldn't hurt."

Arthur tipped it back. As he did, he saw the list of names projected in light above them.

His name moved up the list.

It was back to number three.

Penn's name had sunk to number eight.

He . . . wasn't sure how to feel about that. This had been a victory, though a hollow one born of trickery.

Then again, he had lasted quite a long time against someone with a pure combat card. Him. The guy with the set of skills and a body card he had only scratched the surface of learning how to use.

He allowed himself the tiniest of smiles as he handed back the vial.

"No fighting for the next fifteen minutes," the healer ordered, giving him a hand up.

Penn had already turned his back and walked away.

"Fifteen minutes?" Arthur asked, then looked out where he saw a few Legendary recruits standing by the edge of the translucent wall. He didn't think they were there to congratulate him.

This was going to be a long, long night.

CHAPTER 40

Whitaker looked down from his high box seat, which of course had luxuriously padded seats, angled to view all four quadrants of the arena with ease—as well as looking glasses that magnified objects through some trick of the lenses for those who needed it. Food and drink were brought by courteous servants at the wave of a hand. And, of course, well-appointed lavatories were just around the corner.

If he had any choice in the matter, he would have given it all up in a moment.

Instead of watching the Legendary recruits battling for their right to face the egg, he found his eyes wandering downward to the middling seats where his personal retinue of Rare riders and friends all sat together, drinking and gambling.

They were *truly* enjoying themselves.

Whitaker enjoyed the privileges of being a Legendary rider, but sometimes rank could be a bore.

Valentina sniffed. "Stop sighing. You sound like a child."

She had a slim pair of spectacles held up to her eyes by use of a long wand. An untouched glass of wine sat at her side. Valentina ordered it to be polite, but he had never seen her drink when around other riders.

She could be such a bore.

Whitaker leaned forward to follow her gaze. "Have those two finished beating each other up yet?"

"Nearly. I dare say Kane has him on the ropes."

Whitaker squinted. Perhaps he needed a pair of those spectacles, because the right quadrant was taken up by two boys beating each other up with bare fists alone. Or more specifically—one beating the other. For hours.

The best Whitaker could say about his meeting with Arthur Kane was he hadn't come out disappointed. He was . . . unexceptional. Certainly not worth the two cards Valentina gave up helping his cause.

Cards that the boy at least seemed to be making good use of.

The two combatants paused to exchange silent words before the boy was knocked down once more.

Whitaker sighed again.

"You must admit it's impressive he has lasted this long," Valentina continued.

"Only because Penn Rowantree has allowed it. Why you didn't back *him* is a mystery."

Other than the royals, Legendary recruit cards weren't public knowledge. But all had been watched carefully, and most noble families passed down cards from one to another.

It was semi-public knowledge young Penn Rowantree had a combat-oriented card. This fight should have been over in minutes, if not seconds.

Whitaker began to turn his attention to the farthest quadrant, which was a duel between two temperature card wielders, when Valentina spoke up.

"Doesn't Kane remind you of anyone?"

With another internal sigh, Whitaker dragged his attention back from the more interesting fire-ice brawl. "Don't tell me you have a great-great-grandson floating about . . ."

If that were the case, he would expect the boy to have something more useful than a crafting card. *Crafting*, for pity's sake.

Valentina's eyes didn't leave the duel. "Doesn't he remind you of Lottie?"

"Who?" Whitaker started to say, but then was distracted as the crowd below them suddenly went wild.

It seemed that the one-sided knockdown fight had finally reached a new level.

Whitaker missed the exact moment, but somehow Penn's clothing was ripped, and there was visible blood on his chest.

"It looks like your puppy has some teeth," he said, and then a moment later, "but of course the combat card will always win out." Penn started to punish the other boy for his daring.

"Lottie," Valentina said stubbornly. It seemed like she wasn't even paying attention to the outcome of the fight, even though she was the one who had convinced him—reluctantly—to back Arthur. "Remember Denny's hatching?"

"Denny?" Whitaker frowned, not because he didn't remember the hatching but because he hated being dragged back into a conversation he barely cared about.

He glanced longingly to the seats below, watching several of his fellow dragon riders standing up and cheering, practically spilling their drinks while hollering for more blood. They were having a good time. He wished he were able to sit among him.

"That Legendary that hatched twenty years ago," Valentina said, with a waspish edge to her voice.

"I know who Denny is," he snapped. "Lottie . . . Yes." His frown deepened, and not because it seemed Arthur, at last, had been stabbed well enough to count, but because he hadn't thought of that girl in an age. Pretty thing. Or, she had been.

"What a shame," he said. "That's why I'm glad I didn't have any daughters. You watch one marry the wrong husband, and they die along with them."

Valentina made a noise of frustration, no doubt because her preferred recruit was currently stabbed through the stomach. Why the Buck Moon judges hadn't called the fight and ended this nonsense, Whitaker couldn't say. In fact, Penn Rowantree seemed to be calling for the fight to end, too.

"He has her look," Valentina ground out.

"Who?" Whitaker's attention had been drawn to one of the other matches.

Now Valentina made a sound like someone had trod over a cat's tail. "Lottie."

Whitaker blinked and then looked back at the two boys. His attention was naturally focused first on Penn, as he was the clear favorite. He was a well-built boy and would surely be a strong man. Assuming the egg didn't kill him. It didn't matter how strong a boy was when the unlinked hatchling got in a snit.

The other . . . "Oh, yes, I see what you're saying," he said with a nod. "Lottie was a blonde, too, wasn't she? Fetching color on a woman. Is that why you backed her all those years ago?"

Again, Valentina made that frustrated noise.

Whitaker couldn't question her, as the audience suddenly erupted again.

Finally, a winner had been called.

And it wasn't Penn.

It was Arthur Kane.

Penn, it seemed, had lost his nerve at the last moment and conceded the match. *Huh.*

With a shake of his head, Whitaker leaned back in his seat. "If I've said it once, I've said it a dozen times: a card will only take you so far. You must have the heart to truly wield it."

"You are *impossible*," Valentina said.

He glanced at her. "What?"

But the other Wolf Moon leader didn't reply. She was too busy signaling one of the servers for a strong alcoholic drink. This time, she took the shot the moment it was delivered.

Whitaker rolled his eyes and once again turned his attention to the matches.

Seriously, Valentina was getting too old and too fragile for the rigors of leadership. Her mind wandered to the past.

Recruit Lottie had been a favorite for that egg, but the dragon has the last say. While Denny didn't kill her, he didn't link with her, either.

In the end, she had married the heir to the Rowantree house. A couple years before that scandal broke.

If anything, that should be an object lesson for Valentina: don't back the wrong horse.

Whitaker watched with mild amusement as Valentina's favorite was healed and then immediately set upon by others wishing to duel. The boy was a juicy piece of meat thrown into a barrel full of scourglings. If Whitaker had been in their place, he would've challenged the boy, too.

He remembered his own Legendary recruit duels. Ah, those had been the days . . .

Arthur Kane had to be either touched in the head or truly desperate to enter the arena with a simple crafting card in addition to the little Rare-level tricks he and Valentina had gifted. Really, he stood no chance.

Except . . . the next duel was against a slim young woman with a heat and smoke card as her offensive weapon of choice. The heat/smoke was likely not a Legendary level, though. Either she was keeping their true power in reserve or their Legendary was more of a utility/support role.

Much like Arthur Kane, in fact.

Well, hopefully the girl would have more sense than to drag this out.

The girl acted the moment the duel was started, throwing up a choking smoke screen that coalesced around Arthur.

Arthur responded, naturally, by phasing through the cloud.

She was ready for him just when he stepped out the other side. The few seconds had given her the moment she needed to generate a wave of fire by way of heating the air around her.

In the next second, Arthur had something in his hand—was that a flour sack?—and threw it right between himself and the girl. Flour exploded upward just as the wave of fire rolled through it.

There was an explosion that tested the shield around the combatants.

As the smoke cleared, the audience saw that the girl had been thrown clear across the quadrant and lay in a crumpled heap, unconscious.

Arthur Kane stood where he was. Presumably, he had phased through the explosion. Though from the pinched look on his face, and the way he gasped for air, most of the oxygen in the shielded quadrant had been eaten up by that little stunt.

"He is quite resourceful, is he not?" Valentina said.

"You always like the stupidly lucky ones," he commented idly. "Didn't your favorite from last time, Lottie, have some sort of Legendary sewing card?"

"Something like that."

As the girl didn't stir within ten seconds, the match was called for Arthur Kane.

Whitaker glanced up at the rankings and shook his head. "They're not going to credit him much for stupid tricks. He won't move above third place."

"Which is a victory all on its own," Valentina said smugly. She looked at Whitaker. "Lottie also ranked third place in the duels, did she not? Quite extraordinary for someone with a crafting-type card—"

Whitaker stopped listening to her prattling. There was a boy the next quadrant over who had a fascinating blood-body control card. Now, *that* was a potent card against the scourge . . .

When Arthur Kane was called up again for another duel, it was against a skilled illusionist. Prince Francis Orchardtree, who had been considered one of the forerunners for the egg. Whitaker would have much rather backed *him* than a no-name son of a baron with dumb tricks up his sleeve. Unfortunately, the royals were tied to their city of birth. That meant they were loyal to the hive closest to them. Orchardtree city was placed close to Harvest Moon Hive.

"This should be interesting," Valentina murmured.

"How so?"

She smiled. "You forget so quickly. Arthur Kane was one of the few who was able to resist the mind-mage scourgling."

Whitaker scowled, hating to be reminded of that debacle. So he had chosen to forget it and focus on the future. "You're giving the kid too much credit. You know that Buck Moon Hive was simply elevating him just to rub our noses in that disaster and take the egg from us—"

"Quiet, it's about to start," she said, chastising him as if he were a schoolboy.

For the first time, Whitaker dearly hoped that his officially backed choice would lose. If only to shut Valentina up.

Arthur didn't lose.

Worse, for two opponents in the top three, it was a dreadfully boring fight.

Because of the translucent shields, no hint of the illusions leaked out. Otherwise the rest of the crowd would be at risk of falling under the illusion card's sway. Those powers were a bit too close to mind-mage manipulation for most tastes.

Whatever illusion Orchardtree created, Arthur Kane simply walked through it and up to the other recruit with a pair of scissors in hand.

His snip was much more careful and much less desperate than it had been before. Francis's pants fell down his ankles.

"Oh my," Valentina said mildly over the crowd's roaring laughter. "One would think the boy would be rich enough to purchase underclothing."

Prince Francis Orchardtree hurriedly covered himself. From the way the translucent shields fell, he conceded the match.

Not all the duels that night were so easily one-sided. These were Legendary-rank cards, and some were overwhelmingly offensive based. Too much for a single support card to manage.

Arthur conceded the match twice at the very start. Once against a boy with volcanic powers—understandable—and another against a girl who had a card aligned with salt and sand. It was an odd combination that made people whisper she had two Legendary cards.

For her sake, Whitaker hoped not.

Physically, these elemental type cards were the strongest. However, those cards also tended to be one-trick ponies. While they won most of the matches, their wins didn't gain as many points with the judges.

The losses hadn't hurt Arthur Kane much. He now sat at a comfortable fifth place, with Pennrow Rowantree in second place. Whitaker *knew* he should have backed that one. He had a whole card for fighting, for dragon's sake!

Legendary hatchlings had minds of their own, but most of them didn't choose card wielders with narrow scopes.

Take himself, for example. Whitaker's power was one of telekinesis. He could move inanimate objects with ease. His card's limitation was on self-aware, conscious individuals. He could fling a dead donkey corpse hundreds of feet at a gesture. Maybe half that length if the donkey was asleep. But he wouldn't be able to budge that donkey an inch if it was awake and resistant to being moved. Still, that gave him a wide range of options when it came to combat and utility. He knew for a fact that flexibility was what appealed to his dragon.

But there was too much of a good thing. Take this boy Valentina insisted on backing, for example.

What would he do when faced with a wave of scourglings? Tailor them a pretty dress? Throw another bag of flour? Perhaps a sack of onions this time and hope their eyes started to sting?

People didn't call in Legendary dragon support when things were going well. They were the final bulwark before the king had to step in.

Whitaker sighed.

Valentina leaned forward, the lenses pressed tightly to her face. "This may be a problem."

"What now?"

She gestured below. Arthur Kane had been approached by another recruit.

"Isn't that the Time Prince?" Whitaker asked. "Uh, Martin—"

"Marion Amberlion," Valentina corrected.

Whitaker glanced at the list. From the looks of things, the boy hadn't won a single match yet. He had slipped from number four to number twenty-three. That was a shame for someone with precognition.

"Another boring fight," Whitaker moaned, signaling the attendant for another beer. Once again, he wished he were sitting with the rest of his friends. "The boy with all tricks and no combat versus the ultimate defense, also with no combat."

"No," Valentina said grimly. "Marion is trying to convince our recruit to throw the next match. And I think he just might do it."

CHAPTER 41

"You want me to do what?" Arthur stared at his friend. Or, the person he was beginning to think of as his friend. Now he was starting to wonder.

Marion winced, which struck Arthur as an odd reaction. Almost as if he hadn't anticipated Arthur's question.

But Marion could see several seconds into the future . . . unless he had his Nullify card turned on again.

Come to think of it, the prince was looking worse for wear.

It had been a hard night full of dueling. Arthur himself was exhausted and so was everyone else.

More than a few of the Legendary recruits had ordered their personal servants to bring them cots, which had been set up off to the side of the arena. They now took naps in between rounds.

Arthur had asked Carley to bring him the thickest, strongest tea she could find. It had tasted terrible going down but had kept him going.

Thanks to his Body Enhancement card, it also gave him a mild stamina boost.

Marion, however, looked bad. Wan and pale, the bruises under his eyes looked so dark he would have suspected black eyes if there hadn't been so many healers around.

Marion held up his hands. There was a slight tremor to his fingers.

"I know how it sounds—" he began.

Arthur crossed his arms. "It sounds like you're asking me to throw the next duel against you."

"I have no right to ask you," Marion confirmed. "Except . . ." He glanced meaningfully up at the list. "Echo's done better than anyone foresaw. Even me."

His little half sister had proven to be an absolute beast in the arena, and now sat at number two overall, having just switched places with Penn. It helped she could duplicate opponents to a lesser extent, or mimic a power that worked to counter anyone who opposed her.

Arthur, meanwhile, sat at number five. Not bad for someone without a dedicated combat card.

Marion sat almost at the bottom of the list at number twenty-three.

Marion must have seen the growing doubt on Arthur's face, because he spoke quickly.

"Look, I timed it out. Because I'm at the bottom, the loss will mean less for you. You'll drop three spots. Meanwhile, I'll jump ten. That will put me at fourteen, which is still enough for the second round for the egg. That is my best shot to be close if . . . if things go wrong."

Arthur held up his hand. "Wait, does 'timed it out' mean what I think it means?"

Marion nodded, and now it was Arthur's turn to grimace. No wonder he looked like he'd been run over by a dragon. The last time he used that effect on his time card, he'd passed out.

Then the rest of what Marion said hit him.

"What do you mean by second round?"

Marion raised his eyebrows, once again surprised at Arthur's reaction. "Oh, the Buck Moon leader decided that the recruits will face the egg ten at a time."

"What?!"

The word exploded out of Arthur. He quickly looked around to see if anyone was close enough to listen—they weren't, and most of the audience was paying attention to the duels.

But that interest was fading too. It was so late in the night it could be called morning. People had to sleep and had jobs to do.

Arthur stepped closer to Marion, lowering his voice, though his tone was no less fierce than before. "They're not sending us one at a time, like they do with the Rare eggs?"

"Nooo," Marion drew out the word. "They're trying to reduce casualties after the eruption, and apparently the . . . uh, chances are better if more people face the egg at once." Marion hesitated. "This is a good thing. You don't want to be the fifth to meet the egg, right?"

Indignation warred with . . . well, more indignation. "Then what's the point of the list?" He had been practically killing himself to make sure his standing was as high as possible.

Granted, it wouldn't be all for nothing. He would still be safely within the first group to meet the egg. He had put himself up against Legendary recruits, and while he hadn't come out on top every time, he had won duels with the odds stacked against him. His current standing was proof enough of that.

Other benefits had been more than rewarding as well.

The few seconds he'd faced the guy with the volcanic powers had been enough to earn him **Fire Resistance**. Then his Body Enhancement card had immediately boosted it to level 3.

Then he'd received another level when facing the fire-and-smoke girl. In addition, when the air had gone wrong at the end and all the oxygen had been burned away, he had received **Breath Enhancement**, level 3.

This had the potential to be invaluable, as he could see enhanced breath as an aid to running and other strenuous skills.

Finally, in his duel against Francis Orchardtree, he had received **Charm Resistance** and leveled it up to level 4 in short order.

Francis, apparently, had a strong charm card in addition to his illusions. Arthur had honestly felt bad for defeating him—guilty with a sick feeling deep in his soul, as if he were kicking a puppy or something.

That had all evaporated once Francis conceded the match. It had been a result of his charm card—one that Arthur now had the tools to fight against.

So, yes, he had received some invaluable skills but . . . this was aggravating.

"You know how it is when we all get together. The families have to prove who is better, who has the strongest family to lead the next generation," Marion said. Clearly "we" meant nobles and royals.

Arthur wanted to spit.

He held it in and breathed deep to keep his temper from fraying. Being tired from fighting all day didn't help, but oddly, his new **Breath Enhancement** skill did.

When he concentrated on breathing, he felt more refreshed than he thought he would have.

"Are you *absolutely* certain they'll be letting us in ten at a time?" he asked.

"What? Yeah." Marion waved a hand in the air. "I paid off the servants who were in attendance for the meeting, and they all reported back the same thing. Well, except for the guy who was paid to disseminate false information, but that's standard for high-level meetings."

Arthur snorted. Then he turned serious again.

"Let's say you're right. If I lose against you and get knocked down a few places, that means if I lose again . . ." He trailed off. There was every chance he could get knocked out of the top ten completely.

That was unacceptable.

"No, they'll be calling the duels over soon. Look at the audience," he said and pointed to the visibly wilting crowd. There were more empty seats than filled seats, too.

"But tomorrow . . ." Arthur started.

"Tomorrow is the final rest day. Our last day to prepare." Marion looked grim. He had already hinted he wasn't looking forward to the hatching. It was a duty for him.

So why am I considering helping him out? Arthur wondered. He wanted that egg. He should do nothing to risk that.

Marion had no right to ask this of him. Less than no right, really. Marion was a prince. He could pay someone to take the fall for him.

Except the rest of the recruits were rich nobles.

The only thing Marion could do was to ask Arthur as a friend. Which, of course, was what he was doing.

Arthur made a disgusted sound at himself.

"Fine," he groaned. "But I need something out of this."

Marion brightened. "What? Another bag of coins? I think I have one around here . . ." He started digging in his vest.

Too bad Marion wasn't the type of friend Arthur felt comfortable punching.

"No, I don't want your money," he said. "I want your Instant Competency card."

Marion looked pained. "I'd gift it to you if I could, but those are assigned—"

"No, no." Arthur shook his head. "We have one more day tomorrow? I only need fifteen minutes. It synchronizes well with my existing card." He intended to buy or borrow every tool he could get his hands on and see what skills he could get from them.

Marion's eyebrows rose. "Then I think we have a deal, except . . . there's one more thing."

"What's that?"

"From what I saw, we have to drag out this match until the judges call it a night."

"How long?" Arthur asked.

"Twenty minutes should do it."

Which didn't sound bad, except neither he nor Marion could fight.

Arthur thought he had scraped the bottom of the barrel for silly duels by letting Penn punch him for hours.

But no, it could get worse.

Because now Arthur was the aggressor who was chasing Marion around the arena. And Marion, of course, used his time sense to easily avoid Arthur's strikes.

And Marion being Marion, of course he had to be a know-it-all about it.

"You really don't have any combat experience, do you?" Marion said, easily stepping out from one of Arthur's blows. "These punches are really sloppy."

"I know how to fight!" Arthur snapped. "My recruiter showed me some brawling techniques, but you gotta be within arm's range first." He made a half-hearted grab for Marion, who of course, easily stepped out of the way.

One thing Arthur had going for him was the wicked curved dagger in his hands. Marion had given it to him on the sly, so the duel would look slightly more impressive.

But Arthur had no skills with it. The dagger felt clumsy in his hand.

Honestly, if he were being serious about the duel, he would have brought out the scissors again. Marion struck him as the type who would concede rather than ruin a good outfit.

He swung his dagger again. Marion easily danced out of the way, letting the dagger sail by an inch from his neck. It might as well have been a mile.

"Widen your stance," Marion suggested. "It'll help your swings—No, not that wide. You know what? Never mind. I have some books that may help you."

Arthur brightened, then remembered they were supposed to be in the middle of a duel. He returned his expression to a scowl.

His Mental Bookshelf was depressingly empty, and he hadn't had time to fill it. "I'll take you up on that." He glanced at the audience, which had dwindled even more. More telling was that two of the arena quadrants were empty. The healers around them were looking impatient, as if ready for this to be wrapped up. "Hey, I think it's time for that lucky shot."

"All right," Marion said. "Sorry about this."

Then he came into Arthur's space quicker than Arthur anticipated. Cocking back his fist, he nailed Arthur right in the chin.

They stared at each other for a moment. Arthur hadn't even flinched.

"Seriously?" Arthur said.

"Aren't you supposed to be knocked out now?"

"I would be if you had hit me hard."

"That was my best punch!" Marion objected.

Either Marion was really bad at this or Arthur was just used to Penn's strength.

Or his **Blunt Force Damage Resistance** was just that effective against non-card-enhanced hits.

He made a half-hearted swipe at Marion, just for show, though from the trickle of audience left, he wasn't sure who he was trying to impress.

"Okay, I'll fall the next time. Then just punch me a few more times and I'll give up. Fair? Don't hold back."

He smiled, and Marion barked a laugh.

"All right, you asked for it." He actually managed to hook Arthur's ankle and make him fall for real.

Arthur landed on his back, and Marion followed him down to deliver a few rapid hits.

They felt like taps at best.

Arthur raised his hand, conceding.

He didn't think they'd fooled anyone. Once the semitranslucent walls fell, none of the tired-looking healers even bothered coming in to check on him.

As Marion foresaw, Arthur's name fell to rank eight, whereas Marion's shot to rank fourteen.

Marion helped Arthur up. "Thank you."

He let out a breath. "You'd better not be wrong about this."

"I'm not," Marion said with calm surety. "And now . . . well, if something happens, I might be able to intervene on Echo's behalf." He looked at Arthur. "I won't forget this."

Arthur nodded and looked away. He just hoped he hadn't made a big mistake.

CHAPTER 42

As Marion predicted, the next day was announced as a day of rest and reflection for the final Legendary recruits.

Arthur slept in until noon.

He was woken by Carley barging in and throwing open the curtains he'd pulled across the balcony, letting in light. He would have been angry, but she brought with her a plate of sandwiches.

His stomach rumbled, and he instantly forgave her.

After eating—and of course secreting the extra sandwiches away in his Personal Space because Carley had brought more than he could ever eat in one sitting, but he wasn't going to let it go to waste—and making sure he was semi-presentable, he asked for directions to Marion's room.

Turned out he had been assigned a room just down the hall from Arthur. One of Marion's snooty minders answered the door. When the man bowed Arthur inside, he strode in and stopped dead.

"Did they give you a whole library?"

One entire wall was filled with books. Top to bottom, left to right. More shelves than Arthur had seen in one place other than in the scholar's guild. Only there wasn't any smell of rot. Each visible spine was free of dust.

Marion sat on a chair to the side, a small book in his hand. "Of course not," he said offhandedly. "They're mine. I had them brought from Wolf Moon Hive. Took them long enough," he muttered, flipping a page.

Arthur gaped. "You just . . . travel with all these books?"

"Of course," Marion said, looking at Arthur as if he was being ridiculous for asking. "They're mine."

Arthur couldn't begin to wrap his mind around the logistics involved. Marion must have paid a purple courier—or likely several couriers—for the duty. And a shimmer green to open a portal to the other hive.

"Must be nice being a prince," he muttered.

"It has its perks," Marion allowed. He stood and easily plucked a red-spined book off the shelf as if he knew where it had been all along. "This is the one I told you about last night. It goes over the theory of hand-to-hand combat. There are even pictures to help you along," he added with a smirk.

"Are you two going to spend the entire day reading?"

Echo's exasperated voice drew Arthur up short. He turned to see the girl sitting primly at a table by the balcony. He had been so surprised by the shelves he hadn't noticed her.

Penn sat with her.

Their gazes met. Penn was the first to look away.

Then, just as abruptly, Penn stood and determinedly walked up to Arthur. "Kane."

"Penn."

"You're . . . looking well."

Arthur felt his lips curl in a sardonic smile. "The stab wound wasn't that bad."

His eyes narrowed. "I know. Now."

There was a beat of silence, and Arthur could feel Marion's and Echo's worried gazes on them.

Arthur decided to be the bigger man. He had, after all, wronged Penn several times by now. "Congratulations on fourth place."

Penn's tense shoulders relaxed. "It should have been third, but Francis Orchardtree charmed me, and I lost two ranks."

"He didn't charm *me*," Echo called smugly.

Her words broke the tension between them. Arthur cracked a smile, and then, so did Penn.

Neither apologized or held out a hand to shake. Instead, Penn cocked his head to the table. "We're just sitting down to eat. Join us?"

Despite Arthur having just eaten, he found he couldn't say no.

And even though they were all four competitors, and by all rights should be spending the last day in feverish preparation, the meal stretched long. Conversation was light.

Echo seemed excited about tomorrow, and her enthusiasm was catching, even though Arthur spotted Marion giving her concerned glances when the girl wasn't looking.

"Have you pledged yourself to a hive?" Echo asked the rest. "If you link the dragon, I mean."

Penn shrugged. "I suppose it'll be this hive."

"Worm Moon," Marion said. "It's closest to Amberlion—my city—so it's expected."

"Yes," Echo sighed. "Strawberry Moon for me."

"Wolf Moon," Arthur said.

Penn cleared his throat. "I suppose your barony will be glad . . . if it's you."

Arthur recognized the olive branch but didn't want to give Penn the wrong idea. "For the boon from the king? No, that won't go to my father's lands. I'll take that to Wolf Moon, too." The others looked shocked, so he added, "You've been there—you know it needs all the help it can get."

There was an uncomfortable silence. His declaration not to help his family had shocked the nobles, but from their glances it seemed no one wanted to press. They'd heard what the inquisitor had said about his "sister." Even brash Echo had fallen silent.

Marion cleared his throat and stood. "Well, Arthur . . . there's the matter of business we need to discuss?"

Echo grinned. "You paid him to take the fall in the last match, didn't you?"

"Was it that obvious?" Arthur asked.

"Yes," Echo and Penn said at the same time.

Arthur, of course, needed to stock up on every tool, bit, and bob he could think of before he made use of the card. That meant a shopping trip.

Marion was happy to oblige. They spent that afternoon exploring the Buck Moon Hive commissary. Then Arthur made use of the Instant Competency card.

He only had it for fifteen minutes. But in his Personal Space, that time stretched for hours.

That evening in his room, he spent the time reading the book Marion had loaned him.

It was the first time he had truly experimented with the Mental Bookshelf card. Its capabilities had been overshadowed by the enhancement to his Personal Space card in the same deck.

He read a few pages of the book, closed his eyes, and mentally visited the bookshelf in his mind.

There it was—an exact copy on the shelf waiting for him. Though his mental copy was still slim, as he'd only been through a few pages.

Arthur grinned, flipping through it to check the contents. He found when he "held" the mental book in his mind, he could recall exact sentences and where they fell on the page.

This was a book on combat and wasn't exactly the same as leveling a skill, but he'd take any advantage he could get.

"I'll never have to look up a recipe I've read again," he remembered, and his grin broadened.

Overall, it was a calm evening. Exploring the capabilities of his card helped keep down the building nervousness and the knowledge that tomorrow, if things went wrong, he could die.

He could see his friends die.

The dragon could very well choose someone else.

Maybe it would decide not to hatch out at all.

Arthur shook his head, banishing the thoughts. No. He wouldn't dwell on it. He had a feeling, deep in his heart, that the dragon wasn't the type who liked to wait. Though he couldn't put a finger on why.

Stressing over something he couldn't control wasn't productive.

The dragon would find him worthy, or it wouldn't.

One way or the other, the wait would be over tomorrow.

CHAPTER 43

Arthur couldn't quite describe how, but he could feel the presence of the egg as he stood outside Buck Moon Hive's auditorium—the same one where he'd attended the lecture of dragon colors a few days ago.

There was a pull at his heart. As if something deep inside was reaching out and trying to connect.

This had to be a good thing, surely. He had been the one to find the egg. He had not fainted or faltered when other Legendary recruits had. Even though he wasn't going to be the first to formally approach the egg, the young dragon inside had to consider him.

Right?

Arthur held on to this hope as he and the rest of the Legendary recruits were escorted into the auditorium.

The seats were filled with important-looking people, though, of course, Arthur only knew a few of them. Some were the hive leaders—he recognized Whitaker and Valentina sitting slightly apart from the rest. Ostracized from the company of their peers.

Valentina caught his eye, and her lips curved up in a smile. Whitaker saw him, and his lips curved down in disapproval.

Likely, he didn't approve of Arthur's clothing. He was by far the most plainly dressed of the Legendary recruits. As usual, the men were dressed in stiff fabric, painstakingly brushed clean of any imperfection. The women were similarly dressed in gowns and elaborate hairstyles, but he didn't think that was practical.

Would a baby dragon even know or care about human fashion?

In any case, Arthur had dressed in clean, though plain, clothing. An off-white tunic and a pair of dark trousers with matching sturdy footwear.

He wanted to show the dragon that he had come to work, not to play around. And . . . well, if things went horribly wrong today, he didn't want to die in stiff, uncomfortable clothing.

They were made to stand in a group along one end of the stage in rough order of their rank.

Meanwhile, an elderly man with a silver beard and slicked-back silver hair went to the front to begin to speak, thanking the crowd for their attendance. And not so subtly patting himself on the back for hosting the Legendary hatching.

Great, this was one of the Buck Moon Hive leaders, and there was going to be speechifying.

Arthur rolled his eyes.

Craning his head back, Arthur glanced at Marion.

The other boy looked pale, but not in the exhausted way he had when he had burned the one-hour boost on his time card.

Arthur caught his gaze and raised his eyebrows in a silent question: Do you know what's going to happen next?

Marion grimaced and shook his head, confirming he hadn't used the boost. Likely, he wanted to be at the top of his game today.

Arthur's attention was drawn back at the polite clapping from the audience.

"Now, without further ado . . ." The hive leader gestured to several men and one woman wearing Rare rider badges.

They nodded, and several made lifting gestures with their hands. A semi-translucent shield—the same shield which had separated the dueling arenas—went up between the stage and the audience.

The VIPs were to watch what occurred next, but they were also going to be protected by it. If that shield, which was held by several visibly straining Rares, was strong enough to hold dueling Legendary recruits, it should be strong enough to protect against a wild baby dragon.

But it also meant that all the recruits were trapped within.

Guess Marion didn't have to worry about which group he'd be in after all, Arthur thought. His heart was pounding in his ears, and his own breaths sounded loud.

This was it. This was finally, finally it.

"May I have the top five recruits?" the silver-haired leader said. Then, before Arthur could properly freak out—or turn around and curse Marion for being born—added, "and the next five right behind them. Stand in ranking order, please. Yes . . . yes . . ." He nodded as one by one the first ten stepped up.

The egg itself was placed mid-stage, safely encased on a box on a stone plinth. Several circles were painted around it: green on the outside, blue in the middle, red closest in. Red was apparently considered the dangerous zone.

"Now, the first five will stand at the blue circle. Second five, you stand on the green. You will go up to the egg one by one according to rank. Stand at the red line and bow low to show your respect. Then present an image of your card. If there is no immediate result, and the egg does not hatch, you will step back and allow the next person in line to step forward."

Arthur's mouth went dry. Throwing that last duel for Marion's sake suddenly felt like a boneheaded move. He could have been in the first row. Still with four people ahead of him, but . . .

The recruits did as they were told, but Arthur found it hard to stand directly on the line. He felt as if he were leaning forward at an angle. It was as if he were about to be pulled in and should take a quick step to catch himself before he fell . . . only in reality he wasn't leaning at all.

He blinked and shook his head. Judging from the odd, vaguely uncomfortable expressions around him, he wasn't the only one.

The silver-haired leader gestured, and a force flicked out from his hand. The sides of the box melted away, revealing the egg.

Arthur staggered forward a step, caught himself, and stepped back on the line. Again, he wasn't the only one.

"Recruit Francis Orchardtree," the leader said, "you may begin."

Arthur clenched his fists as Francis stepped up to the egg.

That was Arthur's egg.

I'm not imagining it, Arthur told himself fiercely. *I'm drawn to it—I've always been drawn to it. I'm just a nobody standing among nobles and royalty against all odds. This egg is mine.*

From where Arthur stood at the side, he had a clear view of Francis's face twisted in discomfort as he stepped to the red line.

Then, with a gesture, Francis projected an image of his card out in front of the egg.

Arthur wasn't about to miss this opportunity to check out his opponent's cards.

Illusionary Charmer
Legendary
Illusion
The wielder of this card—

The top of the black egg split.

Arthur's heart froze.

No.

No!

Bits of the shell crumbled inward. Then more and more. It was like watching a figurine of sand fall into dust. Only . . . soon half of the shell was gone, and the dragon was nowhere in sight.

"It's not empty, is it?" someone murmured.

"No," Arthur said. "Can't you feel it?"

But he was worried. The egg wasn't that big to begin with, and the dragon—

"BEHOLD!" boomed a deep, resonant voice. The rest of the shell blasted away, and in its place stood a dark dragon, all four wings spread proudly.

A very, very small dragon.

The body was about as long as a pack of playing cards, the wings the length of Arthur's stretched fingers, from thumb to pinky. It had four wings, just like a purple dragon, and was so dark Arthur couldn't immediately tell if it was black or deeply purple. The only spots of color came from smoldering red eyes.

The dragon flexed proudly as if he were a great beast instead of the size of a largish sparrow.

"It is I, Brixaby!" it said in a deep voice incongruous with its tiny body. "Who among you offers their card to me?"

Shock wore off, and Arthur remembered he was in competition for this dragon.

He was reaching up to break rank and project a copy of his Master of Skills out—protocol be damned. All would be forgiven if he could link the dragon—when Brixaby's bloody eyes fell on Francis Orchardtree.

"Yes," he said. "Your card will do nicely."

Francis, who stood there struck dumb, shook his head and backed up a step. He was rejecting the tiny dragon. "No, I made a mistake. Please choose another."

"Too late. I will have yours first."

Brixaby's four wings buzzed into invisibility like a hummingbird. He darted for Francis, landed on his chest, and with a ripping sound, pulled something away with his claws.

It was a card.

The tiny dragon had just ripped a card out of the man's heart.

Francis collapsed, eyes rolling up.

All around, recruits screamed in shock and fear. Most turned to bolt to the lip of the stage—only to be stopped by the transparent shield.

They all knew they faced danger. However, few seemed to be prepared for the danger to attack the center of their power—the very thing that set them apart from the commoners.

Meanwhile Brixaby buzzed up into the air with his prize. He seemed to absorb the card—even though it was bigger than him.

His voice was as dark as it was deep. "Which is next?"

"Recruits, stand together!" the silver-haired leader yelled. He and a handful of others, including Arthur, hadn't run. "This dragon must be linked, the power tamed! You!" He turned to the dragon, which was flicking back and forth like an uncertain dragonfly trying to figure out which meal to eat next. "That's quite enough."

The man flicked a dazzling silver orb of pure magic at Brixaby. It surrounded the dragon in a cage, temporarily halting him.

But only for a moment.

"Do I smell Nullify magic? Delicious!" Abruptly, the orb shrank until it touched the dark scales. With a soap-bubble pop, it broke, with the remains sinking into Brixaby's scales as if he had just consumed it.

"That power will be mine!" Brixaby roared and buzzed forward.

The leader threw up another burst of nullifying magic, which sank into the oncoming dragon's scales, and it didn't stop him for a moment.

In an instant, Brixaby was at the man's chest. When he withdrew a card, a scream broke through the air, large and outside the auditorium. The thick stone walls shook. The man's Legendary dragon was not happy.

Meanwhile, the rider was seizing on the ground with yellow foam coming from his lips.

If the first card stolen had struck fear into the recruits, this created blind panic. People beat against the transparent shield—one boy threw a bolt of lightning, which cracked against it but did not break through.

There was pandemonium on the other side. Leaders and people of importance shouted at one another—and at those manning the shield. One look told Arthur they were ordering the Rares to keep it up.

This little menace couldn't be set loose among the hive.

"Echo!" Marion yelled. "Behind you!"

The little dragon had just finished absorbing the leader's card, but of course, Marion could see the future. Echo turned, eyes wide, but she had been one of the few to stay in place and not run.

The dragon saw her, licked its lips, and dove.

Arthur finally unfroze. "No!" He sprinted forward to intercept them, to . . . he wasn't sure what he could do.

Either way, he was a few seconds too slow. Marion, who had seen the future, got there first.

The dragon switched directions in an instant, bobbing down and then upward again with a new card in its claws.

Marion didn't collapse like the others. He simply stared down at his chest, a hand over his heart. He looked too shocked to speak.

"That's enough!"

The shout came from Penn, who had stepped up, a gleaming sword in hand. Where had he gotten a sword?

"Come here, you little menace," he growled and projected his card out with one hand, the other holding the sword at the ready.

"You idiot!" Arthur yelled. "He just absorbed a time card—"

The tiny dragon flicked downward, bloodred eyes bright with an out-of-control madness.

The leader had said to tame the dragon. This wasn't a laid-back Common or Uncommon. This was a Legendary, just hatched, full of stolen power, and on the verge of madness.

It was a danger to everyone around it . . . and also to itself.

The dragon clearly had no intention of linking with a recruit. It only wanted more cards.

The moment it came within range, Penn slashed at it. The tiny dragon dodged by a hair. It darted back, then flew in again, hissing.

With a grim look on his face, Penn kept it at bay with the edge of his sword, weaving a deadly pattern through the air.

"Yeah!" someone yelled.

"Get it! Knock it from the sky!"

"That's no dragon! That's a scourgling in dragon skin!"

Someone sent a blast of wind at Brixaby, sending him tumbling. Only his quick flash agility kept him from the point of Penn's sword. If the little dragon had any sense, he would back off, he would use the time card he had just absorbed or one of the nullification or illusionary powers . . .

Arthur didn't know why he wasn't using any of the cards he'd stolen. But he did know that he wasn't the only one who knew there was something wrong with the dragon. The difference was: the rest of the recruits had decided it had to die.

Arthur couldn't let that happen.

A plan born of desperation flickered through his mind. It hinged on one huge assumption.

But it was his only hope.

"Brixaby!" he yelled, took a deep breath, and then projected an image of his Master of Skills card out. "I have a juicy card for you! Come and get it!"

Red eyes fixed on him. With a hiss of hunger and greed, it buzzed up and over Penn's sword slash, and straight at Arthur.

CHAPTER 44

Kane, look out!" Penn yelled.

Arthur ignored him. He set his feet, every muscle clenched, and concentrated with all his might on his Master of Body Enhancement card.

Brixaby the dragon fell on him, little pinprick claws digging into Arthur's shirt. Invisible hands grabbed his Master of Skills card and tugged.

The ripping sensation in his heart was excruciating. It was as if invisible strings attached to his heart were snapping one by one.

But Arthur didn't just have his Master of Skills card in his heart deck. It was paired with another in the same set. Perhaps if Brixaby had been anticipating it, he could have tugged out both. But he was a tiny dragon, and these were a pair of Legendary cards, anchored by the weight of their connected power.

The card came out halfway and stopped.

Brixaby flailed for a moment, taken by surprise. He had ripped out the other cards in a flash, leaving his victims too stunned to react.

Arthur grabbed the little dragon.

"How?!" Brixaby roared.

"Come with me and see," Arthur said, shoving the Master of Skills back where it belonged. The feeling of it slipping back into his heart was one of absolute relief. The invisible strings reconnected, and he was again whole.

He didn't know how this would work. But for some reason, Brixaby must have given him permission. Arthur threw him into his Personal Space.

In the next second, he followed.

Time stopped for every item, animal, or person he placed into his Personal Space. But Brixaby had absorbed a Legendary-level time-based card and a nullify-magic card.

The little dragon buzzed his wings, seemed to freeze in place in midair for a moment, jerk back into motion, then rapidly froze again.

He was fighting the effects of the Personal Space. Arthur could feel the room around him groaning like a wooden ship that had taken on too much weight. It was, after all, only a Rare card.

Arthur hadn't fully uncovered the rules governing time and space here, but he had been able to affect objects before. He had manipulated fabric when he'd practiced his **Snipping** skill.

Maybe he had to touch something in order to unfreeze it?

For the second time, he reached out and grabbed the little dragon. This time he was much gentler. Abruptly, Brixaby stopped stuttering in and out of time and moved smoothly.

He bit down on the webbing between Arthur's thumb and first finger.

His two long fangs actually managed to penetrate Arthur's toughened skin.

"Ow!" Switching the dragon to his other hand, Arthur shook it out. "Don't do that."

"Release me!" Brixaby boomed, his dark head sticking up over Arthur's fist. He added, "Then you may feed me your most delicious card." He eyed Arthur's chest hungrily as if he could see straight into Arthur's heart deck and wanted to swallow it whole. "We are in your heart deck now, aren't we?"

Arthur suspected this little menace would appreciate an argument coming from a position of strength. "You couldn't pull my card outside my heart. I'm too strong for you."

"Yes, how *did* you do that?" the dragon demanded. "Show me."

With a flick of his free hand, Arthur projected an image of both Legendary cards. "I have two in the same set. A pair."

Brixaby wiggled angrily against his fingers. "Then I shall have both!"

"Only if you link with me."

Brixaby was less than impressed with this offer. "Let me out of this prison. I will rip the cards out of every one of the fools outside. Then, when I am strong, when I am whole, I will come and finish you last as dessert."

Arthur ignored the threat. "Whole?"

The dragon fell silent, eyes narrowing. "My card is . . . not right. It's none of your business!" he added quickly.

Arthur tried another tack. "The other recruits are already turning on you. If you attack them again, they'll put you down like a rabid beast."

"I'd like to see them try!"

"They're already trying. Did you not notice the sword?"

"That weakling," Brixaby scoffed. "Though his cards smell like yours. How about I steal his card, then you give me your two cards, and then—"

"That's not happening. Hey, why aren't you using those cards you stole against me?"

"None of your business!" Brixaby roared and thrashed again against Arthur's grip. Arthur just held him steady. Waiting.

In here, he had all the time in the world.

At least Brixaby wasn't trying to bite him again.

Finally, panting, the little dragon stopped. He muttered something under his breath, which was by far the quietest from him Arthur had heard so far.

He brought the little dragon up to his ear. "What?"

"I said," the dragon boomed, "I don't know! I feel their weight, their power, but I cannot fully access them, and I don't know why!"

How could he not know? Unless . . .

A suspicion grew in Arthur's mind, but he kept it to himself for now. If he was right, Brixaby was certain to be prickly about it.

"One thing I've learned about cards is that while the descriptions might be clear, it still takes time to understand them. I had my dad help me out with my skills at first, but I'm still learning things. Especially with my newest card. It's useful to have a friend help you work out the nuances."

Saying this made him feel like a hypocrite. He had kept the details of his cards from Horatio, Kenzie, and Cressida for his and their safety. They couldn't be questioned about what they didn't know.

Of course, he couldn't tell Penn, and Echo was too young even though she was mature for her age.

He might be able to trust Marion, if he wasn't a prince and subject to the king's whims.

Brixaby was silent, staring up at Arthur as if measuring him for something. Arthur shrugged and indicated the projection of his two cards, which he hadn't dismissed.

"What do you think about my cards?"

"They smell deliciously powerful and the . . . the images are pleasing, I suppose," he said grudgingly.

Why Arthur had expected a baby dragon to know how to read, he didn't know. He supposed other dragons felt their way to a perfect match. Brixaby wasn't that type of dragon.

So Arthur read him both descriptions. Brixaby listened carefully.

"There's potential for growth," the dragon said at the end, "though it would take time."

Arthur chuckled. "You're telling me. I found my Master of Skills card when I was twelve, and I still feel like I've barely scratched the surface of what it can do. Now I have the Master of Body Enhancement, too. It feels like there aren't enough hours in the day to do everything. That's why I come to this place. It's outside of time so I can . . . practice . . ." He trailed off, realizing he was talking to the dragon like an old friend. And the dragon was listening.

Arthur cleared his throat. "Anyway, that's what this place is: my own Personal Space."

"Is that why it's filled with junk?" Brixaby asked.

"Those are tools. Mostly. And a lot of food. Look, how about I open up my hand and let you go, but I still think we need to be in contact here, or else you'll slip back into frozen time."

"Release me!" Brixaby announced.

That wasn't quite a yes, but Arthur opened up his hand anyway. To his relief, the dragon didn't immediately dive for his heart. He just stood on the flat of Arthur's palm, stretching out all four wings in relief.

Now that he wasn't darting around, Arthur took a second look at him. Even now, he couldn't tell if he was true black or so deeply purple he looked dark. Though there was no one visible light source in the room, his hide gleamed at the edges.

"You're a shimmer." Arthur turned his hand back and forth, watching the play of light against Brixaby's minuscule scales. At certain angles, he caught flashes of purple, especially through the wing membrane. "But I don't know what grade of shimmer."

"The best, obviously." Brixaby flexed his wings again proudly, then flinched.

Arthur's gaze sharpened. He stopped looking at the color of the scales and closer at his overall conformation.

Not only was he ridiculously tiny, his dark color made it harder to see fine details. But now that Arthur was looking, he noticed swelling at his joints. His stomach was round and tight, too. Too tight.

His **Nursecraft** and first-aid class skills pinged at him. "Are you okay?"

"How dare you! I am fine! I am perfect—ow!" He hissed as Arthur poked at the ankle joint on one of his hind legs. In retaliation, Brixaby swatted at the finger, leaving three miniature bloody tracks.

"You're not well," Arthur said, noticing that the brightness in the dragon's eyes had dimmed, too, though he still thought he spotted lurking madness in there.

Prickly or not, he had to voice his concerns. "Your card is incomplete, isn't it?"

Brixaby swelled in indignation. "It is perfect! You are incomplete in the head! When I am freed, I will tear out your cards and use them as my own and—"

"I've seen this before," Arthur said, "with a Rare that hatched—"

"I am no mere Rare!"

He continued, "Hers presented as breathing problems. But she hatched out too early, and you . . . well, your egg was alone for a long time."

Brixaby snorted. "What happened to the Rare? Did it live?"

"Yes, she did." He smiled at the memory. "Her card was completed when she found someone to link with."

Brixaby went quiet again. He weaved his head back and forth as if having an internal debate with himself.

Then, with a flick, he showed Arthur a projection of his card.

Call of the Void

Legendary

Nullify

The wielder of this card has the ability to take another card of the same rank or lower from any deck. Once placed in a temporary deck, the new card's aspects are slowly consumed and ___ to a _____ to grow the wielder's strength.

This _____ is not transferable and will dissolve upon the wielder's death or removal from core.

This card is part of the Call set. Search out other cards in this set to add to your power.

Arthur's heart pounded. "So, you have a card that takes powers from others, and I have two cards that use skills to grow. I'd like to see what that combination could do."

Brixaby's red eyes gleamed. "Or you can release me and then I take the rest of the cards from those too weak to oppose me!"

"Can you?" Arthur asked. "I don't think you're digesting those other cards too well. It might be because they're Legendary or because your card's incomplete." He poked at his tight, round stomach. "Or you've just taken in too much, too fast."

Brixaby squawked. "How dare you!"

"Meanwhile," Arthur continued, "with my skills and body enhancements, I'm becoming stronger every day." He paused. "Maybe you could too."

"I admit your cards are . . . useful," Brixaby allowed. "But there is a distinct lack of combat skills."

That was almost a yes, but Arthur knew Brixaby wasn't going to like this next bit.

"And if we do link, you're going to have to give back those cards you just stole."

"What?! Why?"

"Because they come from important people, and you aren't absorbing them like you should. They're not just any old cards. They're Legendaries, so that has to be uncomfortable and getting worse. Tell me I'm wrong."

Brixaby growled. He turned and stomped in place, tail lashing back and forth. Arthur had the feeling if he were a red dragon, he'd be snorting fire.

"I'm the one who found you as an egg," Arthur said. "You know that, don't you? Every time I saw the egg, I felt pulled in."

"I suppose our cards are *compatible*," Brixaby said, though grudgingly, as if Arthur had just convinced him to try broccoli. He turned back to Arthur and looked him up and down. "And I suppose you are . . . *acceptable*. No major flaws. That nose is a touch pointy for my taste, though."

"If it helps," Arthur said, "I was hoping for a dragon big enough to *ride*."

"You are *my* steed. Not the other way around."

Arthur smiled. "So, you want to link cards?"

"We can't do that here." Brixaby raised his head proudly. "Transmit me back to the real world."

Arthur hesitated, well aware that Brixaby could just try to steal his cards again. But if they were going to link, be partners, they would have to trust one another.

"Which one do you want to link with?" Arthur asked. "Master of Skills or Master of Body Enhancement?"

"I'm linking to both, of course."

"You can do that?"

"I am Brixaby! Of course I can."

Penn is going to hate this, Arthur thought.

CHAPTER 45

The world was overly loud and bright when Arthur emerged from the Personal Space. He was hit with a wall of sound—people yelling in anger and in fear—and realized he had let himself forget that it had been absolute chaos.

Brixaby launched off Arthur's palm. For a split second, Arthur worried that their deal was off, but the little dragon seemed to be just as surprised at the noise and had startled out of reflex.

Brixaby turned in place, saw Arthur's projected Master of Skills card, and after a second's hesitation, projected his own still-incomplete card.

There was sudden silence as other recruits realized what was about to happen.

"No!" Penn yelled. Dropping the sword, he abruptly projected a copy of his own Master of Combat between them. "You're clearly a fighter. Link with me!"

Had he been trying to kill Brixaby before . . . or had that been Penn's way of trying to impress him?

It didn't matter. Brixaby looked at Penn's projected offering. "Brother cards," he said smoothly. He couldn't read, but he likely could feel the power of the two Legendaries—and how alike they were.

Penn flinched in surprise, and his focus narrowed on Arthur's Master of Skills projection.

Arthur hesitated, long ingrained habits to keep his secrets to himself flaring up. He knew what he had to do, but the old fear made it hard.

Still hovering in place, Brixaby made a deep humming sound. He looked from Arthur's card to Penn's and back again.

"Hmm. Combat *is* more impressive than skills."

"Together, we can be unstoppable," Penn said. "Think about it, dragon! Pure combat combined with your abilities. No one would ever stand in our way!"

In answer, Arthur projected his second card: Master of Body Enhancement.

Penn's eyes bugged out.

Brixaby's deep laughter rang through the room. "Two is better than one. Though I would prefer *three*," he said with an evil draconic smile toward Penn.

Then he zipped forward to push his projected card against Arthur's two.

Penn let out an unbelieving scream as he scooped up his sword. "You son of a—oomph!"

He'd taken one step toward Arthur. Then Marion, his face waxy and pale, hair soaked with sweat, raised his hand, palm out, and summoned a wind blast at him.

It threw Penn across the stage so hard that his back struck against the transparent barrier.

Marion fell to his knees, wheezing with the effort.

But Penn wasn't a Master of Combat for nothing and was on his feet in a moment . . . only to find Echo in her brutish warrior form standing in front of him to bar the way.

At that moment, Brixaby's projected card pressed between Arthur's own.

The rest of the world fell away.

For dazzling moments that felt like eternity, Arthur saw Brixaby not as a tiny, newly hatched dragon, but as a being equal to himself. He felt like he could see through Brixaby.

The dark core that made up his magical being pulsed with energy that drew from the card within.

Arthur had a heart deck, but Brixaby's entire being was constructed and nourished from his incomplete core card.

He felt and saw their energies mixing and sharing. A fourth card, which existed neither in Arthur's heart deck or Brixaby's core, formed between them.

In that moment, Arthur knew whichever of them died or unlinked first would grant the power of the new card they'd just created to the other.

But there was more. As the energy mixed, ebbed, and flowed between them, he realized they had the option to use each other's cards . . . or not at all.

Some dragons and humans kept their core and heart cards separate. Some used the other's almost as easily as if it had been their own. It depended on the comfort level of their link—and depending on how entangled their heart deck and core energies were, how hard it would be to unlink again.

He also felt Brixaby's greed for cards and knew there would be little point in keeping him out.

After all, Brixaby's greed reflected Arthur's own.

As the minimal boundaries were set, Arthur focused on Brixaby again. Specifically, the terrible weight of the Legendary cards in his temporary core.

One day, Brixaby would be able to take and absorb high-level cards as easily as breathing. That was not today.

Casually, he reached out and plucked the three extra cards from Brixaby's core. The little dragon hissed, but the sharp pain of their loss was soothed by instant relief. The swelling in his joints faded, as did the lingering madness in his bloodred eyes.

The final words of his card filled in as the link between them solidified and snapped into place.

A brand-new card rose up between them, filling a place that was both in Arthur's heart deck and Brixaby's core.

Counterfeit Siphon

Legendary

Linked-Utility

While in aura proximity to another active card wielder's power/effect/skill/ spell, the wielder of this card may copy and use it. The copied power/effect/ skill/spell will be effective for the following duration:

Mythic: 1 second

Legendary: 10 minutes

Rare: 1 hour

Uncommon: 12 Hours

Common: 72 hours

This card grants the use of mana.

Search for other Counterfeit cards to add to the same set.

The projections of the four cards—Brixaby's Call of the Void, Arthur's Master of Skills and Master of Body Enhancement, and the newly linked Counterfeit Siphon faded from view.

Arthur was left standing with three previously stolen Legendary cards in one hand and a newly linked dragon sitting on his other.

Arthur was about to check the status of Brixaby's core card when a haggard voice rang out.

"Thief!"

Penn managed to push his way past Echo. Sword in hand, he staggered his way toward them.

Some of the watching recruits yelled in outrage. Anyone with eyes could see Arthur had just linked with the newly hatched dragon. But no one made a move to stop Penn.

After all, if he managed to kill Arthur, the dragon would once again be free to link . . . or to harvest.

Brixaby fluttered to Arthur's shoulder. "Allow me to take his card as punishment for his audacity," he said in what was likely meant to be a whisper. It boomed across the stage.

"Penn, stop. It's over," Arthur said. He didn't want to fight him—he knew by all rights he had wronged him. Even though, arguably, Penn's family had wronged him first.

Penn's eyes were bright with anger and possibly tears. "You stole from my family!" He swung his sword.

Arthur grabbed a piece of firewood from his Personal Space, and the blade bit into the wood.

Penn did not waste a second. With a vicious twist Arthur could not follow, he ripped the wood away.

New Counterfeit skill obtained: Disarm Opponent
Remaining Time: 9 Minutes 59 Seconds

New skill gained: Disarm Opponent (Defense Class)
Due to your card's bonus traits, you automatically start this skill at level 3.

Arthur's eyes widened. The first notice had come from his new linked card.

The second had come from his Master of Skills card.

A moment before, he hadn't been able to follow the disarming move. But now he knew how to do it himself on a basic level.

He stepped into Penn's space, and as his cousin brought the sword down, Arthur grabbed his wrist. He twisted, and Penn's fingers sprang open. The sword clattered to the ground.

Hanging on to his shoulder, Brixaby boomed out laughter.

In the next second, Penn lurched away as if yanked back by an invisible hand.

Arthur looked up to see that the shield had fallen. The audience of hive leaders walked to the stage.

Whitaker had his hand out, telekinesis powers on full display as he used it to drag the cursing, struggling Penn back, or rather, his clothing. With a lifting gesture, Penn rose into the air by his own belt.

"Well," said Leader Ismael, "it seems we have a new Legendary dragon rider."

And as Arthur stood there, amazed, the recruits, who had a few minutes ago been his competition, lowered their gazes and bowed.

PART 4

THE KING

CHAPTER 46

I don't want it," Marion said.

Arthur stared blankly at him, his arm held out with Marion's stolen Legendary time card pinched between his fingers. This had been a rather trying day, and for a full ten seconds, he wasn't sure he had understood the prince correctly.

Blinking, Arthur said, "Come again?"

"He doesn't want the card," Brixaby rumbled from his perch on Arthur's shoulder. He seemed to have claimed that spot as his own, as he hadn't moved from it over the last few hours. He was content to sit there and provide colorful commentary. "That means it's mine again. Gimme."

Arthur ignored him and took a longer look at Marion. He seemed a little pale but otherwise not that harmed for having a card pulled out of his heart deck.

Certainly, he was better off than Francis Orchardtree, who had been left a sobbing mess until he got his card back—a rather sorry state for a bearded man older than Arthur. Or the hive leader, who had been practically comatose and only stirred once Arthur placed the card back into his hand.

Both were now recovering under the care of healers, though Arthur had been assured that once the cards were returned into the heart deck, any damage would be quickly corrected.

He had looked for Marion, only to find him missing. He assumed he was getting some medical attention, possibly for mana depletion.

Sure enough, Marion asked to visit Arthur privately once back in his room a few hours later.

But now he was rejecting the card.

"Marion, just take it. I can't use it."

Brixaby squawked in protest.

Ignoring him, Arthur tried to hand the card to him again. This time, Marion stepped back.

"No." Marion shook his head. "I feel better than I have in a long time. Clear. I don't have multiple futures pecking at me for attention all the time. Do you know what that's like?"

"No, but we *could*," Brixaby wheedled.

"Don't you have that Nullification card?" Arthur asked.

"Yes, but it's only a Rare. It can shield most of the effects of the time card, but not . . . not the sense of the future." Marion chuckled to himself, though his laughter had a strain of stress to it. "Now I can read a book without knowing what the next few paragraphs are going to be. Do you know what a relief that is?"

Arthur shook his head.

Marion sighed. "It was like . . . you know that feeling you get where you see something before an event, or a person's face, and get the feeling it's happened before? I've had that constantly since I was twelve years old. Now I don't. Arthur, I've never felt so free."

"But it's from your heart deck," Arthur pressed.

"Commoners trade out their heart cards, or so I'm told. In times of trouble to avoid being evicted, or they gamble them away."

Arthur had seen that for himself when he had traveled with Red's caravan. It had been seen as unpleasant, but not as debilitating as what had happened to the people today. Granted, those men had been using Common or Uncommon cards.

Maybe Second and his men had been made of sterner stuff than Francis Orchardtree.

Maybe Marion was more resilient, too.

"Excellent," Brixaby purred. "We will use this to enhance my own card—"

Arthur cut him off. "We can't keep the card. You know that."

Brixaby grumbled, though his red eyes didn't leave the card in Arthur's hands until, reluctantly, Arthur put it back in his Personal Space.

The moment it was gone, hidden tension drained from Marion, too. He kept insisting he didn't want it back, but having it right in front of him must have been a terrible temptation.

"No, you can't keep it," Marion agreed. "Officially, it belongs to the king. As soon as my title is officially stripped, he'll want it back."

"What does that mean? You'll no longer be a prince?"

"That's exactly what it means," Marion said, surprisingly light-hearted. He even dredged up a smile. "All the king's heirs have Legendary cards. Removing them is the one sure way to step out of the running." Seeing Arthur's expression, he waved a hand. "It's fine. I can't go back to living the way I did. Plus, Echo is safe, since I doubt another Legendary dragon is likely to be laid soon."

Arthur was torn. Marion seemed set on this path, and by the way he spoke about his time card, he wasn't sure he'd want it back either.

On the other hand, Marion was a prince and didn't know the first thing about being a commoner. Arthur had seen him spend money like water.

Well . . . he'd either learn, or he wouldn't.

"What are you going to do if you're not a prince?" Arthur asked.

Marion smiled slyly. "Maybe I'll join the scholar's guild. I do like to read."

"They could use a few more good men," Arthur admitted, trying not to wince at the memory of Wolf Moon's guild. Surely they couldn't all be men who cultivated scourglings? "If you ever find yourself near the Wolf Moon Hive, come by for a visit."

"Oh? You've chosen Wolf Moon, then?"

Arthur nodded. "That's my home. Besides, I liked the deal Whitaker and Valentina gave me."

A few of the other hive leaders had made offers to Arthur right after the linking, but they seemed half-hearted. There had been some pointed stares toward Brixaby. And, he noticed, none of them had stepped too close.

Almost like they were afraid the tiny dragon would tear the cards out of their hearts as well.

"From what I hear, the Wolf Moon leaders were desperate enough for another Legendary they would have offered you the moon."

Arthur opened his mouth and then closed it again. "Is that a pun?"

Marion's answer was a grin.

Soon after, he said his goodbyes and left. Arthur watched the door close behind him and wished he had an argument to bring Marion to Wolf Moon, too.

But he knew this would be the time for Marion to find himself—to be off on his own for the first time and discover who he really was. Arthur had been through the same thing himself. It was a journey Marion should probably take alone.

"You don't have to give it back." Brixaby said, "When this king guy asks for the card, you can just say Marion took it."

"I'm not throwing Marion under a rolling cart," Arthur said. "Plus, do you really want that card now that you've heard how hard it is to live with?" He poked at his dragon's middle, which was now bloated with actual food instead of sickness.

"Pah," Brixaby grumbled. He swatted at Arthur's finger half-heartedly.

"Besides, you got a pretty good effect out of just having it for a bit."

Arthur smiled to himself as he checked Brixaby's card. The card was whole, now that it had been fully formed by the linking.

Call of the Void

Legendary

Nullify

The wielder of this card has the ability to take another card of the same rank or lower from any deck. Once placed in a temporary deck, the new card's aspects are slowly consumed and added to a list of ten removable/adjustable slots to grow the wielder's strength.

This list is not transferable and will dissolve upon the wielder's death or removal from core.

This card is part of the Call set. Search out other cards in this set to add to your power.

Card Effects:

3/10

Attribute: Charm +5

Spell: Magic Nullification, Level 5

Instant Danger Sense (2-second warning)

That last effect had come from Marion's time card. Arthur was pleased Brixaby would have a head's-up when he was in true danger.

The magic-nullification spell was an interesting one. Arthur himself had no experience with spells, as nothing in his deck was made for it.

He suspected nullification had something to do with Brixaby's natural magic. Much like silver dragons had a natural affinity for pure magic and pinks meta or knowledge. There was something about Brixaby that dampened or consumed magical effects.

"I would rather have a full time card," Brixaby insisted, though it was around a wide yawn. He circled on Arthur's shoulder three times before settling down like a cat ready to nap in the sunshine. "We will discuss this more when I awaken."

"Sure, Brix. You want to sleep on the bed? It's got to be more comfortable."

Brixaby opened a red eye. "You will not leave the room when I'm asleep?" He said this gruffly, as if embarrassed.

Arthur kept a straight face. "I'll be here."

"Very well, then. You may move me to the bed."

Brixaby was more than capable of flying there himself—it would only be a short buzz of wings. Arthur reached up anyway and cupped the little dragon in his hands before he transferred him to a pillow on the bed.

Once there, Brixaby let out a sigh large enough to inflate him completely before he let it out again, then curled up to sleep.

He could be cute for such a little monster.

Emphasis on little.

No one had mentioned it in Arthur's presence, but he suspected a large part of the reason why the hive leaders weren't clamoring for him to join their hive was Brixaby's tiny size.

He was smaller than any newly hatched Common Arthur had seen, even the tiny purple ones.

No one knew what to make of him. He was so tiny it was difficult to believe he'd ever grow to a size capable of being ridden. And his color was . . . odd. He had four wings like many of the purples, with the agility in the air to match. His scales even shimmered with purple highlighting in the bright light.

But he was sharply intelligent and acerbic, whereas purples were sweet and a little dumb.

Was that because Brix was a Legendary rank? Arthur had asked Whitaker and received a non-answer that left him thinking the man didn't know either.

It doesn't matter, he thought fiercely. Yes, the future was unknown, but that's what made it interesting.

One thing was for sure: He and Brix had a lot of growth ahead of them. They had new cards to learn about, not to mention Arthur planned to see if his skills transferred to Brixaby.

Would his Master of Body Enhancement card help the dragon grow?

Would their Counterfeit Siphon card allow him to gain new skills even faster? Arthur couldn't wait to start officially experimenting.

A soft knock at the door interrupted his thoughts.

The door opened before Arthur could answer it. Carley strode in, looking harried.

"Another leader wants to see me?" Arthur guessed.

Carley had been letting them in on a regular basis.

"No, only a message from your Wolf leaders: You're to leave for your new hive in the morning." Carley sent a dubious glance toward Brixaby. Unlike most people, she didn't seem overly concerned that the dragon was about to steal her cards—probably because she didn't have any. "Safe to say you'll be riding on someone else's dragon for the trip."

"I think that would be the case even if Brixaby wasn't . . ." He trailed off and sent a glance to the sleeping dragon, feeling disloyal.

Carley grinned and pinched her fingers together, miming something very tiny.

"Right," Arthur said. "I don't think baby dragons typically carry their riders."

She shrugged. "You'd know better than I, being a rider and all." But there was a bit of wistfulness in her tone.

Arthur hesitated. "You know, I managed to earn a Rare card for myself in Wolf Moon Hive."

"Well, yeah, you're a noble," she said, and though she kept a straight face, Arthur sensed she very much wanted to roll her eyes.

"I worked for every shard," Arthur said. "Two jobs. One in a kitchen, one as a bar-back."

The look she gave him was pure disbelief.

"Oh, you don't believe me? Ever see a noble do this?" Crossing the room, Arthur went to a side table. He had cleaned out the room once already and placed all useful items in his Personal Space. But some of the hive servants had refilled it in his absence—likely because of his new status as an important dragon rider.

That included several bottles of wine.

Arthur grabbed the wine bottles by the stems and started flipping them in the air in a smooth, practiced juggle.

Carley's mouth dropped. "You're joking. That's not some fancy noble party trick?"

"It's not. It earned me good tips for years." Arthur caught the wine bottles and glanced at the labels. Those were good years. Quickly, he stuffed them into his Personal Space.

"My point," Arthur continued, "is that while this hive may be large and grand . . . there's something to be said about swimming in a smaller pond." He paused. "Plus, I'll need an assistant I can trust."

Carley's eyes narrowed. Then she ruthlessly began to negotiate her new pay.

CHAPTER 47

Arthur expected pomp and ceremony upon leaving for Wolf Moon, but the Buck Moon leaders were strangely absent. It might have had something to do with Brixaby's ability—and continued verbal willingness to steal cards.

"I don't see why I shouldn't take from people who annoy me," the dragon loudly grumbled as Arthur strode to the seventh level. Carley had been given her own directions for transport to the new hive. "It was only a Common dragon, and I have seven slots left."

"Brix, I've told you not to speak about your abilities in public." Arthur sighed. "And of course that Common would be missed. All dragons are important to the hive."

Sitting up on Arthur's shoulder, Brixaby fanned two of his four wings. It seemed to be a pose he used for affectation. "Yes, but some dragons are more important than others."

Arthur rolled his eyes.

Deep inside, he was a little worried. The Common dragon in question had been a pretty sky blue they'd happened to pass by in the tunnels. It had been minding its own business, but Arthur had to grab Brixaby to keep his little dragon from swooping at it.

Seeing them, the sky blue squawked, turned tail, and ran in the other direction. Arthur hoped the wet trail it left behind had been some kind of water power.

Brixaby's first instinct was that of a predator. And right now, he saw other dragons as his prey.

The seventh level of the hive was carved out into eerie stone latticework, making the entire floor an open-air balcony.

And since Buck Moon was a larger hive at the base, the open-air floor went on and on. Practically farther than Arthur could see.

Dragons, riders, and others relaxed here and there between the supporting pillars, taking advantage of the pleasant temperatures. Since there were no walls, only supporting structures, larger dragons than usual could fit in and be among their rider friends.

Brixaby let out a happy rumble and launched from Arthur's shoulder.

Arthur felt a stab of worry that he was about to go for a large red he saw in the distance. Instead, Brixaby buzzed in quick circles around some of the lattice-like pillars and through some of the smaller holes. He looked like a dark hummingbird. His four wings even gave him the ability to hover and move backward at a moment's notice.

Arthur smiled. His dragon was playing. Showing off, and happily treating the place like a giant obstacle course.

Brixaby's agility was incredible. If he were to ever grow large enough for Arthur to ride him—

"Arthur!"

He turned at the familiar voice, and his grin widened as he caught sight of Horatio standing near an extended balcony. Behind him was the yellow bulk of his dragon, Sams.

Brixaby saw the two of them as well. Twisting in place, he made a beeline straight for them.

"Brix, no!" Arthur yelled.

The little dragon was far, far out of reach and heading straight toward Horatio as if he was his next meal.

That's when Sams lowered his head and lifted his lips to show very sharp teeth, each as long as Arthur's forearm. "This rider is *mine*."

And Brixaby . . . stopped in place. He hovered for a moment as if considering if the fight was worth it.

"Pah. I have my own rider. Why would I want yours?" he sniffed.

"Good choice," Sams said, then added reluctantly, "Sir."

Arthur caught up, and Brixaby immediately zipped back to his shoulder where he started preening the scales by the base of his wings, as if that was the most interesting thing in the world.

Crisis averted, for now.

"Good to see you," Arthur said to Horatio. "I didn't know if we'd be able to talk again before I left."

Sensing the danger, Horatio had taken a couple steps back. His eyes were still wide, but he regained his composure quickly. "Sams and I are your transport back to Wolf Moon."

"Really? I'm glad, but . . . shouldn't you two still be in training?"

"No other Rare pair wanted to do it," Horatio said in his darkly blunt way. He added, "I can't imagine *why*."

"Cowardice," chimed in Brixaby.

Sams snorted.

"Congratulations, by the way," Horatio said. "It's crazy to think that the guy I used to share a room with in the orphanage is going to be a hive leader."

Arthur shrugged. "I'm not used to the idea either, honestly."

"Hmm." Horatio glanced again at Brixaby, who was still ignoring them as if he hadn't been intimidated by Sams earlier. "Think he'll grow any?"

Brixaby's head shot up from where he'd been nibbling at one of his wings. "How dare you! I am the optimal size!"

"All young dragons grow," Sams said mildly. He stepped forward to look closer at Brixaby, then snorted a gust of hot air that, for some reason, felt like sunshine. "When he matures, he will require a retinue."

Arthur blinked. "A what?"

"You must have seen a small flock of Rare dragons always hanging around Whitaker and Valentina's dragons," Horatio answered.

He had noticed that around Whitaker, but hadn't seen enough of Valentina's to say. He nodded. "Why? Are you offering?"

He meant it as a joke, but Horatio nodded and then said melodramatically, "Being part of a Legendary retinue has great benefits, but why did you have to choose Wolf Moon?"

"I like Wolf Moon." But Arthur's thoughts drifted toward Cressida. Her little pink dragon was a Rare. Would they want to be part of his retinue?

"Why is your face red?" Brixaby asked. "Are you ill?"

"I'm not used to . . . thinking like this. Being in charge of people," Arthur said quickly to cover the moment. Reasserting himself and faking calm by focusing on his **Acting** skill, he looked at Horatio. "Are you sure?" After all, Brixaby hadn't given the best first impression.

"Oh, not at all," Horatio said darkly. "From what I heard I'd be in danger of waking up one day with an empty heart deck, but like I said, the benefits are good. Sams and I don't want to be any old pair of Rares, you know?"

The words sounded right, but there was a look in Horatio's eyes Arthur didn't like. Concern. Maybe a hint of fear.

Of Brixaby? No . . . if that were the case, he wouldn't be volunteering.

And why would Horatio, who talked of nothing but getting out of Wolf Moon Hive, want to go back?

Arthur wanted to ask. But he also had a young dragon on his shoulder who had a carrying voice and no sense of what a secret was yet.

"All right," he said slowly and watched some of the stiffness leave Horatio's frame. "But we might be in training for a while."

"Yes, he does need to grow up," Sams rumbled.

Brixaby puffed up his chest. "Anyone who wishes to join my retinue must first prove themselves. I will only allow those with the most deadly cards to serve me."

"He can fry you to a crisp with light you can't even see," Horatio said.

Brixaby perked up. "I don't suppose you'd be willing to provide a demonstration? Say, on those hatchlings practicing over there—"

"No," Arthur said firmly.

To his surprise, Brixaby listened. Sort of. "Then I shall need to examine your cards. Closely. It will only take a minute—"

He was interrupted by a loud dragon's bellow from high, high up.

Twisting his sinuous yellow neck, Sams barked back a short bellow of his own. Then he turned to the others. "It is time."

"Who was that?" Brixaby demanded, then craned his head up to the sky as Arthur walked to Sams. He jerked in surprise as he saw—sitting on her own thunderhead cloud—Valentina's dragon, Elissa.

The tiny dragon crouched down, lips lifted, not in aggression but in something close to a grimace. He said nothing more, and Arthur got the impression he was intimidated.

Sams crouched, and Horatio swung up to the saddle already placed at the base of his neck. He reached a hand down to Arthur, who easily climbed into his own seat.

"Hang on tight," he told Brixaby.

"Yes, yes. I am the one with wings. You hang on tight to this yellow dragon. I don't know how competent he is in the sky yet."

Was that Brixaby's version of concern?

Arthur didn't have time to think about it before Sams took to the air.

He wasn't the only one. Other dragons had lifted off to Elissa's call—a whole flock of purples, each with cargo or passengers wearing servants' smocks. Valentina and Whitaker didn't travel lightly. Carley, Arthur knew, would be among them.

Elissa was too old and arthritic to flap her wings. Instead, she sat on her thundercloud as if it were a throne and allowed it to move her upward.

In the sky high above, two shimmer greens ripped open a dark hole in the sky. This was their portal home.

Arthur put a hand on Brixaby's back to steady the dragon as Elissa floated in first. Whitaker's Crag, as the next-highest rank dragon, followed.

As they entered the rip, the Counterfeit Siphon activated.

New Counterfeit spell obtained: Spatial Portal
Remaining Time: 11 hours 59 Seconds

Eleven hours? Those were Uncommon-rank dragons?

Arthur was surprised, but Brixaby crowed in delight. He had to hold on to him to keep him from flying off and trying the spell for himself.

"Later. Look, Brix. That's our new home."

Of course, there wasn't much to see. Wolf Moon Hive, apparently, was in the middle of a raging rainstorm. The moment Sams exited the rift, they were pelted by fat drops of rain.

Elissa roared again. The clouds overhead melted away, and instant sunlight beamed over the hive, though the rain continued to pelt the city a few hundred yards out in every direction.

Elissa turned her giant head to look at Sams. She was so large that Valentina looked to be the size of a doll on her back. And instead of a saddle, it seemed someone had placed a throw rug meant for a large room as a comfy place to sit.

"Valentina wishes to speak to the new riders," Elissa said. "You may drop your passengers on my back and return to your hive, Rare Sams."

Sams dipped his head in acknowledgment.

Valentina's own voice reached Arthur's ears, carried by the wind thanks to her card's power. "It's time you and I had a heart-to-heart."

Sitting astride a dragon that was landing on another dragon was an odd experience. Arthur noted how Sams carefully kept his talons lifted and how lightly he landed on Elissa.

There was plenty of room on her giant back. Each one of Elissa's scales was the size of a platter used at a fancy feast. And as she wasn't actively flying—simply floating on a cloud—there wasn't any movement of her beating wings.

Still, Arthur caught Horatio sweating and suspected that Sams would be, too, if he had been capable.

Elissa turned her giant head to watch the process and let out a low rumble of approval.

"You're no youngling, Rare Sams, even though your rider is. It's your second, I assume?"

"Yes, ma'am." Sams bowed his head. "The son of my first rider."

"Ah, excellent," Elissa declared and turned back to watch the sky.

Sams's breath heaved under Arthur as he gave a draconic sigh of relief.

Arthur unbuckled the strap over the saddle and slid off, one hand up to hold Brixaby steady. Once on the ground, he nodded up at Horatio, who seemed to be communicating either *Good luck* or *Hope you don't die* with his wide-eyed stare.

Then his friend signaled to Sams, and the yellow Rare hopped delicately off Elissa's back to the sky.

Arthur turned his head to Brixaby. "Be polite."

"I am always polite!" Brixaby announced, though perhaps not quite as loudly as usual.

Meanwhile, Valentina stood waiting in the middle of the giant throw rug that functioned as Elissa's saddle.

"Come here. Let me take a look at him."

As Arthur walked close, Valentina squinted. Her wrinkly mouth pressed into a line. "Hmm. The size is unusual, though I have seen purple Commons this small before."

"Four wings," Elissa commented, having turned her head back to look at them. "It is a purple, if an off-colored one."

Brixaby, naturally, puffed up. "Four is the optimal number of wings! You should—"

"Quiet."

Elissa's voice wasn't particularly sharp, but there was a resonance in the air that followed her command. It was as if the wind trembled.

Brixaby fell silent.

Valentina caught Arthur's look and smiled thinly. "Don't worry, dear. Dragons have a pecking order among themselves, but Elissa is harmless. In fact, why don't you two have a chat?"

"I'd be delighted to talk to *dear* Brixaby," said Elissa, with lots of teeth.

Arthur felt Brixaby stiffen on his shoulder, but his dragon wasn't the cowering type. "Yes, of course. I'd love to have a chat with my elder."

Then, before Arthur could say any more or warn him to be polite, he buzzed from Arthur's shoulder to circle around the old dragon's head. Elissa snorted a puff of fog, which flipped Brixaby over in the air. Righting himself immediately, he came to rest on the end of Elissa's aged, crooked muzzle.

The elder dragon turned her head away, and whatever they were "chatting" about, Arthur couldn't hear. It may have been a trick of Elissa's wind magic.

"More intelligent than a purple usually is," Valentina commented, then shook her head. "I would have dearly liked to know who his sire was."

"You don't keep track of that sort of thing?"

"We do. But the purple who laid him lost her rider. She fell through the cracks, and no male has admitted it. I suspect he, too, is wild."

"Wild?" Arthur asked.

"The term we use for those without a rider. I forget how green you are." She sighed. "And I'm afraid you will have to learn, Arthur Kane."

He felt a familiar unpleasant jolt at that last name.

Then he felt a second jolt as he noticed Valentina watching him closely.

"I'm a quick learner," Arthur said.

"Yes," Valentina said. "So was your mother."

A third unpleasant jolt in less than a minute couldn't be good for the heart. Somehow, Arthur forged a smile anyway. He'd have to muddle through this somehow. "Oh, you know Lady Kane?"

"Hardly." Valentina's voice was dry. "But I knew Lottie Rowantree."

His smile froze, then cracked.

How long had it been since he heard that name? His father didn't call her Lottie—didn't speak of her at all except to say "your mother"—but her name was stamped just as deeply as the cards in his heart deck were burned on his heart.

Hearing her name was such a shock that for a vital moment, Arthur was knocked out of his **Acting** skill.

He only gaped at Valentina, who watched him, reading him like a book.

"It's rather easy to put together, if one has the pieces," Valentina said. "Your coloring, your estrangement from the baron, and your card."

"My . . . card?" Unconsciously, he reached up to touch his chest.

"As I said, she was a quick learner too." Valentina looked away, out to the sky, which still shone bright and clear above them with a thrashing storm all around. "I assume she's passed?"

"Yes, when I was quite young." Arthur opened his mouth to ask more about the card.

Instead, Valentina turned and spit. It didn't land on her dragon's back but flew out through the air.

New Counterfeit spell obtained: Ultimate Wind Control
Remaining Time: 9 minutes 59 Seconds

He barely noticed the spell—too shocked by Valentina's reaction and her next words.

"The baron is a *pig*."

"I . . . don't disagree," Arthur said.

She nodded once, sharply, and turned back to Arthur. Her eyes were full of sympathy. "I won't be the only one to put two and two together. The story of bandits stealing a Legendary card was always suspect. Though it makes more sense now I've learned he's given it to an illegitimate child."

Wait.

Did she think . . . ?

Arthur felt the blood drain from his face, and he wasn't sure if he should be insulted on his mother's behalf or not.

Valentina had his mother correct but thought that his blood father was actually Baron Kane.

After a pained moment, he decided discretion was the better part of valor and instead asked, "How did you know her?"

"She was a Legendary recruit," Valentina said easily. "Though obviously an unsuccessful one. She conducted herself with grace and honor, and from what I understand, secured a marriage offer from a duke's heir. The boy got on the king's wrong side a few years later for some matter or another—you know how the crown can be," she added acidly, "and that was the last I heard of her."

"You don't . . ." Arthur's mouth had gone dry. He licked his lips to moisten them again. "You don't know what happened between the duke and the king?"

Valentina shook her head sharply. "No, I only take some comfort that a part of Lottie lived on. But," she added, cutting across Arthur's next forming question with a sharp gesture. "That brings me to my next point. The king."

Arthur dearly wanted to ask for more about his mother but set his questions aside for later. Pushing too hard might raise Valentina's suspicions. He was lucky she assumed so wrongly about his father. "What of the king?"

"He requires a meeting with all new Legendary riders shortly after linking, and I dare say, he won't be happy to learn you have a pair of cards in your heart."

Once again, Arthur's mouth had gone dry. "How unhappy?"

"That depends on his mood." She looked at him steadily. "I would not say this if we weren't surrounded by wind and I wasn't confident of our privacy: The king has grown quite unstable over the last decades. I know you must have mixed feelings about your father, but it may be worth it to allow him the traditional Legendary-rider boon—the reward that goes to any noble who gives a child to the hive—if the baron can get you a luck card."

Arthur barked a single laugh, then realized Valentina wasn't joking.

Luck cards, naturally, were some of the rarest and most carefully hoarded. He didn't bother asking if the hive had one.

"What will the king do? No," he said, shaking his head. "Execution, of course. What I mean is, if he . . . takes offense. What will happen to Brixaby?"

He thought he caught a gleam of approval in her eye. "He's still a Legendary dragon and precious to the kingdom. Should that happen, he'll be *encouraged* to pick another rider." She paused. "Penn Rowantree, perhaps."

Arthur winced. "Ah."

"Card theft is a fine tradition in the hives. But as a Legendary rider, you now hold yourself—and your future Rare retinue and their under-riders—to a higher standard. Do not make enemies of the powerful nobles. They may become enemies of the hive."

As consequences went, that was less than a slap on the wrist. Again, Arthur had more questions, but he was still hung up on the fact that the king might execute him for treason against the kingdom.

"What do I do? I can't give up the second card. It's in my heart, yes, but Brix linked with both."

Valentina let out a breath and shook her head. "You have a few days until the king calls for you. We all serve at his pleasure, not the other way around. Until then, I highly suggest you wrack your brain and think hard of what to say to convince the king you are no threat. The fact you're a minor noble at best may help." She frowned. "Or it may hurt. Honestly, I wish I could be more comforting, but the man is erratic."

"Why? What's wrong with him?"

"Dementia," she said pitilessly. "It's not a surprise. He was old when I was young."

He wasn't sure what to say to that.

"In any case," Valentina continued, "we will start you on a schedule as if all is well. Starting tomorrow morning, you and Brixaby are to attend beginning rider classes. As you are a Legendary rider, I expect to hear that you are excelling. After lunch, you will attend either myself or Whitaker for leadership training. The evenings after dinner are yours to train with as you wish."

Arthur nodded.

"Good." She returned the nod with a curt one of her own. "One final thing: You are a dragon rider now. While you are too new to attend regular scourge-eruptions, if another demi-scourgling shows its ugly head, it is your duty to help take it down. Rain, shine, on your deathbed—it doesn't matter. We had a leader from Corn Moon once help fight one while she was in active labor. *All* Legendary dragons answer the call. There are too few of us, and the consequences of having a Legendary-level scourgling running rampant are too high. Do you understand?"

"Yes," Arthur answered, but he couldn't help adding, "I hope the king feels the same way."

"If he's in his right mind that day, and in a good mood," Valentina said dryly, "he just might."

CHAPTER 48

By the time Arthur was dismissed by Valentina, he felt numb by the host of revelations. It was as if he had been bludgeoned over the head several times, and his **Blunt Force Damage Resistance** had not kicked in.

He'd been directed to slide off the gigantic dragon's side to land on the firm cloud below. There, he found Brixaby, who looked about as shell-shocked as Arthur.

"What happened?" he asked as Brixaby landed on his shoulder.

"Eggs," Brixaby said shortly. "Elissa wished to talk to me about making eggs."

He was almost afraid to ask, but he had to know. "You mean, making eggs with her or . . . ? "

The look Brixaby gave him was scathing. "Elissa is revered as a Legendary, but she is *ancient*."

He flipped his top two wings closely against his back before he continued, stiffly, "It is the male's privilege to create eggs with females in his retinue, but Elissa stresses one must do so only with care and feelings of the female in mind, and . . . I do not wish to talk about it further. It is a long time away."

Smiling to himself, Arthur strode to the edge of the cloud. As he did, a piece of the fluffy yet firm cloud broke off with him standing upon it, like an iceberg breaking away from the rest of the glacier. It was unsettling, but he kept his balance, and the bit of cloud started to float down toward the hive.

"This is much like flying," Brixaby mused. "But I like using my wings better."

"One day, you and I will fly together using our own power," Arthur promised.

Brixaby made a show of looking Arthur up and down. "Oh? Do you intend to grow wings?"

The cloud gently sank toward the very top of the hive, where it came to a rather sharp point. A wide, unfamiliar balcony became visible several levels down. The cloud headed, unerringly, toward it. Upon arriving at the balcony, it dissipated into vapor as Arthur stepped down—moving quickly because he and Brixaby were no longer protected from the storm. Brixaby grumbled and flicked water off his wings, which ran icy chills down the back of Arthur's neck.

There was a huge arched door opening ahead. Arthur walked through, then stopped short.

He had expected to step into a hallway, which would then take him further into the hive. Instead, he and Brixaby entered a gigantic room. It was filled with stone and sheer marble, with a skeleton of a bed frame on one side, and the giant gaping mouth of an empty fireplace on the other. Completely free of furnishings, and more than a little dusty, Arthur's footsteps echoed as he cautiously stepped in.

He frowned and headed to the closest side door, only to see it led to a giant bathing room. The empty stone tub was longer than two of his body lengths put together. Along the wall stood a sink with a tap for cold *and* hot running water, on demand. An additional closet beyond indicated an indoor toilet.

Again, all of it was bare of any furnishings or personal touches.

"Wrong door," Arthur muttered, backing up into the main bedroom again.

As he did, he saw a large wooden door at the other end of the bedroom open. Carley walked in. She wore a simple uniform with a badge with a howling wolf pin on one shoulder. Her arms were filled with firewood.

"Oh, you're here," she said, and crossed the room to dump the firewood into the fireplace. "It's going to be a pain to keep this room warm with that open to the sky," she said, waving a free hand to the open archway. "You'd better get somebody with some kind of temperature control card in here to set up runes or anchors or something, or else firewood's going to get expensive really quick."

"Uh . . ."

"And I hope you don't expect me to keep this whole place clean, too. There is dirt encrusted everywhere. I think it's been abandoned for decades."

Arthur wasn't stupid. He immediately picked up on what Carley was saying, but he was still in disbelief. "Wait, are you saying this . . . this is mine?"

Turning, Carley gave him a disbelieving look. "Don't tell me I've been cleaning someone else's room for the last hour."

Well, Valentina did send him here. And now that he looked closer, he saw a pack of his things from Buck Moon had been set on the other side of the gigantic bed frame. Though it was missing a mattress and any other bedding. Turning, he took in the gigantic space.

"I guess it's mine," he said in wonder. "It looks like it's been a while since anybody has lived in here."

"Well, it's not like Wolf Moon Hive has many Legendaries to fill out their suites."

Legendary suites.

Arthur didn't know why, but it hit him all over again. He was a Legendary-rank dragon rider. He was no longer Arthur the bartender, Arthur the orphan, or Arthur the boy from Borderland Village #49. He could now stand shoulder to shoulder with the highest-ranking nobles.

He knew this on a surface level, but he didn't truly feel any different.

Brixaby launched from his shoulder and flew up to explore the thick rafters that crossed the high, bowl-shaped ceiling. Now that Arthur was looking around with a new eye, he noted that the room was large enough to admit a good-sized dragon. Not a truly giant beast like Elissa or Whitaker's Crag, but it would be large enough to hold Brixaby for a good amount of time.

Assuming Brix ever grew that large.

"I shall make my nest up here," Brixaby announced from somewhere among the rafters. "That way I may view my entire territory at once."

Carley craned her neck up. "Is he trying to act like a creepy bat?"

"How dare you!" Brixaby roared. "I will pluck your cards from your heart and eat them for breakfast! I—mmm." He paused. "Arthur, give this obnoxious child a card so that I may then take it from her."

"That's not going to happen," Arthur said mildly. Then he turned to Carley. "Don't worry about getting this whole place cleaned up at once. For now, focus on the main living area, and I'll pitch in to help with the rest."

Carley rolled her eyes. "If you don't mind my saying, *sir*," she said with slight emphasis, "instead of getting on your hands and knees to scrub like a commoner, you could act at your station and hire other people. Only, I still get to be in charge of the new workers," she added.

That wasn't a bad idea. However, Carley was young, and he did not think an adult would appreciate her bossing them around.

But the kids from Freyja's orphanage were always looking for work. And Arthur would pay well. "Let me see what I can do," he said, then held up a hand. "Brixaby, come with me. Let's explore the rest of the place."

He realized belatedly that he was treating him more like a parrot than a dragon, but Brixaby landed on the side of his hand and allowed himself to be transferred to Arthur's shoulder anyway.

Several more doors led off from the bedroom. Arthur chose one at random and found himself in what he supposed was a library. The inset floor-to-ceiling shelves were dusty and completely bare. One side of the room was taken up entirely by glass—also dusty and hard to see through. A small, cold fireplace sat on the other side.

"Boring," Brixaby announced. "I like the other room much more."

Arthur closed the door to give himself and his dragon some privacy.

"Forget that. Brixaby, Valentina told me some things, too. We have to work hard for the next few days and get strong. We'll have an important meeting with the king soon."

Brixaby perked up. "So he can announce my greatness all over the land?"

Arthur winced. "I don't know. He might not like the fact that I have a pair of Legendary cards."

"Why not? They make you stronger."

"That's the problem. He might think they are strong enough for me to challenge him. Though"—he rubbed at the side of his face in thought—"he has a Mythic dragon, so it's hard to believe anything can challenge him."

And he also might be going mad and it won't matter what we do, Arthur did not say. He didn't know if he should burden Brixaby with that knowledge yet. He was only a day old.

Brixaby didn't seem concerned. "I like the idea of getting stronger."

"So do I." Arthur sucked in a breath. "So, let's see what this new spell can do."

Mentally, he checked the timer on the Counterfeit Siphon card and found that he had just over ten and a half hours left on the portal spell.

"How do I activate this . . ." he wondered aloud. He had never done a spell like this before. There was no mention of a cooldown or of a mana cost. It seemed pretty basic.

In the next moment, he found it was as simple as concentrating.

Something inside him twisted, and it seemed to affect the rest of the world, too. It was as if everything around him—the air, the empty shelving, even the glass windows—had turned into a type of fabric. All he had to do was sink his fingers in between the threads of reality and tear it open.

"What are you doing?" Brixaby asked. "You are doing something. I can feel it."

"Concentrate on the portal spell, then help me."

Arthur reached out to the fabric that was the world, poised to tear it open into a portal.

But what would be on the other side?

Logically, he knew he should start small. Test things out. Maybe a portal to the room next door to where he could vaguely hear Carley puttering around. Or to his previous room at Buck Moon Hive.

His heart knew where he really wanted to go.

He thought of his real home, back at the border village. The little two-room cottage where he had grown up alongside his father.

Brixaby buzzed forward and sank his claws into the fabric of the air next to Arthur's hand. Together, they pulled, and as they did, the strings of reality unraveled into a small slit. Arthur concentrated fiercely on the image, the feeling, of his little boyhood cottage. He needed it to be on the other side of the world's fabric.

Brixaby let him direct the spell. He only added his strength and his mana.

Arthur needed all the help he could get. The fabric of the world did not want to come apart. But after using all their strength and concentrating fiercely on the spell, the tear between them widened to a foot tall from top to bottom.

Arthur's mana plunged just from this. He gasped, and suddenly, he was looking into the small wooden cabin. It was as if he had created a window from here to there. The scent of old wood and cooked stew drifted in. It smelled like home.

The portal was too small for him to enter.

But it was the perfect size for Brixaby.

"Hold my side," the dragon said and let go, giving Arthur only a moment to catch his half of the tear before the fabric closed, like a curtain covering an open window.

"Brixaby, don't—"

Ignoring him, Brixaby buzzed through.

"What is this place?" Brixaby called from the other side. "It is quite small, and I smell no cards at all."

"Is there anyone there? Dad, can you hear me?" Arthur called. Sweat bloomed across his forehead. His arms trembled with the strain of holding the portal open.

Just because he could do this spell didn't mean he was practiced at it. Meanwhile, his supply of mana steadily ticked down.

"This is pointless, let's try again, only let's find somewhere better," Brixaby said.

His father was probably out among the villagers. There might even be a dragon-soil shipment to work into a new field. He had never been the type to hang around the house.

If Arthur had planned this ahead of time, he would have prepared a note.

Meanwhile his strength, and his supply of mana, were waning.

"Come back," he gasped.

With the speed of a diving hummingbird, Brixaby shot back through the portal.

As soon as he was through, Arthur released his hold. The fabric snapped closed and reknit as if it had never been torn, leaving Arthur wheezing from exertion.

"Those green dragons didn't make it look hard," Brixaby said.

He buzzed back and forth where the portal had been a moment before, as if testing the air.

Arthur shook his head and wiped sweat from his face with the back of his sleeve. "They probably arranged their entire heart deck to support that one card. Added mana and stamina boosters. Or maybe . . ." He trailed off and shook his head. "Our card is a *Counterfeit* Siphon. We probably only get the basics of their power. And because it's a spell, I don't have a way to level it up."

Brixaby returned to his shoulder. "What I'm hearing is I should steal one of their portal cards and absorb the true power for myself."

Arthur opened his mouth. Then he hesitated. "Let's call that Plan B."

"You're no fun. Wait." the little dragon actually did a double take, looking at him. "Is that a yes?"

"It's a 'Let's keep that in mind,'" he said slowly. "A portal power will be really useful. If we come across one in a card shop, or if there are . . ." he couldn't make himself say it, "other opportunities where no one gets hurt, then we should take it."

He didn't like the way Brixaby rubbed his claws together.

"Meanwhile, let's try opening that portal again in a few hours."

"To the same place? Why? We can open it to a place rich with cards. Then I could gorge myself."

"Because my dad lives in that cottage," Arthur said, quietly but firmly. "And I have questions to ask him about my mother's card."

"Pah," Brixaby snorted.

A knock came at the door, and Carley's voice called out, muffled, from the other side. "You have a visitor."

It made sense. Important people would surely like to speak to the new Legendary rider, but Arthur wasn't in the mood to play politics. "Are they important?"

"Just some Rare rider. Should I send her away?"

Her?

"No." Arthur opened the door and looked past Carley.

Cressida stood in the middle of the bare bedroom, her vividly pink dragon, Joyberry, by her side. Cressida was garbed in a gray training uniform, her bright-red hair pinned up into a bun. She looked both lovely and professional. Joy had grown since Arthur had last seen her. The top of her head now reached Cressida's waist.

Seeing him, Cressida's eyes widened. "So it's true. You really linked the Legendary dragon?"

"Arthur!" Joy cried, springing over to him. "I have a quest for you!"

Brixaby launched from Arthur's shoulder to buzz around the little pink. Joy stopped and craned up her head to watch, her eyes wide in wonder.

Arthur didn't get the notification himself, but he felt something change within Brixaby.

"Now I have a quest, too," Brixaby said smugly.

CHAPTER 49

Cressida stared at him with wide eyes. "So that's true too. Your dragon steals powers."

Arthur's heart sank down to his toes.

Carley, wisely sensing this was a conversation she didn't want to be a part of, backed away to another room with a *good luck* look.

"Nope!" Joy sang out, bouncing up high to get a better look at Brixaby. With a grumble, the little black dragon hovered a bit higher to stay out of her range. Joy glided back down and announced, "I still have my quest!"

Well, that was one question answered.

Arthur hastened to explain. "We're still learning exactly what his card can do, but as far as I can tell, Brixaby only copies active powers, and only when he's close—within the same aura."

Better to let Cressida think this was Brix's main power and not just their linked card. Especially if gossip was already flying around.

Cressida visibly relaxed. "Then you have my apologies for assuming. I've never heard of a power like that before."

"Brix! Brix! Brix! Wait, I can call you Brix, right?" Joy asked, still bouncing. As she did, she flapped her wings for some extra, awkward height. Unlike Brixaby, her body was too large for her still relatively short wings to hold her long in the air.

Now that Arthur thought about it . . . was it unusual that Brixaby could fly so soon after hatching?

"What do you want?" Brixaby demanded gruffly instead of answering her. He hovered in place, just watching her antics with a slightly confused look on his face.

Joy leaped up high again. "What's your quest? I bet it's a good one! I'll tell you alllllll about mine if you want." The latest leap took her to Brixaby's new height—at least until he buzzed upward a few more feet.

Unconcerned, Joy landed easily and leaped again.

"My quest," Brixaby said grandly, "is a worthy one! I have one hour to discover how to grow larger."

"Ohhhhhh. Maybe eat a meal?" Joy said. "Like, a lot, *a lot* of meat. Your tummy will swell, and all that food turns into muscle overnight. That's what my Cressida says."

As the two dragons chatted, Cressida walked over to join Arthur. She glanced up constantly to where Brixaby now buzzed around the high rafters, as if showing off what he could do.

"He's well proportioned," she muttered. "Especially for just being hatched."

Arthur waited a moment, expecting her to comment on his size. But she added, "The only ones in our dragon care class who are flying are purples. He . . . is purple, right?"

"I'm not sure," Arthur admitted. "Have you ever heard of a black dragon?"

"No, just very dark blues. But I'm not an expert." She turned her gaze to him. "I heard about the trials they put the Legendary recruits through. Was it bad?"

Arthur hadn't let himself think much about the last couple days. Every time he did, he got a flash of the wild look on Penn's face: the hurt and the betrayal.

Arthur *had* betrayed him several times in several different ways. He wouldn't have done otherwise if he had to do it all over again, but he didn't like thinking about it.

If circumstances were different—if Arthur wasn't who he was, and Penn hadn't been his cousin who'd lived the life Arthur should have had—they could have been friends.

"It was bad, but worth it," he said, looking up meaningfully at Brixaby.

He almost wished he hadn't.

Brix was now using his feet to hang upside down off the top rafter, watching Joy trying to flap up to him. It made him look more like a bat than ever.

"Yes, I can imagine. You're a Legendary rider now. Congratulations. But . . ." Cressida looked around the bare, dusty suite. "This is where they put you?"

"It seems so."

"Well," she said briskly, "this will never do. I can help you arrange for supplies to be sent up. You need a mattress for your bed at the very least, though I don't know if we can get one tonight."

"No," Arthur said quickly. "I have no way to pay you back—"

She laughed aloud, then quickly stifled it when she saw Arthur wasn't joking. "Most of the upper-tier riders have credit with the hive stores. Though it might take a few days for the hive to establish your official stipend."

He had forgotten about that. Arthur had always worked for his money—he'd never had anyone give him anything just for existing.

Cressida went on. "The lower-tier dragons—the Commons and Uncommons—have only minimal stipends used to feed their dragons and themselves on basic rations. Everything above that is earned through deeds during the eruptions, selling harvested cards and shards from scourglings, or being on specialized teams like the Lobos who do search and rescue. As Joy is a Rare, we're given a decent stipend to fit our needs, but of course, we're still expected to contribute and earn eruption bonuses. But as a Legendary . . ." She trailed off meaningfully and shrugged. "They'll go over it in the dragon care class, I'm sure."

"So, you're saying I can go into a commissary and buy whatever I want?" Arthur asked, half teasing.

"An upper-level commissary," Cressida said firmly. "You'll need quite a lot to turn this cavern into a home. What is your personal style?"

"Style?"

She flicked her fingers. "Most men like forest green, rich browns, or other dark, muted colors. But that can leave a room looking closed in, and that would be such a shame with these wide windows and arch door. I recommend something in gold or cream, perhaps accented in red to fit your new station."

Arthur just stared at her. "Do you have a decorating card or something?"

"No, I was raised to be the wife of a high-powered noble," she said lightly, "but don't change the subject. What colors do you prefer? Do you follow any artists? These walls could support some artwork . . ."

Feeling like a man about to drown, Arthur said, "Uh, what colors do you like?"

He was thankfully interrupted by the dragons.

"Who says I'll help you with your quest?" Brixaby boomed. He had flipped up out of his hanging-bat pose and just looked down at her from his place on the rafters, like a king about to pass judgment. Then he paused. "What is your quest, anyway?"

"I want to join your retinue, when you make one," Joy said, still bouncing.

Cressida whirled to her. "Joy! Remember what we talked about?"

"Oh? Oh! Right." The little pink dragon stopped bouncing, and her head lowered. "Cressida told me we're supposed to be more delicate about asking," she told Brixaby. "Sorry."

Cressida's face flooded with color.

Arthur chuckled. "You know, you're the second person who's asked me about that."

"Not a surprise," she said, not quite meeting his eyes. "It's a high honor for all Rare pairs."

Arthur glanced between Joy and Brixaby and remembered that awkward conversation Brixaby had relayed from Valentina's dragon. "Brixaby just hatched, and no one has explained much about . . . retinues," he said carefully. "Can you tell me what it means, exactly?"

She nodded briskly, visibly regaining her mental balance. "I'm sure they'll go over it in your class. Basically, each Legendary dragon has their own under-riders and outriders—it's a kind of mini hive, or specialized team. They carry out the Legendary's orders during a scourge-eruption and help with the functions of the hive. That's how Joy and I can be of the most use," she added quickly. "I know Joy's card doesn't lend itself to combat, but Rares in the service of a Legendary get extra benefits and better pay. I can buy combat cards for Joy when she's ready. Then we can be a help combat-wise."

"Pah, you're wasted in combat." Brixaby buzzed down to Arthur's shoulder. "Your quest card will be very useful. I only have access to the power for an hour at a time, so I must keep you close. Yes," he decided, puffing out his chest, "Joy and the girl may join my retinue."

"Really?" Cressida and Joy asked in the same breath.

"Well," Arthur said, "it's not like I'm going to say no. I don't know how to make it official, but—"

He stopped as Joy's very vividly pink hide flashed to a brighter shade. It was as if someone had lit a light under her scales, making her almost painful to look at.

At the same time, Cressida's eyes fluttered shut. Wisps of her red hair flew back as if she were caught in her own windstorm.

Just as quickly, Joy's glow faded, and Cressida opened her eyes. She was smiling.

"Quest complete!" Joy chirped. "And I'm part of a retinue now! Yay!" She ran over, throwing her forearms around Arthur's shin in a hug, adding her wings for effect. "We'll be the best under-riders ever!"

"What just happened?" Arthur asked.

Smiling, Cressida explained, "Quest reward. It was a good one—I think joining a retinue is usually a lot harder than this. Joy just got three points added to her charisma, and I got two added to my base intelligence. You have heard of attributes, right?"

"Yes. That's quite the reward."

She nodded. "But the reward isn't why we came here. You should know that Joy and I intend to take our duties seriously. Even if we're in training, and . . . well, you know that I'm already in your debt for helping me out with Joy's hatching. I haven't forgotten that, and—"

Arthur held up his hand. "I don't need people in my debt. I just need good people on my side. Plus," he admitted, "your quest card is really useful."

Now she practically beamed. "I'm glad you see the use of it. Some of the combat-oriented dragon pairs don't understand."

"They're big meanie-heads," Joy agreed.

"Then I'll show them what true power looks like when I rip their cards from their cores," Brixaby said.

"Ohhh," Joy said. "Can you really do that? There's one green who—"

"No," Arthur and Cressida said at the same time.

"He can't really do that," Cressida said, "can he?"

"Not to allies," Brixaby confirmed. "Because it upsets Arthur."

Arthur winced. "I'd rather that didn't get around."

Cressida's eyes went very wide, then narrowed as if she was studying Arthur for something, then she nodded. "Of course I'll be discreet, but young dragons usually . . . aren't."

"Yeah," Arthur sighed. "This is Brixaby's indoor voice."

"What is wrong with my voice?" Brixaby boomed.

Using diplomacy with the deftness of a high-leveled skill, Cressida changed the subject. "They *are* having you join dragon care lessons, right?"

"Yes, first thing in the morning."

"That's our class!" Joy cried. "We're going to have so much fun. Today we practiced diving down on scourglings. Like this!" She flapped heavily in the air and then dropped again, claws outstretched as if preparing to land on something and start tearing into it.

"It's part combat, part hatchling daycare," Cressida said in a low aside to Arthur. "The trainers separate the classes by month, so the hatchlings grow up together."

Arthur frowned. "They expect you and Joy to hunt scourglings?" That didn't seem to be a good use of Joy's quest talents. And the fierce little snarl on her muzzle as she pretended to dive on scourge didn't look right on her face.

"No, we're hoping to be in tactics, planning, or search and rescue," Cressida said. "But everyone is trained in physical combat regardless of card powers, in case of emergencies. And I have my flame bears in case we get into trouble."

Arthur nodded.

It seemed like tomorrow's dragon care class would be interesting.

"Brixaby," he said, interrupting the two dragons who were talking about who was the better diver. "Looks like we have a big day tomorrow. Let's see if feeding you up completes your quest or not."

Cressida soon excused herself, saying she wanted to get a start on purchasing things on his behalf to "Make this room livable."

Arthur was a little surprised she had been serious about that, but he knew better than to argue against the steely glint in her eye.

So with only a quick stop to find Carley and explain Cressida was authorized to come and go as part of his retinue, he took Brixaby to the kitchens.

The hive had giant kitchens on the lowest level where the bulk of the population lived and worked, some restaurant-sized ones on the mid-levels that housed most of the dragon riders, and some exclusive ones on the higher levels for the elite of the hive.

Arthur knew which one he was expected to visit—or where to send a servant to fetch for him—but he was feeling homesick.

Three weeks ago, he'd been a nobody with a couple of jobs to pay for an apartment in a middling part of the city. Now he was someone of importance. He would be expected to lead people.

Right now, he just wanted to sleep in a familiar bed. He'd rather it be back in his old apartment in the city, but smuggling Brixaby out of the hive would be too problematic.

So Arthur settled for his quarters inside the hive. The one Kenzie had gotten for him.

It was near enough to the sprawling lower-level kitchens that he was able to stop in with little trouble. Brixaby kept silent for once, a small dark spot on his shoulder, and the servants were busy enough not to give him much of a look. Arthur collected two bowls of beef stew.

On his way out, he passed by a man who was using the ample workspace to carve a melon into a flower. Likely, that melon wouldn't be displayed in the lower levels but some upper-tier rider's room.

Huh. Maybe he should host a fancy party and have one of those—

New Counterfeit skill obtained: Decorative Vegetable Carving
Remaining Time: 71 Hours 59 Minutes 59 Seconds

New skill gained: Decorative Vegetable Carving (Cooking Class)
Due to your card's bonus traits and your existing Cooking Class, you automatically start this skill at level 5.

Arthur stopped so fast he slopped stew over his hands.

The man working on the melon looked up, saw Brix, and paled slightly. "Can I help you, sir?"

Arthur didn't have to force a smile. "No, thank you."

He moved on.

"As my steed, you should make your movements more fluid and less jerky," Brixaby complained.

"I worked in the kitchen for years," Arthur said in wonder, hardly listening to him, "and I never picked up that skill. Then again, I didn't try for it, but now, now I have Decorative Vegetable Carving. Just like that."

"Decorative vegetable carving?" Brixaby repeated. "What use is that?"

"You'd be surprised. I saved myself quite a few times using basic skills. Speaking of which . . ." He glanced at Brixaby. "You've been riding on my shoulder off and on all day and you haven't gotten a, uh, human-riding skill?"

"No? Should I?"

"I received a dragon-riding skill my first time on Tess."

Brixaby bristled. "Who is this Tess? How dare they! I am your dragon. Not—"

He went on like that, but Arthur wasn't listening.

He was still deep in thought by the time he and Brixaby made it back to his old room on the lower levels.

Though he hadn't lived there nearly as long as he had with the apartment he shared with Horatio, stepping inside felt like home.

Brixaby wasn't as impressed. "This is quite small and dark, and there are no rafters for me to roost from."

"It's palatial compared to some places I've lived." Arthur set down the bowls on the small table. "Here, try some of this. You might like the broth and the chunks of meat."

He had never seen a dragon eat human food, but he'd heard that some of them liked fruit as an occasional snack. This probably couldn't hurt.

It might even help Brixaby to grow.

Jumping to the table, Brixaby sniffed his bowl of stew and then cautiously dipped the tip of his muzzle in. A moment later, he'd ducked his entire head under and was slurping greedily.

Arthur grabbed up a spoon and dug in his own bowl. It had been a long day.

The simple stew also had an indefinable sense of home. Buck Moon Hive treated him well, and the food had been several orders above what he usually ate. But the mix of spices was slightly off. It was as if the cooks were used to adding a few pinches more spice and sugar to everything. Not bad, just markedly different.

It was good to be home.

Brixaby finally came up for air, long tongue licking at his chops.

"I just received a new skill."

"What is it?" Arthur asked eagerly. It was his first skill he'd gotten on his own, without copying from someone's aura first.

"Culinary Appreciation."

Arthur grinned. "You really are my dragon."

"Yes, was that in any doubt?" Brixaby speared a floating chunk of stew meat and started tearing it apart with his needlelike claws.

Eating good food hadn't helped Brixaby's quest to grow larger. It timed out within the hour.

Arthur wasn't too surprised. Nor was he worried: They were going to spend a lot of time with Cressida and Joy. Either Brixaby would get another crack at that quest or perhaps another one that would be easier to complete.

"Why are you smiling?" Brixaby asked.

Arthur shook himself. "Nothing, I was thinking." He didn't want to tell the dragon that he was thinking about his size. Brixaby could be sensitive about it.

The dragon narrowed his red eyes at him.

Not wanting to explain, Arthur said, "Let's talk about your skills."

"Yes!" Brixaby perked up at once. "Is there a rending skill? A skill to see which cards are best to steal? Perhaps a dark of the night skill . . ."

"There's a stealth skill," Arthur said. "That one has helped me out quite a few times."

The little dragon's tail flicked in satisfaction. "Yes, that will do nicely. How do I achieve this skill?"

Arthur almost said "By being sneaky," but . . . that wasn't quite it, was it?

"You have to be deliberate," he said. "Back when I was first learning about my Master of Skills card, my father advised me to think about what I was doing. To . . . to practice with intention. A person does hundreds of actions each day, but only when you slow down and think about it do you start to master the process . . ." He trailed off and shrugged. This was a concept he knew, but until now he hadn't truly put it into words.

Brixaby, however, had listened raptly. "I see. So that is why I hadn't received a human-riding skill. Or a flying skill at the expert level," he added. "This room is much too small for me to adequately practice."

With that, he made a light leap to Arthur's shoulder. "But you may pace around the room."

Arthur stood from the table. "Focus on moving with me. Your center of balance isn't important now, but it will be when you start to grow."

Brixaby adjusted himself so that his long, dark tail lay across Arthur's neck. "Like this?"

"Yes, and it may take some repetition. Three times is the magic number for me."

With Brixaby hanging on and concentrating, Arthur crossed from the table to the other end of the room, turned on his heel, and crossed again.

Because he was focusing on Brixaby so intently, he once again felt something within him change. No, that wasn't quite right. It felt as if something tiny, deep inside, had just grown.

The seed of a new skill?

"Aha!" Brixaby cried. "I received my human-riding skill at level four."

"Perfect." Arthur looked around the room, searching for inspiration. His gaze landed on a nearby bookshelf. It was empty, but he'd taken a few dry books of hive history from his room at Buck Moon Hive.

"Next," he said, "reading."

* * *

He spent the next half hour or so going over the ABCs with Brixaby. The dragon had a keen sense of memory and picked it up faster than Arthur had when he was a young boy.

Once Brixaby received **Basic Reading** at level 3, Arthur taught him to count.

"Oh," Brixaby said once he got the basics down. "Is that what those attribute numbers mean in my core?"

Arthur slapped his palm to his forehead. "Right, why didn't I think of it? You're linked to my Master of Body Enhancement, too. Of course you can see your own attributes."

He didn't ask how Brixaby knew the word "attributes," even though he had just learned the fundamentals of reading. When a card entered the heart deck, the details were imprinted on the soul. He assumed dragon cores were the same thing.

"Can you show me?" Arthur asked.

"They are very good numbers. Some of the first people count, which means they're the best," Brixaby said proudly and showed the list.

(20 = Average)
Strength: 5
Stamina: 7
Dexterity: 4
Perception: 21
Charisma: 20
Intelligence: 29
Wisdom: 15
Luck: 20

Some of those were . . . not great. The strength and stamina explained why Brixaby was so small, though.

Brixaby's expression was of expectation, and Arthur didn't want to hurt his feelings.

"Your intelligence is higher than my own," he said grudgingly. "Very good perception, too."

Brixaby preened.

The night was growing late, and they had a big day in the morning. Brixaby had eaten his fill of the stew, as well as the dregs on the bottom of Arthur's bowl, and was looking round and sleepy.

Arthur checked the time on the portal spell.

A little over two hours remaining.

"I'd like to try the portal again," he told Brixaby. "Oh, wait—" Then he went to his writing desk, pulled out a piece of paper, and started writing.

He kept his note brief and impersonal—aware that Baron Kane's men could search his father's cottage at any time for contraband. He also kept his reference to the children he had helped escape the village as discreet as possible.

Calvan,

I am well, and everyone is settling into their new lives. There's no easy way to ask this: I've come across information about your wife, Lottie. I need to know: What was her card?

I don't know when I can see you again. If we cannot talk, please write me a letter and leave it on the table. I'll receive it.

Arthur bit his lower lip and decided against signing it. There was far too much incriminating information on the page for his liking already.

Hopefully he wouldn't need the letter and could simply talk to his father face-to-face.

Brixaby was dozing on the bed and grumbled when Arthur poked him awake. He eventually woke up enough to help lend his strength to tearing open the fabric of the world again.

The cottage on the other side was dark, with not even a glow of embers from the woodstove.

Arthur called out his father's name without an answer.

With Brixaby visibly wilting, Arthur shoved the letter through, where it fell down to the wooden table.

Then he let the portal snap shut.

"Can I go to sleep now?" Brixaby asked grumpily.

"Yes, Brix. You did good." Arthur set aside his worry for his father long enough to guide the dragon to curl up on Arthur's own pillow.

Brixaby took this as his due, yawned big enough to show every one of his tiny razor teeth, and settled down to sleep with the tip of his tail curled over his nose.

Arthur stroked one fingertip down the length of his dragon's purple-black spine.

Why hadn't his father returned to the cottage?

Everything was in good order—nothing broken as if there had been a fight or a search from the baron's men. And the cottage was too well built to go empty for long. If the worst had happened, there would be another family living in there within days, perhaps hours.

Perhaps Calvan was busy. There wouldn't be much of a reason to stop by the cottage other than to eat and sleep.

Arthur hoped Calvan had found someone special who he was spending time with. It had been years since Lottie died.

There was no point worrying about it for now. He had to find a way to survive his upcoming visit with the king.

But before that, he and Brixaby had dragon care class.

CHAPTER 50

Arthur walked into the giant indoor arena that hosted the dragon care classes, Brixaby on his shoulder.

At a quick glance, there were ten other dragon pairs. They were of all shades and sizes, though none smaller than Brixaby or larger than a dog.

Most of the young dragons were gathered in a group, wrestling while making "fierce"—frankly adorable—growling noises. Two of the smallest dragons, who were about the size of cats, fluttered around the fray on four rapidly beating wings. Those were the purples. One was a light lilac, the other a darker shade. They were the only two in the air, though other young hatchlings occasionally rose up on their hind legs to beat stubby wings in order to exercise them.

Joy sat off to the side of the main group, watching with a sad look on her face. It faded the moment she spotted Arthur and Brixaby.

"You're here! You're here! *Finally!*"

She bounded up to them, and some of the other dragons broke off from their play to see what she was doing. One by one, they fell silent when they noticed the newcomers.

Joy skidded to a stop in front of them.

Arthur braced himself for a notification from the Counterfeit Siphon card, but nothing came. His guess was Joy didn't have a currently running quest, so there was nothing for the card to siphon from.

"I am never late," Brixaby told her. "I arrive exactly when I plan to."

"Yes, but I haven't seen you for hours," Joy explained.

Looking around, Arthur caught sight of Cressida. She, too, was separated from the main group of people and stood next to an older woman with steel-gray hair.

Brixaby flew off to circle around Joy's head, so Arthur left him at it to go join the others.

"Sir," the older woman greeted, dipping into a curtsey. "My name is Instructor Athena, Rare rider to orange Brooks. I'm honored to have you in my class."

"Arthur, Legendary rider to purple Brixaby." It was the first time he had ever introduced himself as such, and it felt odd. He decided to go with purple as Brixaby's main color, though he had his doubts. "And I can't wait to get started. Brix, too." Turning, he pointed just in time to see Brix buzz over to the grouping of baby dragons.

Several squealed and tumbled out of the way, one rolling head over tail in its haste, another two running to hide behind the legs of their own riders.

Apparently rumors of Brixaby's abilities had circulated around the hive.

Not all ran, however. One sturdy red hatchling stood stock still and let out a reasonably loud roar at Brixaby. A blossom of fire bloomed out of his mouth—literally—and the yellow-red flame was shaped like an unfurling flower.

Several people cried out. Arthur tensed in instinctive fear.

He shouldn't have worried. Brixaby might be vulnerable to physical harm, but his natural nullification magic had him well covered from standard card spells.

The fire curled around Brixaby, but what flames made it close disappeared into wisps.

"That is a fine spell!" Brixaby boomed out. "And now it is mine!" He laughed, and out of the tips of his claws bloomed a winding vine of pure flame that wound its way to the floor.

"Oh dear," Cressida murmured.

"Stop! Right this instant!" Instructor Athena's voice cut through the air with the force of a card's power behind it. Arthur saw a slight distortion in front of her mouth, as if the words had a weight.

Brixaby flapped backward a few feet, the vine-fire dissipating.

Athena charged to the two, and Arthur quickly followed with a sinking sensation in his gut.

That sinking sensation turned to surprise within a moment.

"Zaxes!" Athena barked to the red dragon. "You have been told there are no card powers allowed in the arena. Bad dragon! Where is your rider? Jorine, come here at once."

A young girl with straw-colored hair jogged up. "Sorry, Instructor. She . . . she got nervous. It won't happen again."

"See that it doesn't. Three laps around the arena. Go!" Instructor Athena snapped.

The girl gestured to her dragon, who quickly scuttled to her side. Without a backward glance, the two made their way to the outer wall to begin their laps.

Arthur braced himself for his own reprimand.

Instructor Athena turned to him and in a softer voice said, "With your permission, sir, I'll be starting the class now. I'll be working with the Commons and

Uncommons first. Meanwhile, I recommend you stand with Rare Rider Cressida and observe."

"I . . . uh . . ." Completely thrown, Arthur nodded. "Sure."

Then he raised his arm. "Brixaby, come here."

Brixaby landed, proud again now that the surprise from the woman's voice-blast had worn off. "I have a fine fire spell for the next twelve hours."

"Yeah," Arthur muttered as he walked back toward Cressida, "and showing off like that isn't going to help the rumors of you stealing powers."

"Why should I care what others think of me?"

"You're supposed to be leading them. That means setting a good example." Though his words felt flat since the instructor, apparently, had seen nothing wrong with Brixaby's behavior.

She might have been going easy on Brixaby because the rules hadn't been explained to him yet, but Arthur didn't think so.

They joined Cressida and Joy and watched as Instructor Athena organized the Common and Uncommon dragons into two groups—or flocks. Then they were to practice traveling back and forth while in neat rows without stepping out of formation or stepping on each others' tails or wingtips. As the two purples could fly, they were allowed to follow along on the wing.

The human riders accompanied them to try to keep order.

This was easier said than done, as the newly hatched dragons all seemed to be at a different level of physical ability, were different sizes, and had the attention spans of young children recently given sweets.

Arthur wasn't thrilled at being excluded, but after watching several pileups, he couldn't complain about it, either.

"Is it always like this?" he asked Cressida.

"They've gotten better." She sighed. "Now at least most of them stay awake during the class."

Arthur stared at her.

"They're hatchlings. I don't think you were much better when you were born," she said with a smile.

"But Brixaby and Joy . . ."

"Are higher-tier dragons. Their magical cores are more developed in order to handle their higher level of magic." As she spoke, she rested her hand on Joy's head.

The little pink dragon sighed happily and leaned against her thigh. "One day we'll be allowed to practice fighting with card powers. I can't wait to see what kind of quests I get . . ."

Instructor Athena returned shortly after, dipping her head toward Arthur in a move that was short of a bow. "Thank you for your patience, sir. When the flocks come in from this last loop, I'll have yours join the formation." She paused. "If you could possibly restrict your dragon from stealing powers while they practice . . ."

"Nothing is stolen," Arthur said quickly. "Just temporarily copied."

"Why would I want Common cards anyway?" Brixaby asked, disgusted.

She didn't look convinced. "As you say, sir." She looked out to the motley group—the red who had stood up to Brixaby had tripped, creating a pileup of three other dragons behind it. "I admit, they don't look like much now, but give them six months and they'll be fighting fit."

"They'll need to be," Cressida muttered, still petting Joy's head.

There was a darkness in her tone that caught his attention.

"Why's that?" Arthur asked.

She shrugged. "Because scourge-eruptions are coming more frequently."

"That's enough of that," Instructor Athena said sharply. "Scourge-eruptions happen in cycles. We just happen to be at a high point."

Cressida frowned at the older woman, then caught Arthur's gaze and shrugged. "They do come in cycles," she agreed, "but this one seems to be a particularly . . . vigorous one."

"Why haven't I heard much about it?" Arthur asked. "I've lived in the hive for years."

"The cycles generally last decades. If you'll excuse me . . ." Athena walked toward the flocks, which had merged more or less into one group as they rounded the last bend to return to the starting line.

Arthur watched. "Hard to believe they'll be ready to fight in half a year."

"No offense to our instructor," Cressida said with such a dry tone that she clearly meant the opposite, "but I believe dragons do better once they're in the air. Look." She pointed out through the wide-mouthed opening of the arena. A large slice of sky was visible, and through it, multicolored dots against the blue. It was another flock of dragons. As Arthur watched, they wheeled to the left and did a neat turn, all in formation.

"That's a class a few months ahead of us, I think." Cressida sighed. "I can't wait to fly with Joy."

Arthur couldn't say how he knew for sure, but he suddenly felt Brixaby's sharp attention on the conversation. Reaching up to his shoulder, he patted the little dragon. "We'll be flying too," he said, "even if I have to find a wing body-enhancement card to do it."

"Why find one?" Brixaby asked. "It's much easier to steal it."

Finally, Instructor Athena gathered everyone together.

"Now, we will integrate the Rare Joy and our new Legendary Brixaby into a formation. Lower tiers: What is your duty?"

"To protect the high tiers," the riders and a couple of the dragons repeated by rote, though Arthur caught a few disgruntled looks thrown his way.

He didn't blame them.

Athena nodded. "That's right. This is all to lay a foundation for later. Riders, you must make your dragons understand that when you are assigned to flock with a high-tier dragon, they are to be protected from all scourgling attacks so they can complete their missions." She nodded to Arthur. "This is especially vital when a Legendary takes the field."

Now all the dark looks were aimed squarely at Arthur. Brixaby puffed out with pride.

The little dragon was deflated a few moments later when he was informed he would be walking—not flying—with his flock.

The formation was a simple one: a diamond of dragons, one forward, one rear, and one to the right and left of Brixaby. The formation would escort him across the arena and back again three times.

As the two Common purple hatchlings would not be expected to ever escort a high-tier dragon in battle, they were excused for basic flying practice.

Brixaby watched them with open envy.

The remaining dragons would form a smaller escort for Joy as they crossed the arena.

It was a simple exercise in theory—but not in practice. Out of all of them, the red dragon was the largest, and she was now terrified of Brixaby and kept either darting ahead or slowing down to fall out of the formation.

Meanwhile, a slithery-looking green somehow managed to trod on the tail of the lead dragon: a sunset orange who kept looking over his shoulder at Brixaby in worry, as if he didn't trust him. The brown dragon on the left side of the diamond kept yawning and dragging his feet. At one point, he stopped completely and demanded his rider carry him the rest of the way, saying he was too exhausted to go on.

Brixaby turned with a snarl to the brown. "You are in *my* formation, and I don't tolerate useless dragons. Either you walk, or I'll rip out that Uncommon card I can smell in your core and give it to a dragon who will!"

Within seconds, the entire formation fell apart in fear. The other dragons scattered while the brown's rider—a large boy built on the scale of a mountain, advanced on Arthur.

"Legendary or not, if your dragon threatens mine again, I'll shut both of you up."

Arthur held up his hands in a peaceable gesture. "Now, wait a second. They're all learning to get along—"

"That wasn't a threat," Brixaby boomed, "that was a promise."

Rage flashed across the other rider's face. He threw one balled fist right at Arthur's belly.

The fist phased right through. Arthur had been ready for it and activated his Phase In, Phase Out card.

The brown's rider lurched forward, taken by surprise from his hand passing through air. Arthur took the opportunity to step to the side and retrieve a pair of scissors from his Personal Space. He was on the verge of snipping the belt from his pants—normal scissors couldn't do such a thing, but he had advanced the skill quite far—when he sensed a flash of darkness from the side.

Brixaby leaped up at the other rider, and from the gleam in his red eyes, he meant to go for his card.

Arthur caught him in midair. "Oh no you don't!"

"ENOUGH!"

Instructor Athena's voice had a stunning effect that knocked Arthur back a few steps, all thought lost in blank white shock.

New Counterfeit spell obtained: Verbal Stun
Remaining Time: 59 Minutes 59 Seconds

The effect lasted only a moment—or what felt like a moment. By the time Arthur blinked and came back to himself, the Rare instructor was between them. Standing on her tiptoes, she jabbed a finger into the brown rider's barrel chest. "How *dare* you strike at a Legendary rider! I could have you sent to the dragon-soil fields for this!"

"No!" Arthur and Brixaby said at the same time.

Arthur was horrified—the rider had been only defending his dragon. Brixaby had been . . . well, his charming self.

Brixaby had another take on the situation. "That lazy brown and his rider are part of *my* formation. If anyone sends them away, it will be me!" He paused. "But I'd rather they just do the work so I can copy their powers later. You do have useful powers, don't you?" he demanded of the little brown who was standing by his rider, now wide-eyed awake and trembling.

"Q-quicksand," the brown whispered.

"Excellent! Arthur, unhand me. We will continue the rest of this training . . . Wait, where did everyone go?" He craned his neck around, just realizing the other hatchlings had fled in fear.

Arthur watched Athena nervously. Surely she couldn't be happy about being undermined.

"If those are your orders, sir," the woman said, voice deadpan.

This . . . was going to take some getting used to. "Yes," Arthur said quickly. "There was no harm done. He stays in the class."

Eventually, the rest of the hatchlings were coaxed to come back. The dragons were visibly afraid, and their riders were stiff and cold. All kept as much distance from Arthur and Brixaby as possible.

However, the formation kept a perfect diamond shape.

* * *

The class soon came to an end. Arthur saw Carley hovering nervously just inside the arena entrance. He beckoned her over, and she presented him with a tiny scroll.

"I was told it was from Leader Whitaker," she said.

Nodding, Arthur opened it.

Our leadership lesson is canceled today.

That was it. No explanation. Between this and the way the hive leader had not spoken with him when he'd returned from Buck Moon Hive, Arthur was starting to wonder if the man was avoiding him.

It didn't matter.

"Good," Arthur said, letting the scroll roll back up. "Brix and I have better things to do."

"What's that?" Brixaby asked.

"We're going to train," Arthur said grimly. "We need to get you and me up to level twenty in as many body-enhancement skills as we can."

CHAPTER 51

The first thing Arthur did was to take Brixaby down to the hive entrance on the bottom level. He stood off to the side from the wide-mouthed arch and pointed down the road to the gate, which was manned by guards clearing people to come in.

Brixaby watched the comings and goings of traders, carters, and a variety of people and horses in all shapes and sizes with keen interest.

To Arthur's relief, he didn't attempt—or even threaten—to steal a card from anybody. Arthur would have suspected it was a sign of new maturity, only he knew better. The truth was, these common folk likely didn't have a card worth Brixaby's time.

"The first thing we're going to do is work on getting you a flying skill," Arthur said.

"Hmm. Yes. It's odd that I haven't gotten one before now. Perhaps I am an expert," Brixaby said, standing up on his hind legs to extend his upper pair of wings, while his lower pair beat the air furiously.

"I suspect that it's because you've used pure instinct," Arthur said. "Remember: in order to cultivate a skill, you must focus and work with deliberate practice."

He must be getting better at reading Brixaby's expressions, because doubt tinged with contempt was written large on his scaly muzzle.

"Plus," Arthur continued, "if you get a class, or even a single skill up to level twenty, you get additional bonuses. That should be *easy*, considering you're an expert and all."

"Of course," Brixaby said quickly. "So, how do you propose I improve what I already do so well?"

"Like I said: deliberate practice. Think about how you move your wings, and how the air flows around your body." Arthur was hardly an expert on flying, but he had lived in the periphery of the hive for years, and he'd heard dragon riders talk at the bars. "Some dragons use warmer air to fly up higher, and some seek out colder currents because the air is denser. The thicker air gives them fine control to maneuver."

Brixaby bobbed his head in a nod. "You want me to fly up high?"

Arthur's heart jolted in his chest at the thought of his little dragon flying out of his sight. It was a completely unexpected sensation, and he had to pause for a moment to collect himself. "No," he said carefully. "Right now, let's just work on speed. I want you to fly to that gate and back as fast as you can. Do you think you can do it three times in a row?"

"Of course," Brixaby said scornfully.

Then he shot off Arthur's shoulder—a streak of darkness heading straight for the gate.

Some of the cart horses shied and tossed their heads. Men called out, pointing, and Arthur heard a few loud questions, wondering if that was a bat or a dragon.

Brixaby reached the arch of the gate within a few breaths and looped around in midair, flying back nearly as fast.

However, his second lap there and back was noticeably slower.

Now people were watching for him, saw Arthur, and put two and two together. Most of the carters ducked their heads and went about their way. This was dragon-rider business, which meant a fair chance of dealing with somebody with a high card.

However, many of the children pointed, stared, and laughed aloud when Brixaby zipped by.

Brixaby came back for his third and final lap, and as he passed over Arthur's head, Arthur heard rapid, labored breathing.

However, Brixaby was not going to give up that easily. Though he was no longer a dark streak, he was still about as fast as a man running full out as he made his way to the gate and back.

"Maybe we should put some of those points into stamina," Arthur murmured to himself.

Focused as fiercely on Brixaby as he was, he felt the moment Brixaby got the skill.

He couldn't see the notification, but again, it was as if something had expanded—just a little, within Brixaby's core.

Sure enough, when Brixaby flapped heavily back to land on Arthur's shoulder, his wings were drooping, but he was exultant. "I satisfied the requirement of two skills," he said, proudly, between panting breaths.

"Very good," Arthur said warmly.

There was a water trough meant for horses nearby. Walking over, he reached down and cupped some of the water, which was cold and sweet, from a nearby well. He brought it up to Brixaby, and the dragon sucked it down greedily.

New skill gained: Basic Dragon Care (Dragon Rider/Magical Animal Husbandry Class)
Due to your card's bonus traits, you automatically start this skill at level 3.

Arthur smiled but kept his new skill to himself. He didn't want Brixaby to think he was taking care of him just for new skills.

He waited until Brixaby's breathing had evened out to ask, "So, what levels did you start at?"

"Level nine in Basic Flying," he said smugly. "And level five at Flying Sprint."

Arthur blinked. "Those are high starting levels. Good job."

"I told you I was exceptional. I don't know why you continue to be surprised."

"You're almost halfway to twenty in basic flying," Arthur murmured. "Those are body-enhancement skills, so when you reach level twenty, you'll gain points to add to your attributes. Basic Flying and Flying Sprint are both in the same flying class?"

"Indeed."

Turning, Arthur regarded the distance between where he stood and the gate again. "Getting a flying class will help you with your attributes, too. Do you think you could manage more laps?"

Brixaby hesitated, but only for a moment. "Yes, but while I do, you can fetch me a proper bowl to drink from. The water cupped in your palms tastes salty."

In answer, Arthur grabbed a small bowl from his Personal Space. He just hadn't thought to use it before.

Brixaby snorted and took off for the gate again.

Eventually, a guard came by and asked, in the most painfully polite tone Arthur had ever heard, if they could move their training elsewhere. The sight of a tiny purple-black dragon, of whom uncomfortable rumors were already swirling about, zipping over commoners' heads was starting to cause a disruption.

By that time, Brixaby had leveled his **Basic Flying** to 12 and his **Flying Sprint** to level 7.

The **Sprint** skill was coming along at a slightly slower pace due to the fact Brixaby's stamina bottomed out, usually around the second lap.

He was taking longer and longer to recover between sprints, too. Arthur had upped his **Basic Dragon Care** another level.

"That's fine," Arthur said. "We have other places to practice."

He smiled in reassurance, but if anything the guard looked more nervous than ever.

"Begging your pardon, sir," the man said, actually doffing his guard's cap. "You can of course use this area in the future, but if it wouldn't be too much of a burden, perhaps send one of your servants down to tell us ahead of time so we can plan to reroute traffic to the southwest or southeastern entrance."

Arthur winced. There were several entrances through the hive, but though those two were the closest, that was quite a hike.

How often did high-ranking dragon riders swoop in and upend people's lives on a whim? Arthur wasn't sure he wanted to know.

After thanking the guard, and fending off offers to speak to the guard's supervisor should Arthur be in need of them in the future—"And also, sir, we're always here to help. We didn't mean any disrespect toward you or your illustrious dragon"—Arthur finally made his escape.

He decided to visit one of the rider training areas, hoping people wouldn't scrape and be so subservient there.

The gym was on one of the lower sublevels and markedly smaller than Buck Moon Hive's had been. Though it appeared to have a sauna, which Arthur looked forward to.

He felt eyes on him the moment he stepped in and people made way—almost comically abandoning their spots on the track or obstacle course as he passed by. As if they feared Arthur would turn and start climbing one of the cargo nets over the mud pit, just for fun.

Setting his jaw, Arthur went to one corner, where a series of weights were set up. Large blocks of dull iron had been drilled through the middle with a bar stuck through. An identical block of iron sat on the other side of the bar, giving it a perfect counterweight.

Brixaby had fallen asleep on Arthur's shoulder, legs and wings sprawled on either side and wings dropping as if he were dead instead of exhausted.

Arthur gently moved him to a spot off to the side. He wanted Brixaby to train hard, but the little dragon had only hatched a few days ago. His newfound **Basic Dragon Care** skill told him that pushing him too far at this stage would be detrimental.

Arthur returned to the weights, set his feet, focused on determined practice, and got to work lifting.

Brixaby roused just when Arthur hit level 10 in **Weightlifting** (Strength Class).

This was somewhat of an accomplishment even though he had started at level 5. Apparently his years of hauling boxes of produce, slabs of meat, and heavy pots of soups in the kitchen had given him some foundation to work on.

Like with **Running**, hitting the tenth level had given extra bonuses.

For reaching this threshold on a body-enhancement skill, you have gained a 5% bonus to all strength while lifting heavy objects. In addition, you gain a 10% temporary bonus while lifting an object greater than your own weight.

"I'm hungry," the little dragon announced, flitting to the end of the weight Arthur was currently lifting. Thankfully, he was so small it didn't do much to upend the balance.

"Do you want raw meat?" Arthur asked in between reps. "Or do you want human food?"

Brixaby cocked his head and considered for a moment. "I will have both."

"All right, watch yourself: I'm setting this weight down."

Arthur had already planned for this, and after setting down the weight, he reached into his Personal Space and plucked out a small plate full of raw beef, shaved down to small bite-sized chunks, and a bowl of multicolored fruit. This was all thanks to Buck Moon Hive.

Arthur had spent a few days in that luxurious room of theirs, with a practical feast brought in for every meal. He'd stuffed every scrap that wasn't eaten into his Personal Space for later use, as well as everything he'd been given for Brixaby's first meal after he'd hatched. Thanks to the fact time didn't move in his Personal Space, the food was just as fresh as when he'd stored it in there.

Waste not, want not.

Brixaby looked at the bowls, wrinkled his snout, and looked up at Arthur.

"Am I not to have those tools humans use to eat food?"

"Tools?" he repeated blankly. "Oh, you mean utensils?"

"Whatever you call them," Brixaby said. "Do you expect me to eat like a common animal?"

The answer was yes, but Arthur kept his face blank. Other dragons ate like hogs at a trough, especially as they got older and killed their food.

But Arthur had loosened the tie on this sack of problems by introducing him to human food. And Brixaby didn't eat with the other dragons. Most of the Commons and Uncommons all ate together, socially.

Brixaby had only seen him eat, and that was with a fork and a knife.

Arthur took a moment and searched his mental list in his Personal Space. He had taken to throwing all sorts of odds and ends in there. But had he brought—oh, he had.

Arthur brought out a tiny three-pronged fork meant to help clean out the shells of seafood. He had, of course, taken it from Buck Moon Hive after one of their extravagant meals.

"I don't have a knife that'll be, ah, appropriate," he said tactfully, meaning one that would fit Brixaby's size. "But you can start with this."

Brixaby took the seafood shell fork delicately in his claws. "It will have to do. Now, show me how to hold this thing."

Arthur spent the next few minutes giving the basics to his dragon until Brixaby received the **Basic Eating (Utensil)** skill.

Then Arthur went back to weightlifting.

* * *

Brixaby hit level 20 in flying before Arthur hit 20 in **Weightlifting**, but not by a large margin.

His speed in flight had increased by a visible degree. Whereas before he had been a dark streak, now Arthur could easily lose sight of him against the shadowy gym corners. He could go from a top speed to a hover almost instantly, and even the sound of a low buzzing drone from his wings had diminished. He was becoming more efficient in the air.

However, he still needed breaks between sprints.

"I shall put all my points into stamina," Brixaby announced, then, uncharacteristically hesitated. He brought one hand to his chin and scratched it. "Or perhaps one to strength and two to stamina . . ."

Arthur took a breath. "One to stamina, the rest to luck."

"Luck?" he repeated, shocked.

"Luck," Arthur confirmed. "I'll be putting all three of my points there, and whatever else I manage to scrape up before we meet with the king. Brix," he said seriously, "we're going to need all the luck we can get."

The dragon looked doubtful, and Arthur was certain he was going to do what he wanted to do anyway. It wasn't as if Arthur could stop him.

"As you say," Brixaby said, and then assigned the points.

One to stamina.

Two to luck.

CHAPTER 52

Two days later, Arthur's luck attribute finally hit level 27.

Part of it had happened quite by accident. As it turned out, one aspect of **Weightlifting** was breathing correctly.

He already had a **Breath Enhancement** thanks to his time dueling, but he only started to level it when he focused on his breathing correctly—smoothly in and out as he lifted and lowered the progressively heavier weights.

It had interesting bonuses at 20, too.

For reaching this threshold on a body-enhancement skill, you have gained an additional 10% performance boost when breathing correctly during a strenuous task. In addition, you may now hold your breath up to 2 minutes with no ill effects.

Between getting his **Weightlifting** up to 20 and the **Breathing Enhancement**, he had added six attribute points.

The temptation to stick them into strength, especially after several days of grinding work, was nearly overwhelming.

Instead, Arthur stuck with the plan and added them all to his luck attribute.

He still had one temporary bonus point of luck. As his luck attribute had started out at a base of 20, that made 27 in total.

He only hoped it would be enough.

Brixaby had been working hard, too. After his **Basic Flying** hit 20, he focused more on **Flying Sprint**.

That eventually hit level 20 as well. He stuck one point in stamina, and the other two into luck.

That brought his total luck attribute to 24.

From there, Brixaby worked on **Trick Flying**, which was a skill he had accidentally picked up while doing loop de loops for fun.

With his four rapidly beating wings, Brixaby could stop in midair, shoot up at nearly a vertical angle, dive with ferocious accuracy, and even fly backward.

Trick Flying was an easy offshoot skill to pursue, and by the end of the third day, he had it to level 17—a stone's throw away from another level 20.

And that was when the official notice from the king arrived.

Carley came down to the gym at once, flanked by two guards in high livery. Apparently, they were there as witnesses to ensure the message reached the correct person.

Carley held a thick scroll in her hands, the edges gilded, and multicolored ribbons of rank covering the whole thing.

"This came for you." Carley's usually unaffected voice shook slightly. "It came through portal and dropped right on the floor outside your balcony."

"Oh?" Brixaby asked as he landed on Arthur's shoulder. He peered down at the scroll with interest. "Is it for me?"

"I believe it's for both of us," Arthur murmured. Then he reached out to take the scroll.

The thick creamy paper must have been hiding magical runes or a card-anchor spell. Something that was keyed to him. The moment Arthur's bare skin touched the scroll, the entire thing flexed and warped.

Arthur did not receive a notification from the Counterfeit Siphon card because this magic was outside of the card wielder's aura.

He took a startled step back. Carley did, too, losing her grip on the other end of the scroll.

Instead of dropping to the ground, the scroll stayed in place midair, still twisting, flexing its size from large to small and back again. To Arthur's eye, it seemed to be flexing in and out of this reality into . . . somewhere else.

"It's a flesh-locked scroll, sir," one of the guards said, seeing his startled look. "These unlock themselves only after the intended recipient touches it."

"Is that what it's doing? Unlocking?" Brixaby asked.

No one answered because a moment later, and with a twist that didn't make sense to Arthur's eyeballs, the scroll was suddenly unwound and hovering flat in air in front of him. Many ribbons decorated the bottom, signifying the king's rank.

Cautiously, Arthur reached out and took the scroll. Whatever magic was holding it up in the air drained away, and the paper relaxed into a normal page.

Arthur Kane, Legendary Rider

You and your dragon are summoned to King Elizar's court at your earliest convenience.

First scribe for King Elizar, Mythic Rider, First of His Name, Father of the Kingdom, Savior of Candlewood City . . .

The titles took up the majority of the page.

"At my earliest convenience?" Arthur repeated aloud. "How am I supposed to get there?"

One of the guards cleared his throat. "Begging your pardon, sir."

"Yes?" Arthur asked.

"My brother works for the palace, you see, and I know it's not my place to advise you. I would never presume—"

Brixaby growled. "Just spit it out."

The man visibly paled but forged on. "'At your earliest convenience' is palace speak for you're expected to head there immediately." He paused. "Like your tail is on fire, sir."

"Oh." That put a different spin on things. Arthur still wasn't sure how he was going to get to the palace, however.

Quickly making a decision, he handed the scroll to Carley. He was momentarily concerned the thing would roll itself up and relock if someone else touched it, but the magic seemed to have faded entirely. It remained a decorative piece of parchment in her hands.

"Take this to Valentina immediately."

He didn't include Whitaker, not having seen hide nor hair of him for the past three days other than curt messages saying their lessons were canceled.

Arthur was certain the man was avoiding him, and from the sounds of it, he didn't have time for games.

"Yes! At once!" Carley could be snarky, but she knew when to take her duties seriously. Gripping the page, she sprinted off—not to the stairs, because that would take an absurdly long amount of time to reach the top—but outside to where the purples usually sunned themselves in the day. A ride to the upper levels would only be minutes.

Arthur would have taken one himself to the suite, but Cressida insisted his rooms weren't "fit for habitation" yet, so he had been spending the last three days in his old quarters.

In any case, everything Arthur needed was in his Personal Space, so he headed for the small sauna to change.

He had no idea what to dress in other than "nice clothing," so he wore the same fashionable shirt and pants he wore during Brixaby's hatching.

If it was good enough to meet his dragon, it was good enough for the king.

Meanwhile, Brixaby took the time for a sand bath, which was generally how most of the young dragons cleaned themselves. There was a large pit of sand set to the side of the gym. By rolling over and over, the harsh grit polished the scales and didn't leave dust behind.

By the time Arthur came out of the sauna, as reasonably clean as he could get, Brixaby's scales were polished to a shine. Literally. He flashed iridescent purple under harsh light.

Arthur admired him for a moment, feeling a swelling of pride. Though he hadn't grown so much as an inch over the last few days, he had worked hard to improve his skills. His fine control in the air had improved by leaps and bounds, as had his speed.

This was only the bare beginning of Brixaby's journey. Arthur couldn't wait to see what kind of dragon he would grow up to be.

"Yes, yes, I am quite handsome, aren't I?" Brixaby said, turning himself from side to side and twisting his neck around so he could admire his own scales. Then he looked at Arthur's outfit and snorted. "You ought to trim your cloak with deep purple so that we match."

"I'll commission something when we get back," Arthur promised, then considered. "Or make it myself. I could use more tailoring skills."

"No, your clothes represent me. Let an expert handle it."

Arthur rolled his eyes but then grew serious. He held out his arm, and Brixaby obediently landed on it.

He met Brixaby's bloodred eyes. "We're going to meet the king."

"Yes, yes, I'm aware—"

"Which means," Arthur continued, "you must be on your best behavior. Brix . . . this is important, and the man may be unstable. He holds our future in his hands."

Brixaby paused. "I understand the king has the largest card library in the kingdom."

"Where did you hear that?" Arthur asked, thrown.

He shrugged a wing. "People talk, and that talk echoes."

He had spent a lot of time flying loop de loops around the giant gym area. Arthur put that mystery to the side for now in favor of frowning at his dragon.

"I suppose, being king, he would have only the best."

"So if we please him," Brixaby continued, "it stands to reason he will give us a gift. After all, he has so many cards, and I am newly hatched and have only a few. Plus, you need a combat card."

Arthur was torn between agreeing for the best chance of getting Brixaby to behave and getting his dragon's hopes up.

Briefly, he wondered if this was what being a parent was like.

"I've never heard of the king giving away a card," he said, "but I suppose anything is possible. I don't know what he will do, Brix. That's why we both have to be careful."

Brixaby bobbed his head in agreement. "Yes, I understand." Then, "I wonder how big the card library is?"

Arthur sighed, even though inside, he wondered the same thing.

He didn't have much time to wonder before a servant came to retrieve him, explaining Leaders Valentina and Whitaker were there to meet him.

Aside from when Brixaby's egg was discovered, Arthur had never seen the two leaders outside the higher hive levels. The idea of Valentina standing outside the main entrance along with commoners was enough to make him smile, despite his rising nerves.

It wasn't to be. Instead of Valentina, a cloud stood waiting right outside.

The servant started to direct Arthur toward it, but he already knew what to do. He stepped up and was unsurprised to find the misty cloud as solid as a stone.

Brixaby clung onto Arthur's shoulder, and the two quickly rose up the great height of the hive.

Arthur's ears popped several times, and he idly wondered if he would someday get an altitude resistance.

Valentina and Whitaker were indeed waiting for him—both dressed in fine cloaks along with spotless outfits. They also wore glittering jewels—Whitaker had so many adorning his fingers Arthur wondered if he had trouble closing his hand.

On seeing Arthur, Whitaker frowned and turned to Valentina. "I don't like this. Not only is the dragon too small to ride, he'll look as poor as a pauper in comparison to the rest of the court. Let me at least fashion him some gemstones." He gestured to a bit of craggy rock that detached itself from the cliff and broke apart—presumably in preparation to be remolded into something new.

"No," Valentina said, "the humble look suits him. He may be seen as less of a threat."

Arthur looked down at his own, best clothing. "It's not that bad, is it?"

"No, she's right." Whitaker sighed. "Besides, if the king is in one of his moods, it won't matter what you look like."

Brixaby spread his wings. "I shall shine for the both of us."

"Enough." Valentina made a sharp cutting gesture with her hand. "The portal will open shortly. We don't have time for this. Arthur." She turned to him. "When you are presented to the king, bow low, rise, and then answer any question he asks with strict politeness. Even if it's odd. Even if it's insulting. Chances are, this will be a formal welcome to the court. The king will treat this as a bit of administrative work and send you on your way. Be polite," she emphasized again, "address him as 'sire' or 'my king,' and do not speak unless spoken to."

Arthur started to nod and then stopped. "A formal welcome to the court?"

Her gray eyebrows rose. "Yes. As a Legendary rider, you are part of the king's retinue, just as you will one day choose Rares for your own." She turned a searing look to Whitaker. "Didn't you explain this to him?"

"Not sure I should bother teaching him anything until the king accepts him in or not," Whitaker said bluntly. "Don't give me that look. I haven't seen you preparing a grand festival for the hive's newest Legendary."

Arthur's stomach had gone from nervous flip-flopping to outright sinking down to his shoes.

"I don't have time to plan parties. I'm too busy doing the job for two people by running this hive," Valentina snapped back to him. Then she pressed her lips together, visibly controlling herself, before she turned back to Arthur. "We don't have time for this. Arthur, do you have any final questions?"

"Too late," Whitaker said, and pointed directly to the side of the balcony.

There was an oddity in the air. A bright light, like a miniature sun, grew from a pinpoint flame to a rapidly expanding ball. Though Arthur was more than a dozen paces away, he still stepped back in alarm.

Brixaby, too, hissed.

As the ball expanded, it became a ring with a hollow middle. Then, within a few heartbeats, the flaming ring was the size of a door.

Through it, Arthur saw a hallway of white stone chased with gold.

"That's the portal," Valentina said. "Go. And do us proud."

You're not coming with me? Arthur wanted to ask, but he knew the answer.

She wasn't his grandmother there to hold his hand. Arthur was a Legendary rider. He was expected to stand on his own.

So, squaring his shoulders and reaching for his **Acting** skill for confidence he didn't have, he strode through the portal.

New Counterfeit skill obtained: Sun Ring Portal
Remaining Time: 9 Minutes 59 seconds

That was a Legendary-level portal.

Arthur didn't have time to think much about it. The next moment, he found himself standing in a huge, opulent chamber.

He didn't know anything about the king aside from rumors. His unconscious expectation was he and Brixaby were to meet with a servant who would conduct him to the king. There would be some grand affair with lots of bowing, speech-making, and either a very good or bad outcome.

Instead, Arthur stood at one end of a beautifully stark chamber. The cold marble and golden edging deserved a long look, but his attention was drawn to the focal point of the oddly shaped diamond room.

Three men stood in attendance on either side of a carved wooden throne.

And on that throne slumped a blond teenager no older than Arthur. Possibly even younger.

With one leg hanging over an arm of the throne, he looked as bored as any schoolboy attending a tedious class.

Raising a hand, he gestured Arthur over. "You there," the teen said in a light tenor voice. "What are you waiting for? Step forward and greet your king."

CHAPTER 53

Is he the king?" Brixaby asked in what he likely thought was a quiet voice. It boomed through the hall.

However, the teen—the king?—made no indication he had heard.

The three richly dressed men surrounding him as advisors frowned.

Best to proceed with respect, just in case, Arthur figured. Though he spared a moment to be annoyed at Valentina. The woman had told him that the king was old when she had been young.

He wasn't an idiot. What he was seeing could be a powerful illusion or an anti-aging card power.

Still. She could have warned him.

Instead of answering Brixaby directly, he strode forward in an effort to regain that confident air. But it had left him, and every echoing footfall through the room sounded hollow and weak.

He quickly reached the foot of the throne. Now that the initial shock had worn off and he was properly taking in the room, there was some sort of lumpy, glittery substance surrounding the back of the high-backed chair. In fact, that odd lumpiness—a ghostly translucence that was almost visible—stretched across the borders of the room.

Arthur got the impression of vast limbs he couldn't quite make out the shape of. If that were the case, he was walking right up to a vast belly.

Shoving that thought away as unproductive and alarming, he executed his best low bow.

"My king," he said, "I am Arthur Kane. Allow me to introduce your kingdom's newest Legendary dragon, Brixaby."

There was silence from the throne. The back of Arthur's still-bowed head prickled, but he did not rise from his bow.

This was a trick he had seen nobles pull with servants they were unhappy with. Nobles kept them in a subservient pose for an extended few seconds to prove a point.

"I have never seen a dragon so tiny," the king remarked in a bored yet vague voice. "It's fascinating."

Arthur stayed in place, knowing better than to take the words as permission to rise. That was a trick he'd seen played on servants, too. "Yes, Brixaby is unique, but his power is strong."

Brixaby stirred, his weight shifting upon Arthur's shoulder. But his little dragon stayed silent.

"Unique," the king repeated. "That is one word for it. Rise, Arthur Kane. There is no need to grovel at my feet like a dog."

Arthur straightened, but he felt something was . . . off. His movements were a bit too jerky, as if his fine muscle control had fled and his limbs weren't sure what to do with themselves. He found he had trouble meeting the king's blue eyes.

Automatically, Arthur grabbed for his **Acting** skill. It wouldn't automatically restore his equilibrium, but at least acting the part out as if he were in a play would give him a false persona to hide behind.

His **Acting** skill did not activate.

Arthur could feel the skill resting in his heart, but when he mentally reached for it, his fingers found only air.

"Kane . . ." The king reached to tap a long, elegant finger against his bottom lip. "Kane . . . Kane . . . Not one of the high noble families. A outskirts barony, am I correct?"

Why wouldn't his **Acting** skill work?

"Yes, my king," Arthur said, and to his horror he heard his own voice tremble. Hurriedly, he cleared his throat and continued, "My father runs a small barony on the outskirts of your kingdom."

The bearded man by the king's side spoke. "Untruth."

Arthur froze.

The king's eyebrows lifted.

Arthur knew he should say something to cover for this moment. He should have guessed the king had someone who could tell the truth from lies among his trusted men.

Why hadn't the man called him out when he'd given his false name?

Was it a false name, though? Arthur was known as Kane by many people. He used it freely and couldn't remember the last time the name made him flinch.

Perhaps he had adopted it as his own. Enough not to trip the senses of the Truth Seeker.

These thoughts bounced around his mind, and Arthur found himself completely at a loss for words. His **Acting** skill was out of reach, as was his **Breathing Enhancement**.

He knew that because he felt like he couldn't get enough air. His throat was tight with rising panic.

And the silence stretched on, becoming awkward.

Finally, one of the other men leaned toward the king and said in a low voice that nevertheless carried, "Sire, there is also the matter of the dispute."

The king turned to him with a scowl that fit his young face. "What dispute?"

"The duke, sir."

Oh no, Arthur thought. That did not help his panic. He knew without anyone saying which duke they were talking about.

All his luck had failed him. Just like his skills.

"Well, he can wait," the king snapped. "Who is the king here? That's right, I am. And I'm interested in getting to know our new friend."

He turned back to Arthur, who found himself frozen like a rabbit under the searching gaze of a hawk. He had to actively work to keep his breaths normal and not hyperventilate.

For so long, his lies had been his shield against the rest of the world. Now it was about to be ripped away.

"Well?" the king asked after a moment. "Are you going to stand there like a dog waiting to be kicked, or are you going to properly introduce yourself to your king?"

What?

Was he mad, or playing with him, or asking for him to try again and not lie this time?

Arthur hesitated, then swept into a bow.

"My king, I am Ernest Kane, though my friends call me Arthur," he said, willing himself to believe that he was indeed who he said he was. "Please, allow me to introduce the newest Legendary to your kingdom, Brixaby."

"What's going on?" Brixaby asked, puzzled.

The king leaned forward, squinting his eyes at Brixaby. "I have never seen a dragon so tiny. Huh. Fascinating."

Despite his pulse pounding so hard he could hear it in his ears, he had to resist the snarky urge to repeat the exact line from last time. "He may be small, but he is a dedicated servant to the kingdom. As am I."

There. A little flattery couldn't hurt. Right?

"Yes, yes, you all are. So . . . Kane . . . Kane . . ." The king drummed his fingers on the side of the throne, then tapped his chin. "Where have I heard that name before?"

Arthur's estimate tipped a little more toward "mad" than "playing with his food."

"The Kane family is not the highest ranked of nobles," he said firmly, not looking at the bearded Truth Seeker. "Baron Kane's land is on the outskirts of the kingdom. He runs several border villages."

The Truth Seeker remained silent.

Arthur had, after all, spoken the absolute truth about the baron. It wasn't his fault if his words implied they were related.

The king slumped, visibly bored again. "Oh, one of those." He flipped a hand at Arthur. "So, what is the acreage you've managed to reclaim for the kingdom this quarter? You outer baronies are always so proud of that."

"I'm not sure of the recent numbers," Arthur said. "I have been away from that area for some time."

"Untruth," said the Truth Seeker.

"I have been back for a brief visit, of course," Arthur amended. "But not long enough to see the lands that were reclaimed. As you can imagine, my time has been spent in the hives."

Without his **Acting** skill to aid him, he couldn't tell if he was overselling his story or not. But he felt he should shut up now.

The king looked at him.

Arthur looked back.

The silence, again, stretched on.

A wild thought flitted across Arthur's mind: *Is he going to ask me to introduce myself again? Am I going to be at this all afternoon?*

In the next moment, a high, thin voice pierced the air. And though it whistled like a gust of wind, it was *big.*

"Elizar, my love, Duke Rowantree requests an audience."

Brixaby jerked in startlement. From the corner of his eye, Arthur caught the little dragon looking around frantically.

Then Brixaby froze, looking behind him.

Arthur turned, too.

A pair of slit-pupiled yellow eyes hovered behind him.

There was the barest hint of a ghostly shape that might have been a large dragon head, but the lines were so translucent, Arthur couldn't say where the actual dragon began. The only thing solid were the eyes.

Brixaby jumped up to put himself between Arthur and the strange dragon, then seemed to recall himself and bobbed a greeting midair. "Oh, you are the—"

"Mythic," the voice said, and Arthur heard scales shifting across the floor.

He looked back toward the throne, and his mind finally puzzled out the faint lines he'd seen before: The hint of an outline of a belly and a back leg, tucked up against the throne.

The dragon was in a position to always protect its human.

From what little Arthur could tell, the rest of the Mythic was thin and stretched long, coiled around the room like a massive snake.

What kind of a dragon was shaped like that?

"Pleased to meet you," Brixaby said. "Those are fabulous cards in your heart."

"They are," the Mythic confirmed. "Do you wish to steal them, Legendary Brixaby? I have heard of your powers."

"No, no! Well . . . I wouldn't say no to perusing your library—"

"Brix!" Arthur hissed.

The Mythic dragon gave a gentle laugh that blew Arthur's hair around.

"Serve me and Elizar well, Legendary Brixaby. Perhaps you will someday earn your way into my card library."

Brixaby visibly brightened.

"Elizar," the Mythic said, "remember the duke."

"Eh?" The king straightened. "What are you talking about? Which duke?"

One of his men spoke in the same tone as he had the first time. "Duke Rowantree requests an audience."

If Arthur's heart beat any faster, he suspected he was in danger of a heart attack.

He executed a bow. "Sire, if that is the case, Brixaby and I will trouble you no longer. We would be glad to be on our way."

But the luck he had fought so hard to earn was not with him. The king snapped his fingers. "Right, right. The dispute. No, you stay here, Kane. This involves you."

Then he nodded to a second advisor who had stayed silent so far.

That man turned and waved his hand in a grand circle. Ten feet away, another bright ring of fire opened into a portal.

Arthur didn't feel a twinge from his Counterfeit Siphon card. That confirmed it: his powers were blocked here.

The portal expanded to show a cozy library with shelves stocked with books. A man sat with his back to them at a heavy wooden desk.

Some instinct made him turn: It was Lional Rowantree.

The moment Lional saw the portal, he nearly fell out of his chair in his haste to make a perfect bow.

"My king, thank you for answering my petition."

"Yes, yes," Elizar said on a yawn, "make it quick."

This is bad, Arthur thought.

And a moment later, it got worse.

Lional looked to the side. "Penn, wake up. It's time."

There was a creak of cot-springs, and Penn stepped into view, looking rumpled.

A distant part of Arthur realized the duke had no idea if—or when—his petition to the king would be answered. Once applied, he had to be ready at a moment's notice.

The rest of Arthur, of course, was dumbstruck in horror that his worst nightmare was about to come true.

Lional and Penn stepped through the portal to join them in the king's court.

The moment they arrived, they fell onto their knees in front of the king. Though Penn's angry glare never left Arthur.

"My king," Lional said, "I formally beg for a reconsideration. I ask for justice."

"Get to the point, Duke Rowantree," the king said, looking bored.

"This boy"—Lional spared a moment to glare at Arthur as if it wasn't perfectly clear whom he meant—"linked with a Legendary dragon under false pretenses. My king, he is a threat to the kingdom."

Arthur did not currently have access to his **Acting** skill, but he still had common sense. If he were an actual noble, he'd consider his honor thoroughly insulted. Actually, he had to stop thinking that way. He was now a rider linked to a powerful dragon. And his honor *had* just been insulted.

Arthur stepped forward. "Of course, that is the duke's opinion. He expected his son to link to my dragon. And now that didn't happen, he wishes for the king to intercede."

He meant for his words to spit venom back at Lional. But even to his own ears, his phrasing was wooden and lacked a certain force. How much had he come to rely on his skills over the years? Who, or what, was suppressing them? And how long until he got them back?

A new thought hit him. What if it was one of the men surrounding the king? A mind-mage might be able to block a card's power . . .

Automatically, he reached for his mental blocking skills. Of course, he couldn't get to them.

They were just as out of reach as everything else.

The king looked at Lional with a bit more interest. "Is this true?"

"Yes, it's true," Brixaby said dismissively, and gestured with his head toward Penn. "I considered that one right there, but Arthur—"

Arthur coughed sharply before Brixaby could let something slip about his pair of Legendary cards.

The little dragon hesitated. "I liked Arthur better."

"You mean you liked his card better," Penn said bitterly. "A card that Arthur Kane stole from our family."

Arthur knew this accusation was coming, and there was likely worse down the line. He still couldn't keep down a slight cheek twitch—something he would have easily suppressed had he had access to his skills. Meeting Penn's eyes, he focused hard, thinking about the cards that should have been his by birth. "That card is mine by right."

Penn shot to his feet, hands balled into fists. "That is a lie!"

In answer, Arthur looked to the man who had called out his lies before. The Truth Seeker watched the exchange impassively without comment. It seemed he was not going to weigh in one way or another. He didn't work for them. He worked for the king.

Finally, the king waved his hand at the Truth Seeker to give his permission. "So? What say you?"

"There are shades of truth within both of them," the man said.

The king rolled his eyes as if he were truly a teenager and not a man of importance. "Yes, so it seems our newest young Legendary rider purchased a card that you now claim is stolen. I find it interesting, Rowantree, that I am only hearing about a missing Legendary-level card now."

"It has been a family matter," the duke said tightly.

Arthur took in a breath. Keeping his mouth shut might be the smart move. The king did not seem impressed with Lional's claim. But he knew that Lional wouldn't let this go, and they had much more damaging information on Arthur to reveal. The stolen card was only the opening act. Arthur's best bet was to distract from the issue by introducing a whole new one and possibly regain the momentum of the conversation. Lional or Penn would surely still bring out the ace up their sleeve, but by then, Arthur *might* have the backing of legitimacy.

He didn't want to rely on luck, especially since it seemed everything else was suppressed. But he didn't have much of a choice. The only other option was to let Lional accuse him on his own terms.

"I am sorry to correct you, sire," Arthur said evenly. "I didn't purchase the card, either. You see," he said, knowing that his next few words would change everything, "that card I have in my heart is mine by right of blood."

The king turned bright blue eyes on him, eyebrows raised. If nothing else, it seemed this little show was entertaining him.

All of this time, Lional had been respectfully kneeling in front of the king. But at Arthur's words, he stood and turned to Arthur. "What nonsense is this?"

"Probably a lie," Penn said, bitter. "Everything that comes out of his mouth is a lie."

Arthur continued, "While I am now known as Arthur Kane, I was born Arthur Rowantree. That card is my rightful inheritance."

Lional lurched forward as if someone had clubbed him on the back of the head. He stared at Arthur, looked him up and down, and a new light came into his eyes. "You . . . You're Calvan's son?" Then his expression crumpled to be replaced by one of growing outrage. "So you are the one who opened the blood lock. Does your traitor father still live, boy? Answer me!" He moved toward Arthur, every line in him dark with menace.

On Arthur's shoulder, Brixaby hissed, "Take one more step, and I will rip that Rare card I can smell out of your heart."

Lional stopped, and one hand flew to his heart as if to cover it.

The king barked out a laugh and clapped his hands once like a child who had just seen an entertaining puppet show. "The reports are true! That dragon is fierce!"

"Sire," Lional turned to him, horrified and exasperated, "this rider has just admitted he is the son of Calvan Rowantree."

"Who?" the king asked.

"My king, you sent him to the borderlands for his treachery yourself. Don't you remember?"

Within an instant, the king's face took on the look of a thunderstorm, ominous and angry. "Don't you dare presume to tell me what I remember or what I don't. I am your king, your sovereign, and better in every way! Remember your place!"

The blood drained from Lional's face, and he once again fell into a kneel in front of the king. Reaching up, he tugged at Penn to do the same, but his son resisted him. He was too busy staring strangely at Arthur.

"What are you saying?" Penn asked, looking a little lost. It was as if he had missed the king's outburst altogether.

"We're cousins," Arthur said bluntly.

Penn looked from Arthur back to Lional, and maybe he was imagining it, but he thought he saw a little bit of accusation in his eyes toward his father. Then that accusation turned fully on Arthur. "How long have you known?"

"It doesn't matter," Arthur said.

"I think it does," Penn said. "Have you targeted me from the very beginning?"

Feeling an unexpected stab of guilt, Arthur looked away. "I couldn't tell anybody. My father was sentenced to the border. He is your father's *older* brother." There. Let Penn make the connections himself.

Meanwhile, one of the king's assistants had bent next to the king and was speaking quietly into his ear. Likely reminding him of something he refused to admit he forgot.

The king slowly lost his annoyed expression and said, "Oh, yes, Calvan Rowantree. Greedy man. Such a shame."

"And his son shares the same flaw," Lional hissed. "My king, if you can forgive me this one request, I ask that you treat my son and heir equally as you do the son of a traitor. I ask for special dispensation, not for myself, but for Penn."

The king eyed him. "Choose your words very carefully, Duke Rowantree."

"I only ask for equality and justice. This son of a traitor is a traitor himself. He has two Legendary-level cards of the same set in his heart. I ask that one be removed—"

"No," Brixaby boomed, and Arthur had to quickly grab the little dragon as he launched himself toward Lional's heart.

Lional continued, ". . . and that card be given to my son, who has shown his loyalty to the throne. Let this mistake be rectified. If the little dragon linked to this set once, he can do it again."

The king's expression had lost all trace of amusement as he looked back at Arthur. "So, the son of a traitor is a traitor himself. How boring. I thought by linking a unique dragon, there would be something special about you."

"My king, I didn't know the terms of my father's sentence. I left the village behind a long time ago," Arthur said with an internal wince. To his own ears, his voice sounded thin and weak. "I only took my inheritance, what was mine."

". . . and in doing so, you broke our highest law," the king replied. "Very well, let's get this over with. You could prove your innocence right now by showing me your cards."

Arthur hesitated. There was no way he could prove his innocence since he was very much guilty of having a pair. Nor could he think of a way out of this. Plus, he didn't just have those two linked Legendary cards. He had a three-of-a-kind in Rares as well.

There has to be a way. There has to be something, Arthur thought. Nothing came to him that wouldn't get him into more trouble.

"Show them to me, or I'll have my men force you to do it," the king said, sounding bored again.

It was better to show some of his cards voluntarily than to have all of them forcefully revealed. Arthur gestured to his heart and projected his two cards: Master of Skills and Master of Body Enhancement.

"Then it is as Duke Rowantree claims," the king said. "Very well, Lional, for bringing this to my attention, you may have this special one-time dispensation. I reward those who are loyal."

Lional rose. "Thank you, my king."

The king looked at Brixaby. "Dragon, your rider must die. When he does, you will have the option to relink to another. You would do well to consider this boy here."

For a dumbfounded second, Arthur didn't understand. His own death was being discussed so casually that it didn't seem real. But it was.

"Brixaby isn't going anywhere," Arthur said and reached for his last resort, which was his Return to Start card. Activating it would transport him back to his keyed-in point back at Wolf Moon Hive. He still had Brixaby firmly in his grip. Perhaps it would take the little dragon too.

But like everything else, the card did not work.

"What is this madness?" Brixaby asked, struggling against Arthur's hold.

Numbly, Arthur put him back on his shoulder. The dragon puffed himself out and put a possessive clawed forepaw on the side of Arthur's neck. "I'm not linking with anybody else."

"Elizar, my heart," said the massive voice that was the ghostly Mythic dragon, "this Legendary is but a mere hatchling. Until he gains his own strength, his rider's death will backlash and kill him as well."

Arthur felt a brief jolt of hope. It was dashed a moment later.

"It would be far better for one of the heart cards to be removed and the link sundered before the traitor is executed," the dragon continued. "Fortunately, Brixaby's unique ability can be put to good use. Brixaby, pluck the card out of the traitor's heart—whichever card you want, and bring it to your new rider."

"What?" Brixaby asked dumbly, as if the Mythic had just told him to rip off his own arm and beat himself with it. "No!"

"And the other Legendary card will go into my library," the king said. "Yes, I like this plan very much."

On cue, Penn stepped forward and once again displayed his Master of Combat card for Brixaby to see. "This card is of the same set," he told the little dragon grimly. "Think about how powerful we could be if we add Master of Body Enhancement to Master of Combat. No one will stand in our way."

"Th-there has to be something else, some other way I can prove my loyalty . . ." Arthur said, feeling numb all the way to his heart deck. But his words were weak, and he was flailing without his normal skills.

"Fighting is pretty great," Brixaby said. "But Arthur has done more in his life with his regular skills card than you have or ever will. I'm going to go further and grow stronger with Arthur."

"I'm afraid this is not up for discussion," the king said. "Hurry up. Pick a card from the traitor."

Desperately, Arthur tried his skills one by one. He even reached for the Sun Ring Portal spell, even though the ten-minute timer had elapsed. Nothing worked.

He hadn't picked up any more abilities from the people in this room, even though he knew powers had to be activated. He was utterly and completely blocked.

This can't be happening, he thought uselessly, over and over. Though he feared for his life, the thought of being separated from Brixaby was far more worse and immediate.

Brixaby growled at Penn. "I don't want that boy. He is weak inside, and Arthur is strong. I have the rider that I want."

Arthur backed away from the throne, though he didn't know what he was going to do. He had no plan. He felt completely helpless.

And he forgot about the Mythic dragon.

There was a flash of translucent movement. Arthur turned just as Brixaby was snatched off his shoulder by a giant hand.

As he was, he felt a shroud fall between himself and the dragon. Brixaby shrieked and clawed at the ghostly hand surrounding him.

"No, Brixaby!" Arthur yelled, and lurched toward him but fell short. He still had his cards, but it was as if his heart had been cleaved in two.

A crackle of fire behind him made him look over his shoulder. The Sun Ring Portal opened, and through it was a brick stone room. Two of the king's advisors stepped forward and grabbed Arthur under the arms. They hauled him to the portal and tossed him through.

He landed hard and scrambled up, looking back through the portal to the king's room and caught a flash of Penn's triumphant face, and Brixaby fighting hard against a grip that he could not see.

"Goodbye, cousin," Penn called.

Then the portal snapped shut.

Arthur mentally reached for his Counterfeit Siphon card, knowing he had been close enough to the portal maker to possibly recapture that power. But, like everything else, the card was inactive. He still couldn't use any of his powers.

And he was alone.

CHAPTER 54

Frustrated, Arthur struck at the spot where the Sun Ring Portal had been a moment before. His hand struck the brick wall, sending a bright burst of pain up his arm. Hissing, he shook his hand out.

Of course. His **Blunt Force Damage Resistance** was gone, too. That was just great.

Arthur resisted the urge to kick at the wall. With his luck right now, he'd probably break a toe.

Did it matter? He was going to die.

This can't be it, he thought frantically. *This can't be the end.*

He looked desperately inward for inspiration, for anything. All his cards were blocked. He couldn't even retreat into his Personal Space. He was as helpless as someone uncarded.

That was when a voice, breathy with song, drifted through his mind.

"At last . . ."

Arthur froze, and the hair on the back of his neck stood up on end.

He looked around the small room—it was more of a pit with a low ceiling he could stretch up and reach, and just enough room to move three paces. No entrances or exits. No windows. This was a room meant to stash prisoners using card portal powers.

The only light came from a low-glowing brick in the ceiling. It wasn't strong enough to cast shadows, and there were no places to hide.

But Arthur felt he was not alone.

"Wh-what?" He licked his suddenly dry lips. "Who?"

"*Let us not play games, Arthur. You know exactly who I am,*" the voice crooned, the words almost lyrical.

With a shudder, Arthur clapped his hands over his ears, though he knew it was hopeless.

"Mind-singer?"

He hadn't thought much about the scourgling that had helped cause so much trouble during the Legendary recruitment test. Once he was safe in Buck Moon Hive, his time had been taken up by Brixaby's pending hatching.

Arthur's lips lifted back in an involuntary snarl. "I'd hoped you'd died along with the other scourglings."

"*We suffered losses,*" the mind-singer whisper-sang. "*The most grievous was suffered by your hands.*"

A memory flashed in front of his mind so intensely it was like being back, fighting the batlike scourgling by hand.

"*You killed my sister,*" the scourgling hissed.

Yes, he had. And he had harvested its mind card. Though for the sake of morality, he hadn't used it.

Arthur choked out a laugh. How could this day possibly get any worse?

"What do you want? Wait, how are you speaking to me? All card powers are blocked."

"*They are blocked while you are in the Mythic dragon's aura range. However, they have put you at the edge of its power. A place where someone suitably strong enough may break in. And at last,*" she crooned and repeated herself, "*at long last you are not shielded against me.*"

"What . . . ?" he said again, but something in the way the scourgling spoke gave him a clue to figure it out. "You mean I have been shielded against you? Unconsciously?"

"*Yes!*" it—no, *they* hissed.

Because the more they spoke, Arthur got the impression there were two voices twined together in a duet. One that was stronger and more coherent than before.

However, it used to be a trio.

He summoned his courage from somewhere and spat back, "Well, too bad for you. It won't matter if you take over my mind. I don't have access to my cards. And the king is going to have me killed shortly, so whatever you have planned won't work."

"I am aware of your limitations, but you are wrong. My plan has a chance at succeeding. Arthur Rowantree, you and I are on the same side."

He stiffened. "No, we are not." Then he looked around again. "Where are you?"

"Outside the palace, hiding in plain sight, like I have always done."

He received flashes then, of Buck Moon Hive, of following Valentina through the portal to Wolf Moon. The mind-singer sisters had been close as a breath at times and no one, not even the Legendaries, had sensed them.

"*We were waiting for the right moment to strike,*" the mind-singer said. "*For you to use our sister's card and for us to become a trio again. But you did not. And now the card is at risk of being lost to us forever."* A pause. *"Tell me, what happens to the contents of your Personal Space if the card is harvested from your body?"*

"I don't know."

"The card is in your heart, stamped to your soul. You know."

He did.

It wasn't written on the card. It was intuition. As the mind-singer said, it was stamped on his soul.

"The items inside will be lost forever. Personal Space . . . It's personal. It's my space. If someone had my card, they'd create their own Personal Space."

"*Thus, our dilemma,*" the mind-singer said. *"I want that card back."*

Arthur frowned. He hadn't used that card for very good reasons—mind magic felt like a slippery slope. Now that he knew it would link him in a minor way to the mind-singer, he knew that instinct had been sound.

Still, he wasn't about to give a scourgling what it wanted.

"Maybe I'm saving it for a rainy day."

"That rainstorm is about to descend on you. Even now, the duke and his son are trying to convince your little dragon to pluck out cards from your heart and pass them around like treats before they dispose of your body."

Arthur's breath caught. "You know what's happening now? Is Brixaby okay?"

"He is not bending to their wills. Yet. But soon the duke will tire and ask the king to use his mind-mages to convince him. Or they will retrieve you and hurt you until your dragon gives in and they give you mercy at the end."

Arthur shuddered.

Ruthlessly, the mind-singer continued, "*And then your dragon will bond with Penn Rowantree. They are compatible. And after some time, Brixaby's resentment may turn into grudging acceptance. You have betrayed Penn many times,*" it added almost gleefully. *"I can see the hurt in his mind. He thought of you as a friend."*

"I didn't have a choice," Arthur ground out.

"You tell yourself that, and you shove the guilt down deep under a layer of childhood scar tissue built over trauma. But you know the truth. You blame that boy for the sins of his father . . . and the inadequacies of your own."

"Shut up!" he roared. And for a second, he felt his **Telepathic Blocking** skill activate.

The mind-singer's voice faded.

Then the skill was crushed down again, and she returned.

"My, I think you do have some natural affinity for the mind arts."

"What do you want?" Arthur demanded. "You have no chance of getting my card while I'm in here. So unless you can break me out—"

"*I can,*" the mind-singer said.

Arthur stopped. "What?"

"Of course, I cannot influence the mind of the king or anyone near that dratted dragon which suppresses powers," it corrected. *"I am a Rare, and it is Mythic. But I have ways of influencing humans outside of the Mythic's reach. In doing so, I can give you a chance at freedom in exchange for a price."*

"What price?" he asked warily, though he knew.

She laughed—and the laugh had two voices. *"What else? The card, of course."*

He shook his head. "I'm not giving it to you. I haven't fallen so far that I'm willing to aid the scourge."

"Arthur," it said with a mental tsk-tsk, *"you could hardly fall any further. Do you think you are the only one who has worked with the scourge? Do you think those scholars you freed me from allowed my sisters and I to spawn and then educated us with knowledge cards for fun?"*

"Why . . . Why did they? Why would anyone?"

"Many reasons. They told themselves it was to establish a line of diplomacy between themselves and the enemy, but really it was for power. Their inner thoughts spoke of jealousy over the strength of the hives, and how they wielded it over the rest of the kingdom. They wished to undermine that power, and they thought the king would reward them."

Arthur shook his head. He didn't know what to think of that—or if he should trust it. And establish diplomacy with what? Other scourglings? Ridiculous.

"I'm still not going to give you something you could use to hurt people."

"Arthur, I could have hurt you at any time. I could have whispered to one of your little friends." Images of Cressida, Horatio, and Carley flashed through Arthur's mind. *"But in the end, we want the same thing."*

"And what's that?"

"Freedom," it sang.

The word echoed like a bell through his mind.

He shook his head. "I need to think."

"Don't take too long."

Arthur paced the two and a half steps it took to reach the other end of his cell.

He was in dire straits, but to aid a scourgling was to betray humanity.

He had done things he knew weren't kind or good—most of them directly impacting Penn—and he had even used his skills in ways that weren't legal or bordered on cheating when gambling.

Nothing like what he was contemplating now.

Was the scourgling influencing him?

He didn't think there was an easy way to tell, but . . . at the same time, he didn't think so. Logic said any influence would quickly fade away once he got closer to the Mythic. So there wasn't much of a point.

What if he did agree?

He could tell himself that whatever harm he did today would be offset by the good he could do when he was a full Legendary dragon rider. But he didn't know that for sure.

The fact was, Arthur wanted to live. He also didn't want Brixaby to live a sad, mediocre life with Penn while they learned to not resent one another. Arthur had plans. He wanted to rescue people in his borderland village. He couldn't do any of that if he was dead.

But . . .

He stopped, sighed, and said, "I can't."

"Why not?" The mind-singer sounded taken aback, which was another point to him not being influenced.

"Because I've seen scourge-eruptions. I've seen what they do to communities, to the land. If I gave you this card and you tried to raise another Legendary demi-scourgling . . . every death would be on me."

The scourgling scoffed in his mind. *"We were not responsible for the eruptions—nor the increase in eruptions. I merely took advantage of the opportunity that was presented. I am a mere Rare, not one of the Mythic Scourge Gods."*

"The . . . what?"

"*Seven Scourge Gods*," the mind-singer all but sang, "*and seven Mythic dragons to balance them. Oh, but only five dragons right now, so the balance slips further and further toward us. Also not my doing, but so sweet to think of . . .*"

There was only one Mythic-level dragon in the kingdom. Did that mean . . . "Are there other kingdoms?"

"Obviously. Perhaps you should eat some knowledge cards of your own."

Arthur's heart raced. Other kingdoms!

A pang of instant regret followed that thought: Other kingdoms he would never learn about and certainly never be able to see.

"*What if I promise to take this card and go to one of the other kingdoms. Far, far away*," the mind-singer suggested slyly.

"Are you reading my mind?" he demanded.

"Does it matter?"

He scowled. "How do I know you will keep your promise?"

"You don't."

"That's what I thought," Arthur grumbled, then looked at the brick wall. He sighed, and his shoulders slumped.

"*Perhaps I will go to another kingdom, which would welcome my talents and see me for what I am,*" the mind-singer mused.

He didn't believe that any kingdom worth living in would welcome the antithesis of life. Nor did he feel good about making the mind-singer someone else's problem, but . . .

He didn't want Brixaby to face a lifetime of resentment with someone else.

Arthur wanted to live.

"How would you get me out?"

He sensed hesitation from the singer. *"It is not guaranteed. I can provide a distraction—there is some sympathy for your plight by allies. But you will have to be the one to convince the king. His mind is feeble but too well shielded. I cannot influence him."*

Arthur nodded once.

"*Then when you are free*," the singer continued, "*you will give me the card as payment*."

"Okay," he rasped. "Give me that chance."

CHAPTER 55

Brixaby growled. He bared teeth and claws. He alternately ignored the demands from the pathetic boy who would *dare* to call himself Brixaby's equal or yelled curses at him. After all, he had picked up quite a few interesting words over the last few days in the hive's training yard.

Still, these pathetic humans dared to drag him into an empty chamber aside the king's throne room and tell Brixaby that they knew better than him.

Who was the Legendary dragon here?

Brixaby longed to rip out their hearts and laugh in their faces as he absorbed them. That would teach these arrogant fools where the true power laid. That would teach them to keep Arthur away.

But the only magic left to him in this terrible place was that of his natural flying affinity. Even then, the skills he had worked so hard to attain were not available to him.

He could only imagine how Arthur felt.

Brixaby did not enjoy thinking from others' points of view. It was an uncomfortable sensation. Case in point, every time he allowed himself to imagine what Arthur must be going through in that strange stone room where they had stored him . . . he saw red. It took everything he had not to fly into a whole new rage.

"My duchy has fertile fields," his would-be new rider prattled on, as if Brixaby cared. "Lands of fertile fields with livestock grazing upon them, fat from all the harvests. Whenever we visited, you could have your choice of the harvest. A cow? A pig? It would be freshly slaughtered and brought to you."

"Foolish idiot moron!" Brixaby roared. He had been doing that so much in the last few hours his throat was getting a little sore. Not that he would ever admit it. "I live in a hive, not a nowhere duchy, and I do *not* dine on unprepared meat like an animal."

He regretted the words the moment they were out of his muzzle. He had let something about himself slip.

Penn Rowantree's eyes lit up. "Well, as you know, my family is well-regarded, and I can hire the best chefs for you. Whatever you desire will be on hand. Just like that." He snapped his fingers.

What Brixaby desired was for Arthur to make him a delicious plate of food. They had not had much chance for relaxation over the last few days while working on their various skills. But at one point, Arthur had taken a break long enough to visit the hive kitchens.

Brixaby had been working on pinpoint turns for **Trick Flying**. He had been surprised to see Arthur return with two plates, both loaded with a dark brown meat Arthur had called "steak."

"I cooked yours rare," Arthur had said and pointed to a fluffy white cloud next to it with a well of brown sauce. "With a side of mashed potatoes and gravy. I'm not sure you'll like it, but give it a try."

Brixaby had liked it all. The meat was almost raw inside, and the outside crust was delicious with salt and spices. The potatoes were odd but filling in a way that was similar to meat. And the gravy, Brixaby could smell, was created from other meat juices and fats, which he found quite delightful.

"You will make this for me again," Brixaby demanded after he had eaten his fill. "I especially enjoy the . . . what do you call it?"

"Garlic."

"Yes. You will double the amount of garlic tomorrow," Brixaby announced.

"If we do that, we run the risk of people smelling you before they see you." Arthur had then suggested other meals Brixaby might like as well.

But he had not gotten those meals because they had been summoned to see the king soon afterward. Then, this nonsense happened.

And now these half-wits dared to suggest—no, worse, insist—that Brixaby pluck out a card from Arthur's chest and hand it over to a boy that Brixaby had already refused?

"I would rather pluck out the card from your heart and give it to Arthur," he snarled, coming to hover an inch from Penn's nose. "Then I would be certain it would go to someone who would do something useful with it!"

Brixaby had the pleasure of seeing Penn's pulse jump in the big vein of his neck, but the idiot did not have the good sense to move away. He continued trying to convince him.

"Surely you can see that this is the better solution for you. Arthur is a traitor to the kingdom—"

"Why do I care about that?" Brixaby snorted.

Lional spoke. "Because you are a dragon, a service animal bound to our kingdom."

"I did not give you permission to speak, Rare card," Brixaby said, not bothering to turn in his direction. "This is a conversation for your Legendary-rank betters."

The man reddened. "You dare—! I've pushed out turds bigger than you!"

Brixaby's lips pulled away from his teeth in a draconic grin. "And yet here you are, begging me to take your son as my rider. Pathetic."

"Father, that's enough! Brixaby . . . Honored dragon . . ." Penn turned to him, and Brixaby got the impression that he would be on his knees, literally begging, if he thought it would help. It wouldn't, but Brixaby would like to see it nonetheless. "What do I have to do to prove myself?"

"Nothing," Brixaby answered with the greatest of satisfaction. "I have chosen, and I chose well. Go bother the next Legendary hatchling."

"But that could be years from now," the boy whined.

"I fail to see how that's my problem," Brixaby replied. He reached up to tap his bottom claws on his chin in thought—a motion he had seen Arthur do. "Switch out your card with your father, and try to trick a Rare to link with you. Maybe if you happen to link a useful one, and you please me enough, you may serve in my retinue."

Lional audibly ground his teeth. "This is useless. We should kill the traitor's son. Then, if this beast survives, he will be desperate enough to take anybody."

"I will never be desperate enough to take him." Brixaby pointed his tail at Penn. "I would rather become a wild dragon and live off the land than be in either of your presences."

It looked like he had found Penn's last straw. Balling his fists, he glared at Brixaby. "I should have killed the traitor myself when I had the chance. Well, I won't make the same mistake twice. I'll prove my loyalty to the king, and you'll have no choice but to link with me."

Brixaby made himself a silent vow. If they hurt Arthur, then he was going to spend every minute of every day for the rest of his life taking down the Rowantree family. He would gut every man, woman, and child of their cards, one after the other, add them to his own power, and nobody would be safe from his wrath.

It was at that moment that the door to their chamber blew open. Brixaby buzzed straight up in startlement and got the impression of a ghostly dragon head—narrow with a delicate nose—snaking in with a long, sinuous neck following. It was the king's Mythic.

The Mythic spoke in a high voice like the wind. "An urgent summons has arrived for Duke Rowantree."

"What?" the man barked. "What summons?"

"I am not your messenger," the Mythic said. "Read it yourself."

Brixaby snorted to himself.

The duke remembered who and what he was talking to and hastily kneeled.

Penn did too, though with a sour look on his face. He didn't like kneeling for dragons, yet another flaw in a long list of flaws.

"Of course," Lional said. "Please allow the messenger in."

The dragon's head withdrew, and a startled-looking servant arrived, a scroll in hand. The man bowed, and Duke Rowantree gestured for him to bring it over.

The man took a step, and Brixaby zipped down and snatched the scroll. He didn't actually want the thing—though he was somewhat proficient at reading. Or he would be if he still had his skills.

Reading wasn't why he grabbed it. Annoying the duke was.

"Give me that, you overgrown bat," the duke roared and snatched at him.

Dropping the scroll, Brixaby chose to latch on to the back of the man's hand instead, dragging all his claws down deep into flesh.

The duke howled, and Brixaby launched off, back through the still open door the way the servant had come.

Freedom! Now to find Arthur . . .

He didn't forget about the Mythic. He just hoped that it would not prove to be a problem. Unfortunately, like the rest of this rotten day, luck was not with him.

A ghostly dragon-hand shape he could not see wrapped around him, and Brixaby snarled again, biting at it. Not that it did any good. The scales were like steel.

The Mythic held him up, and Brixaby felt like he was being examined.

"I take it that you were unhappy with your new rider?"

"He is not my rider! He was unworthy even before I picked Arthur," Brixaby snarled. "Get me back to my true rider, and we will face whatever's to come together."

The dragon laughed low. "I'm afraid you will get your wish if you push the duke too far."

"So? He is a mere duke. I am a Legendary dragon."

The hand he could not see briefly tightened in warning. "And I am a Mythic dragon. Yet you have not treated me with courtesy."

Shame tinged with resentment washed through him: shame that the Mythic was right. Resentment, also, that the Mythic was right.

For the first time today, Brixaby stopped struggling. "Release me."

Perhaps the Mythic sensed the change, because the grip loosened. Brixaby crawled on top of the fist and, doing his best to guess where the head was that he could not see, bowed low, spreading all four wings. "I, Brixaby, greet and acknowledge Mythic . . . uh . . ." He wrinkled his nose. "My apologies. I don't know your name."

"You have not been hatched long enough to be properly educated." The Mythic sighed.

And then, to Brixaby's shock, it—she—became visible.

She was . . . unlike any dragon he had ever seen.

Her head was pointed like an elongated spear, with two swept-back horns. Her body was indeed snakelike and coiled around the room in loops. She had almost comically short legs. Brixaby stood on one forelimb, and he saw how she had to raise the top part of her body to allow it. Her narrow wings were equally short, set somewhere in the middle of the body.

They looked like they should not be able to hold her weight, yet Brixaby knew they could because she was a gleaming, polished silver except for a stripe of bright blue down her spine.

This was a Mythic with a natural inclination to pure magic and water. And she was the loveliest creature he had ever seen.

Fully revealed, her power swept over Brixaby, making it feel as if he had suddenly found himself buried under a ton of boulders. He was pushed flat by her mere presence and lay on the side of her forepaw, trembling.

"I am Lung Bai. Now, you may rise," she said in a voice that was no longer a ghostly whisper. It, too, had become real.

The power lessened just enough for Brixaby to climb back to his feet, though his legs were shaking. The thought of the cards she must be holding made him want to salivate, but . . . to steal one would be unthinkable.

She regarded him for a moment. "Brixaby, you are becoming a pain in my tail."

"I don't mean to," he said. "But I have chosen, and he is a good, worthy rider. He is clever. And he is right for me."

"From what I understand, Penn Rowantree has a combat card."

"He can stuff his combat cards under his tail," Brixaby snarled, but then thought he might be coming off as rude to the Mythic, so he bowed his head. "Forgive me, but the only way *that one* can attain power is by getting his father to tattle on my rider."

Lung Bai watched him solemnly. "You claim your rider is clever. I have not seen this yet."

"He is, though he could use some polishing. That's where I come in," Brixaby said.

"Hmm. You are arrogant, but think I we need arrogance for the trials that are to come. I will give your rider one more chance."

Brixaby's heart leaped.

"If he impresses my king, I will not stand in his way. He is young, and so are you. Perhaps you will both take this as a teachable moment."

Brixaby resented the chastisement, but if it meant getting out of Penn's presence and having Arthur back, he could swallow it. "My rider is an excellent cook. Have you ever had steak?"

Lung Bai cocked her delicate head. "Steak, as the humans eat?"

"It is delicious. My rider makes it. Perhaps if you had some, you would understand why I am so loyal." Brixaby meant this wholeheartedly, so he did not understand why the other dragon smiled.

"That may be the case, young Brixaby. Now, it seems that we have an opportunity."

"An opportunity?"

"The scroll."

At that moment, she turned and went invisible again, releasing Brixaby from the last of her power.

Brixaby buzzed up into the air just as Penn and Duke Rowantree came into the room. The duke was clutching his freely bleeding hand to his chest, and from the stormy look on his face, they had been discussing the scroll—and Brixaby.

They stopped short just in the room, perhaps sensing the Mythic dragon within.

"You have read the summons," Lung Bai said.

"Yes," the duke said. "It *seems* a terrible occurrence has stricken the Rowantree duchy."

"Bandits, it would seem." The dragon seemed incredibly amused. "That conveniently needs someone with great combat power to stop them. How very unfortunate that this news should happen . . . now."

Penn raised his arm. "Brixaby, come join me. I will show you my power and drive away these bandits."

As loath as he was to admit it, Brixaby was mildly tempted. Not because he cared what Penn could do, but because bandits might have juicy cards in their hearts.

It was with reluctance that he turned away. Arthur really owed him one. "Sort out your problems for yourself. I'm not your dragon."

With a gesture of a barely visible Mythic hand, the door to the throne room swung open. One of the king's men strode out as if he had been waiting for this moment.

"Return Duke Rowantree and his son back home," Lung Bai said.

Penn finally caught on. "Wait, no, I'll stay—"

His father pushed forward in front of him. "Honored dragon, my son will stay. We have strong men to sort out any bandit attack."

"What a poor example you make to the king. Your duchy should be your first priority," she tsked.

Brixaby got the impression that the dragon was very much enjoying herself.

Penn looked at Brixaby. "Will we be able to return?"

"In due time. Meanwhile, I will spend time with *dear* Brixaby."

He could tell that the duke and his annoying son did not like the idea, but no one was going to countermand the Mythic.

The duke tried again. "If I could speak to the king—"

That, it seemed, was a step too far.

"The king chooses when to speak to his subjects. Not the other way around. Wilber, open them a portal."

In answer, the king's man gestured, and the Sun Ring Portal opened. It led back to the library.

Brixaby thought that it was quiet outside for a supposed bandit attack.

"Bye," Brixaby said, then fluttered to the other side of the room, just in case someone tried to use a power on him to drag him through.

"No, I'll stay," Penn insisted, but with a puff of air from the Mythic, he was pushed through the portal.

The duke walked through under his own power, then turned around and opened up his mouth.

"Please send word to His Majesty—" The portal snapped shut.

Brixaby let out a huge sigh of relief.

"Don't think that you are in the clear," Lung Bai said.

Though Brixaby could not see the Mythic's face, he got the impression of eyes carefully watching him.

"We cannot countermand the king. As his loyal friends, we can only . . . *help* him along with his decisions. Make no mistake, Legendary Brixaby, if the king is not impressed, he will kill your rider and force you to link to the man of his choosing."

"But not Penn Rowantree, right?" Brixaby asked.

She paused. "As I said, that is up to the king. Now, Wilber, if you please . . ."

The portal man—who Brixaby guessed was Wilber—once again opened up the portal.

A second later, Arthur stepped through. He looked pale and grim-faced, but very much in one piece.

And the next second, Brixaby slammed right into Arthur's chest.

"Oomph! Brix!" Arthur cradled him in one hand and looked around curiously. "Are you okay?"

"Those people were horrible! I cannot believe they're your relations." Brixaby crawled up to his regular shoulder perch, where he made sure to curl his claws deep into Arthur's shirt. Then, for extra effect, he twined his tail around the back of Arthur's neck. He wouldn't allow himself to be easily snatched off his shoulder again.

Leaning over, Brixaby spoke into Arthur's ear. "You must speak to the king again. Mythic Lung Bai has given us a second chance. We have to do better this time."

"Is that so?" There was some flatness in Arthur's voice Brixaby didn't understand or care about.

"Yes!" Brixaby said. "And you must be more clever this time. Tell me you spent that time working out a plan."

In answer, Arthur turned. "Where is the Mythic now?"

Brixaby pointed with his head toward where he thought Lung Bai to be waiting.

Arthur turned and bowed to her. "With your permission, I would like to speak to the king. I have a . . . proposition for him."

CHAPTER 56

Arthur took a breath to steady himself. Then, he took another.

This was it. This was for the entire pot of gold, as some old gamblers he'd played cards against used to say.

He had one last chance to convince the king not to kill him. While he didn't have his **Acting** skill, he had years of experience. And, he hoped, common sense.

Arthur squared his shoulders, told himself to act like the Legendary dragon rider he was, and looked to the closed throne room door. He nodded.

There was a burst of wind from the ghostly Mythic dragon he could barely see. The thick throne room doors creaked open.

The king was visible across the open space, lounging in his massive throne like a loose-limbed teenager. He was clad in a different-colored robe of state, this one of red and gold.

How long had Arthur been locked up in that small stone room? Enough for a new day to pass?

As usual, the two advisors to the king flanked him on either side. As Arthur walked in, the portal user quickly made his way to the king's side. The three men exchanged glances with one another, full of meaning.

But Arthur's attention was focused on the king. As he got closer, he saw the man was playing some kind of board game on a side table with marbles.

The king placed a marble into the slot, examined his work, then turned his attention to Arthur. "Well, well. An unexpected visitor. What is this about?"

There was the sound of scales slithering over stone, and a ghostly voice spoke. "Arthur Rowantree, Legendary dragon rider to the newly hatched Brixaby."

Arthur held his breath, but there was no immediate outrage from the king. Instead, the man looked intrigued.

"So, you are the new Legendary rider. Come closer." The king waved an errant hand. "Don't just stand there like a dog waiting for its master's call."

Good thing Arthur had already decided on his course of action. Striding up to the throne, he kneeled down on one knee as he had seen his uncle, Lional, do.

"Sire, I have come to you to introduce myself and my dragon, and to plead for a special dispensation," Arthur said.

There was a pause.

"Is that so?" The king's voice was bland. "We have barely met, and already you are asking for favors from your king. This is not the start of a promising friendship."

"I understand," Arthur said quickly, "and the last thing I want is to be rude at the start of our . . . friendship, but I have something I think you will appreciate."

"And what is that?"

"It is a card stored within my personalized storage space. Since the space is a card's power, I unfortunately do not have access to it at this moment," Arthur explained. Then he shut his mouth and waited.

Silence stretched on between them, and he felt Brixaby shift on his shoulder nervously. But Arthur did not speak again and risk digging himself into a hole with the erratic man.

"This had better be good." The king sighed. "What was your name again? Rowantree? Hmm. Any relation to the duchy?"

Did he not remember, or was he playing with him?

"Yes, sire. Lional Rowantree is my uncle," Arthur replied.

"Lional . . . Lional . . ." The king drummed his fingers on the throne. "Oh, yes. Him. He asked for a dispensation for a pair of cards recently, did he not?" He looked to the Truth Seeker among his advisors, who nodded once.

"Yes, sire. But from what I understand, he was not able to secure that second card." The advisor glanced at Arthur, and Arthur could swear he saw sarcasm in his eyes.

The king let out a long, exaggerated sigh, flopping back into his throne again.

"Very well, Arthur Rowantree, but don't try anything stupid. My man here"—he waved to the biggest of his three advisors, and the only one who had a massive sword strapped to his waist—"is armed with every Legendary-level combat card my dragon could stuff into him without his heart deck exploding, so this had better not be an assassination attempt."

As he spoke, the stern man stepped forward to put himself in between Arthur and the king.

"Of course, I would never . . ." Arthur stopped himself from saying "imagine doing such a thing" because he could, and considering the deal he had made with the mind-singer—yeah, he was definitely *capable* of such a thing. "This is no trick," he said flatly.

Although the king had not given him permission to rise, Arthur stood to his feet. As he did, a tingling sensation came over him, traveling up and down his spine.

He felt lighter. It was as if an invisible weight had been lifted off his heart deck—one he had not quite sensed before.

Brixaby felt it too and extended his wings as if he felt less shackled down. It was a lifting of restrictions. At least, one of them.

Arthur reached into his Personal Space and nearly gave his own sigh of relief when it actually worked. His concentration settled, briefly, on the mind-singer's card.

Instead, he grabbed Marion's Legendary time card.

He held it up in front of the king's armed guard to inspect. The guard looked at the card for a hard moment, then at Arthur, and finally stepped to the side to allow him access to the king.

The king had been reaching again for his marble board game, but stilled when he glanced at Arthur.

"Oh! A Legendary card." He clapped his hands once, clearly pleased.

Arthur figured he would be, since Harvest Moon Hive was known to ply the king with Legendary cards that they took from battles with demi-scourglings.

"Yes, my king. This is the card that once belonged to Prince Marion Amberlion."

The room stilled around him.

"He speaks the truth," called the Truth Seeker.

The ghostly Mythic dragon's voice spoke up. "The prince is dead, then?"

Arthur realized his mistake. "No, sire. Forgive me. He still lives. I got to know Prince Marion during the Legendary recruitment process, and I consider him a friend. After Brixaby hatched, Marion expressed his wish to relinquish his title of prince."

The king glanced to the Truth Seeker, who nodded and said, "Truth."

"I wish to return this card to its rightful place," Arthur continued. "Back to the kingdom."

"What a shame," the king said. "That boy had talent, though I worried about his nerve." The king focused behind Arthur. "How many siblings are in the Amberlion line?"

"None," the Mythic Dragon answered.

"Well, somebody make a note to discuss that with his mother later."

Arthur remembered that all princes and princesses had different mothers. Well, hopefully by now, the woman would be forewarned of a pending royal visit.

"So," the king continued, "you have come to return the card to its rightful place, but we both know this is a bribe. So, out with it. What do you want with this special dispensation? I suppose you want me to double the Legendary-rider boon to the Rowantree house?" His eyes were unusually sharp as he gazed at Arthur. "I understand that they have run into some financial difficulties over the last few decades."

"No, sire," Arthur said quickly—too quickly by the warning glance the bodyguard gave him. Arthur chose his words very carefully, though he knew they would not come out as prettily as he would have liked. It just wasn't possible without his skills. "First and foremost, I seek forgiveness. My king, I confess that in my travels, I intercepted a Legendary-ranked card that was meant to be sold on the open market. In my greed, I put it in my heart. It is part of a set of one of my own."

And then, over the Truth Seeker's announcement of "truth," Arthur gestured to his chest and projected a copy of his two Legendary-level cards: Master of Skills and Master of Body Enhancement.

Again, he felt the room grow cold with the king's displeasure.

"Rumors of your dragon's talent have reached my ears, Arthur Rowantree," the king said.

These kinds of statements made Arthur wonder if the man was experiencing dementia or if he was playing games. How could he possibly remember this, and who Marion was, but not yesterday's events?

The king continued. "Am I to believe that you did not take this card from somebody's heart? One of your own illustrious relatives, perhaps?"

"I did not," Arthur said.

The king looked to the Truth Seeker, who nodded.

"Truth."

"Then you stole it fair and square, did you?" The king's voice dripped sarcasm.

"I did, sire. I believe that the sale of Legendary cards is strictly regulated—"

"If you had knowledge of it, then you should have come to me or one of my men," the king said. "Lung Bai." Again, he glanced at the Mythic dragon lurking just behind Arthur. "Are you familiar with . . . Which card was it that you stole?"

"Master of Body Enhancement," Arthur said, and to his surprise, the Mythic Lung Bai answered right on the heels of his words.

"Duke Rowantree mentioned it was missing from his card library."

The king's eyebrows rose. "The plot thickens. So, Arthur, you stole it from your relatives, and . . . come to think of it, I don't believe Duke Rowantree mentioned that he was looking to sell the card in the first place. That is interesting, and worthy of my attention."

Feeling the conversation was close to spinning out of control—if the king called Lional back to the throne room, all was likely to be lost—Arthur tried a new tactic.

He bowed his head. "I am well aware that I have made mistakes," Arthur said as humbly as he could, "which is why I had hoped to show I am worthy of your favor by immediately coming to you with Prince Marion's time card." He hated scraping like this, but the alternative was even worse.

But he could tell it had limited effect. The man might not be totally cognizant of dates, but he was not an idiot. He was not happy with Arthur.

"You are aware that I could have you executed for this, and your dragon forcefully relinked to somebody else—yes, it's possible," he added sharply, even though Arthur had not voiced an objection. "Do you think that we would allow a young Legendary dragon with such a unique talent to go without a rider?"

"I . . ." Arthur opened his mouth, unsure what to say.

"My king," the Mythic spoke, interrupting him. "If you would permit me a question to the new rider . . ."

Instantly, the king lost his stern expression. His face softened, and he turned to the voice of the dragon. "Of course, Bai."

There was a movement through the air, a ghostly impression of a narrow dragon head, though Arthur could not quite focus on the entire shape of the dragon, which seemed very odd to him.

"Arthur Rowantree," the dragon intoned, "tell me true. Do you wish to complete a full set of Legendaries and ascend?"

"Ascend?" Arthur asked, caught off guard. "I beg your pardon, but I do not understand."

The Truth Seeker's voice rang out. "Truth!"

With a disturbance of air, the Mythic turned to the king. "I believe that this is a child who worked in ignorance. He has also tried to correct his mistakes—albeit clumsily."

"Ignorance of the law is not an excuse to break the law," the king said, then sighed and slumped once again in his throne, rolling his eyes. "But you belong to . . . which hive again? Oh, Wolf Moon, wasn't it? A very tiny hive. Inconsequential. I can't imagine that anybody would ever gain a dangerous amount of power there." He focused on Arthur. "You do understand that by becoming a Legendary rider, you will be officially slotted into the royal retinue? That means an oath of loyalty to *me*."

This had been briefly mentioned to him before—emphasis on briefly.

Arthur kept his expression as calm as possible and nodded once. "I will do whatever I need to do to serve the kingdom." He was able to say this with a clear conscience only because he had made the mind-singer promise to go to *another* kingdom. It wasn't necessarily better, but it was enough.

"Truth," the Truth Seeker said.

However, it didn't relieve all of Arthur's concerns. An oath? He should have guessed something like that was coming. But if the king required him to swear that he had always been true to the kingdom, or even true to the king . . . he couldn't.

Oaths, as far as he knew, could be as binding as a promise between friends or lovers. Or, when they were done in more serious circumstances, on the strength of a card whose power was to enforce a contract between two parties.

He was willing to bet an oath to the king would be the latter. And if the king demanded that he would always remain true to the kingdom and to him . . . he didn't know if the oath would be accepted.

But though he didn't have his **Acting** skill, Arthur knew it would be suicidal to show any kind of hesitation. This was his last chance.

So he inwardly girded himself and added, "I'm willing to do whatever needs to be done." That was the truest statement he had spoken so far.

Arthur would do whatever needed to be done to save himself, to save Brixaby, and eventually, save the people he cared about. Meanwhile, he pushed the guilt and his inner disgust of his deal with the mind-singer far, far down.

"Of course you will," the king said, then waved to his warrior bodyguard before he returned back to his marble board game.

The bodyguard strode up to Arthur, and with a flourish, produced a glowing orb on his palm.

"That's a Legendary-level power," Brixaby said with interest. "What does it do?" He cocked his head and looked down at the orb greedily.

"This is an oath anchor, which is binding to any other Legendary-level user and below," the man said solemnly. He watched Arthur with an expression that Arthur could not quite read. "Rest your hand on the orb."

"Me too?" Brixaby asked.

The man hesitated. "This is for humans only."

Brixaby grumbled, and Arthur got the impression he'd just wanted a taste of the power.

Holding his breath, Arthur did as he was instructed.

"Repeat after me," the man said. "I, Arthur Rowantree . . ."

Arthur dutifully repeated the man's words.

"Do solemnly swear on the strength of the cards in my heart deck, that I will join His Majesty the king's royal retinue as one of his riders. In doing so, I swear to always come at the king's call, to obey his direct and lawful orders, and that I will always serve the kingdom."

As Arthur spoke the last sentence, he concentrated fiercely on the idea that he had told the mind-singer to go to another kingdom. That meant he wasn't helping an enemy of this kingdom. It was a fine line, and not a very ethical one.

The stone in the man's hand pulsed white with every word.

Then, abruptly, the man stepped back. "Very good."

Wait, that was it? Arthur thought, and had to actually bite back a laugh of relief.

Then again, this oath would usually be taken by nobles who had their own agendas and plans. "Serve the kingdom" was a phrase with many shades of meaning.

The man nodded and strode over to the king. "Sire?"

The king sighed dramatically, turned away from his board game, and slapped his hand on the stone.

"As king, I swear to take Arthur Rowantree into my retinue and treat him as a loyal subject," he said quickly, on yet another sigh.

The stone pulsed white again, and as he lifted his hand away, it cracked in two.

Pure horror washed through him. Had it cracked in two because it knew, somehow, about the deal he had made with the scourgling? Maybe it considered him a disloyal, unworthy subject.

But no one else looked alarmed. The two halves of the stone flattened themselves into sheets. Then writing appeared on the front, one half etched in Arthur's usual handwriting. The other in a flowing, practiced script.

No, they weren't sheets. They were . . . cards?

The process took only a moment. The man holding the two new cards bowed and presented one to the king, who lazily took it and put it in his heart deck without even looking at it.

Then the man walked over to Arthur and held the other card out to him.

With trepidation, Arthur examined it. But . . . it was not a regular card. Just a repeat, word for word, of the short oath Arthur had made and the even shorter acceptance from the king. Each oath was in their separate handwriting.

He looked around and saw that people were watching him with expectation. He knew what he had to do and quickly added the card to his heart. Afterward, he felt unusually full, as if he had overeaten on a large meal.

However, there was a sense of loosened tension throughout the room.

"Well, that's done," the king said, bored. "Congratulations, new rider. I know that you will serve me well."

"Thank you, sire." Arthur bowed again. His heart hammered. Was this it? Was this finally over?

The king's attention once again returned to the board game.

Arthur and Brixaby glanced at one another.

The throne room doors opened with a puff of air, and Arthur saw the ghostly visage of Lung Bai make her way out.

Arthur followed, and the portal user did as well.

As soon as they were outside the room, Arthur felt a lifting of his restrictions. His skills flooded back to him, and if not for the lingering sense that this was not over, and the impact of his **Acting** skill, Arthur would have broken into a huge grin.

"Oh, yes, that is very nice," Brixaby said, shaking himself all over, as if shedding a layer of uncomfortable snow off of his scales. "Not having my cards was very unpleasant," he added pointedly to the Mythic.

The Mythic ignored him with dignity. "One moment, if you please." The doors to the throne room shut once more, and then she became fully visible.

Arthur took a staggered step back. Not because of the dragon's odd looks . . . though her shape was striking and unlike any dragon he had ever seen. He could hardly take his eyes off her beautifully polished silver scales.

But the pure force of her—of magic and power he could hardly comprehend but could almost taste—made much more of an impact. He realized he had been sharing the room with a being of monstrous power.

Being in the Mythic's presence made him feel small, like a grasshopper trapped under the gaze of a massive snake.

Lung Bai's gaze shifted slightly as she relaxed the scales around her sharp yet delicate-looking muzzle. Abruptly, she was less like a snake ready to strike and more like a disapproving mother.

"I hope you recognize how fortunate you have been, young Arthur Rowantree," she said sternly, "and how many strings were personally pulled for you to leave that throne room alive."

Arthur nodded, falling to one knee once again. "I understand, and I'm grateful."

"Could the king really make me link to someone else?" Brixaby asked.

"Yes, though the mind-mage with that card would have to be called in, which is an inconvenience," she said. Then her stern gaze again fell on Arthur. "And I hope you are intelligent enough to recognize that your king, who you have just sworn loyalty to, can be . . . forgetful. It would behoove you not to remind him of your set of cards."

Arthur swallowed hard. "I understand."

"Do not make me step in on your behalf again."

The Mythic hesitated for a long moment, and Arthur glanced up. She seemed to be waiting.

"Is there something else that you wish to tell me?" she asked at last.

New sweat broke out on Arthur's brow.

Brixaby, not understanding, bowed again. "We will work hard and serve the kingdom well," he said. "Also, about that vast card library . . . if there is any way that I could perhaps earn a visit to such wonderful treasures—"

He stopped as Arthur rested a hand on his back.

"There is something else," he said, hoping with everything that he was not about to make yet another gigantic mistake. "While in isolation in that stone room, I was contacted by an enemy . . ."

The scales around the Mythic's muzzle shifted again. Arthur wasn't quite certain, but she seemed to relax.

"Go on," she said.

Arthur winced and then told her about the mind-singer, and their agreement.

Brixaby was visibly shocked. "Wait, you agreed to aid the scourglings?"

"I didn't agree to aid her. Just to . . . Look, I didn't have a choice," he said.

"Of course you did. You could have told the scourgling to stick that card up its tail. Or better yet, use the card yourself. No, wait." Brixaby caught himself. "Your cards were blocked, weren't they? How inconvenient." He sent a slyly annoyed look at Lung Bai.

"Have you used the mind card?" the Mythic asked.

This, at least, he was not guilty of. He looked at the Mythic and said, "No."

Since the Mythic had not yet mentally or physically stepped on him for his confession, he decided it was time to be direct. "I hope I'm not overstepping myself, but you do not seem surprised about the mind-singer."

"I am not. I felt interference of a Rare mind card throughout the palace, and especially on the messenger who gave me the opening to send Duke Rowantree and his son back home. It was a transparent ploy. I suspect the scourgling is not as powerful as it pretends to be. It, too, is young."

Brixaby perked up. "If you know where it is, we should kill it now. I'll tear out its cards, and we can wrap them in a bow for the king, since he enjoys card sets. Maybe then I'll be granted access to your library."

Lung Bai laughed softly. "One thing that you will learn as you grow up is that there do need to be lines of communication open. Yes, even with a despised enemy. The king knows this and has tasked the scholar's guild with researching such a thing. It seems one branch guild was successful in the end."

The scholars were working under the king's orders?

Arthur doubted that was the whole story. He also dearly wanted to ask about the five Mythics left in the world and the seven Scourge Gods, but knew he was on very thin ice.

"I do not like it," Brixaby growled.

"You do not need to like it. As part of the royal retinue, you only need to accept it," she said and let out a large sigh. "I will speak to the royal inquisitor mind-mages about reinforcing our mental shields and contacting this high-handed scourgling. In the meantime . . ." She curved her head to the side and looked directly at the man who had followed them in, and who'd stayed silent until now. "I believe it is time for you to return home."

"But the mind-singer . . ." Arthur continued. "Isn't it a danger?"

"A Rare is no danger to me. Besides, it will soon be another kingdom's problem by the sounds of it." She sounded smug. "If it's open to suggestions, send it to Palath. They could use a kick in the tail."

That did not sit well with Arthur, though he knew he was being somewhat of a hypocrite.

The king's man gestured, and a new Sun Ring Portal opened.

Through it, Arthur saw Valentina's room in the Wolf Moon Hive. This ordeal was almost over. He and Brixaby could go home.

Finally, they could start their lives as a dragon-rider pair.

Brixaby shifted his weight on Arthur's shoulder, and Arthur sensed that he desperately wanted to argue the points. With his hand firmly on Brixaby's back, he stepped through the portal.

New Counterfeit skill obtained: Sun Ring Portal (Spell)
Time remaining: 9 Minutes, 59 seconds . . .

The portal closed behind Arthur the moment he stepped through.

He heard a gasp, looked over, and saw Valentina and Whitaker sitting at a wooden table with papers in front of them, a carafe of juice between them. It looked like he had interrupted a grim meeting.

Valentina dropped her papers and half stood. "Arthur? You're alive?"

Whitaker barked out a laugh. "Well, guess the king's messenger was a little premature." He looked at Valentina. "I told you there was nothing to worry about."

"I'm alive," Arthur said grimly. "No thanks to you two."

They knew he had been a long shot and had treated him like one. As such, Arthur had gone into his audience with the king almost completely unprepared. Nor had he any indication that they'd tried to step in on his behalf, despite badly needing another Legendary rider for the hive.

Instead, it had come down to a sympathetic Mythic and the mind-singer.

A scourgling had put its neck out for them further than these two.

He would have to learn to work with the two hive leaders—perhaps even earn their respect.

Right now, he wasn't in the mood. The timer was counting down.

Valentina snapped something at him about respect, but Arthur wasn't listening.

Turning, he reached for the Sun Ring Portal spell.

It was shockingly easy to activate. All he had to do was picture the place he wanted to go the most . . . and there he was.

With Brixaby on his shoulder, Arthur stepped through the portal to the tiny cottage he'd grown up in. The fire in the woodstove had burned down to coals, warming the place, and his father's once-familiar snores filled the single room.

Arthur shut the portal behind him.

He had ten minutes.

CHAPTER 57

Stepping through the portal, Arthur let it snap shut behind him.

The only sound he made was a single footfall, but in order to survive in the borderland village, one must always be prepared. His father's long snore cut off immediately. A dark shape lying on a simple bedroll on the other side of the room stirred.

"Who's there?" his father rasped. "I'm armed."

A feeling of relief threatened to overwhelm Arthur, tightening his throat. He had tried not to let himself worry too much about why his father had been absent from the cottage, but concern had been a constant companion in the back of his mind anyway.

Plus, it had been a long, trying day.

"Dad, it's me, Arthur."

"Arthur?"

Sitting up, his father reached for the woodstove. The cottage was small enough that nearly everything was within arm's length. He opened the door, which let in more light.

"Arthur!" he said again, then stumbled out of bed to pull him into a rough hug. "I got your letter, but I didn't expect you so soon. What's—" He caught a glimpse of Brixaby—or more likely, the red glint of his eyes—and stepped back.

"Greetings!" Brixaby boomed, extending all four wings. "I applaud you on the procreation of my rider. He has proved quite useful!"

"This is Brixaby," Arthur said. "He is my dragon."

Calvan simply stared, then glanced back at his rumpled cot. Arthur suspected he was wondering if he was dreaming or not.

"He just recently hatched," Arthur explained. "Dad, I don't have much time, but we need to talk. I just came back from a meeting with the king."

"The king?" Instantly, Calvan's attention turned back to Arthur. He looked him up and down as if checking to make sure he was still in one piece.

Arthur knew the feeling.

"It was close," he said, and Brixaby snorted. "Dad, I'm sorry to hit you with this, but I have"—he checked the timer on the Sun Ring Portal spell—"less than nine minutes before I have to return to the hive. I need to know why our family was sent to the border. What exactly was your crime?"

His father looked like someone had just knocked him over the head. "That is . . . a long story, son."

"Then you must speak quickly!" Brixaby said. "Arthur, perhaps there is a quick story skill . . . ah, you would need an appropriate card for that. Never mind."

Arthur stepped forward. "I know it's painful, but living in ignorance is going to come back and bite me."

It already had.

"I . . . yes." Calvan nodded. "You're a man now, and it's . . . it's well past time." He sank down to the cot, gathering himself.

Arthur wanted to scream at him to hurry up because this was only the first of his questions, but the man still looked shocked.

Calvan spoke. "When I inherited the dukedom from my father, your grandfather, I discovered a rot within the kingdom. It's something all high-level nobles come to learn. If you've met the king, you know how he is: an old man trapped in a young man's body. But his mind has not been so well preserved."

"I noticed," Arthur said grimly.

"He is not the only ruler like this. Some are worse, some are better, to less and greater degrees."

"You mean other kingdoms," Arthur said.

Calvan nodded. "We are so cut off from one another that rumors of other kingdoms have become no better than myths. But from what little information there is, the rulers are in agreement: none want to give up their power and few wish to see anyone climb the ranks."

"Ascend the ranks, you mean." Arthur's fists clenched. "Are you saying that Legendary cards can move up to Mythic?"

Again, Calvan nodded. Though the motion was heavy, as if he carried a great weight. "It's said only a full set of Legendary cards can make that leap. An entire set becomes one Mythic card."

His heart raced. "Only Legendaries, though? If I had a full set of Commons, could they become Uncommon?"

"That is the million-gold-coin question, son," Calvan said. "And a dangerous one. It would make sense, but think of the difficulty. How many Common cards are there in the world? In this kingdom? And how many are still active? If there is an accident and a Common forester dies out in the woods with his cards unclaimed, that card will eventually rot away. It will never be replaced, and the set can never be completed."

It was difficult but not impossible. Arthur had seen a complete set of Commons with his own eyes when he was a boy, back when he stayed with Red's trader caravan. Though the set had been smuggled under a thick pile of tobacco leaves that disrupted magical seeker cards.

If a set of Legendaries became a Mythic . . . that went a long way to explaining why the king was so adamant against somebody obtaining pairs or better.

People must have tested it out on lower ranks at some point. He bet the scholar's guild had the answer.

He wanted to ask more, but they were pressed for time.

"There are seven Scourge Gods," Arthur said, "and five Mythic dragons."

"Five?" His father looked up and then snorted, shaking his head. "Last I heard, there were six Mythics. But that was years ago." His lip curled in self-disgust. "I was so worried then that if the Scourge Gods ever made a move—if two were to attack at once, the king's beast would find itself overwhelmed and there would not be enough Mythics to help. Now it's even worse."

"Dad?" Arthur asked carefully. "Did you want to make a Mythic card?"

"No!" he said sharply. "Arthur, you must understand that this was a long-term plan. I never expected to advance the set myself, or even for you to do so. Finding a set of Legendaries is the work of generations. It was started with my father's father, and in all that time, we'd only been able to scrape together two—"

"What about my mom's card?" Arthur asked.

Calvan looked at him blankly, clearly not understanding.

"Hive Leader Valentina knew Lottie," Arthur went on leadingly.

"Yes, she was a Legendary recruit for one of the hives before I knew her. Your mother—" Calvan sucked in a breath, as if saying those words hurt. "It was an arranged marriage, but a happy one. Her father was a traditional man and wanted her card returned to the family. She understood it and was given two powerful Rares as recompense, though . . . it's not quite the same." He reached up to touch his own chest. "Then the ploy to build a set of Legendaries was discovered. And the king . . . well, I lost everything. I wanted to give Lottie, you, and your sister the best life that I could. I failed so many times—"

"Dad," Arthur said sharply. He had sympathy for the man, but he simply didn't have time for self-recrimination. "What was my mother's card?"

Calvan looked at him. "She never spoke of it. I didn't want to push, as it was too painful. But my father had done research into cards with similar powers for the set, and . . ."

Arthur knew where this was going. "My mother's card might have belonged to the same set as yours."

The strained look on his father's face was all the answer he needed. "It was a possibility. I had hoped to give her time to heal, and then through the work of years, possibly acquire it within the next generation as an in-law."

Arthur checked the time. A minute and a half left. He'd spent more time than he wanted on questions. Now he had little time to convince his father to save himself.

"Lional Rowantree knows I'm your son now. He's probably going to send men down here for you. He might even contact Baron Kane to do it, if he hasn't already. You need to leave."

"I can't."

"Do you still have any of those cards I left with you?" Arthur continued. "Or I can give you one? I have some in my anchor I can give—"

"I cannot, son. I swore an oath to stay."

Arthur considered letting the timer for the Sun Ring Portal run out and then going back to the hive via his Return to Start card. Brixaby could come along in his storage space.

But that was a last-resort escape card. He would rather it stay secret for as long as possible.

Time to brute-force the issue.

"Brix, do you sense an oath card in his heart deck?"

"Ohh." Brixaby's eyes were little pinpoint specks of red in the gloom.

Sensing his attention, his father stepped back.

"There is something," Brixaby said. "Not in the heart deck, exactly. Just outside of it, but latched on like a parasite."

"Take it," Arthur said.

"Now wait a minute," his father said. "You can't just—!" He broke off in a sharp shout.

Brixaby, always eager for any new card, zipped over to Calvan and ripped it out of his chest before the man could begin to swat him away.

Calvan gave a choked gasp, looking like the wind had been knocked out of him.

Brixaby returned to his perch on Arthur's shoulder.

Taking the card, Arthur looked it over.

The oath his father had been required to take was like a wrapping of heavy chains compared to the light leash of Arthur's.

In Calvan's handwriting, the card read he swore he would give up all claims to his lands and individual rights, that he would never again take any cards, that he would stay within Baron Kane's lands until his death.

The king's handwriting was much simpler: *Witnessed.*

Even as Arthur read the card, it disintegrated to dust between his fingers. Arthur looked up to see his father staring.

"Dad, are you okay?"

"I feel . . . good." He took in a deep, bracing breath. "The oath is gone. It's really gone. You . . . taught your dragon to do that?"

Brixaby bristled. "Stealing cards happens to be my specialty."

"Amazing." Calvan stood up straighter. He blinked, and his eyes looked suddenly clear.

"Dad," Arthur said urgently. The seconds were counting down. "Come with me to the hive. I can hide you."

"No, Arthur." He shook his head. "There is . . . well, a very special lady here. Now, I can see you were right. I need to hide. But I won't leave her."

That helped explain why his father had been absent from the cottage. Arthur was glad. He deserved someone in his life.

"Is she bound by an oath? Brix could—"

"Twenty-three seconds left," Brixaby said. He looked regretful, like he would very much enjoy taking another card.

"Go," his father said. "I'll manage. Don't get trapped here, Arthur."

With a frustrated sound, Arthur turned and reached for the Sun Ring Portal. It took a few precious seconds to open it back up to his new suite in the hive.

Before stepping through, Arthur looked over his shoulder. "Tell the parents of the children I took that they're doing well, and . . . and I'm not done with this village. Brixaby has to grow up, and I have to train to get stronger. Once we're ready, I'll be back for anyone else who wants to leave."

His father smiled. It was a clearer expression than he remembered seeing. "I'll tell them. I'm proud of you, son."

Arthur stepped through just as the last seconds counted to zero.

EPILOGUE

Arthur sat on the lip of his balcony, legs dangling off the side. There was no safety railing, but he wasn't worried. As high up as he was, he'd have a very long time to fall. Plenty of time for Brixaby to arrange for another dragon to catch him.

A dozen feet beyond, Brixaby was flying a quick whirlwind twirl that made him look like a spinning top. He claimed it was to level up his **Trick Flying**, but Arthur couldn't see the utility in it. He suspected Brixaby was just having fun.

He couldn't wait until they could fly together.

What form it would take—whether Brixaby would ever grow large enough to carry him or if Arthur had to find an extreme body-enhancement card, he wasn't sure.

But one way or another, it was going to happen.

It was an almost perfect evening and unusually warm for Wolf Moon Hive, especially this high up where the wind could be cutting.

Arthur had a whole host of new cards to learn about and explore, and nothing planned for the foreseeable future except leveling his skills and helping Brixaby grow up.

He had wealth in the form of a generous hive stipend and friends who would soon be close at hand, as soon as Brixaby was old enough to officially form a retinue—until then, it was more an informal arrangement—and power in the form of rank . . . even though the hive leaders weren't happy with him.

That was okay. Arthur wasn't happy with them right now, either. They would learn to work together.

Life was good.

The only thing that darkened Arthur's thoughts was, of course, the tiny matter of his betrayal to all of humanity.

The mind-singer had not yet come for him. He suspected he and Brixaby had left it behind during his quick exit from the palace. Lung Bai had probably delayed it further.

He had many thoughts on the subject. None of them were pleasant.

The fact that the king had ordered the scholar's guilds to create a way to contact the scourglings made him wonder if the uptick in scourge-eruptions was truly part of a cycle . . . or a more worrying trend.

Were the scourglings building up for a massive attack now that there were five Mythic dragons to seven Scourge Gods?

And what exactly would Arthur do when the mind-singer came to collect her card? Could he in good conscience help his enemy in any small way?

"What are you stewing about?" Brixaby asked, hovering up just beyond his nose.

Arthur blinked and jerked back, having been so caught up in his thoughts he hadn't seen him approach.

"I'm worried about the mind-singer," he admitted.

Brixaby made a disgusted sound. "I don't see why you believe you owe the thing."

"She got me out of the palace."

"Lung Bai did that."

"She provided the opening for Duke Rowantree and Penn to leave," he said. "If they were still there . . . I'm not sure what Lung Bai could have done."

"From what you told me, you and Joy's rider were the ones to release the scourgling from the scholar's guild in the first place," Brixaby said. "So your scales are balanced."

Arthur paused. He . . . hadn't thought of it that way.

"I gave the thing my word," he said.

"Well, *my* word is that I don't like you helping out the scourge."

"Neither do I," he replied with irritation. "I don't want to! I know it's wrong, but I'm also someone of importance now. And when you're powerful, it's too easy to go back on your word because it's convenient or you changed your mind. I don't want to start down that path."

Brixaby heaved a sigh. "Well . . ." he grumbled, "I suppose it's only a Rare card. Not important like a Legendary. Since you want to be *a good man.*" This last part was said with the utmost sarcasm.

Arthur ignored his tone. "I haven't decided what I'm going to do. I'm just telling you that it's not an easy decision. It's the sort of thing that defines a man's character going forward."

"Yes, yes, you are so very conflicted and virtuous. What's so special about this card anyway? Show it to me so that I at least know the details when it inevitably comes back to bite us."

Arthur sighed and withdrew the card from his Personal Space. He flipped it around so Brixaby could read it. The dragon was leveling up his **Reading** skill quickly and—

Brixaby darted forward, snatched the card, and shoved it in his own chest. That was quite the feat considering the card was bigger than himself.

"Brix! What are you doing?"

"Taking a card out of circulation," Brixaby said, smugly buzzing backward when Arthur reached for him.

Arthur, however, was terrified for his dragon. "That might link you with the mind-singer. You'll be a part of its trio!"

"Oh, please. There's nothing like that in the card's description. Besides, I'm a dragon: the antithesis of scourge. My dung revitalizes scourge-touched land. Their powers have no hold on me."

He calmed down somewhat. "Are you certain? You didn't add it to your core, did you?"

"Of course not," Brixaby snapped, offended. Then he rubbed his stomach. "I'm absorbing it. Soon I'll have some nice new Rare power to add to my list."

Slowly, Arthur relaxed. Brixaby was right. And he could destroy cards without them going to rot because he was a dragon.

Arthur smiled. "The mind-singer isn't going to be happy. You're amazing, you know that?"

"I'm a Legendary dragon. Of course I am. Ohh . . . Um. Something's happening. Something . . . big." He sounded unsure. "Arthur? I . . ."

He burped sparkles that looked like mana made real.

Then, in a blink, Brixaby became notably larger. He was now the size of a large parrot.

He let out a short sound of surprise, dipping in the air until he regained his altitude. His limbs were longer, head that much more defined. There were larger purple-black bumps up and down his spine to indicate future ridges.

Brixaby had *grown*.

. . . Some.

"Brix!" Arthur gasped. "Are you okay?"

"I . . . I grew!" Brixaby flew in a happy loop. The buzz of his wings had taken a deeper tone now that he displaced more air. "That was what Joy's stupid quest was about. Quick, we must find her again so I can reacquire it. Then you will feed me more cards."

"We'll start with shards, first." Arthur was amazed and happy for him. Really. But he was still concerned. "What about the mind card?"

"I'm still absorbing its shards," Brixaby admitted. "I can feel it now: that was the initial burst of magic after the card's magical structure splintered. I'll be adding its power to my own over the next few hours."

This was his first time absorbing a card since hatching. That first time had given him trouble because he hadn't had a fully formed card in his core and had been trying to absorb Legendaries. Now he had matured a little, had a full card, and this mind card was of a lower tier: It was a perfect test case.

Arthur let out a soft chuckle and leaned back to rest on his arms. "I wonder how much of its power you'll be able to absorb?"

Brixaby rubbed his now-larger and more wicked-looking claws together. "I can't wait to find out."

Arthur couldn't wait to see for himself.

ABOUT THE AUTHOR

Having selected banker as her profession and purchased sturdy oxen as well as all the ammunition she could afford, Honour Rae loaded her family into a wagon and set out to establish a homestead. Unfortunately, she could only keep two hundred pounds of the deer, elk, bears, bison, squirrels, and rabbits she massacred along the way. Soon, dysentery set in and attempting to ford the river proved to be a huge mistake. Somehow, Rae and her family pulled through—albeit with the loss of any extra wagon parts. The Oregon Trail conquered, and having made it to the Willamette Valley, she sat down to write this book.

THANK YOU

FOR SUPPORTING HONOUR RAE

CONNECT WITH THE AUTHOR
BY VISITING THE FOLLOWING:

@HonourRae

PATREON.COM/HONOUR_RAE